Forbidden Things Book One

Dissident

By Nikki McCormack

Published by
Elysium Books

Written by Nikki McCormack
www.elysiumpalace.com

Cover Art by Robert Crescenzio

First Edition 2015
978-0996319614

To my mom, Linda, who knows the characters in these pages almost better than I do, and Michael, whose support and love helped make this dream possible.

CHAPTER ONE

There were too few things to enjoy in this life. She would be a fool to squander a lovely day.

Indigo inhaled the rich smell of a recent rain and tipped her head back, closing her eyes to let sunshine fall full upon her face. Gritty cobbles crunched underfoot. Snippets of conversation from other walkers and the clacking hooves of occasional equestrian traffic blended into a meaningless hum.

Her feet knew the path. She and Andrea walked the same route home from the academy every lesson day for nearly two years. Behind them, the twin spires of Caithin Healer's Academy twisted towards the sky like the gold horns of some great beast. In the bright sunshine, they were almost blinding in their brilliance, and she fancied she could feel reflected light from them on her back.

Her student's robes dangled over one forearm, and the backless summer dress she wore left her skin exposed to warm afternoon sunlight. With her hair pulled over one shoulder, the sun's touch fell hot upon the tattoo between her shoulder blades. The symbol of her studies to become a healer, the blue rose of the Caithin Healer's Academy, on display for anyone to see.

"Indigo, are you listening?"

Opening her eyes, she glanced at Andrea and smiled an apology. "Sorry. It's a beautiful day for this early in the year. I got caught up in it."

"Judging by that dress, you think it's summer already."

The other woman's huffy tone stifled her enjoyment. The colorful dress might be better suited to a midsummer party, but the playful style bolstered Indigo's withering spirits. In contrast, Andrea's conservative blue dress did nothing to emphasize her shape or set off her features. Not the type of garment that could bring the bounce back to one's step.

"It's just a fun dress."

Andrea responded with a sour look. "No wonder Jayce gets edgy every time you step outside."

Distress rose in response to the comment, and Indigo slapped it down. She spotted a woman stepping out of a nearby building in a bright yellow dress that cut low in front and clung to her hips, emphasizing feminine curves. She raised her eyebrows at Andrea, wiggling her fingers in the woman's direction show she was not the only one dressing for the day.

Andrea dismissed the woman with a roll of her emerald eyes. "While you were flouncing about in your early spring daydreams, I asked if you had decided on flowers for the wedding."

Indigo adjusted her bag on her shoulder and then started picking at her fingernails, making soft clicking sounds with them. "I haven't had time to think about it."

"Well, I have. Neither of you is upper nobility, so violet would be presumptuous."

Indigo struggled not to bristle at the superior tone. Andrea's parents trained her in the fine art of looking down on anyone of lower status. It never occurred to her that it might be insulting, though Indigo intended to point it out someday, just not today.

Andrea pressed her lips together, then a bright smile lit her face, her enthusiasm for the subject leeching away Indigo's better mood. "You know, if you lean into your uncle's

status, I imagine you could get away with pink or maybe...
And there you go again."

Indigo startled. "What?"

"Every time I bring up the wedding, you get gloomy.
What is wrong?"

Andrea placed a hand on Indigo's arm and stopped.
Indigo allowed the other woman's gentle pull to turn her. She
avoided Andrea's eyes, glancing first at the early spring
flowers in a window box behind her before gazing back the
way they had come.

Some distance back, an Ascard Watchman leaned on a
light post, his tan military uniform accented with the deep
maroon of his special division. His hooded gaze took in the
late afternoon traffic. Prickles of fear crept up her spine.
Despite a few years of living in the city without incident, she
couldn't stop dreading the day they would find her out and
punish her for her deception.

Never let them know your true strength.

Hadris and her father must have told her that a thousand
times as a child. Did it matter now, with them both gone?
Would the Watchmen do anything to her other than force her
to use her ascard ability in service to the crown? Her father
would have detested that, but it didn't seem so disagreeable
from her current position.

Besides, maybe they were wrong. Maybe her ability
wasn't that strong. Hadris had helped her construct barriers
around her inner aspect as a child, and she couldn't bring
herself to take them down to find out. It chilled her blood to
remember how they had beheaded Hadris for hiding her own
ability, but Hadris had been a Lyran slave.

And I am the daughter of a traitor.

She liked her head where it was.

She forced her attention back to Andrea. "I haven't got
enough time to keep up studies and plan a wedding. I had

hoped to wait until I finished my schooling, but Jayce insists."

When she suggested waiting, he had accused her of infidelity. His face had gone ruddy with rage, and he had thrown a vase at the wall—one of her few keepsakes of her mother—shattering it. If only she could do more than postpone the wedding, but it was too late. It had been too late the moment her uncle accepted his proposal. In proper society, one didn't back out of an engagement, and her noble status depended upon this marriage because of the scandal surrounding her parents' deaths.

You tried to do so much good for others, Father, but what did you do for me?

Andrea tittered, disregarding her deepening melancholy. "He worries someone will steal you away."

How true. Indigo held her tongue. Andrea and Jayce were friends long before she moved into the city. She was the outsider.

"Honestly, I am surprised you're not in more of a hurry to see this marriage through, considering."

Indigo swallowed a foul taste. "Considering?"

"It is difficult to find a man of noble birth willing to marry someone with your background."

"I know." How could she forget with Andrea and Jayce always willing to point it out?

Her attention wandered to the fountain sprouting up in the center of a nearby courtyard, simple and elegant like a great stonework lily. A man stood by the fountain, watching water droplets falling with the shimmer of multicolored gems in the bright sunlight. Long silver hair hung to the middle of his back like a frozen waterfall. His smooth pale skin and unusual hair marked him as Lyran, but his regal bearing and rich attire didn't befit a slave or merchant.

Curious. "Have you seen him before?"

Andrea turned, following her gaze. "Who?"

"The man beside the fountain."

"There is no one by the fountain."

Andrea's reply tugged at her awareness, but the silver-haired Lyran was turning toward them now. His pale eyes met hers, and the air pressed from her lungs as if a corset were being pulled too tight. The buildings lurched and spun in her vision.

"Indigo?" Andrea's voice came to her across a vast gulf.

She sank to her knees. Andrea crouched down with her, her eyes wide and frightened. She held Indigo's shoulders tight, her lips moving. Indigo heard only the pounding of blood in her ears. Bowing her head, she closed her eyes. The pressure eased, and her heartbeat slowed to some semblance of normal. At a tug on her arm, she opened her eyes and let Andrea help her to her feet.

"Are you well?"

Leaving a hand on Andrea's arm for balance, she glanced at the fountain. No one was there now. Where had he gone? She scanned around them and spotted a Watchman striding over. His shrewd gaze picked apart the area around the fountain, then settled on them with open suspicion.

Indigo's breath caught in her throat. Her hand tightened on Andrea's arm.

"Are you ladies all right?" His tone was polite, but his gaze bored into them, into her.

Was her ability still hidden? Had her masking slipped? Did he know what she was hiding? She didn't dare access her ability to find out for fear he would notice. She opened her mouth to respond, but her voice caught on the lump of fear in her throat.

"Indigo?" Andrea's worried tone broke through the cold terror.

"Yes, we are fine." She forced a light tone. "I had a dizzy spell."

She started turning as if to continue home, and he raised

a hand to stop her. Her pulse pounded, a thousand drums beating triple time. How could he not hear it?

"You are students from the academy?"

"Yes, sir," Andrea answered, sparing Indigo the effort.

His suspicious gaze lingered on Indigo for seconds that threatened to stretch into eternity. He gave a curt nod. "Best be on your way."

They finished the walk to the student residence in strained silence. When they arrived, Indigo dashed up the stairs and to her bedroom past a startled Jayce. She closed the door and leaned against it, her heart racing at the thought of facing her fiancé in such a flustered state. Forcing slow breaths, she listened to Andrea greet him in the next room.

"I'm guessing that passing breeze was Indigo."

Andrea responded in a voice so low Indigo had to put an ear to the edge of the door to hear. "Something peculiar happened on the way home. We were talking near the Healer's Courtyard, and she said she saw someone by the fountain. The strange thing is, there was no one there. Then she swooned and sank to her knees, gasping. She wouldn't respond to me for almost a minute. I'm worried. I think you should keep an eye on her."

Indigo touched her neck, remembering the terrifying sensation of suffocation. Had it been as long as a minute?

"Who did she see?"

The edge of suspicion in Jayce's voice made her skin prickle with alarm. *Don't tell him.*

"Some man, she said, but there was no one there."

Her palms grew sweaty in the brief silence that followed.

"Thanks, Andrea. I'll take care of her."

"Tell her I will see her tomorrow."

Indigo sat on the edge of the bed and focused on making her breathing regular. The outer door clicked shut. Seconds later, the door to the bedroom creaked open, and Jayce stepped in. His hazel eyes narrowed, the short cut of his brunette hair adding severity to the expression. It was exhausting dancing around his temper. Where had he hidden his possessive jealousy when he was courting her?

Perhaps if his parents knew where he spent his nights out, they would insist he stay home, though they didn't appear to care what he did in private so long as he didn't publicly disgrace them. She could talk to her uncle, but he was away too often to have much influence as her guardian. Besides, if she got her fiancé into trouble, regardless of the reason, it would reflect badly upon her.

She turned away, her gaze following the rays of late afternoon sunlight that trickled through the window. The residence maids had missed a smudge in one corner of the glass pane. An inconsequential thing. A dingy spot on the glass, just as she was a dingy spot upon society. One misstep and they would wipe her away as they had her father.

Did she deserve any better?

The mattress sank a little when Jayce sat next to her. He rested a hand on her far shoulder and gave a gentle squeeze. She leaned into him. Maybe he wasn't angry. Maybe he would be supportive the way he always had been before their engagement.

"Are you well?" He brushed her hair back over her ear to see her face.

"I had a little dizzy spell. I'm fine now."

"Maybe you should take a few days to rest." He kissed her neck, and a small shiver of pleasure ran through her despite her trepidation.

"Tomorrow *is* a rest day. It will be enough."

His breath tickled across her ear, but his hand tightened on her shoulder, crushing any enjoyment she might have gotten from the sensation. "Who was the man you saw?"

She pulled away and went to stand near the window. "No one, Jayce. There was no one there."

He stood, muscles in his jaw jumping, his eyes closing to angry slits. "A hallucination then. Of whom?"

She took a deep breath. One of them had to remain calm and rational. Why did it always have to be her? "It wasn't anyone I remember seeing before. Maybe a face from my childhood. I don't know."

"Was he handsome?"

So very handsome. "I don't recall. I couldn't breathe. That was a little distracting."

He clenched his fists, and she cringed inside. Letting him see her fear would only encourage him though, so she lifted her chin and met his eyes.

"I think you should stay home for a few days."

"I can't fall behind."

His face flushed, and his gaze roamed her body, contemplating what he stood to lose to this hallucination. "What if it happens again?"

"Then I will be among healers. They are equipped to handle such things."

He stared at her for a long time, but even he couldn't come up with a good argument against that. Instead, he walked over and kissed her hard. A possessive, angry kiss.

* * *

She lay awake long into the night after Jayce finished showing her she belonged to him. Every detail of the man by the fountain was vivid in her mind, from his intense gaze to his ethereal highborn Lyran allure. She had never encountered a pure-blooded Lyran who was not a slave. According to her Uncle Theron, whose work for King Jerrin put him in a position to know such things, true Lyran nobility possessed an uncanny grace and beauty. Given that, what else could the stranger be?

But why would a Lyran nobleman be wandering the streets of Caithin?

She listened to Jayce sleep for several minutes, his breathing deep and even, hers quick and fearful. Then she slipped out of bed and donned a pair of fitted riding pants and a blouse. It wasn't appropriate attire for a woman of noble breeding in the city, but it would set her apart from any courtesans and whores about at this hour. As an after-thought, she snatched a deep blue shawl from the vanity, the one her uncle had given her because it matched her eyes, and wrapped it around her shoulders on her way out.

The education district had a livelier nightlife than all but the market and low-town districts because of its young populace, but her destination was close enough to academy grounds that it should be quieter. The Healer's Courtyard sometimes drew pairs of lovers. Tonight, it was empty and solemn, lit by the soft glow of a half-moon.

Trepidation slowed her steps as she approached the fountain. She stopped beside where the Lyran man had stood and watched the surface of the lower pool ripple with droplets falling from above, shining like clear crystals now in the moonlight. It was mesmerizing watching the play of a single ripple colliding with others and rebounding from the edge of the pool. So much like life itself. Each decision a droplet hitting the water, the ripples reaching out and affecting countless others.

She became aware of someone standing next to her, and her lungs contracted in response to the extraordinary power surrounding him. She stared hard into the fountain, fighting the urge to flee.

This was why she had come, to see if he was real.

Unnerved by his silence, she forced a deep breath into her tightened chest and spoke in the Lyran trade dialect in case he didn't speak Caithin. "Might I ask your name, my lord?"

"Where is this place?"

His voice was deep, melodious. The refined Lyran dialect he used reinforced her suspicion that he was aristocracy. How then had he come to be here?

"That was not an answer, my lord." She dared a glance at him. He was gazing into the fountain. His eyes were pale silver-blue, like glacial ice, beautiful and cold. She turned back to the fountain, terrified and excited by the mystery of him. When he said nothing, she relented. "The education district."

"What city?"

Startled by the question, she looked at him again. He was looking around at the rest of the courtyard now. Was he serious? How could he not know what city they were in?

"The Caithin capital, Demin."

A faint smirk touched his lips. He looked at her then, and she felt again as if the air was being pressed from her lungs. An icy spike of fear froze her to the spot.

"Who are you?" she breathed.

He took one of her hands in his, his grip warm and gentle. "Help me."

The courtyard faded around them. The sharp tang of sulfur stung her nose. Their environment transformed, moonlight vanishing behind thick storm clouds. A rugged black landscape surrounded them, riddled with cracks emitting a red glow and stifling heat. The Sinner's Hereafter of passionate priests' sermons given solid form.

Any who use the ascard for aught but good shall burn in the Sinner's Hereafter.

He who turns his back on his countrymen shall burn in the Sinner's Hereafter.

Any woman unfaithful to her husband shall burn in the Sinner's Hereafter.

A panicked cry ripped from her throat. She yanked her

hand away and fell back, landing hard on the cobbles in the courtyard.

When she looked up, she was by the fountain again, and alone.

Her heart pounded, and the sting of sulfur persisted in her nose. She grabbed her shawl, scrambled to her feet and ran back to the residence. At the stairwell, she sank panting on the bottom step and covered her mouth to muffle frantic sobs. Panic faded. When the frightened tears stopped, she stood and made her way up the stairs, still trembling like the last fall leaf clinging to its branch before the onslaught of a rising storm.

In the bedroom, she lit a candle and sat at her vanity to check her elbows in the mirror. Both had raw scrapes from her fall on the cobbles. She chewed at her lip as she dabbed them clean. How would she hide this from Jayce?

She could heal them with ascard, but they forbade students from using those skills outside of the academy until their third year. Punishment for breaking that rule wasn't severe, but she couldn't afford any negative attention.

Ascard Watchmen, with their fine-tuned ability to sense ascard use, enforced that rule and other laws governing ascard use. Any use of ascard outside of healing was illegal and immoral, except for the Watchmen themselves. They were the reason her father had Hadris teach her to hide her ascard ability. He hadn't wanted them to take his daughter away. Now, with Hadris and her parents dead, she had to manage on her own. Her engagement protected her noble status. Becoming a healer gave her value in Caithin society.

Do those things matter if I am miserable?

Jayce moaned in his sleep, and her heart jumped.

When he didn't move, she relaxed and stared into the mirror. She could still see those glacial eyes piercing into her, the need in them powerful and captivating. The hand that held hers had been strong, but he hadn't tried to hold her against her will.

He asked for your help, and you ran away.

She scowled at the mirror, then shuddered, remembering the smell of sulfur, the red glow, the broken landscape. Power was involved in this beyond her understanding, forbidden power that enticed her with the visage of a handsome stranger.

CHAPTER TWO

Indigo struggled up from the depths of sleep to the sound of someone rapping on the front door. Early morning light crept in through the window, and her gaze returned to the smudge in the corner. Tentative fingers touched her elbows. Her throat constricted when she felt abrasions there. It hadn't been a dream.

"Jayce!" Andrea's voice bounced jubilantly through the rooms. "Lord Caplin will be here any minute. He has invited us to join him for a picnic. I told him the two of you would come. I hope you don't mind."

"Of course not."

Indigo scowled. Jayce's reply was far more cordial than it would have been if she had made such plans without first consulting him. She threw back the covers. Despite her exhaustion, there was relief in knowing she wouldn't have to face the day alone with him.

She pulled on a blue dress with long, off-the-shoulder sleeves and an open back. It maintained the casual summery style they would expect from her while hiding evidence of her nocturnal outing. A glance in the mirror revealed tired circles under her eyes that she did her best to conceal beneath a light powder. When she felt presentable, she opened the door to find Jayce reaching for it on the other side.

He smiled, his hand hanging in the air where the handle had been. "I see you decided to get up?"

Returning the smile, she offered her hand. He took it and

kissed it. She would at least start the day with charming Jayce. Another small relief.

He escorted her out front where Caplin already waited, indulging Andrea's nervous prattle with a patient smile.

Fondness bubbled up in Indigo like happy laughter.

After her parents' deaths, her Uncle Theron had taken her in, taking her to the city with him on his frequent visits. She and Caplin had spent long days together while Theron and Caplin's father attended the royal council meetings of Caplin's uncle, King Jerrin. They consumed hours making a game of trying to lose Caplin's attendants in market crowds or racing horses down the river road. Those were special days when she could forget what it meant to be a traitor's daughter and just be a child. Now they were older, and Caplin had his own seat on his uncle's council, but those memories still connected them.

Caplin beamed at her when they came down the steps in front of the building. His dark hair hung in deliberate disarray, and the shadow of stubble gave a whisper of rebelliousness. Though his father detested the look, court ladies fawned over him, a simpering bunch of lovebirds he had more than mastered.

His confident strides consumed the distance between them, then he bowed.

She withdrew her hand from Jayce and curtsied with an overstated flourish, offering the hand to Caplin along with an impish grin to counter the formality of the gesture.

"Lord Caplin Duvox." She batted her lashes in playful mockery of the court ladies.

"Lady Indigo Milan, you look stunning." He smothered her hand with an exaggerated kiss. "If not for the exquisite Lady Andrea, I would woo you away from Lord Jayce." He gave Jayce a good-natured wink.

Seeing the storm rise in Jayce's eyes, she withdrew her

hand. "You jest sweetly, Caplin."

Andrea hurried forward and set a hand on Caplin's arm. "Shall we be off?"

"Certainly! Your carriage, my lady."

He took Andrea's hand in his and spun her around, sweeping an arm out to present his new carriage drawn by a pair of matching blood bay geldings. Crafted with elegant sweeping lines and a deep red lacquer finish that darkened to black at the edges, the carriage looked fit for the king himself. It even had new heavier springs underneath designed to give the smoothest possible ride.

Caplin watched Andrea expectantly. When she didn't comment, the enthusiasm lighting his eyes faded, and Indigo stepped forward, making a show of admiring the carriage.

"It is magnificent."

"Thank you." Caplin gave her a troubled glance before offering Andrea a hand up into the waiting conveyance.

They settled on cushioned velvet seats, and the carriage rolled off, its motion akin to the rocking of a cradle along the cobbled streets. Indigo drew aside the black brocade curtains and closed her eyes, letting the morning sun peek in the window to warm her face. The mysterious Lyran nobleman appeared in her mind as if painted on the inside of her eyelids. Her pulse quickened.

Who was he?

A poke in her side startled her. She opened her eyes to find them all watching her. Although Caplin looked amused, Jayce was scowling and Andrea, sitting beside her, pursed her lips into a thin, disapproving line.

"What?"

"Lord Duvox was talking to you," Andrea snapped.

She turned to Caplin. "I apologize."

He waved a dismissive hand. "I only said that your uncle asked after you at council yesterday."

Theron was in Demin? Why hadn't he come to see her?

Was a brief visit too much to ask? She forced a polite smile. "I had no idea he was in the city."

"He is not anymore. He did check after you though and said to let you know how impressed he is with your progress at the academy."

She flushed and started picking at her nails. "Did he?"

"Yes."

"Where is he off to now?"

Caplin gave her an indulgent smile. "High Council business, my lady. You know I cannot talk about that."

She shrugged. It was worth a try. "Thank you. It is nice to know he asked about me."

"My pleasure."

Jayce frowned at them, and she yearned to chastise him for his misguided jealousy, but that wasn't appropriate, even among friends. She turned back to the window.

They were passing through the bustling merchant district. Hawkers bellowed out the excellence of their wares while the smells of food, spices, cured leather, and other goods blended in an olfactory collage. She spotted a woman picking through an array of bright Kudaness fabrics and imagined the textures of those extraordinary weaves under her own fingertips.

Because Caithin had little direct contact with the Kudaness, many Lyran merchants turned a fine profit offering fabrics and rare spices from the desert tribes of Kudan alongside their Lyran goods. Those merchants all bore traits of the pureblooded Lyran, though the influence of other races was always apparent. The stubble of a beard there, dark eyes on another, one with a round face and dark hair. The active slave trade discouraged most pureblooded Lyrans from crossing the Gilded Strait by choice.

The man by the fountain had been pureblooded Lyran. That was reason enough to doubt the encounter. Still, the light fabric of her dress catching upon the scrapes on her elbows was hard to dismiss. Was it possible she had injured herself fleeing her own imagination?

After the guards waved them through the city gates, they followed a rutted trade road meandering along open farmland on one side and eventually turned into a sheltered meadow within the line of trees bordering the river on the other. A thicket of willows gathered around the meadow like a ring of bearded scholars standing in silent contemplation, blocking out sounds of traffic going to and from the city. The footman set out a blanket and an elaborate spread of food in the shade. Goblets of wine leaned, precarious on the uneven ground around plates piled with fresh fruit, teacakes, crisp bread, meat paste and an uncommon array of cheeses. Picnicking with Caplin had a distinct flavor of luxury.

Indigo savored some meat paste on crisp bread and listened, finding little to pique her interest today in talk of politics and local gossip. During a lull in conversation, she excused herself to go sit by the river, where she pulled off her shoes and dipped her toes into the cool water.

Andrea joined her a few minutes later. "Are you better today?"

Indigo gazed at her inconstant reflection on the water's surface. She looked the same, but she felt like a fledgling poised on the edge of a cliff, knowing that a step forward could bring death or glorious flight. She kicked her foot, disrupting the reflection.

"I had a restless night, but I'm fine."

"Maybe you should talk to a healer."

"Perhaps tomorrow."

"I think you should." Andrea reached over and squeezed Indigo's shoulder. Then she pulled her own shoes off and dipped her toes in the water with a squeak of surprise. "It's cold."

Jayce and Caplin sauntered off chatting. After the footman collected the remains of their meal, Indigo and Andrea pulled the blanket into the sun and stretched out on it.

Indigo closed her eyes, her thoughts turning to the Lyran man. He had asked for her help. What help did he need that she could provide?

The Lyran people possessed knowledge of ascard use far beyond healing. Knowledge Caithin's leadership went to great lengths to keep away from the populace. Citizens with the ability to manipulate ascard energy went to one of the larger cities to train as healers, or, when deemed appropriate, as Ascard Watchmen.

Her father had not wanted that future for her. He fought to abolish slavery, leading raids on slave camps and caravans. During one of those raids, he hired a freed slave to teach her to hide her ascard ability. An elegant and kind, yet firm teacher, Hadris had been a pureblooded Lyran noble and adept prior to being condemned to slavery for a crime she said she hadn't committed.

Perhaps the stranger was also an adept. The possibility was exciting and frightening. If she were of a bolder disposition, she might not have fled, but then what would have happened? Thinking about it made her gut clench. Memories of Hadris shoved to her knees before a headsman's blade brought a cold sweat to her palms. The last thing she needed was to be caught associating with another Lyran adept.

* * *

"Indigo."

She woke to the murmur of her name. Jayce leaned over her. The sun had moved well across the sky. It was late afternoon. Accepting his offered hand, she let him help her to her feet. They joined Andrea and Caplin by the carriage as the footman went to gather the blanket.

"You looked so peaceful we didn't want to disturb you,"

Caplin said, "but I must get back."

"I apologize. I had not intended to fall asleep."

He waved the apology off and offered Andrea a hand up into the carriage.

On the return trip, Andrea leaned on Caplin, and he rested an arm around her shoulders. When he caught Indigo's eyes, she gave a subtle nod in approval of the match. He smiled back and continued his conversation with Jayce.

Indigo gazed out into the fading light.

They were passing a slave wagon fitted with a large rusty cage in which five men and two women huddled. She searched their features for a glimpse of the beauty and strength she had seen in the man by the fountain. They were dirty, their clothes threadbare, and their eyes shadowed. Something—perhaps nothing more profound than their natural lack of facial hair—gave the men an air of refinement out of place in the rusty enclosure. One woman looked at Indigo. Pride and stubborn defiance shone in her pale eyes. Untouchable beauty rose from the strength there.

Tears stung Indigo's eyes.

"More of Raving Rylan's discards," Andrea muttered.

Indigo bristled. Her father's voice rang out in her mind. *Never judge by appearances, child. The important differences lie within.*

A belief he lived and died by, fighting the slave trade until it put him in his grave. She admired his conviction, even if it left her life in chaos.

A crush of sorrow made her turn from the Lyran woman. The man next to the fountain could not have been real. There were no pureblooded Lyrans in Caithin who weren't slaves, aside from the rare dignitary who came to treat with the king. Such a man would never wander nighttime streets without protection.

She blinked back tears. The prospect of losing her mind

didn't bother her as much as that of never seeing him again.

* * *

Indigo and Jayce supped that evening in silence. Invested in her brooding, she neglected to acknowledge that he had slipped into a darker mood. The silence suited her. When she rose to go to bed, he stood, bumping the table hard enough that it scraped the floor, and grabbed her arm. Startled, she jerked away.

His eyes narrowed, a storm of emotion boiling within them. "You are jealous, aren't you?"

She shook her head, confused. "Jealous of whom?"

"Andrea. I saw you and Caplin share your little moment in the carriage."

Frustration flashed like lightning, bowling over caution. "Caplin and I have been friends for years. How can you be such a fool?"

She hit the floor, her raw elbows stinging with the fresh impact. Shaking fingers touched her lip. They came away smeared with red. She stared up at Jayce. He shifted his feet, his hand still balled into a fist. Then he sneered.

"That's what you get for provoking me all the time!"

His words burned through her daze. She spat blood at his feet. "Provoking you!"

Using a chair for balance, she got to her feet.

"Yes!" He threw a hand in the air, warming to the argument. "Dressing like you are on the market. Flirting all the time. Going to that ridiculous academy."

She backed away, shaking so hard her legs threatened to give out. "I have always been faithful to you, and I have no choice about my training."

His gaze flickered from her eyes to the hand reaching behind her toward the front door. "What are you doing?"

"Going for a walk."

"You are not going anywhere."

She continued backing toward the door. He lunged, grabbing her arm. While his balance was forward, she twisted away, forcing him to release her to keep from falling. She yanked open the door and ran down the stairs, rushing out into the darkness. He screamed her name into the street a few seconds later, but she didn't slow, running blind through the tears in her eyes. She sped past two couples strolling in the moonlit streets and a well-lit house where a gathering had spilled out the front door. The sounds of merriment amplified her misery.

When she reached the Healer's Courtyard, it was dark and empty, like the hollow in her chest. She sank against the edge of the lower pool and pulled her knees in, clenching her teeth against more tears.

The Lyran stranger wasn't there. He had been a hallucination. She had skinned her elbows on the cobblestones fleeing her own desperate imagination.

Tears burst free. There was nowhere to go from here, nowhere except back.

"Help me."

Her heart stuttered. She looked up, her lungs constricting when she met his eyes.

"What are you?"

"Come with me and I will tell you."

When she didn't move, he knelt beside her, and she sank willingly into his beautiful eyes.

I would go anywhere with you. Away from here. Away from Jayce and this endless apprehension. She yearned to say the words, but memories of the molten landscape stopped them in her throat.

"Do not be afraid." He brushed tears from her cheeks with careful fingers.

At his touch, her head began spinning. She closed her

eyes. He took her hands and guided her to her feet, his effortless strength both shocking and comforting. The smell of sulfur filled the air, and oppressive heat closed in again. She whimpered, afraid to look.

Then his lips touched hers.

The brief flare of indignation at his inappropriate advance faded before pleasure and a desire to prolong the tender contact. When he moved away, the spinning stopped, and she opened her eyes. She could breathe again, but the black, broken landscape surrounded them.

Fear rushed back in. "No."

He took her face in his hands, making her meet his eyes. "Stay with me."

She grabbed his wrists. "I don't want to be here. This is..." His charmed smile baffled her into silence.

"It is not the Sinner's Hereafter." There was a hint of laughter in his tone, but it faded along with the smile. "Give me a chance to explain. Please."

She met his eyes, captivated by those complex depths. Fear dwindled before the intensity of his gaze. The landscape lost importance. She let go of his wrists.

He leaned in as if to kiss her again, then hesitated. She held her breath, longing twisting in her chest. He did kiss her then. A voice in her head insisted that she stop him. Engaged women didn't behave this way. It was a small voice, however, and loyalty to Jayce was the least of her concerns if this was real, and of no concern at all if it wasn't. She returned the kiss, letting forbidden indulgence and the sting from her split lip ground her. When they parted, he looked inappropriately pleased, and embarrassment rose hot in her cheeks.

He took her hand. "Follow me."

CHAPTER THREE

After three tries that evening, Yiloch had almost walked away, but he had given it one last effort. She had been there. He hadn't planned to kiss her, but he had needed to distract her from her fear, and her injured lip drew his attention to her mouth, and his delight at her return overwhelmed his better judgment. The second kiss simply happened. The touch of her lips sent a barrage of neglected desires pounding through him. Her beauty, while a striking and welcome contrast to the hostile volcanic scenery, proved distracting.

When it looked like she might stay in spite of, or perhaps because of, his inappropriate advances, he took her hand and began a careful traverse across the hardened black crust. Active flow ran molten below the surface, and the crust was fragile in places. His nerves, charged with excitement for the freedom she represented, crackled like lightning with the stress of navigating the dangerous terrain.

When her delicate hand started trembling in his, he spun to face her, and she jerked back in surprise. Careless. He could not afford to frighten her.

He looked her over, noticing more detail this time. Someone had struck her recently, judging by her split and swollen lip. Acting on instinct, he brushed away a trace of drying blood below her lip and forced what he hoped was a comforting smile. "I will not let you get hurt."

Her slow nod was full of reservations. Fear showed plain in her pallor and the rapid pulse along her slender neck, yet she stayed. Somewhat drunk on gratitude, he turned away to hide a ridiculous grin and led the way on.

It took most of an hour to reach the nearest shelter, every second of which he expected her to disappear. The shelter was a chamber encased in cooled lava with an entrance small enough to keep out the monstrous hounds that roamed there. A natural skylight in the ceiling admitted enough light for him to guide her to the crude bed he had constructed, a weaving of flexible branches from berry bushes and scarce grasses arranged upon a shelf of hardened lava. The chamber exuded a musty smell, but he doubted she would notice after her fresh inundation in sulfur stench.

At his direction, she sat and watched him light a fire under the skylight. When he finished, he sat on a rock to one side, close enough to talk without being threatening.

"What is this place?"

Despite her extraordinary circumstances, she still spoke Lyran. That was an unexpected consideration.

"This is a prison created specifically for me." He held up a hand when she shifted away from him. "Do not judge too hastily. I was organizing a rebellion against Emperor Rylan, but someone betrayed me, and now, here I am."

"Here I am," she echoed. A flicker of interest caught in her eyes. "You were trying to fight Raving Rylan?"

He crushed down a preposterous swell of defensiveness for his father. "Is that what the Caithin call him?"

"Some do. He claims to be immortal—at least that is the gossip—and he sells his own people into slavery. That doesn't seem especially rational."

Her expression darkened, and disapproval tightened her voice when she mentioned the slave trade. How encouraging. Her pulse still ran wild under the soft bronze skin of her throat, and her hands trembled in her lap, but she was looking around now. Then, her vibrant blue eyes locked on him with a commanding intensity.

"Who are you?"

"Lord Eldrian Seraff." He had to give her a false name. If she knew much about his father, the "raving" Lyran emperor, she would know about the Blood Prince as well. Given the rather infamous past mistakes that earned him that hated nickname, telling her who he was could make securing her cooperation impossible.

"How…"

He held up a finger to silence her. She obliged and began picking at her fingernails, making little clicking noises with them. Exhaling a soft laugh, he reached over and touched her hands to quiet them. It had been so long since he last laughed that it surprised him to find he could still do it.

"I'm sorry. I do that when I get nervous." She folded her hands in her lap. The light bronze of her skin deepened with a hint of rosy flush.

She was exquisite.

"I said I would explain." He stared into the fire, struggling with a surge of longing. He had prepared to face disbelief and fear in his subject. The possibility of that subject being a beautiful woman had never crossed his mind. "This prison is a fabricated ascard environment. It exists everywhere and nowhere at once."

"That makes no sense."

"Have you heard of Symphanie Serroc?"

"Many times."

Her wistful smile surprised him as much as her words did. It was a Lyran tale, not something he expected a Caithin woman to know. He nodded, encouraging her to continue, both to find out what she knew and to get her engaged in the conversation.

When she spoke, her voice picked up the cadence of a storyteller, rhythmic and entrancing. "When she was born,

Symphanie Serroc was the most beautiful child in all of Lyra, and she grew to be the most beautiful woman. Her beauty was so extraordinary that her own father fell in love with her. Madness grew within him for want of her until one day he killed her mother and insisted that she marry him. When she refused, he commissioned a…"

She paused, searching for the right word in Lyran, he suspected. Her fluency was impressive, and he appreciated her using it with him. It showed a consideration of others that seemed to come naturally to her. That too could work in his favor.

"He commissioned a… creator?" She met his eyes, continuing when he nodded at her choice of words. "… to make a special prison for her. The prison he created was an ascard fabrication as extraordinary as the woman it confined, a beautiful forest environment that she could never leave and only her father could enter. He swore to release her only if she married him, but she never consented, choosing instead to grow old and die alone in her prison.

"I see what you are implying, but it is only a story," she added when she finished.

"How do you know it so well?"

"I had a Lyran tutor as a child. She told it to me whenever I got upset with my father to illustrate how much worse he could be."

Although her response to him and her comfort with his language supported her claim, he found it hard to accept the idea. "It is rather uncommon in Caithin, is it not, to let a Lyran slave tutor one's children?"

"She… My father…" She chewed at her lower lip for a few seconds then shrugged. "My family was not typical."

How he wanted to dig deeper, but there wasn't time and it didn't matter. Theirs wouldn't be a long relationship. "Do you know the rest of the story?"

"There is no rest of the story." When she shook her head,

some of her wavy dark hair fell around her eyes. She brushed it back; her slender fingers tipped with neatly trimmed nails. Not a woman accustomed to physical labor.

"There is more. Symphanie did not die of old age. Before her father passed, he gave the secret of the prison to another."

"If he was so jealous of his daughter, why would he tell anyone?"

"Everyone has their price." Her expression darkened, but she didn't argue. "This man went into the prison. Symphanie was old, her beauty depleted by time and sorrow, but the man was not there for her. He had been sent to study the prison. He was unable to manipulate it with her inside, so he killed Symphanie. Then he took the secret of the prison to a group of powerful creators and had others like it made. We are in one of those prisons."

"You are implying that Emperor Rylan took the secret of the prison." She sat in contemplative silence for a minute, picking at a bit of grass in the woven bed, then asked, "Why would he not simply put you to death if you were organizing a rebellion? Why go to this trouble?"

Because he is my father and a fool. "I am not certain. They call him Raving Rylan for a reason." He pressed on before she could question further. "I discovered faults in the prison, places where I can contact the outside world. That is how I was able to appear to you in Demin."

"But Andrea was with me the first time, and she was unable to see you."

She was trying to understand. He respected that, but too many questions and he was going to give away something he should not.

"Few people can. I have tried countless times." The most success he had prior to her had been a Kudaness priest who tried to run him through with a spear when he appeared. Not the most encouraging encounter. "Perhaps you saw me because you were willing to. I am unsure how it works. What I do know is you could see me and feel my touch even though I was never physically there. I cannot leave through the faults, but I could bring you here."

"You were far more finely dressed by the fountain," she remarked with a pointed glance at his tattered clothes.

"Illusion," he countered, pleased by her increasing boldness. She was relaxing into a conversational tone, which he hoped meant his explanations had satisfied her. "Would you have come with me if I had appeared to be a vagrant?"

"Perhaps not. Why did you bring me here?" An amused smirk turned her lips. "For a romantic tryst, the location lacks something."

"You have me there." He cracked a genuine smile. It felt awkward on lips that had not done so in many months. Her fortitude and lack of prejudice were refreshing, precious rays of sunshine in a world of storm clouds. "A tryst with you sounds delightful, but I brought you here because you can help me escape. I must resume my campaign against Emperor Rylan."

Her gaze turned inward. Years of practice in politics gave him the poise to sit quietly, waiting to find out what thoughts churned behind her pensive frown. When she focused on him again, fiery determination burned in her blue eyes.

"What must I do?"

Tension lifted. Long-bound muscles relaxed. She was willing to try. That was a victory by itself.

"I have done my own research into these prisons. This place was created to hold one specific person. If you come to the gate with me, your presence should trigger a safeguard in the prison makeup that will, for lack of a better term, unlock the door. Then you can return home. The prison cannot hold you against your will because you are not the one they created it for."

Her eyes widened a fraction. "So, I could leave at any

time?"

Do I lie to her?

No. Some measure of trust was necessary. It had to be her choice to stay. If she didn't understand that she could pull herself out without meaning to. He nodded.

"And if this does not work?"

"Then I remain imprisoned, and you return home."

"As easy as that?"

I hope so. He nodded.

Her gaze shifted to his arm, and her nervous fidgeting stopped. "Are you injured?"

Forgetting her caution, she came around the fire and knelt beside him, reaching for the bloodstained tear in the arm of his shirt. He pulled away, and she gave him a chastising look, then took hold of the arm. With careful fingers, she removed the crude bandage and inspected the wound he had sustained that morning in an altercation with one of the hounds. She placed a hand over the gash and closed her eyes, delicate furrows forming on her brow. The pain of flesh knitting back together brought understanding. She was a healer. The prison muted his connection to the ascard, but it appeared to have no such effect on hers. When she took her hands away, the wound had closed.

She met his gaze. "I hope that was not too painful."

"Not at all." How wonderful she smelled, like warm spring and roses. He ached to touch her. Desire burned hot in his blood. It took substantial effort to bury that longing. "You are a healer?"

"A student, actually." She smiled, proud of her achievement. "They do not permit us to heal outside the academy until our third year, but I can't imagine they will find out about this."

"What of your injury?" He touched her lip.

She jerked away, her expression darkening. When she

turned to return to her seat, he noticed the Caithin healer's rose tattooed between her shoulder blades. Intrigued, he reached out to trace the stem with one finger. She gasped and spun, glaring an explicit warning at him.

"I apologize." He tried to look repentant. Now that she knew she could leave of her own free will, he needed to be more cautious, but it was hard to resist an excuse to feel how real and alive she was.

The warning faded, and she sat back on the makeshift bed. Her fingertips touched the split lip. "I think I will keep this for now."

Such sorrow in her eyes. "I still don't know your name."

"Indigo. Lady Indigo Milan, if you wish to be proper, though the situation does not seem all that proper."

She was nobility then. Not a surprise given her apparent education and the fine fabric of her dress, not to mention the expensive ring of promise she wore. The last name sounded familiar, but there was no chance they had met before.

"It is a pleasure to meet you, Lady Indigo."

A fleeting smile touched her lips, and her fingers picked at the thin fabric of her dress. "Where is this gate?"

"A little over a day's walk east. We can leave in the morning."

She glanced up through the skylight at the roiling black clouds. "Does it brighten up at all?"

His chuckle was dry, devoid of genuine humor. "Marginally. Enough to make navigation easier."

She dropped her gaze to her lap, where her hands lay clasped, perhaps to keep them still. "Normally, I would object to spending the night with a stranger, but since this cannot possibly be real..."

He moved to kneel before her and placed a hand on her cheek. She inhaled in surprise, her eyes widening as they met his, but she didn't pull away. Surrendering to impulse, he kissed her again. She didn't pull away from that either.

"Was that real enough?" His lips lingered close to hers. His pulse pounded so fiercely he could barely hear himself speak.

"Yes."

He might have backed away then, but her breathless reply shattered his will. For seven months, he had been without human contact. How could he resist such temptation? He kissed her more insistently, and her mouth opened to him, her response hinting at a need almost as strong as his. He ran one hand over the bare skin of her back, and she shivered, pressing closer. Her hand slipped around the back of his neck, the light touch of her fingers fanning the flames. She offered no resistance when he pressed her back onto the bed.

He gathered up the silky fabric of her dress and slid his hand under it, up the inside of her thigh. She tensed, and he stopped, drawing back enough to meet her eyes. He wanted her more than he had ever wanted anyone, but there was one thing he wanted more. His freedom. This wasn't worth driving her away.

Her other hand came up and hesitated inches from his face. Her gaze pulled him in, holding him there while she searched his eyes. Then her hand on the back of his neck tightened, drawing his mouth to hers. Her body relaxed, and his hand resumed its path as he gave himself over to the hunger raging within.

Later, he lay on his side with her warm back pressed to his chest and his arms wrapped around her, feeling her heart beating in time with his. She trembled in his embrace, and he brushed the backs of his fingers against her cheek. They came away damp. What could he say to ease her sorrow without knowing its cause? Was it guilt over betraying whoever had given her the ring? Whatever prompted her to give herself to him, he was grateful, so he kissed her head and held her until she fell asleep. It was no bother. She fit perfectly against him.

CHAPTER FOUR

L ord Caplin?" The tentative voice crept through the door, accompanied by an equally tentative knock.

Caplin rubbed his eyes. Was it time for the council meeting already?

He glanced through the window. The pale gray of pre-dawn glowered back. It was barely morning. The meeting wouldn't start until noon. There was no good reason for him not to sleep several more hours.

He rolled onto his side, putting his back to the door, and closed his eyes.

"My lord?" The voice was softer this time, more uncertain. "Lady Andrea is in the foyer."

Caplin groaned.

Why now? Hadn't they spent the previous day together? How much attention did the woman need?

Guilt poked at him through a fog of sleep, and a stray thought tugged at his awareness. Wasn't Andrea supposed to be in class at the academy? If she were here instead, something must be wrong.

Concern snapped him awake. Rolling out of bed, he went to the door and stuck his head out. He met the eyes of a grim-looking portrait of his grandfather staring at him from the opposite wall of the hallway, a reminder that he came from a long line of important, grumpy men and that he should be forever thankful to have inherited his nose from his mother's side. He looked down at the Lyran boy standing outside the door.

The boy bowed his head.

Caplin opened his mouth to speak, and his mother's voice popped into his head.

"Calling someone by their name acknowledges that they are a person. Remember that even the lowest man is still a man."

He exhaled and searched his mind for the boy's name. "Sheyv?"

A faint head bob. That was confirmation enough.

"Tell Lady Andrea I shall be down momentarily and see that someone offers her tea."

"Yes, my lord. Shall I send Durin to assist you, my lord?"

A headache threatened at the mere thought. "Absolutely not. The last thing I need is him trying to organize my room again. I couldn't find a blasted thing the last time."

Sheyv made a small noise that might have been a strangled laugh before bobbing a hasty bow and scampering off down the hall.

Caplin gave the portrait across the hall a frosty scowl before shutting the door, then sorted through clothing lying at the foot of the bed, sniffing at them to see if they were suitable for the council meeting later. Once dressed, he arranged his mussed hair, nodded approval at his reflection, and left the room.

Andrea was waiting in the sitting room at the foot of the grand staircase. She sat in a high-backed chair, her spine rigid, staring out the window and twisting a lock of dark red hair around her finger. A rim of red around her eyes suggested she either hadn't slept well or had been crying, maybe both. A steaming cup of tea sat untouched on the table.

She jumped to her feet when he entered and looked past him as if expecting someone else to be there. Disappointment dimmed the light in her eyes.

"Lord Caplin. I am sorry to drop in unexpectedly, but..." she lowered her voice and glanced past him again, "... is Indigo here?"

For a second, he thought she was accusing him of having

relations with Indigo. Then other potential implications behind the question struck him. "Why do you ask?"

Andrea placed a hand on his arm and drew him into the room with her. Lowering her voice even more, she said, "Indigo and Jayce had an argument last night. She left and never came back. She didn't tell him where she was going. Have you seen her?"

His pulse began racing, and a metallic taste rose on his tongue. Where would she have gone at night? He kept his voice even and reassuring. "I'm sure she's fine. She's probably in class now..." He trailed off when Andrea shook her head.

"I went to class after I talked to Jayce, hoping she would be there. When she didn't show up, I requested permission to leave and came here. I didn't know where else to go. You two have been friends for a long time. I thought you might know where to find her. Jayce is in an absolute fury."

And what did our dear Lord Jayce do to chase her away?

Indigo's training at the academy was important to her. She believed that becoming a healer would somehow erase her father's treason from people's memories. He couldn't imagine her missing class over a simple argument. The twisting sensation in his gut warned of something more sinister.

He clutched Andrea's arm. "What did Jayce do to her?"

She took a step back and jerked her arm away, her eyes widening in surprise. The moment of stunned silence was short-lived, however, then her eyes narrowed and her hands settled on her hips.

"He didn't *do* anything," she snapped. "She overreacted to a little argument."

Caplin bit the insides of his cheeks, fighting not to say something he would regret. He had known Indigo for a long time. The Indigo he knew was considerate and sensible. It wasn't like her to storm off in a fit of pique. She wouldn't have run out into the night without good reason. Jayce must have done something substantial to provoke that reaction. Still, Andrea was as quick to defend Jayce as he was to defend Indigo, and fighting with each other wasn't going to help them find her.

"I do not know where she would go if she didn't seek out one of us. I can check a few places this morning. There is a council meeting later. If I haven't found her by then, I will ask Lord Serivar if he has heard anything."

Andrea's expression softened. "Yes. Headmaster Serivar should know regardless, in case she doesn't show up for her other classes."

He gave her shoulder a comforting squeeze. "I am sure she will show up soon. Don't worry about it."

"Thank you, Caplin. I knew you'd help." She beamed at him, her anger forgotten. "I had best get back."

He escorted her to the door and watched until she passed out of sight, then shoved it shut and turned into the house. Panic threatened again. What if something terrible had happened? Someone might have attacked Indigo, even killed her, if she had wandered down the wrong streets at night. Demin might be one of the safest cities in the kingdom, but there were still places where a woman walking alone at night would draw the wrong kind of attention.

The mere thought caused painful twisting in his chest. He had to find her. She was his sanity. Whenever he got discouraged by the politics of the High Council or demands of upper nobility, he sought her out for the calming effect she had on him, albeit less often since her engagement. Her pleasant conversation and open smile were a soothing balm to any frustration.

Stepping back into the sitting room, he pulled the string for the servant's bell. Sheyv darted out through a hidden door. Caplin didn't give the boy time to complete his bow.

"Have Terun saddle my bay gelding, Nissin. I will be out

in a few minutes."

Picking up on the urgency in his tone, the boy rushed to the door, pausing for a quick bow before vanishing outside.

"Father!" Caplin took a few steps toward the staircase and paused. He didn't know where his father might be in the big house at this hour. Perhaps in a sitting room or his study. He was an early riser. "Father!"

As the second shout rang through the house, the door under the staircase that led to the kitchens flew open. His mother, a handsome woman whose refined features complimented her gentle nature, stepped through the doorway amidst a waft of aromas that made his stomach growl. The cook was hard at work on something.

His mother raised her eyebrows at him. "By the Divine's grace, Caplin, are you trying to wake the district?"

"Where is Father?"

She walked to him and lifted one hand toward his head in a familiar attempt to smooth his hair. Caplin caught her slender wrist in a firm grip, and she searched his eyes, frowning.

"Is something wrong, dear?"

"Indigo has gone missing. I need to go look for her."

He released her hand, and it went to her chest. "Dear me. I hope she is all right. I am afraid Gavin has already gone to the palace. A messenger came for him early this morning. Emperor Rylan must have snubbed some part of the trade agreement again."

Caplin ground his teeth in frustration. How ironic that Indigo's calming influence would be such a boon right then. He placed a distracted kiss on his mother's forehead. "I'll see him at the meeting then."

"Will you be home for supper?" she asked when he spun away and strode to the door.

He jerked it open and stepped through, pausing with one

hand gripping the ornate handle tight enough to hurt. "I don't know." He shut the door, blocking out the disappointment in her eyes.

The day was bright, though a chill lingered in the morning air. He stopped in the courtyard and closed his eyes, picturing Indigo. Her smile came to mind—a beautiful smile that lit her vivid blue eyes with its sincerity. Aching filled him, and he opened his eyes, his glare cutting through the morning calm as he stormed toward the stable.

The groom, Terun, his ice-white hair bound in a long tail, met him at the door with Nissin saddled and ready to go. Caplin took the reins and swung into the saddle, managing a hasty nod of recognition for the man before he trotted the gelding out into the morning street.

There were only so many places Indigo might go. She was too absorbed in her schooling to build up many close friends in the city, and her Uncle Theron's estate was too far outside the city for a spontaneous visit. The meadow by the river was a favorite place. He couldn't imagine her spending the night there, but it was the best lead he had.

A few hours later, Caplin returned to town disappointed. He found no sign of her near the river. She might have shown up at the academy or her residence by now. He couldn't verify either possibility in the time he had, so he went to the palace. If nothing else, he might have a minute to talk to his father about her before the meeting. Gavin referred to Indigo as his incidental daughter. He might think of something Caplin overlooked.

King Jerrin's hearty bellow met him when he stepped through the council room door.

"He is going to get a war if he keeps this up!" The king's face flushed beneath his heavy beard, his dark eyes pinching in anger.

Gavin and Lord Serivar, the Healer's Academy headmaster, were also present. Jerrin paused in his tirade, and the three men nodded greetings. Caplin bowed to his uncle first before offering a nod to his father and Lord Serivar.

"Am I interrupting?"

"Not at all." Jerrin gestured to a random chair.

Caplin took his usual seat as Jerrin resumed his rant.

"That Divine forsaken Emperor Rylan has raised prices on slaves again, and he increased taxes on Lyran exports of wine and fabric for the third time in two months. He is making a mockery of our trade agreement."

It was a testament to the state of things that his mother already guessed the cause of the king's distress. The Lyran emperor had been abusing the terms of the trade agreement in subtle ways for several years. In the last several months, he had progressed to openly disregarding much of that agreement, and Caithin's nobility was beginning to feel the impact of his actions in rising costs. Jerrin could no longer afford to let it slide and risk losing the support of his people.

There was a long silence while the king composed himself. Then he turned to Caplin. "There is another issue we have been discussing. I know you have friends in the education district. Perhaps you might have insight to offer."

Caplin longed to talk to his father about Indigo, but he didn't dare brush off his uncle when the man was already in a sour mood. He stared at Jerrin, trying to generate interest.

Gavin read him like a book and held up a staying hand to his brother. "You look troubled, Son. What is wrong?"

With no small relief, he turned to his father. "Lady Andrea paid a visit this morning to ask for my help. Our mutual friend, Lady Indigo, has gone missing."

The meaningful look Gavin and Jerrin shared then gave Caplin a dreadful chill. They knew something and, judging by their solemn expressions, it wasn't good.

Serivar glowered at him. "Who is Lady Indigo?"

"Indigo Milan," Caplin snapped. "She is a student at your academy."

Serivar's eyes bored into him. "Do you honestly think I have time to memorize the names of every individual enrolled in the academy?"

Caplin opened his mouth to snap back, but his father's harsh look silenced him. "I think we have identified our mystery woman. The description fits."

Caplin glanced around at them. "What do you mean? What mystery woman?"

Jerrin nodded to Gavin, who leaned back in his chair and inhaled deeply. He scratched his chin through his well-trimmed beard, and his dark eyes gazed down the broad family nose Jerrin also shared, but that Caplin had fortunately escaped.

"There was a strange flare of ascard energy in the Healer's Courtyard the day before yesterday. It happened again that night, a little stronger. The Ascard Watchmen increased patrols in the area yesterday, but we assumed someone was playing around illicitly with their healing skills. Such things happen on occasion. With a few Ascard Watchmen tuned to the area, a third offence would have given them an ascard signature to work with. When nothing else happened around there yesterday, they resumed normal patrols."

Gavin glanced at Serivar, perhaps seeking verification of the story. The academy headmaster worked closely with the Watchmen on matters of student misconduct.

Serivar stared at the table, his long fingers steepled in front of him, and gave a faint nod.

Gavin continued. "Last night, a Watchman saw a young woman going to the Healer's Courtyard alone. A few minutes later, there was a powerful surge of ascard energy from the area. When he reached the courtyard, there was no one there. They started investigating and found a couple who had been near there the night before. They said they had seen a young woman running away from the courtyard. The description they gave matched that of the woman the Watchman saw. It also sounded familiar to me when I heard it, though I was not sure why until you mentioned Lady Indigo."

Caplin felt faintly ill. "They haven't found her then?"

"No. They will continue searching, and now we can at least tell them who they are searching for. I am afraid we cannot do much more than that."

Caplin stared at his father. Something inside him broke, leaving a hollow in his chest.

"The young woman has a lot to answer for," Serivar snapped.

Gavin's look of warning kept Caplin from lashing out in response. Perhaps one student among hundreds mattered little to the headmaster, but the callous tone infuriated him. What if something bad had happened to her? What if she had tried to protect herself with ascard or someone else had used it against her? The possibilities were endless, and he didn't like any of them.

The door cracked open, and a servant stepped in, bowing to Jerrin. "Your Majesty, the other council members are arriving."

Jerrin nodded. "Send them in. We have a great deal to discuss."

CHAPTER FIVE

Indigo didn't have to open her eyes to know she wasn't with Jayce. He had never held her like this. Her heart sped up. She opened her eyes to the sight of jagged black stone pressing around them. Dingy light shone on the packed dirt floor where the remains of a fire smoldered in the center.

Not a nightmare.

Like the shelter, the long muscular body pressed against her was very real.

Or a dream.

What have I done?

No matter how wrong it might be to wake up in another man's arms, the warmth of his embrace muffled her guilt and quieted her fear. Savoring the sensation, she lay there until he stirred next to her. His hand came up to caress her cheek.

"Eldrian," she murmured.

He said nothing, and she wondered if he had heard her, then he slipped his arm out from under her and rose on his elbow. She rolled onto her back. The gray light became beautiful where it touched his long silver hair.

"I didn't hurt you last night, did I?"

She shook her head, the concern in his voice soothing her inner turmoil more than her own attempts at justification could. Right or wrong, it was easy to forget everything else while gazing into his stunning silver-blue eyes, so cold at a glance, hiding such extraordinary passion.

"I should not have been so bold." He traced the line of

her jaw with one finger. "You have lovely eyes."

She exhaled a small laugh, and he raised his brow in question. "I was thinking the same thing about you."

He kissed her then. She reciprocated willingly and with none of the awkwardness she might have expected after such sinful indulgence with a stranger. Perhaps that was because of the peculiarity of the situation. The thought of Jayce out searching might have caused her guilt if not for the sting of her lip as they kissed. Classes would go on without her, and she hated to fall behind, but that was far away. Part of another world.

Within this nightmare landscape, she was free for once to do as she pleased, and it pleased her to experience all of him. He was keeping things from her, but since he only needed her to help him escape, they didn't need to know one another's secrets. The lack of long-term obligation provided a sweet sense of liberation.

He ended the kiss and got up to gather his tattered clothes. The fabrics were expensive silks, satins, and other fine cloth, still beautiful despite the wear. Upper nobility indeed, if that was his typical attire.

Lyran grace poured out of him, evident in every move-ment. Lean muscle rippled beneath his pale skin. A long scar ran along his ribs, and another marked his left thigh. Perhaps battle wounds given his situation. A good healer might have prevented such scarring, but she appreciated their stark con-trast to his almost surreal perfection.

He glanced at her over his shoulder, and she looked away, her cheeks warming. He chuckled and finished dress-ing. Aware that he now watched her, she rose and pulled on her wrinkled dress. His open admiration made her cheeks flush hot, more with desire than embarrassment.

When she finished, he handed her some dry purple berries. She followed him from the shelter, munching on the sour morsels. The landscape was more desolate in the grayish light seeping through dark clouds. It wasn't active here like the area they had traversed in the night. This appeared older with patches of dirt and sparse brown grass nestled amidst black basalt and spotted with gnarled little trees and bushes.

He led her to a nearby spring where they drank their fill, then turned his somber gaze on her. "Are you ready?"

"Lead on, my lord." She hid discomfort behind her smile. The berries only amplified her hunger, but, from the looks of the place, food was in short supply.

He started walking, his strides confident. She took a deep breath and followed. The sulfur stench was less bothersome now. She was growing used to it.

They hadn't gone far before the sting of rubs began on her toes and heels along with a building ache in the arches of her feet. Her dress shoes weren't made for traversing such rugged terrain. When the pain became intolerable, she would heal her feet, but only then. Healing was draining, and she didn't dare waste too much energy on it.

Hours passed with the dark sky churning overhead. Needles of pain began shooting up her lower legs, muddling her thoughts. Bleak surroundings faded before the substantial effort of putting one foot in front of the other.

When he noticed her falling behind, he stopped. She sank down on a weathered rock and took off the shoes, exposing bloody rubs on her toes and heels.

He gave her a reproving look. "You should have said something."

"And what would you have done, carried me?"

At least he was sensible enough not to argue the point. Instead, he turned to picking tart berries off a nearby bush while she placed her hands around one foot and then the other, healing the wounds. With considerable dread, she slipped the shoes back on. Sticky smears of blood inside them promised more misery.

He gave her another handful of berries and frowned at her feet. "I hate to make you continue."

She said nothing. She had a choice. If he spoke the truth, she could leave this place, and him, behind at any time. There would be no more of this pain, but...

Dodging those thoughts, she said, "My father gave his life fighting the slave trade."

"Desgard Milan!"

She stared, startled to hear her father's name, the pronunciation skewed by his accent. "You knew my father?"

"His name is well known in Lyra. He and those who fought with him are heroes to many. People tell stories of their exploits. They caused my... They caused the emperor quite a few headaches."

She lowered her gaze to hide the sudden well of tears. "Headaches. He died for the sake of causing a few headaches."

His hand rested on her arm, strong and comforting. "Your father was fighting an impossible battle, but he restored many lives. The emperor chooses to sell his people into slavery. It will take more than a handful of fighters to stop him."

"Why does he do it?" She looked up, searching his pale eyes, savoring his touch. Melancholy swept in when he withdrew his hand.

"To eliminate those who oppose him and frighten the rest into behaving. I admired his cunning until I was old enough to understand that it is the product of cowardice and an inability to lead. You should be proud of your father. He was very courageous. A trait he seems to have passed on to his daughter."

She rolled her eyes and started turning away, but he caught her jaw and forced her to look at him.

"I mean that. Not many people would stay here to help a

stranger. You are a more remarkable woman than I think you realize."

Not many would sleep with that stranger either. What does that say about me?

She squirmed under the intensity of his gaze, wishing he would kiss her or release her. Unfortunately, he chose the latter.

"Why are you fighting Emperor Rylan?"

His jaw tightened, and he narrowed his eyes, their striking depths darkening with anger. "Lyra is a proud and beautiful country with a rich history. Her people are proud and beautiful as well. Rylan is destroying that, undermining a magnificent empire that was the greatest single power in the known world not so long ago. I will not stand by and watch my country and its people crumble."

A wave of affection surprised her. She pushed the berries around her palm with one finger and smiled. "You sound like my father ranting. He would have liked you."

"Is he the reason you agreed to help me?"

"This kind of behavior does seem to run in the family," she replied, "but there's more to it than that."

"Such as?"

Yes, such as?

She stayed because of Hadris and her father, two of the dearest people to her heart, but that wasn't all.

She averted her eyes and put a few berries in her mouth. The tart morsels did nothing for her hunger or her growing thirst. "Is there water nearby?"

He smirked at her evasion and let the question go unanswered. "There is water at the next shelter."

"I don't suppose a carriage will be by soon?"

He shook his head, a glimmer of amusement in his eyes, and took her hands, lifting her to her feet. "No."

"Lead on then."

He continued at a more deliberate pace now that he was aware of her pain, which also allowed for conversation. "If I recall the stories right, your father was not a fan of mandatory academy training for adepts in Caithin. He couldn't have appreciated watching them take you away."

"They didn't. Hadris, my Lyran tutor, was an adept. She taught me to mask my ability."

"But you *are* training as a healer?"

She was, because they were both dead now. All their efforts to protect her and she had nothing to show for it but fear and haunting memories.

"Go, Indigo. Please don't watch this," Hadris pleaded, her violet eyes overflowing with tears.

The Ascard Watchmen shoved Hadris to her knees and pulled her pale hair forward. Indigo wanted to look away, but her eyes wouldn't close, her head wouldn't turn. The blade was sharp. She wept and screamed when her tutor's head fell away in a spray of blood, her body slumping to the ground like a dropped sack of flour.

Judgment and execution were immediate for a Lyran slave caught using ascard in Caithin. Her father's death must have looked much the same, though she had been spared that sight.

She swallowed the lump in her throat. "They executed Hadris for using ascard a few months before they caught my father and executed him for treason. Mother chose not to go on living without him, so my uncle took me in and negotiated to preserve my noble status. Still, I am marked by my father's deeds and my exposure to a Lyran adept. I am a stain upon society, so I let some of my ability show in order to train as a healer and better my standing."

"*Some* of your ability?"

A spark of fear danced along her nerves. A few careless

words and he now knew more about her than anyone alive. Still, even if he got free of this place, it was not likely to come up in his life again, and telling someone her secret was as terrifying as it was cathartic.

I have gone this far.

"Hadris and Father warned me not to reveal my full strength. I can't bring myself to ignore their warning. I keep much of it hidden."

He picked his way through a section of broken basalt, and she followed precisely in his footsteps.

"I assume you know there is more to using ascard than healing."

"Not where I'm from," she replied.

"You cannot be satisfied with that."

"Can't I?"

"Not knowing the power you use to heal has so much more potential. You already use it to mask part of your strength and to prevent conception."

She stumbled, wincing from a flare of pain in her foot. "How..." She bit off the question, her cheeks burning, and scowled at his back.

The first thing female students learned from peers at the Healer's Academy was how to use ascard to prevent pregnancy. Most students were away from supervision for the first time in their lives, and much discovery went on in the residences that polite society turned a blind eye to. The ascard method of protection was easier than other options and required no pre-planning. Senior students passed on the knowledge like sacred doctrine. The Watchmen had to be aware of the practice, but such a minute amount of ascard energy wouldn't alert them unless they were within a few feet of the guilty party.

"I don't think about it."

"Of course not." He glanced back, his enigmatic smile

snaring her curiosity.

"What do you know? Are you an adept?"

"The academy is a good thing to a point," he said, side-stepping the question. "Caithin channels their adepts down a specific path and provides necessary training. In Lyra, people choose their own path, but healers are rare because we have no organized training. People can use ascard as they choose. Since healing requires intimate knowledge of the human body, few put forth the effort to learn it."

"Lyra should create schools. Healers are an asset to any nation."

He gave her a measuring glance and nodded. "I agree. Why does Caithin control the use of ascard so rigorously?"

"Because uncontrolled power is dangerous."

"They drill that into your heads to keep you out of trouble. Do you honestly think the military potential has escaped them?"

She stumbled again and glared at the rocks as if they, and not her unease with their conversation, were responsible. This discussion alone would be grounds for arrest in Demin. "You think they have military-trained adepts they're keeping secret. That's ridiculous."

"Is it?"

"I..." She trailed off. Ingrained fear made her defensive. If she thought about it, his words made more sense than the assumption that Caithin's leadership would ignore an obvious military asset. "No, it isn't."

Silence followed, and her thoughts wandered while she struggled with ever-increasing pain. Why was she putting herself through this when she could leave at will?

The answer lay in a man she barely knew, whose every look made her feel needed, whose every touch made her feel wanted. A man who challenged her to see her world with fresh eyes. Being with him forced her to acknowledge how flawed her relationship with Jayce was and how much she longed for someone to confide in. The mere act of mentioning her masked ability was like throwing off shackles she had worn most of her life. Shackles that would click shut again the moment she returned home. For those reasons, she would stay, even doomed as this relationship was.

"Indigo."

His urgent whisper sent a spear of panic through her seconds before he grabbed her arm and pulled her down beside a table of basalt.

"What?"

"We have company." He gestured beyond the rocks with a jerk of his head.

She rose high enough to peek over.

"Are you mad?" He yanked her back down.

Before her head dipped below the rocks, she saw the beast. It was a way off still, moving in a course that would intercept their path several yards back. It looked like a hairless hound, only the size of a horse. The long head swung back-and-forth close to the ground, milky white eyes staring ahead.

Her heart stuttered frantically in her chest. "Is it blind?"

"Yes, but it has a fine sense of smell."

"Do you have any weapons?"

He gave a cynical sneer. "Oddly, when they sentenced me to this torment, they chose not to leave me a sword."

"So it was a stupid question," she snapped. "What now?"

"We wait and hope it does not come after us."

"And if it does?"

He met her gaze. "I am working on that."

CHAPTER SIX

Fear gripped Indigo, and the sudden pressure on her lungs made her gasp. The landscape shifted out of focus.

"No." Eldrian brushed his fingers across her cheek. "I need you here."

A hint of desperation shone in his eyes, yet he remained poised and gentle. Her throat tightened at the thought of disappointing him, and the constriction around her chest eased, the landscape coming back into focus.

"I will take care of this. I promise." He looked back the way they had come, his brows pinching together, then held a hand out to her. "Give me your shoes and heal your feet."

Odd as the command was, she handed him the shoes and began the healing process. The beast's claws made a shrill noise, scraping over exposed basalt.

Indigo shuddered.

He placed a hand on her arm when she finished healing, seizing her attention with unsettling intensity.

"Stay hidden and be ready to cover your ears."

Another odd command. She gripped a ragged knob of basalt tight enough to cause pain, distracting from her fear, while he crept over to crouch behind a jut of rock further back along their path. The head of the hound, its pasty white eyes shifting, came into view a few yards beyond his position. Crusted blood around a wound on the creature's head exaggerated its grotesque appearance.

The hound stopped, its scabby black nose pressing to the

ground where they had passed, its breath coming in excited huffs. She tightened her grip on the knob of rock.

The beast turned in their direction and started following the scent trail. Eldrian tossed one of her shoes toward it. When the shoe struck the ground, the creature's head swung toward the sound with the precision of a sighted hunting dog. A growl thrummed through the air like distant thunder, and she covered her mouth to muffle frightened breathing. It lunged, pinning the shoe in place with front paws and tearing at it until shreds of tan and blue material lay strewn about its feet.

Indigo broke into a cold sweat despite the heat of the dismal environment, distantly aware that she had let go of the knob of rock.

Eldrian tossed the other shoe out beside his hiding place, and the beast advanced. Oversized teeth had shredded the flesh around its mouth, distorting its lips with the bloody swelling of continuous injury. There was nothing right or natural about the beast.

Eldrian picked up a rock, testing the weight in his hand like a sword hilt. The warrior in him emerged, his posture and expression taking on a fierce aspect barely more human than the hound. The transformation made her feel very alone. She held her breath while he moved to the edge of his hiding place. The creature began tearing at the second shoe, bloody drool dripping from tattered lips.

Eldrian sprang out, bringing the rock down hard on the existing head wound. A piercing shriek emitted from the abomination, making sense of his warning about covering her ears. It lunged and missed, barreling into the outcrop next to him. Blood ran thick and dark from the wound on its head. It shrieked again and twisted, its mass swinging into him with enough force to send him sprawling.

The hound staggered and shook its head, its nose working hard to sniff out its opponent. Eldrian started to rise, but he moved slowly, dazed and injured by the impact. The beast turned toward him.

How much did she care for this man?

Indigo grabbed a rock and stood, hurling it at the beast. It struck the creature's flank with a meaty *thwack*. The hound spun toward her, staggered to the side, then righted itself and advanced. She froze, time slowing as she stared into those sightless eyes. The beast bunched to lunge.

Bursting into her field of vision, Eldrian rammed his shoulder into the hound, and it toppled. He went down with it and slammed the rock into its head again, pounding it repeatedly into the bloody wound. The sound of cracking bone made her stomach turn. The beast thrashed, throwing him off. Then it sagged, twitched a few times and was still, its skull lying open like a shattered bowl.

Eldrian attempted to rise and stumbled. His hand went to his side. His face twisted in a pained grimace, and he sank beside a large rock. She hurried to him, trying not to see the pulp that had been the hound's head. Moving his hand, she placed hers against his side and used ascard to assess the damage. Five broken ribs.

"This is not good."

"I could have...told you that," he said around a pained gasp.

Could she heal this? If she accessed more of her ability, she could, but what if she couldn't hide it again as it had been before? What if she couldn't control it?

Fear stalled her, but his harsh, shallow breathing compelled her. He couldn't continue this way, and she refused to leave him. Cool sweat broke out on the back of her neck. She reached into her inner aspect and stripped away part of the masking that hid much of her ability. Tuning out his agonized groan, she began to set and heal the bones. The injured flesh around his ribs also required careful attention. It was better to deal with major injuries in stages, allowing time for natural healing to occur between efforts, but it wasn't always possible. The abrasions on his arm and side she left to heal on their own.

Finally, too exhausted to care about rough rock poking at her backside, she sat and pulled her knees to her chest, then rested her arms across them and let her head fall on the table they formed. Her inner aspect was up to the task, but she had never worked with so much ascard energy at once.

His hand touched her shoulder. When she lifted her head, his mouth claimed hers in a long, ardent kiss. When he backed away, his regard boiled over with pleasure and disbelief. "You stayed."

She started to smile, but something else caught her attention, and she wrinkled her nose instead. "What is that smell?"

With a wry grin, he sat back and pulled off his boots, the stiffness of his movement betraying the ache that would remain in his healed side for a few days.

"Our late friend." He nodded to the dead hound as he handed her the boots. "Put these on."

"They are much too big."

His uncompromising scowl convinced her. He stood with a stiffness to match her exhaustion, and they resumed their trek. The boots were too big, making her footing less sure, but at least she wasn't going without.

"You should have warned me about that thing."

"I hoped we would not run into one. I had an altercation with that wretch yesterday." He gestured to the arm she had healed the night before.

"How do they survive here?"

"They are ascard creations. The hounds do not eat, sleep, or drink. The adept who created this place put them here to harry me and kill me if I get careless."

"You have imaginative enemies." His choppy, painful strides made her feet ache in sympathy. "Please take your boots back?"

He spun and his eyes cut into her, the coldness behind them reminding her how little she knew about him. Hiding apprehension, she lifted her chin in defiance of his aggressive stance. His eyes warmed, fondness chasing away the cold.

"In my normal life, I rarely go out of my way to be chivalrous. Consider this my penance for that and stop being foolish. Besides," he added, turning away, "I have you to heal me. We will be at the shelter soon."

Gloom of dusk darkened the landscape when they reached another rock shelter. Several stubby trees and thorny berry bushes formed a partial fence around the entrance. Stomach growling, she dove into picking berries.

He caught her hands and shook his head. "I have something better. Come."

They ducked into the shelter, and the glorious crisp smell of fresh water beckoned from a pool in the back. She snatched the rough-made wooden cup he offered and knelt by the pool. The first cup of cool water ran down her parched throat, a celebration of refreshment. When she had drunk her fill, expunging dryness from her mouth, he moved a rock to reveal a carved-out hollow full of dried meat and berries. Clutching a fistful of meat, she kicked off the oversized boots and sat, biting into it. It had an unusual musky flavor, but was still a welcome change from berries.

Eldrian left smears of blood in his wake when he walked to the pool. She set the meat aside and stood, taking the cup from him.

"Sit."

"As my lady wishes." He sank to the floor with weary grace.

She filled the cup and handed it to him. Then she sat and

took one of his feet in her hands. The raw scrapes were quick to heal. Once she had tended to his feet, she refilled the cup for him before returning to her meager meal, hunger and exhaustion amplified by the strain of more healing.

She held up a strip of the meat. "What is this?"

"There are a few lizards around. Fewer now."

She swallowed a bite. "It's not bad. Better than more berries."

"I am looking forward to anything else. Wine particularly." The yearning in his voice hung heavy in the air between them.

"How long have you been here?"

"Seven months."

He pointed to her left, and she turned to see rows of scratches on the wall. She traced them with a finger, ragged grooves in hard black stone. To be alone in this place for so long would be torture. She turned back, catching a flicker of misery in his expression before he hid it behind a faint smile.

"I'm so sorry."

"I brought it on myself."

His cutting tone encouraged her to let it go.

As miserable as the prison was for him, it was an edifying experience for her, and it let her be with him. His beauty, confidence, and determination were captivating and inspiring. In their short time together, he had needed her more than once and, unrestricted by social or legal boundaries, she had proven equal to the challenges. Here, in his prison, she had freedom and purpose.

Outside the cave, the dingy light was nearly gone. Another night would fall away from the comfort of home, and she didn't mind. On the contrary, it was going back that she dreaded. Submitting to the demands and expectations of society, living in constant fear of discovery and now, more than ever, fearing the wrath of her fiancé.

Her appetite waned. "When do we reach the gate?"

"Tomorrow morning." His response was distant, his gaze focused somewhere she couldn't see.

"I won't see you again, will I?"

Warmth suffused her when he focused on her.

"No."

She lowered her eyes, fussing with her ring so he wouldn't see the sorrow his answer caused. He knelt before her and took her hand, then slid the ring off and set it aside. When he leaned in to kiss her, she let everything else fall away, yielding to their effortless intimacy. His kiss promised a more deliberate approach this time, and she was happy to return it.

* * *

"Good morning." Yiloch traced her jaw, his touch feather light.

Her entrancing blue eyes blinked open, and a smile lit her face. He hungered to run his hands over her soft, bronze skin again. To feel her and taste her and let the world go on without them. They could have reached the gate last night, but he had postponed his long-awaited freedom for one more night with her. That freedom beckoned. She was the prison he had to escape now.

He dared a kiss before getting up to dress. Temptation would be easier to resist with clothing between them. When he reached for his boots, he spotted her ring on the ground and picked it up, slipping it into a pocket. He tossed her the boots.

"Wear those."

"But..."

He silenced her with a stern look. "I appreciate your concern, but it is not far enough now to worry about."

Her face fell at his words. In morose silence, she donned

her dress, torn and dirtied by the previous day's travel. Then she sat, tucking her hair behind her ears to keep it out of her face when she leaned over to pull on the boots.

She was beautiful, brave, and willing, and she possessed precious skills. If only he could take her with him, but he couldn't send her through ahead of him, and once he was gone, the gate would vanish. She would go home then, he hoped. Guilt nagged at the thought of leaving her behind. She had proven herself competent. He had to believe she could get herself out.

"I am ready."

He smiled at her sorrowful determination. She made him smile often despite this place.

Think of wine and a proper bed. Better yet, think of your father's flesh splitting before your blade, of the surprise on his face in that final moment.

His sword. He curled his fingers around the remembered hilt. He would have it back soon.

"Thinking about life after prison?"

He took her hand and led her outside without an answer.

The rough ground under his feet made little impression. Freedom was too close for it to matter. He guided her into a canyon. They walked for most of an hour along the bottom where a thin layer of dirt and sparse brown grass made traveling barefoot easier. Seven months, but he remembered the way like it was yesterday. He turned down a small branch in the canyon. Two unremarkable rock columns stood a few feet apart before the cliff that marked the branch terminus.

They approached the columns, his stomach twisting in knots. At first, nothing happened, then the air between the columns shimmered. Glorious triumph burst through him.

"I win this round, Father," he murmured.

"What?"

"This is it." He embraced her, lifting her off her feet, and kissed her.

His body responded eagerly to the desperate passion with which she returned the kiss. When he lowered her down, sorrow shone in her eyes, but she would let him go without complaint the same way she had endured the rest. He kissed her once more, unsettled by his own reluctance.

"I must go. There's much I need to do."

"Good luck."

Her brave smile was a dagger to his heart. He touched her cheek. "Remember your reality. Make it more real than this. That is how you leave."

She nodded.

Resolutely, he turned and stepped between the pillars.

The sudden pressure on his lungs was welcome. If he understood the prison, he would return to his rooms in the stronghold, the place he had been taken from.

His head spun, and he stumbled. His knees struck down hard on the pale marble floor of his bedchamber. He ended kneeling like a man at worship before the stand on which he kept his sword. The weapon waited there, a seamless blend of Lyran and Kudaness design tempered with ascard. The gentle curve of the blade's razor edge glinted in the light, sharp and clean.

A slow smile spread across his lips, and he laughed. When the laughter faded, he stood and grabbed the sword belt lying beside the weapon. He had to tighten it several notches past the old wear marks. He gripped the pale wood hilt, delighting in the balanced weight of the lethal blade. It felt natural in his hand, an extension of his being. In a life full of frustration, the weapon was simple and pure. There was no doubt as to its purpose and no question of how it would serve him. If only people could be so simple.

He held his breath, listening to the song of the blade sliding into the sheath. It was exquisite. It sang of blood and vengeance.

With one hand still on the hilt, his gaze drifted to the door leading out of his chambers. "Shall we see who's home?"

CHAPTER SEVEN

Why are we still doing this? Prince Yiloch isn't coming back."

Renkle's voice set Yiloch's blood on fire, the sound of betrayal.

He leaned against the wall outside the council hall, fortified by the ancient structure. The stronghold stood little changed from its original state when the first Lyran Emperor, Yiroth, built it using an army of adept architects to reinforce its walls. It served as Yiroth's last stronghold before he conquered the region and founded Lyra's capital, named in his honor. A fitting place for Yiloch to organize his campaign to take the empire from his father and restore Lyra to the glory it had known in Yiroth's reign.

That legendary emperor's blood ran in his veins. He belonged here. Renkle's presence was a scourge upon those ageless halls.

Drawing a breath to harness his rage, Yiloch eased out his sword and listened with calculated patience. His captains' voices carried the length of the long open room.

"Renkle has a point," Ferin said, ever practical. "It has been seven months."

"If you wish to leave, you are welcome to do so. I worked hard to get here. I'm not ready to throw everything away." Adran. His voice as welcome and dear as Renkle's was despised.

A discreet glance allowed Yiloch to take inventory of the

seven individuals standing around the map table on the far end. Dalce and Paulin stood to the right, across from Ferin and Eris. Renkle and Hax stood with their backs to the door. Adran was across from them, his defiant expression mirrored by his twin sister, Eris. These people were his family. He had missed them all except Renkle, the viper lurking in their midst.

Renkle sold out to Emperor Rylan for the promise of land and a title, sending Yiloch into his father's prison. The traitor would pay for seven months of misery, all in a moment.

Uncomfortable silence lengthened in the room.

Yiloch drew upon the full strength of his ascard ability for the first time in seven long months and stepped through the doorway. Adran's eyes popped wide, his jaw dropping. Before he could speak, Yiloch swapped himself with the ascard in the air immediately behind Renkle. With ascard-enhanced strength, he thrust his sword into Renkle's back. The point punched out through his chest, sending a bright spray of blood across the map table. The others all flinched back from the spray, most of them dropping hands to their weapons.

Yiloch inhaled, savoring the intense satisfaction of long-awaited vengeance. Then he twisted the blade and Renkle choked, gurgling blood.

Putting his lips next to the dying man's ear, he whispered, "I spent many miserable days dreaming of this moment. Your dreams are over."

He yanked the blade free and let Renkle fall, then swept his gaze over his remaining officers. They stared back in shocked silence. None drew weapons, but their hands remained poised to do so. He would expect no less.

"Anyone else care to betray me?" When no one spoke, he bent to wipe blood from his sword on the dead man's shirt, then sheathed it. "Good, I'm exhausted."

He spun and strode from the room. His steward, Galen,

nearly ran into him when he stepped into the hall. The man reeled back, his face draining of color and his mouth dropping wide as if he had seen a ghost.

Yiloch paused. "Send someone to clean the council hall."

Galen jerked his mouth shut and bowed as Yiloch resumed his course. "Yes, my lord."

"Yiloch!"

He turned, weariness weighing down his movements now that vengeance no longer fueled him. Adran trotted up and threw his arms around him.

He staggered from the force of the embrace. "Please, Adran, I want nothing more than a glass of wine and to sleep in a real bed." Despite his words, he returned the embrace before pushing free.

Adran's broad smile split his face between the beard and mustache he had grown. "I've been telling them you would come back for so long." His light amber eyes looked Yiloch over, and the new worry lines etched in his brow deepened. "I almost lost hope. What happened? Where's Kardyn?"

"Later." The blue-gray slate that floored most of the stronghold felt icy under his bare feet.

"Yes, my lord. I'll bring some wine." Adran started to turn away, then hesitated, wrinkling his nose. "Would you care for a hot bath?"

A bath? "Yes. I try to take one every seven months or so."

Adran chuckled, then his gaze went to the doorway of the council hall. "About Renkle?"

"Tell the others I will explain everything this evening."

Adran nodded.

Yiloch walked away. Renkle was dead, which meant that threat was gone. He could afford to rest and recover, if only for a few hours.

Back in his rooms, he eyed the soft linens on his neatly made bed. How glorious it would be to undress and climb in, but a clean bed would be sweeter when he himself was clean.

After setting his sword on the stand, he began undressing. His hand brushed a small lump in his pants pocket, and he smiled. Pulling out Indigo's ring, he placed it on the stand next to the blade. The deep blue center stone shimmered, like her eyes. Three small clear stones nestled on either side of it on an elegant band. An expensive piece, something she would regret forgetting, though he hadn't noticed her complaining when he removed it. He turned it so the blue stone reflected in the blade, then, discarding the rest of his tattered clothes into a heap on the floor, he stretched out on the long lounge at the foot of the bed.

A soft knock on the bathing chamber doors woke him from a restless sleep.

"Yes?"

A serving woman opened the doors and knelt between them, bowing her forehead almost to the floor. "My lord, your bath is ready."

"You may go."

"Yes, my lord." She got up and backed into the bathing chamber, before ducking through a hidden door to the servants' passages.

A large round marble basin inset into the floor steamed with hot, scented water. He walked down the steps into it and sank onto the bench that ran around the outer edge. Heat eased tired muscles, and the sting of the scrapes from his fight with the hound provided welcome proof that this luxury was real. He closed his eyes and rested his head back, inhaling aromatic steam.

The outer door opened, and Adran's careful footsteps approached. "You've gotten thin."

He opened his eyes. Adran walked with almost feminine grace, carrying two goblets to the basin edge. He knelt, setting the goblets down, and tested the water with a finger.

"My dining options were limited."

"May I join you?"

"If you wish."

The water rippled when Adran entered. Yiloch took a goblet of wine and held it under his nose, inhaling the complex aroma of the ruby liquid. He sipped it, letting its warmth flow through him.

He let out a sigh. "That's what I needed."

Adran watched him sip his wine again, waiting for him to initiate conversation.

Yiloch appreciated his patience. He was tired, and his mind raced with things he needed to do now that he was free. The single overriding need to escape the prison had consumed him. Now, everything else rained down upon him like a barrage of barbed arrows.

"I haven't used ascard that way in some time."

"Appearing behind Renkle like that was impressive," Adran commented. "Terrifying even."

"Good. I like to be terrifying."

"You often succeed."

Yiloch set down his wine. The heady satisfaction of killing Renkle was already fading, and he found his mind dodging the tasks before him to wander back over the past two days. The memory of vibrant blue eyes calmed him. She would escape. She wasn't the intended victim, so the prison couldn't hold her against her will. Still, their unexpected intimacy might undermine her ability to return to her own reality. If she clung to thoughts of him...

As I do of her.

"I can't believe you're back."

Jarred from his musing, Yiloch held his breath and sank under the water. Adran was fishing for explanations he was not ready to give. He needed to gather his thoughts. He rose, gentle fingers of water running through his hair. It felt glorious. This life blazed with fresh vitality after the gloom of the prison. The scented water overpowered the persistent stink of sulfur.

Adran was watching him.

He smiled with weary humor at his longtime friend. The other man had grown a beard and mustache, as pale blond as his hair. It called attention to his mixed blood.

"You should shave."

"Anything you ask, I will do," Adran answered.

So much devotion behind that immediate response. He could depend on Adran for anything. "Good. When I've finished bathing, I intend to sleep. Wake me in a few hours, and we'll reconvene in the council hall."

"Done." Adran got out, dried, and quickly dressed.

When he was gone, Yiloch scrubbed at the grime and washed his hair until he felt clean for the first time in seven months. He finished the wine before climbing out to dry off. Back in the main chamber, the pile of ruined clothing was gone, and he bid it silent farewell before ascending two steps to the level of the bed. Throwing back the covers, he fell into exquisite softness and sleep.

When Adran woke him later, he could almost believe the prison had been a long nightmare, but for the aching of his body and familiar nag of hunger. Before eating, he needed to find out how much Renkle's betrayal had compromised the years of careful planning he had put into overthrowing his father.

"Have a meal, something bland, prepared for after the meeting. I want proper food."

"Certainly, my love." Adran gave him a teasing smile, more obvious now that he had shaved.

Yiloch raised an eyebrow at him but said nothing. The man at least had the decency not to say such things in public. "You didn't sell off my wardrobe, did you?"

"No. Like your sword, I meticulously preserved your

attire."

"Thank you for keeping things in order." He infused his tone with the deep gratitude he felt.

"Of course."

Yiloch took out dark pants, a fitted white shirt, and tall black boots, all clean and comfortable. When he pulled the boots on, a wistful smile curved his lips. Was Indigo still wearing his other boots? Would she keep them? The possibility broadened his smile as he ran a brush through his hair.

"You look marvelous. Shall we?" Adran gestured to the door.

"Yes."

He strapped on his sword belt, ignoring Adran's frown when he grabbed the weapon and sheathed it. His officers knew nothing about where he had been. They might be jumpy after his sudden reappearance given the dramatic entrance, but they would settle, and he wasn't going without the sword for their comfort.

The others waited in the council hall. Dark stains on the map stretched over the table were a reminder of Renkle's well-deserved death, refreshing his waning satisfaction.

Eris probed him with her amber eyes, her dusty blond hair, bound in a tight braid, adding sternness to her sharp features. She looked a lot like Adran. The whisper of masculinity in her features no more unflattering on her than the hint of femininity was on her brother. Commander Dalce, mixed blood apparent in his thick beard and the dark color of his close-cropped hair, sat back from the table, eyeing Yiloch guardedly. Ferin, Hax, and Paulin followed his approach with uncertain eyes, all three pale and elegant, their bloodlines as pure as his own if not as ancient.

"You all look like you are awaiting execution. Renkle is dead because I know he betrayed me. If any of you have done the same, or plan to, you had best be certain I don't find out.

Otherwise, you have nothing to fear.”

"My lord.” Hax twisted a finger in her satiny blond hair, betraying a rare hint of apprehension. “How exactly did he betray you? And where have you been?”

"You know my father had creators studying the Serroc prison?”

Slow nods answered him around the table.

"He had a secondary key created—a portal into a Serroc prison in the guise of a scroll. Renkle handed that scroll to me in my chambers the day I vanished. Captain Kardyn had a hand on my shoulder, so it transported us both into the prison. My father’s pet adept, Myac, killed Kardyn when we arrived because they had no need of him.” A twist of fresh sorrow came with the words. Myac would pay for Kardyn’s death and for the freakish hounds he had created to hunt Yiloch in the prison. He pushed away his anger. “I won’t bore you with the details. What matters is that I found a way back.”

"Should we send word to Leryc of his uncle’s death?” Paulin asked.

Yiloch negated the idea with a firm shake of his head. “Leryc is already at risk. If he starts entertaining ideas of avenging Kardyn, he will end up dead or worse.”

Dalce cleared his throat. “Not to question your judgment, but are you sure Renkle knew what he was giving you?”

"I am. Father gloated about buying out one of my officers when I arrived. I have always said every man has a price. My failure was in not applying that rule to my most trusted.” He met each of their eyes in turn as he spoke, pleased that none of them looked away.

"The emperor had your brother beheaded for treason,” Eris blurted.

"Delsan? Delsan doesn’t... didn’t have the nerve to kill a spider.” Yiloch searched her face for a hint of what reaction she hoped to get with that abrupt revelation. She had been fond of his younger brother, and her slight flinch at his callous reply hinted that there was depth to that fondness. Was she seeking a reassuring display of emotion? Having essentially grown up with his family, it would surprise him if she expected so much. It was unfortunate, but everyone knew he had little love for his brother.

"Why would he make a show of killing Prince Delsan and say nothing of imprisoning you?" Her words cut off with an edge of bitterness now. She met his eyes a second before looking down at the map table. Her fingers touched one of the bloodstains.

Yiloch scowled, irritated by unspoken implications. "My father hated Delsan because he was spineless. You know that, Eris." She flinched again, and he glimpsed the shimmer of moisture in her eyes. Had she loved Delsan? Could he have missed something like that despite all their years together? "Me, he always respected. More so because I defied him. Perhaps he thought it amusing to preserve me like a pet he might take out and play with some day. Whatever the reason, he would not have wanted to give my allies hope by letting them know I still lived."

"What about Delsan?" Eris looked up.

There really were tears in her eyes.

"What about him? I cannot bring him back." Yiloch held her gaze. He refused to waste time on things he couldn't change. Still, he needed her support. He forced a softer tone. "You knew Rylan would never let him have the throne. His death became inevitable when he stayed in the capital."

Eris's jaw tensed, perhaps recalling that Yiloch had never asked Delsan to go with them. He would have let him come if his brother had asked, but that made no difference now.

She held her silence this time. Adran's hand touched his

sister's arm, a gesture meant to comfort, and she jerked away from him.

They were wasting time.

"What I need from all of you is a full accounting of Renkle's activities while I was away. Any way in which he may have planted the seeds of failure. The influence he has had on our plans. Where we are with those plans, assuming you continued to follow them."

"We did." Adran straightened, proud.

"Adran. Ever dependable." Yiloch acknowledged him with a nod. "Thank you for not giving up. You can begin with your account of things."

Adran shifted his feet when they all gave him their attention, but he nodded and began.

CHAPTER EIGHT

Indigo stared at the place Eldrian had been seconds ago. With him there, even the beasts couldn't drive her away. Now that he was gone, icy fingers of dread crept up her spine. She wanted to be anywhere else. In scant seconds, everything changed, and all she had left of him were memories and a pair of boots.

Looking at the oversized boots, she grinned. Though she barely knew him, something about him fit her. His arms felt like home more than any place she had ever been. Jayce would be a poor substitute for this exotic man who made her feel so wanted and alive. Such was the price she would pay for her father's treason.

She stepped closer to the pillars, pulse racing, but the shimmer was gone. He was gone, and she couldn't follow. In that instant, she would abandon everything to go after him. Placing a hand on either side of one pillar, she closed her eyes and pressed her forehead against the rough gray stone. If only...

The sound of movement behind her shattered her musings like so much fragile glass. Her heart leapt into her throat, and she spun to see a hound ambling into the canyon. She looked into its sightless eyes and recognized death in them.

Escape. She had to escape the dead end.

She ran, aiming for the gap between the beast and the canyon wall. Its head snapped up when she darted past, homing in on the sound of her movement, and it charged after her. She couldn't hope to outrun the lanky beast in shoes that didn't fit.

Remembering Eldrian's last words, she bit hard on the healing split in her lip. Sharp pain and the taste of blood brought back the moment Jayce struck her—the surprise, the hurt, and the anger. She remembered running to the fountain in the Healer's Courtyard. Images and emotions pummeled her. Pressure built on her chest, making it hard to breathe. It wasn't happening fast enough.

The hound snarled, so close. Terror spurred her, and she discarded the remaining barriers masking her ability. Ascard energy flared, the tremendous force nearly driving her to her knees. Daring a glance over one shoulder, she saw the beast bunching for a lunge and seized the wild energy. It was beyond control.

She yearned for home more than she would have ever thought possible, even yearned for Jayce, for anything but this. The beast slammed into her, its oversized claws tearing into flesh under her rib cage in a blast of white-hot pain. The collision propelled her forward. Desperate, she lashed out with ascard. The hound shrieked. Then the sound cut off, and she hit cobblestones with bone-cracking force.

Confusion. Then the pain of her arm snapping under impact, while agony seared through her side where the beast's claws had torn in. She rolled off the arm, expecting another attack, and her eyes focused on the fountain.

"Did you see that?" a woman shouted.

A man leaned over Indigo. Someone's hands held her down.

"Keep still. You're hurt."

"Get healers. Quickly!"

A hand moved into her line of sight, covered in blood. Someone was bleeding. She opened her mouth to tell them, but the words wouldn't come. The man's face hung over her, his features blurring. Black closed in around the edges of her vision. She fought to push it back.

I will not die!

The blackness swept in.

* * *

Caplin jumped up from his seat. "I should go check on her."

"That's what I said." Andrea looked quite cross. "Were you even listening?"

"You said they found Indigo."

"And?"

Caplin stared. He had stopped listening after that revelation. Unable to come up with a graceful way to convince her otherwise, he asked, "Is she all right?"

Andrea's eyes flashed with irritation before she looked away. "As long as you two have been friends, I would have expected you to care more."

You have no idea.

He struggled to keep the impatience grinding away at his nerves from coming out in his tone. "Apologies. I have a lot on my mind."

"I told you. She's in the east hospital building. They refuse to let anyone in to see her, not even Jayce. With your status, they might let you in to check on her. We're quite worried."

"As am I. I will see if I can get in or at least get more information."

She stood, and he kissed her on the forehead the same distracted way he always did his mother, barely noticing that the one was not the other.

As the king's nephew, he would only get so far, but as a member of the High Council, he could get past most restrictions.

"Thank you, Caplin."

Something in her voice caught his attention. Looking at her brought faint surprise. *Andrea, you're talking to Andrea.* He brushed his fingers against her cheek. "Anything for you."

Anything for Indigo.

Less than half an hour later, he walked through the east hospital building on the Healer's Academy grounds behind an older woman. She stalked along with her lips pressed in a tight, irritated line. As a member of the High Council, they couldn't deny him, and they weren't happy about it. They turned a corner in the hall, and she stopped so fast he bumped into her and backed off with muttered apologies. A faint, satisfied smirk tugged at her lips when she turned and knocked on the door beside them. A long silence followed, and Caplin started shifting from one foot to the other. He wanted to see Indigo now, to know that she was alive.

The woman gave him a sharp glance, and he forced himself to be still.

"Maybe they didn't hear you." He reached up to knock again.

Her hand darted out like a striking snake and smacked his away. Before Caplin could express his indignation, the door cracked open, and a man peered out. Dark skin and curly, graying hair suggested an uncommon helping of Kudaness in his lineage.

"Master Siddael, this is Lord Caplin Duvox from the High Council. He insists on seeing your patient."

The dark man scowled at Caplin, his lack of deference disconcerting. "I sent the king's inquisitor away so more healing could be done. She needs rest now."

Caplin raised an eyebrow. Chasing off an inquisitor was harder than getting rid of a bad cold. Then again, this man was a master healer. He could probably get rid of a cold easily enough.

"I came to get a full update on her condition," he stated

with practiced confidence.

"The broken arm and the wound to her side need more healing, but she'll recover. She's resting and shouldn't be disturbed. We will allow her to wake after another healing."

His heart skipped a beat, and he swallowed, trying to maintain composure. "What happened to her?"

"The arm broke when she fell in the Healer's Courtyard. The other injury was from some kind of animal we think, something large."

Caplin shook his head, trying to make sense of what he was hearing. "How did she get to the courtyard?"

Master Siddael's dark eyes narrowed. "As stated in the report, several witnesses saw her appear by the fountain in the Healer's Courtyard, falling as though she had been thrown or shoved. The wound on her side was fresh. She broke her arm when she hit the cobblestones."

He stared. It was all he could do. She had *appeared* by the fountain. How was that even possible? Where had she come from?

"The report explained all of this, which is why King Jerrin wants his inquisitor to speak with her when she wakes. Why would he send you as well?"

Shoving confusion aside, he met the man's gaze. "She knows me. The king thought a familiar voice might help her."

"She is resting."

"I would like to see for myself."

"She needs quiet and rest," the Master healer persisted.

"I will be quiet," he countered.

Master Siddael shook his head, and Caplin prepared another argument. It died on his lips when the healer opened the door enough to admit him. He hurried through into a long room full of cots. Four candles near the center added their meager illumination to the dim light from several small windows at the far end. All the cots were empty except for one sitting amidst several lit candles.

Dodging the healer's reaching hand and ignoring the small sound of protest he made, Caplin rushed to the bedside. Indigo lay still. So still he wondered for a sickening moment if she had died. Her skin was paler than usual. Then he saw her chest move with slow, shallow breaths. Thick locks of rich brown hair framed her soft features. Long lashes brushed her cheeks, fluttering. Perhaps she was dreaming. She looked beautiful and fragile as a child. He yearned to look into her vivid blue eyes.

Caplin sank into a chair beside the cot. The flood of relief left him weak, and an ache filled him, coursing through every fiber of his being. She was alive. She was perfect. Everything he wanted and nothing he could have.

Moving as one caught in a dream, he lifted a hand toward her.

Master Siddael hissed, "Do not touch her."

He pulled the hand back, but not before his fingertips brushed the soft skin of her face. Thank the Divine she was alive. What right did he have to ask for more than that?

"I'm sorry. May I sit here a moment?"

The healer scowled, but a tiny glimmer of sympathy softened his eyes. "You may if you sit quietly and do not touch her."

Caplin nodded.

Siddael gave him a last look of warning before retreating to a desk tucked in the far back corner of the room.

Caplin looked at Indigo. At some point, she had become more than a friend and sister figure in his life. The change snuck up on him, and discouragement from his father made him reluctant to express that new affection. Before he could work up the nerve to defy his father and tell her how he felt, she was engaged to Jayce. The moment he would have offered her his love, she had slipped beyond his grasp. She would never be his partner now. That didn't change his heart.

What had Jayce done to her to make her run? Where had she gone?

A low moan came from her. He glanced up to see if the healer had heard. Siddael was reading something on the desk, unaware of the soft sound. Caplin started when fingers brushed his arm. Indigo's hand reached out searching, her eyes still closed, moving rapidly behind her lids. He took the hand, and a tremulous smile curved her lips. Then she spoke so softly he couldn't make out the words.

He leaned closer. "What is it?"

"Don't leave me," she whispered in Lyran, her hand clenching his.

Caplin looked at her eyes, hopeful, but they had yet to open. She wasn't speaking to him. Dreaming then, but of whom and why in Lyran?

Sighing, he answered in kind. "I won't leave you."

The eye movement stopped. Her hand relaxed. Caplin moved to place the hand back on the cot, and something, or rather the lack of something, caught his eye. Was it the wrong hand? Glancing at her other hand, he confirmed that her engagement ring was indeed missing. After placing the hand back on the cot, he stood and walked to Master Siddael. The man looked up at him, folding his hands together on the desk.

"May I?" Caplin gestured to a chair.

"I suppose so."

Sitting, he considered the other man, deciding which of many questions to ask first.

Master Siddael tapped his foot. "Well?"

"Did she have anything on her when she was found?"

Siddael gave a weary exhale. He would have answered the same question from the inquisitor. "Yes. She had her clothes. They were rather tattered."

"Nothing else?"

"And those boots."

Following the healer's pointing finger, Caplin saw a pair of worn, fur-lined boots sitting on the floor to one side of the desk. They were too warm for Demin or any place very near the capital city. The make and materials weren't Caithin either. If those things alone weren't odd enough, they were also men's boots.

He thought of her words a moment ago. "Are those Lyran?"

The master healer nodded.

None of this made sense. "You said she was injured by an animal?"

"Yes. Her side was torn open. The wound was ragged, as though claws or teeth had done the damage. Whatever did it was powerful. She nearly bled out before we could close the wound sufficiently. If we had gotten to her a few minutes later, she would be gone."

Caplin shuddered. How close he had come to losing her. "But they found her in the Healer's Courtyard. There are no animals in the city that could do something like that."

"They didn't find her, Lord Caplin. She *appeared* in the courtyard."

"Appeared out of the air?"

The healer nodded.

"How is that possible?"

"If I knew that, boy, I wouldn't have the High Council and inquisitors plaguing me, would I?"

Caplin bristled at the disrespectful address, but he held his temper. The man probably wasn't used to this much harassment over a single patient.

"It's just..." Caplin ground his teeth and glanced over his shoulder at the still figure on the cot. He turned back to Siddael, struggling with helpless frustration. "We have no idea where she was, how she got there, or how she got back.

What if she is still in danger? What if..." He cut off, clenching his fists and glaring into his lap while he fought to keep his temper.

He snapped to his feet, stepped away from the desk, and ran a hand through his hair, staring at Indigo. Siddael came to stand next to him and placed a hand on his shoulder. With gentle pressure, he guided Caplin to the foot of the cot.

"Whatever she is to you, Lord Caplin, believe that I will do everything I can for her. Beyond that, she is in the Divine's hands and none of us can do more than He can for her."

Caplin wanted to argue that the Divine let this happen to her in the first place, but that argument would gain him nothing. He nodded, understanding and appreciating the healer's good intentions.

"We will let her wake tomorrow. Perhaps we can learn more then."

Caplin choked out a hoarse thank you, allowing the hand on his shoulder to steer him to the door.

He knew he should find Andrea, but Jayce would likely be with her. The last person he wanted to see right now was Indigo's fiancé. There was little doubt in his mind that Jayce had done something to force her out into the night, which made this his fault. He wasn't sure he could face the man right now without assaulting him. That would only complicate things. Andrea would forgive him in time if he sent a messenger in his stead to let her know that Indigo would recover.

CHAPTER NINE

Indigo clawed her way to awareness through a sticky fog of exhaustion and, intending to assess her condition, opened herself to the ascard. Power erupted within her. For a few terrifying seconds, she flailed in a river of wild ascard energy—shocking, excruciating, and magnificent. She wrestled the connection to her inner aspect closed and snapped her eyes open, expecting to see Watchmen storming toward her.

She lay on a cot in a long room that smelled of sterile floors and over-washed linens. Similar cots, all empty, lined the walls on either side of the room. In a chair next to her, sat a man with hard brown eyes and dark hair cut in a casual style that he somehow made look harsh and militaristic. He wore disdain like a cloak. It stiffened his posture and pinched his features. His stern, unfamiliar face in this stark, unfamiliar room left her frightened and confused.

When she met his eyes, his bored glower morphed into an abrupt, emotionless smile.

"Good to see you awake." Polite words spoken in the tone of a man who never truly grasped the point of civility.

Puzzling images flitted through her mind, not quite solidifying into anything coherent. Pain in her side restricted her breathing. "What happened?"

"That is what we would like to know." He gave her the cold, appraising look one might give a devious criminal. "You vanished four nights ago amidst a powerful burst of ascard energy. Less than two days later, during another such burst, you allegedly tumbled out of the air alongside the fountain in the Healer's Courtyard. You suffered a broken arm in the fall and had a ragged wound on your side. You were also wearing those boots." He gestured to the floor near his chair.

One look at the worn, fur-lined boots set off a dizzying rush of memory. Lord Eldrian, the prison, the hound that attacked her. Those were his boots, which meant the memories were real—the bad ones and the good. The good ones made a warm flush blossom in her chest. Tucking those memories away, she clung to her mystified expression, buying time to evaluate her situation.

The man peered at her, a hawk waiting for the perfect moment to strike down its prey. She sat up, taking care not to aggravate her injuries and propping up pillows to lean on while he huffed impatience. This way, she might not feel so small and helpless before his predatory gaze.

"Might I know your name, my lord?"

"Captain Rezvan, of the king's inquisitors."

Dread raked away the remains of the warm flush.

An inquisitor? Inquisitors questioned traitors. An inquisitor had interrogated her mother before they executed her father.

"We need to know where you were. Those boots are Lyran. Were you kidnapped?"

She stared at the boots. Arguably, she had committed treason of a sort. She helped free a Lyran man planning to overthrow Emperor Rylan, with whom her king had a long-standing trade agreement. Everyone knew the emperor had not been honoring the terms of that agreement of late, but it still might not go well for her if the truth came out. They had already marked her as a risk because of her father. Besides, if word got to Emperor Rylan of Eldrian's escape too soon, the choice she made to help him might be wasted.

I've picked sides in a war on another continent. What good can come of this?

People said you couldn't lie to an inquisitor. They could always tell. A rumor likely started by the inquisitors themselves. If you were confident, you could lie to most anyone. Hadn't she lied to everyone about her love for Jayce after any semblance of such faded? Hadn't she deceived them all about her ascard ability?

The masking? Had they discovered her true strength?

Her nerves danced. Her heart raced. Somehow, her voice remained steady. "I'm sorry, my lord. I remember nothing."

"You must remember something." His disgusted sneer strengthened her resolve.

"I went to the fountain after an argument with my fiancé and..." He leaned forward eagerly, and she hesitated, enticing him with a drawn-out, introspective silence, then shook her head. "And then I woke up here."

"I am certain, Captain Rezvan, that she would share anything she remembered." The newcomer had entered so quietly that even the captain startled when he spoke. "She has been through quite an ordeal. Give her time to recover."

The captain stood and offered a cursory bow to the tall, slender man now standing at the foot of her cot. "Lord Serivar," he greeted, his tone caustic.

The headmaster smiled and inclined his head as though responding to a much nicer welcome.

"You will let us know immediately if she remembers anything. It could be of critical importance. If this is part of a slave uprising—"

"Of course. We must keep those willful Lyran slaves in line." The headmaster nodded toward the door. "Right now, she needs rest. The strain of answering inane questions will only hinder the healing process."

The captain stiffened. "I shall take my leave then." He

bent down and snatched up the boots.

"Wait!" The boots were all she had left of Eldrian.

Rezvan turned to her, blinking rapidly in apparent aggravation, his face flushing.

She thought fast, surprised she could do so before his molten glare. "You say I was wearing those when they found me." He nodded. "Perhaps if you left them here, they might trigger my memories."

The captain hesitated, reluctant to relinquish his only evidence.

"Very clever." The headmaster inclined his head in approval. The slightest hint of a smile tugged at his lips before he faced the captain. "It is a reasonable argument, Captain. The boots could act as a catalyst to bring her memories back."

The captain closed his eyes for a second and shook his head, but he set the boots down. "Very well. Keep them. Good day to you both."

Without allowing time for a reply, he spun and stormed from the room. The door thumped shut, and the headmaster lowered himself into the now empty chair. He took time to smooth his soft gray robes and the full-length scarlet stole draped over his shoulders to denote his rank.

Headmaster Serivar was a narrow man with a narrow face, rather light of complexion for a Caithin. Perhaps he didn't get outside much. She recognized him more from the painting in the dining hall than from any personal interaction and had always assumed the portrait was old because he looked so young in it. Yet he looked just as young in person. Far too young to be headmaster of a respected academy and a member of the king's High Council. He was either very ambitious or he aged extremely well.

"I would love to know your thoughts, Indigo." He straightened one cuff with a sharp tug.

The informal address made her feel awkward, but she

wasn't about to complain. Nor was she going to tell him any-thing more than she told the captain, despite the panicked voice in her head warning that she was walking down the same road as her father. He might be the headmaster, but also being a member of the High Council meant anything she told him would get back to them as fast as it would through the inquisitor.

"Thank you for sending him away, Headmaster. I wasn't up to that right now."

His smile was enigmatic, warm hazel eyes shining with amusement. "You were more up to it than you care to admit." He didn't pause long enough for her to question the com-ment. "Your injuries were quite severe. How are you feeling?"

She took inventory of her physical state without using ascard this time. The Watchmen could sense ascard energy in use. If she didn't use it, they wouldn't detect her strength, but at some point, she had to use it to reestablish her barriers, which left her in a predicament.

"My arm aches a little. My side hurts more."

"The break was clean. It should require only one more healing. Your side was torn open as though a large predator had attacked you. A bear or large wildcat, perhaps?" He raised his brows in question.

A mutant hound created by a Lyran adept. She stared back.

He relented. "It will take a few more healings to repair all the damage."

She shivered, remembering the beast and the pain too well. "How long have I been here?"

"Two days."

Sorrow twisted in her chest. Why was no one there for her? "Has anyone..." she swallowed, unable to finish.

"A few people have tried to visit, but Captain Rezvan in-sisted on being the first to speak to you."

Rather than comfort, his answer sparked intense longing, though not for any of the people who might have visited. She forced a smile. Let him think his answer pleased her.

The door opened, and the headmaster stood. "Master Siddael will tend you now. I would like to see you in my office when you are ready. Heal well."

"Thank you, Headmaster."

He picked up the boots and set them beside the head of the cot, then smiled, winked, and left her to wonder.

The older man who entered wore tan healer robes with the pale blue stole of a master healer over his shoulders. His dark skin, darkened further by myriad wrinkles, and curly black hair struck through with splashes of gray, suggested strong Kudaness in his lineage. She hadn't seen him before, but healers working in the hospital had little interaction with students early in their training.

"This healing will be painful." His tone was apologetic, and his warm voice soothing. "Would you like a priest to sit with you?"

Perhaps she had spent too much time with Hadris as a child, absorbing the Lyran skepticism of their Divine. Or perhaps it was all those years watching her parents fight, each twisting the teachings of the church to support their argument. Whatever the reason, the thought of a priest at her side wasn't a comfort. She shook her head.

The healer put his hands on her arm, and her world became agony.

When the healing of both injuries was through, she sat on the edge of the bed for a time. The healer gave her permission to leave so long as she returned in a day for one last healing on her side. Hunger and thirst nagged, but she would visit the headmaster first. After all, he was the headmaster.

Wary of causing more pain, she slipped gingerly into a set of beige student robes lying on the stand next to the bed and put on the simple white shoes lying under it. Then she noticed what was missing.

My ring.

Her heart skipped a beat as she stared at her conspicuously bare finger. She had left it in the prison. Her cheeks burned when she recalled the exact circumstances that led to its absence.

Jayce will kill me.

There was nothing for it now. At least he would never know the truth of how she had come to be without it.

Wincing with every stride, she made the short walk to the headmaster's office in the administrative building, nestled between the two hospital buildings. The building's cold stone halls were bare and unwelcoming, bereft of the tapestries, carpets and other décor that warmed the halls of the hospital buildings. At least it didn't smell of sickness or medicine.

The office door stood open. She peeked inside.

The headmaster looked up from behind a heavy wooden desk, smiled, and gestured to a chair opposite him. "Please sit."

A platter of bread, cheese, and tarts tempted, sitting on the desk between two tidy stacks of books along with water and a goblet of wine. The splendid aroma made her mouth water. Her stomach growled like an angry dog, and her cheeks flushed.

The headmaster chuckled and waved a hand at the platter. "Help yourself."

She sat and selected a piece of cheese to nibble. As soon as the creamy morsel touched her tongue, hunger took over, and she shoved the rest into her mouth. She grabbed bread with one hand and water with the other, not quite finishing the first bite before stuffing in another. After a brief eating frenzy, an assortment of crumbs was all that remained of a fourth of the platter.

The headmaster reclined in his chair, hands folded, with

a little smirk tugging at his lips.

She glanced at the tart in her hand, mortified. "I'm sorry. I don't know where my manners went."

"You need not apologize. You should feel famished after what you've been through. How did the healing go?"

She washed the tart down with water. "Painful, but my arm is done now."

"What happened?"

His demanding gaze made her more aware of the escape route behind her. It would avail her nothing to walk away, but it was still tempting. Lying to a stranger was easy enough. Lying to someone she respected, and who had the power to shape her future, was another matter. Yet, if she told him the truth, he would tell the king. Given her history, she didn't think her actions would surprise anyone. She could almost hear the king saying how they should have expected it from her as he condemned her to death.

And what would happen to Eldrian?

"I don't remember."

"I don't believe you."

They stared at one another across the desk. Her gut twisted in knots. If the silence held, she might break before that calculating gaze. She had to distract him.

"Why don't we train people to use ascard for more than healing?"

He straightened. "Why do you ask?"

She swallowed, feeling as though she had stepped off the gallows with a rope around her neck. That it was a poor choice of subject was apparent, but she couldn't take it back now. "I was curious."

His gaze sank to his wedding ring. He twisted it around his finger with the thumb and pinky of the same hand.

She took another tart, feigning indifference.

"I am not convinced the timing is right, and yet..." He

stared at the ring, his brows drawing together in deep deliberation. Finally, he nodded to himself and looked past her. "Close the door, Indigo."

The last bite stuck in her throat. Muscles in her shoulders and neck tightened as she went to shut the door. Once seated again, she took several long sips of the wine to calm her nerves.

"There are many ways of using ascard that we do not openly teach here because they are too dangerous."

She sat up a fraction, homing in on his choice of words. "You said *openly* teach."

He inclined his head, that knowing smile tugging at the corners of his thin mouth again. "You are attentive at least. Given your history, you have undoubtedly heard of some ways Lyran adepts use ascard energy. Perhaps you've even encountered some of them recently?"

A lifetime of fear warned her to caution. "I've heard very little."

The headmaster's eyes narrowed with a trace of frustration, but his voice remained calm. "Lyran adepts and creators have explored countless ways of using ascard, everything from reinforcing structures with it to myriad ways of using it as a weapon. They even nurture creators—adepts who can draw ascard energy from anything and manipulate it into something completely unrelated. To understand the risk in such varied applications, you must truly understand what ascard is.

"Ascard energy exists in us and in everything around us. A small percentage of people are born with a strong enough connection to the ascard within themselves—their inner aspect—that they can learn to control it effectively. How much someone can do with ascard is determined primarily by the strength of that connection. Unfortunately, because of the dangerous potential of many applications, healing is the only skill we are permitted to teach. The Caithin High Council ruled long ago that anything else posed too great a risk."

She sat at the edge of her chair now, eager and terrified. "But doesn't that put us at a disadvantage if we go to war against a country like Lyra, where they've developed it for use in combat?"

"It would, but as you caught earlier, I said we could only *openly* teach healing."

Butterflies swarmed in her stomach. "And that means?"

"Caithin cultivates adepts and creators apart from our healers. I won permission from the High Council almost ten years ago now to develop a covert group of powerful ascard users we call the King's Order. When we find individuals with particularly strong connections to their inner aspect, we separate them and teach them other skills. Some hold permanent positions working for the crown. Others only get called upon occasionally to perform special assignments."

Tension in her neck and upper back built until her head started aching. That the king had the Healers Academy secretly training adepts and creators in other skills somehow didn't shock her that much. What frightened her was that the headmaster was telling her about it.

Her feet itched with the urge to leave. "Why tell me this?"

"Have some more wine." He leaned in and handed her the goblet.

She accepted the drink, sucking down a large swallow. The burst of pungent flavor, pleasant only in sips, made her choke.

He sank back again. "The Order has adepts trained to sense and assess the strength of an individual's connection to their inner aspect when they first come to us."

She choked on a second mouthful of wine and set down the goblet to hide the shake in her hands.

Serivar continued when she stopped coughing. "They

filter our students, letting us know their potential so we can place them properly in classes and identifying those who might be valuable additions to the Order. Before your disappearance, your connection was average at best. Now, miraculously, it is so strong we cannot quite assess its full potential."

Was it too late to play ignorant? "How is that possible?"

"As far as I know, it is not. A person's ascard connection never changes. From birth to death, it remains static. That suggests that somehow you have been concealing most of your strength. I am willing to accept it could have been a defensive response to traumatic events in your childhood. The Divine knows you had plenty of those. Regardless, something that happened during your disappearance must have broken down your barriers.

"The King's Order does not usually recruit women. They rarely possess the proper disposition for many of the assignments we give. I would make an exception in your case based on your potential alone, but you also have a certain moral versatility and do not seem intimidated by authority."

"What does that mean?"

He leaned back in his chair and steepled his long fingers, gazing over his fingertips at her. "You lied successfully and, I would venture, guiltlessly to Captain Rezvan. A representative of your king, I might add. You have lied to me, and I sense no remorse for that either. We are both people you should respect and defer to for our status if nothing else."

She held her silence. He had mistaken terror and desperate evasion for moral versatility and lack of intimidation. It didn't seem advantageous to correct him at this point.

"See, you are defiant still. I expect you will be difficult to work with, but I make the offer knowing that. Will you join the elite ranks of the King's Order?"

She considered the terrifying power hiding inside her. Could she ever control that? "If I say no?"

"If you were to say no and mean it..." his tone suggested

he didn't think that likely, "... then I would put you to sleep and you would wake remembering nothing of this conversation."

She shivered. "Can you do that?"

"We have someone who can. We would have to watch you, however. It is unwise to ignore that much power."

She gazed past him at the shelves of books lining the back walls of his office. A deep inhale brought the soothing smells of old paper, ink, and leather binding to her.

Jayce wouldn't approve, but she suspected he could never know. Eldrian would encourage her to learn what she could. Despite the brevity of their time together, she felt confident about that.

Was this a punishment or an opportunity? She might learn things she had never dreamed possible, but if she couldn't share it with anyone, it would be a lonely adventure. Yet, finally controlling that power instead of fearing it might be worth the cost.

"You can reveal this to no one," Serivar said, predicting her thoughts. "Once you finish training, you can lead a relatively normal life. Given the strength of your connection, I would advise that you also continue studying to become a healer. You can marry and have a family. The only stipulation is that you remain willing to drop anything and accept an assignment at any time. You must also become accomplished at lying to those you care about. I am afraid there is no way around that."

The hint of sorrow in his voice made her wonder how long he had been lying to his own family.

"You must be confident in your decision. Should you change your mind later, we cannot allow you to remember this, and there is an escalating risk of mental scarring inherent in memory removal over time."

"I'm getting married in five months."

"If you accept, I will arrange to have the wedding postponed. You should not have that to deal with so soon after such an ordeal."

Even better. This might be her chance to improve her place in the world, and she could put off the dreaded wedding.

Serivar wanted her to accept. She could see it in the gleam in his eyes and the faint curve of his lips.

"What happens if I accept?"

There was a twitch at the corner of his mouth. A hint of a satisfied smirk. "Publicly, you will spend evenings in therapy to restore your memories of the incident. Inquisitor's orders of course. In reality, you won't have to deal with more interrogation from charming Captain Rezvan or his ilk. You will also receive immunity from the Ascard Watchmen in Demin. I give them a list of special students who have permission to use ascard outside of the academy for practice. You will take accelerated classes in the mornings to stay up to speed on your healing, and I will take over your training in the afternoons." His smile turned faintly ominous. "I intend to work you particularly hard, at least until you explain your disappearance. Then I may ease up and pass you to another instructor."

"I can't tell you what I don't remember."

"Not even a blink," he remarked appreciatively. "Shall we start your training in three days, when you are fully healed?"

She felt like throwing up. "Yes."

He stood and walked to a table set against the wall, then filled a goblet from the wine decanter there. He swirled the contents as he spoke.

"There is one thing I want you to do immediately. Your connection is strong enough to draw unwanted attention. You were masking it before. I want you to resume doing so. I have my office shielded, so this would be an opportune time to reestablish it."

He paused, savoring a sip of wine, and she accessed a tiny portion of her connection. The process Hadris taught her for constructing the barriers returned slowly. This time she wouldn't be blocking most of her ability from herself as well as the rest of the world but simply hiding it from outside detection. After some nervous floundering, she figured out how to adapt the process to solely external masking.

"I also want you to practice masking your actual workings so that you can eventually use your ability to its full potential without alerting anyone. We have several adepts who focus part of their ability on such masking. They describe it as a process of blending the ascard signature of their workings with the signature of the ascard around them. Practice until it becomes second nature. Can you do that?"

"I'll try."

"You will succeed." It sounded like a warning rather than a vote of confidence. He returned to his chair and held his goblet up over the desk. "To the newest member of the King's Order."

She lifted her goblet, and the two touched with a soft metallic chink, like the sound of a lock clicking home.

CHAPTER TEN

Yiloch relaxed on his bed, his back against the pale wood headboard carved to resemble a flourishing tree, its branches winding up and out over the high wall. Unlike the rest of the stronghold, he had arranged the redecoration of his private chambers after he took over. Light marble floors and ornate pale wood furniture created a faint echo of the beauty of the royal palace in Yiroth.

With an arm draped across one raised knee, he swirled his wine, thoughts lingering again on the last few days of his imprisonment.

Adran sat cross-legged on the white chaise at the foot of the bed wearing a wounded look. "You made love to her?"

Yiloch's hand stilled, fingers tightening on the rim of the created glass. He gave his friend a long, level look. "I summarized seven months of misery, and you fixate on that. It's not as if I will ever see her again, nor as if she's the first woman I have taken to bed. We had sex. After seven months of forced celibacy, it was a welcome change."

Adran's gaze darted to the graceful sword on its stand. The perfect blade gleamed in the cool light shining through the windows. Indigo's ring glittered at its base. "Obviously, it was nothing. That's why her ring sits beside your precious sword."

Yiloch's hand tightened more. The created glass would never break. It was almost disappointing. "Why does it matter? Did you hope I would be so starved for intimacy on my return that I would be desperate enough to want you?" Too cruel, perhaps, but the words were out. "You know I am not interested in men. That's never changing."

Adran clenched his jaw. His hands closed into fists. "You can be a real horse's ass sometimes."

Yiloch let out a sharp laugh. He knew well how to irritate Adran after so many years of friendship. "Sometimes? I would have thought it chronic by now."

Adran snapped to his feet, a flush rising in his face. "I've had enough of your mockery."

"You know where to find me when you want more."

Adran stormed to the door and jerked it open.

Yiloch softened his tone. "And Adran…" The other man stopped. Yiloch made him wait, taking a sip of wine before continuing. "You will come to Caithin with me, won't you?" He could demand it, but for the sake of their friendship, he made it a request.

Adran stared into the hallway, and Yiloch felt a pang of guilt. He was quick to anger since his return. Frustrated with the time he had lost in the prison. That wasn't Adran's fault, but familiarity made him an easy target.

"If you go, yes." He left, slamming the door behind him.

Yiloch gazed out the window at the glacier-spotted mountain peaks and sipped his wine.

He would meet his principal officers in the council hall soon, their numbers reduced by Kardyn and Renkle's deaths. Their reports suggested Renkle's dealings with the emperor might not have extended beyond enabling Yiloch's capture. Most of his preparations were intact because Adran and the other captains refused to let things fall apart, courting allies, gathering resources, and training troops as if nothing had changed. Very little needed rebuilding, but he couldn't assume his father knew nothing of his plans. He needed something more. Some advantage that would catch the emperor by surprise. It was time to present his new idea to the others.

Ten minutes before the appointed time, he filled his wineglass and strolled to the council hall. The map table stood like an island in the center of the far end, with a row of chairs lined up against one wall. He approached the table and traced a bloodstain on the map of Lyra with one finger, letting the satisfaction of Renkle's death soothe his frustration. Then he took a chair from the wall and sat, putting the heels of his worn black boots up on the edge of the table. He sipped the wine.

Hax nodded a greeting on her way in and grabbed another chair. She dressed in tight-fitting pants and a loose-laced shirt that revealed the soft upper edge of her breasts. She didn't mind men admiring her shape, but no one dared test her fierce devotion to her dark-skinned Kudaness warrior, Cadmar. Unsworn though he was, the man's fighting skill and his calming effect on Hax earned him a place in Yiloch's army.

Ferin and Eris arrived together, a stately bird and a wildcat strolling along in good-natured disharmony. Ferin transferred a chair over with a small expenditure of ascard and settled into it. In harsh contrast, Eris dragged a chair noisily over and plopped down on the seat.

Hax grimaced. "Honestly, Eris, could you try not to grind the legs off on the slate in the process?"

Eris rolled her eyes.

It was refreshing to see them behaving normally. The two women reminded him of stallions posturing over turf, but they worked efficiently together when it mattered. After a few days spent gathering information from them regarding events during his absence, they were relaxing into business as usual.

Dalce and Paulin joined them, entering through the rear

of the room and pulling up chairs. Dalce added his feet to those on the table, a small cloud of dust puffing off his boots when he slapped them down. They waited several minutes more before Adran arrived. He walked up and bowed to Yiloch with a sarcastic flourish.

Yiloch ignored the gesture. "Take a seat. We have much to discuss."

Adran grabbed a chair.

Yiloch considered them, letting them wait under his scrutinizing gaze. They were his top officers; the people he relied on most. Did he still trust them after Renkle's betrayal?

Eris bit off a torn nail, spitting it onto the floor. Hax sneered in disgust, and Dalce shook his head at them.

Yiloch stifled a smile. "Based on your accounts and the reports from Leryc, Emperor Rylan is alienating nobles and peasants alike at a rather perilous rate. It won't be long before the populace revolts or one of our neighbors declares war. We need to act decisively before either of those things happens. We need something extra. An advantage my father can't be expecting, even if Renkle told him everything. We need to court a powerful ally. Given the emperor's offensive disregard of trade agreements with Caithin and their strategic position across the Gilded Strait from Yiroth, I have decided to seek an alliance with King Jerrin."

Hax and Dalce sat up.

Eris fiddled with the laces on her leather vest, feigning disinterest, though he knew she would be attentive to the reactions of the other captains. She never missed a word and was skilled at deciphering body language. Too skilled sometimes.

Paulin was already nodding. Adran picked industriously at dirt under one fingernail. Only Ferin managed a complete lack of reaction.

"You said nothing of outside alliances." Dalce's flat tone

suggested disapproval.

"I think it's an excellent idea." Paulin glanced around at them with his cold gray eyes, inviting challenge. "We have no power on the seaward side. At the very least, Caithin could meet that need."

"The Caithins have always disrespected our people," Adran grumbled.

Yiloch gave him a warning glance, and he smirked, enjoying the chance to get some payback.

"Caithin has a formidable military," Yiloch stated. "They will insist on continuing the slave trade, but if we are flexible there, we can practically guarantee our victory. In the aftermath, we would have their support to dissuade opportunists from moving against us while we clean up my father's mess. Once we are stable, we can reconsider the relationship and see to ending the slave trade."

"Makes sense. I'm in." Hax put her feet up again and leaned back in her chair, lifting the front legs off the floor.

Eris gave the unbalanced chair an opportunistic smirk.

Yiloch tapped the table once, enough to discourage her, and she exhaled a soft put-upon sigh, reining in mischievous inclinations in response to his look of warning.

He gave a tiny nod of appreciation before turning back to the conversation. "Thank you, Captain Hax, Captain Paulin, for your support." He nodded to each of them. "What about the rest of you? Captain Ferin?"

Ferin lifted his slight shoulders in a shrug, creating a cascading ripple in the silken blue tunic he wore. "If we can convince King Jerrin that our chances for victory are good and his slave trade will continue, he won't have much cause to disagree. The emperor has been abusing his relationship with Caithin enough that all we should need to do is offer them a better option."

Eris nodded. "And we best do something before Kudan

does. That border's growing restless."

Yiloch caught the many sour looks that met her comment. The Kudaness usually spent too much of their time preoccupied with bickering between tribes to pose a threat, but they were lethal when joined against a common enemy. If they were angry enough to consider unification, things were dire indeed.

"Adran?"

"I stand behind you as always," Adran relented.

"Thank you." That left only one. "Commander Dalce, you are my second. I must have your support. What say you?"

Dalce scowled. "I don't like dealing with Caithin. The slave trade is an affront to all of us."

There were a few subtle smirks around the table. It was an odd comment coming from the shaggy bear of a man whose traditional Caithin looks overpowered any trace of Lyran blood, but no one dared remark upon it. He was sensitive about his mixed blood, and a blow from him could leave a person reeling for days.

"The only way the trade will end is if we get Prince Yiloch on the throne," Paulin countered. "It might be necessary to make some concessions now in order to effect greater change later."

Dalce pinned the pale man with his stare for a second before turning to Yiloch. "I say we try it then."

Yiloch smiled. "I knew I could rely on you. Do we still have a creator in residence? I need a secure missive created."

Eris shook her head. "Ian's here, but you know the Caithin are terrified of creators. Sending a created document may not be the best way to open negotiations."

"You are partly correct. They have conditioned the general populace to fear any ascard user who doesn't dedicate their ability to healing, but I believe King Jerrin has his own specialized adepts. His subjects just don't know about them."

"Really?" Eris leaned in, her interest piqued.

"We know they allow the teaching of ascard use for healing. No kingdom practicing ascard manipulation is going to pass up its military advantages. Except Kudan," he added when Hax opened her mouth, "but that is a religious restriction. Caithin is hiding something. Besides, we can't afford to have the missive intercepted. My father may not know I am free, and I would prefer to keep it that way as long as possible."

"I'll get Ian." Eris popped up and strode from the room.

When she returned, a lanky boy in plain brown pants and a tan, shapeless tunic scuffed along behind her. His shoulders hunched and his white-blond hair hung down around a long, skinny face trained into deliberate neutrality. He tried to fade into the background, but his remarkable aptitude for creation at such a young age made him impossible to overlook. Because of that, his cousins, Eris and Adran, brought him into Yiloch's service to keep him out of the emperor's hands.

"Creator Ian." Yiloch gestured for him to sit in the chair Eris had been using.

"Your Highness."

Ian's awkward bow morphed into a graceless slump into the indicated chair while Eris dragged another one over and plopped down in a new spot by the table.

Ian began tracing a bloodstain on the map with one finger, his brow furrowing. "What happened here?"

"It's Renkle's blood," Dalce grumbled.

Ian paled. He pressed a palm down on the map. "I can get rid of it."

Yiloch snapped up and shot his arm across the table, pinning Ian's hand. The youth stared wide-eyed at the hand on top of his, his light skin draining of what little color it still had.

"Thank you, Ian, but I am rather fond of it this way."

Yiloch tried to keep his expression gentle to balance the edge of warning in his tone. He released the slender hand and coiled back into his chair.

Ian drew his hand back from the table. His hands shook as he brought a rolled parchment up from his lap and unrolled it, placing his palm over the blank surface.

"You needed a missive created, my lord?" His voice also trembled, and his gaze stayed riveted on the parchment.

"Yes. To be viewed only by those at this table and King Jerrin Duvox of Caithin. It will read as follows. Most Respected King Jerrin Duvox of Caithin." Ian closed his eyes. Words formed on the page in elegant script. "I, Prince Yiloch, rightful heir to the Lyran throne, formally request an audience—"

"You plan to go yourself," Hax interrupted.

Yiloch took a sip of his wine, enjoying the flicker of impatience in her pale gold eyes. He knew his officers well enough to know when and how far to push them, when to be firm and when to be supportive. It was an art, learning to maintain enough aloofness to remain their respected leader without letting them become distant enough to forget why they followed him.

"Why not? Dalce can run things here, and negotiations will go faster if the king is dealing with someone he considers more of an equal. Besides, I could stand to do a little traveling after being locked up for so long."

She glanced at Dalce. The big man was as expressionless as a statue. Somehow, that appeared to reassure her. "Then I expect you'll go," she conceded.

He glanced around the table, giving the others an opportunity to raise objections. No one spoke. Ian waited, his hand poised over the parchment. Yiloch continued.

CHAPTER ELEVEN

Myriad butterflies fluttered in Indigo's stomach when she entered the headmaster's office. After a frantic morning spent working to catch up in accelerated classes, the smug smile he greeted her with grated on already frayed nerves. She had an appalling urge to slap him. Instead, she offered a stiff curtsy.

His eyebrows lifted. "Trouble at home?"

"What?"

"I thought that might explain your scowl."

"I'm not scowling."

He chuckled. "Shut the door."

She knocked the door shut with her heel and sat across from him. At which point he stood, a glimmer of amusement rising in his eyes, and motioned her to follow him. She got up, clasping her hands before her to keep from picking at her nails. Eldrian's smile when he stilled her restless hands with a touch in the prison flickered through her mind. Straightening her back and lifting her chin, she followed him to the rear of the office.

With a decorative dagger from a nearby shelf, he pried a small square of paneling from the wall, exposing a hole with a lever inside. He raised the lever, replaced the panel piece, and then pushed the wall. A hidden door swung open onto a narrow hallway. He gestured for her to go ahead of him.

She peered down the dark corridor. Her feet didn't want to proceed.

"Did you think we would train in public classrooms?"

"I suppose not." She swallowed and started walking.

He followed, carrying a candle from his office that made her shadow leap and dance ahead of her. The chill corridor led to a heavy, iron-banded door. He urged her on, so she pushed it, shivering as it creaked open. The room beyond was dark and cool. She hugged herself against a chill and entered.

"Am I the only one?"

"No." He shut the door. The bolt screeched when he slid it home. "There are other rooms. You won't meet many others in the Order. If you do not know each other, you can't betray one another."

He swept one arm out, and candles flickered to life around the room.

The heat of excitement chased away her chill. "You did that!"

"Yes." There was a hint of smugness in his smile.

"Are you a creator?"

"No. My connection is not strong enough for true creation."

The candlelight revealed a room twice as long as it was wide. A carpet ran most of the length, the colors and patterns long worn to a blur of reddish brown. Two battered archery targets bearing ominous scorch marks cowered in the shadows at the far end. A chair and table waited at the near end before shelves laden with books, weapons, and other more curious objects.

At the headmaster's gesture, she sat in a chair facing the wall of shelves. The rest of the room skulked, its shadowy emptiness pressing against her back.

The headmaster perched on the edge of the table. "As I said before, ascard is a controllable energy that exists in everything. The ascard within you is your inner aspect. The ascard in everything around you is the external aspect. To control it, you must be able to manipulate your inner aspect to form a link between it and one or more external aspects. The strength of your inner aspect and your connection to it are what determine whether you can control ascard and to what level.

"In most people, their inner aspect or connection to it is too weak to manipulate. In some, it's moderate, and those individuals often make effective healers. Fewer still have the strength to become true adepts or creators."

Novice information. Her attention drifted, wandering over to pick at titles on the shelves. Most were volumes that could get a person thrown in prison. *Controlling Fire: From Flicker to Inferno*. *Basic Creation Theory*. Some titles were in elegant Lyran characters. *Ascard in Architecture*. *The Legacy of Yiroth*. There were even titles in cryptic Kudaness and other written languages she didn't recognize.

He slammed a hand on the table, making her jump. "Do you see any other students here?"

She shook her head, a flush of humiliation burning her cheeks.

"You, Indigo, have an extraordinarily strong inner aspect and connection. Given proper training, I believe you can become something truly remarkable, but you must pay attention. No getting lost in thought and no outside interference."

She understood the last part too well. "Jayce can be... protective. He likes to know what I'm doing."

A flicker of sympathy touched his eyes, but his words offered none. "If you can't handle your fiancé, then you are not strong enough for the King's Order."

She bit back a flare of anger. "I'll figure it out."

He nodded, the approval in his eyes irritating her more. "I know you will. Now let's start with something easy." He walked to a shelf. "A finesse exercise."

He returned and set a brown, egg-shaped object on the table.

"Beneath the clay surface is an eggshell, its contents

removed using ascard to keep it from spoiling. I want you to separate the clay from the shell without damaging the shell."

"This is easy?" She considered the object. What if she wasn't as strong as he thought? Worse, what if this were an elaborate setup to prove she was an untrustworthy law-breaker like her father? Her nerves crackled like the air before a storm.

"There are lessons from your healer training that will help you." He went to another shelf and picked up a book, then retrieved a chair from the shadows of one corner and sat down across from her. With a last nod to the egg, he commenced reading.

It was too late to turn back.

Healing required understanding of the patient's body and the illness or injury they suffered from. Here, the patient was the eggshell, so the illness would be the casing of fired clay. To solve the problem, she had to break away the clay without injuring the patient.

She grinned. Maybe this was easy.

Wary of releasing the flood again, she opened a limited connection to her inner aspect and set a fingertip against the clay surface to initiate contact. Envisioning ascard as a liquid seeping from her finger into the clay, she advanced until she felt the ascard signature that identified the shell's surface. When she had ascard energy wrapped around that surface, she used it to push out. The clay resisted. She focused more ascard, pushing out with greater force.

With a popping sound, fragments of clay sprayed out from the center of the table. The headmaster lifted the book to shield his face, apparently expecting this outcome. Then he lowered the book and considered the ivory object on the table.

"That was decisive." He picked up the shell to examine it. "Well done. Not a crack."

She closed her eyes. Her head spun, and beads of sweat

cooled on her skin. "If that was easy, I could be in trouble."

A touch on her hand made her open her eyes.

"Your exhaustion is from lack of practice, not a drain on your ascard energy. An inner aspect as strong as yours could do that all day without fading. Besides, that is one of the more difficult beginner tests. I figured you would be less intimidated if I lied to you about it. You did well."

"Slipping in lessons on the art of deception already?"

"It's never too early to start," he replied, unruffled. "Take a minute to recover, then we will try something else."

The candles around the room drew her attention. The manipulation of fire had tremendous potential.

"Wasn't lighting the candles a kind of creation?"

"No. That was simple borrowing. I was carrying a lit candle. It's easy to borrow ascard from one flame and use it to light another."

"But you lit," she counted the candles, "twelve flames at once."

"Practice. When you can reconstruct the ascard around you into something completely different, like starting a fire using ascard from water, then you are a creator. Although creators have limitations. A single working using that kind of ascard manipulation often requires the commitment of an adept's full strength. The test with the clay egg would drain a dedicated creator. You will never be a creator."

She picked at a spot of dirt under one fingernail. "Why not?"

"You are not limited to one or even a paltry few chosen skills. You have the capacity to learn many skills, creation included. Now, if you have the energy for questions, you have the energy for another test."

She shifted in her seat. His confidence in her ability was unnerving. Perhaps Hadris and her father were right about keeping it hidden. What might the king want to use it for once she finished training? Would they give her a say in that?

"I'm ready."

"Let's see if we can get you past the need to touch your subject. That is a dangerous and unnecessary handicap. The sensation of touching something with ascard comes from the interaction of your inner aspect with the ascard in that item. For example, the sensation of *feeling* the eggshell within the clay was the ascard signature of the eggshell being identified by your inner aspect. You can project your inner aspect onto anything you want to manipulate. Once you truly understand the relationship, it will take mere seconds to sort through thousands of ascard signatures to find the one you are after."

The candle on the desk went out. "Light that. Without touching," he snapped when she lifted her hand.

She folded her hands in her lap and, remembering his words about borrowing, focused on a lit candle nearby. She visualized ascard closing in on the flickering flame.

The candle went out.

He chuckled, and she set her jaw, focusing on the next candle along the wall. Seven snuffed candles later, the room was much darker, and she yearned to kick something repeatedly.

"I can't do it."

The seven candles relit at once. "You are trying to take the flame. You need to connect to ascard within the flame and split it, taking only part of it. On the positive side, you are proficient at putting fire out."

She ground her teeth.

"Let's try something else." He strode to the shelf and returned with another clay egg. "Remove the clay without touching it this time."

She rubbed her eyes.

Serivar looked expectant, so she returned her hands to her lap and focused on the egg, visualizing ascard as she had before. After a brief mistaken connection to ascard in the table, she found the signature of the clay and sank through it to the eggshell. Then she wrapped ascard around its surface. She pushed out, increasing the pressure by tiny increments. A few cracks appeared. Then more formed, multiplying rapidly until the outer shell fell away.

Something akin to greed flickered in the headmaster's eyes. "Excellent. You had perfect control this time."

The effort left her breathing hard and sweating again, but she grinned, giddy with accomplishment.

They continued until early evening. The borrowing of flame continued to elude her. After countless attempts to light the candle, she dropped her head to the table and closed her eyes.

"Indigo."

"No. I can't do it."

"Not yet, but you have done exceptionally well for your first day."

She opened her eyes and sat up. Was he teasing? His gentle smile looked sincere.

"I have?"

He nodded. "Yes. You must not practice any of this outside of this room. Do you understand?"

"If you promise to let me go home now, I promise not to practice outside this room."

"Don't test me. I will keep you here." His smile hinted at humor, but she got the feeling there was some truth behind the threat. "Are you comfortable walking home alone at this hour?"

"It's not far." Passing through the fountain courtyard still put her on edge, but there would be no beasts coming after her now. Unfortunately, there would be no Lord Eldrian coming for her either.

He escorted her to his office. "Same time tomorrow."

"Yes, Headmaster."

Outside the administration building, she rubbed at her eyes and succumbed to a yawn before starting her walk. Cool night air made her sluggish; her efforts to keep up a swift pace undermined by exhaustion. Her mind drifted. At the Healer's Courtyard, she stopped by the fountain and held her hand out into the cascade of falling water, transfixed by the droplets that splashed on her skin. She was too tired for memories of the beast to unnerve her. Eldrian filled her thoughts, his silver hair shimmering in the sunlight the first time she saw him.

"Lady Indigo?"

She jerked her arm to her side like a child caught stealing. Her heart raced, but she managed to smile when she turned.

"Good evening, Caplin."

He flashed an uneasy smile. "You're heading home late."

"I'm doing therapy sessions after class to recover my memories." How effortlessly the lie came, even with someone as dear as Caplin. Perhaps exhaustion made it easier.

"Any luck?"

She gave a tired shrug. "Not yet."

"Might I walk with you?" He offered his arm.

Grateful for company to move her along, she rested her hand in the crook of his elbow. "What are you doing out so late?"

"Walking and... thinking." He glanced sidelong at her. "Can I ask you something?"

"Anything."

"What happened between you and Jayce the night you disappeared?"

The question caught her off guard. She started bringing her free hand up to her healed lip and caught herself, dropping it to her side. Telling him the truth would only cause conflict between him and Jayce. She needed to figure things out on her own. "We were both in a poor mood, and we had a minor falling out."

"A minor falling out that drove you into the streets?"

She made a show of a sheepish smile. "I wanted to get some air and cool my temper. I didn't know it was going to lead to all of this."

His brows pinched when he looked at her, seeming unconvinced by her explanation.

As I would be. She clung to her smile.

"You know how to find me when you are ready to talk about it." His look warned her they would discuss it again. "I wanted to ask you something else too."

"Go ahead."

"Seeing as how you're taken"—he grinned, and she nudged him playfully with her elbow— "and Andrea is a lovely woman from a respected family. Do you think she would..." he trailed off.

She laughed as his discomfort finished his thought for him. "Andrea would marry you in a heartbeat. It would be a fine match."

He gave her a wary glance. "You think so?"

She shook her head at him. "Men can be so daft. Ask her, Caplin. You shouldn't be alone. You need someone to keep you out of trouble."

His arm relaxed under her hand, though she caught a glimpse of sadness in his eyes.

"I was planning a private supper at the manor for the proposal. Or should I use a dining room in the palace?"

"The manor. You don't want to overwhelm her."

"Yes, you're probably right." He retreated into fretful silence.

She squeezed his arm. "Don't worry. She would marry you if you proposed in an alley by the Kilty docks. Whatever you do, she'll love it."

"Then it's decided, unless..." They were outside her

building now. He turned, taking her by the shoulders, and looked into her eyes.

"Unless what?" Again, that hint of sorrow. She searched his face for some hint of the cause.

He looked away. "Thank you. You are a good friend."

"And glad of it." She gave up her silent inquest.

He kissed her on the cheek and struck out toward the palace district. She went to her rooms to find Jayce waiting at the table. Sitting, she inhaled the delicious aroma of the meal laid out between them.

"Thank you. I'm famished." He simply stared at her, and she stared back, trying not to let weariness drive her to quick anger. "What's wrong?"

"Will you be this late every night?"

She took a bite of bread to quiet her nerves. After she washed it down, she said, "I don't know. It depends on how much they want my memories back."

His gaze drifted to her unadorned ring finger. "Did you remember anything?"

She shook her head and turned to eating. After a time, he ate too. He hadn't raised a hand against her since the night she disappeared, but their relationship remained tense, and repeated lies would only make it worse. She preferred to avoid conversation altogether.

Before climbing into bed, she sat at her vanity and brushed out her hair. Slipping off her shoes, she used her toes to touch the top of one of the Lyran boots she had tucked into the shadows under the vanity. Her image faded from sight, and she focused on Eldrian in her mind, smiling to herself.

"I think it's brushed enough."

The mirror showed Jayce watching her, his eyes hooded with desire.

She longed to refuse, but knowing another assault might be an unwelcome word away made her reluctant to do so. She forced a smile and joined him. He mounted her with the passion of a rutting deer while she clung to memories of those two nights in the prison, letting past pleasure hold back her tears.

Despite her exhaustion, she stared into the dark long after he drifted to sleep, rubbing her finger where the engagement ring had been. What use was there in being powerful if she was doomed to this for the rest of her life? There had to be another option.

CHAPTER TWELVE

Myac stood silently at Emperor Rylan's right hand.

The magnificent throne room of the Imperial Palace in Yiroth rose around them like a grand cavern of ice. Overhead, the soaring arched ceiling of ascard-worked crystal captured the splendor of both night and day through its many faceted surfaces without allowing glare in the room below. The ascard woven into it protected it from the elements even now, hundreds of years after its creation.

Pale blue marble panels, inset between marble columns along the walls, displayed scenes of dancing, lovemaking, battle, and other passionate moments. Each one masterfully etched and highlighted in the softest colors so that the images evaded the eye, playful and secretive like a lover's whisper, becoming clear only when viewed from the exact center.

The floor was of marble a few shades darker, with patterns in pale granite worked through to form a natural flow, like a river carrying the eye to the finely wrought throne of silver and ivory on the marble dais at the far end of the room.

Filling the wall behind that dais, a vast mural portrayed the Founding Battle in which the first emperor, Yiroth, had taken this land and established the capital of Lyra. Cavalry and infantry clashed with spear-wielding tribes in glorious chaos on a battlefield carpeted with the fallen. Yiroth himself rose above the fray on a rearing stallion, his sword captured forever in mid-sweep, his refined Lyran features immortalized in an expression of magnificent, savage determination.

Emperor Rylan sat upon the throne before the mural like a precious stone in an elaborate setting, as beautiful, hard, and cold as his surroundings. His silver eyes regarded the room without emotion. His refined features, reminiscent of Yiroth himself, were statuesque. With a gleaming mane of pearlescent hair, he was striking as only a Lyran of purest blood could be, as his sons were, or had been.

Knowing both the emperor's sons were out of the way brought a contented smile to Myac's lips. He never could stomach so much perfection in a single room. The head of Rylan's youngest, Delsan, hung above the inner gates. The gentle younger son received more recognition in death than he earned in life, becoming a martyr for simple folk. Rylan hadn't even flinched when the axe fell, its ascard-honed blade slicing through the young prince's neck like soft cheese. In a single stroke of the headman's axe, Rylan lost the confidence and support of many allies. Whispers on the streets and in the royal court claimed he had truly gone mad. They weren't wrong. Rylan was often quite lucid, but the madness Myac would use to justify taking the throne once both sons were dead was becoming more apparent.

The eldest, Yiloch, was more difficult. In his current state, Rylan might not inspire enough confidence and loyalty in his people to be capable of defeating Yiloch if the exiled prince built his own army. Yet, even with rumors abounding that his son intended to overthrow him, convincing the emperor to imprison his eldest was harder than convincing him to put the younger to death. Now, locked in the Serroc prison, the prince could no longer cause trouble, but he still needed a public death. Arranging that was the final challenge. Then deposing the mad emperor would be easy, and people would support Myac's humble ascension once he revealed his blood ties to the royal family.

The last of those seeking an audience with the emperor

were gone. Other than an attendant knelt near the foot of the steps, only he and Rylan remained in the room. He often stayed to watch night fall through the crystal ceiling, and Myac shared his appreciation of that view. The first stars glinted like diamonds in a sea of deep blue, their presence multiplied a thousand times over through facets of crystal. The beauty of the sight on such a clear evening was without compare.

Myac watched the night arrive with a sense of satisfaction. He had a true claim to the throne, though no one there knew it. Black hair and eyes, discolored in the ascard-based healing of severe burns, veiled the purity of his blood. That suited him for now. This way, he could work his manipulations at leisure. He would see Yiloch put to death in some slow and deliberate manner, assuming the arrogant prince survived the prison, and see Rylan fall in disgrace. They would pay for the wrongs they had done him and the lives they had destroyed. If fate were kind, he would get the chance to tell Rylan why before he died.

The almost reverent silence in the room shattered when the doors at the far end swung open.

"Your Eminence."

The robed creator scampered toward the dais like a frightened mouse, bowing every few steps. His face was a pallid mask of dread, and Myac sensed fear rolling off him, could taste the sour tang of it in the air.

"Why do you interrupt me, Creator Cathis?" The emperor's rich voice flowed across the room like melancholy music.

"Your Eminence." Cathis sank to one knee at the foot of the dais. "Your son, Prince Yiloch..." The man swallowed, his eyes darting between Myac and the emperor with open fear.

Rylan leaned forward, impatient. "Speak."

"He's gone."

"What do you mean by gone? Was he killed? Was it a

hound?" The tightness in Rylan's voice betrayed his enduring affection for his eldest son.

"No, Your Eminence. There would be residue from such an incident in the prison's composition. The prison is in flux. Its purpose for existence is no longer there. He's simply gone."

Myac didn't need to see the emperor's face. Through his ascard ability, he felt the man's rage flare up like lit straw, matched by his own.

"When did you last check on him?" The emperor's voice shook with barely contained fury.

Cathis licked his lips. Swallowed. "Over a month ago," he muttered.

Rylan's wrath turned from fire to ice, and Myac inhaled sweet anticipation.

"Do you know how long he has been gone or where he went? Do you know how he got out?" The emperor was calm now. That boded ill for Cathis.

"N-no, y-your Eminence."

"Myac."

Cathis stiffened, his fear spiking. His gaze flickered to Myac, the whites of his eyes showing like a terrified horse.

Rylan waved a hand in the vague direction of the creator. "Take care of this."

Myac embraced his ascard connection with almost sensual pleasure. He had so much rage to take out on Cathis. At best, Yiloch's escape delayed his plans. At worst, it could destroy everything he had worked to accomplish. For that, the creator's death would be excruciating.

Reaching out with his inner aspect, Myac took hold of the ascard in the air around Cathis and began shaping it to his will with an artisan's care. With refined skill, he constructed an invisible barrier around Cathis and sank it through the man's skin.

Cathis met his eyes. Tears streamed down his face, his

resignation so absolute he hadn't even connected with his inner aspect. Myac sneered and made the barrier solid under the man's skin, splitting connective tissues holding the skin to the underlying muscle. Then he compressed the barrier with massive force. A fluid choking sound emerged from Cathis, and bones crackled as everything beneath his skin crushed into pulp. Myac released him, and he collapsed in a limp, misshapen heap, blood streaming from all visible orifices.

"Effective, if untidy." Rylan turned to the attendant, who was staring wide-eyed at the dead creator. "Get this..." His lip curled with revulsion when the attendant doubled over and retched. "And that, cleaned up."

The attendant wiped his mouth on his sleeve and scurried from the room.

Myac savored the mild, sated exhaustion that followed his efforts, letting it counterbalance his anger.

Rylan reclined on his throne. "You were right, Myac. Cathis was a fool. Does that please you?"

"It pleases me to serve you, my lord," Myac replied, wary of angering the emperor now that he was stuck serving him a while longer.

Rylan rubbed his temples. "What shall we do about my son? And do not tell me how I should have killed him when I had the chance. You have no children. You could not possibly understand. Yiloch is the only child of my blood who was ever worthy of the line."

Worthy of a slow death, perhaps. "My lord, I would venture that he feels the same. He will come for his birthright eventually."

"Yes, I believe he will. That is why I love him, but I cannot have him in my way. I need no heir coveting my throne so long as you can keep me young."

Myac said nothing. Instead, he sat on the upper step of

the dais before the throne and gazed at the dead creator, admiring his handiwork. It was easier to destroy than to create. The power it took to rejuvenate the emperor's body was exponentially more draining, but it amused him to see how the promise of unlimited youth influenced a man on the brink of madness, and it secured his position for as long as he had to play this game.

He turned to the emperor. "You know where Yiloch's stronghold is. He will have returned there, though he may not stay long."

"I shall send a troop to investigate."

"Had you allowed me to interrogate Renkle, you might even know what your men should expect when they arrive."

"You speak out of your place, Myac." Rylan emphasized the warning with a dark look.

"Apologies, my lord." Myac turned to keep the emperor from seeing the ridicule in his smirk. Rylan was more defenseless before him than Cathis had been, but he was too arrogant or delusional to acknowledge the fact. Power drove him, and the promise of keeping it made him manageable.

The attendant returned with two others, and they began cleaning up the remains of the unfortunate creator. While they worked, Myac gazed at the darkening sky and caressed the faceted crystal ceiling with fingers of ascard. A remarkable creation. No more magnificent example of ascard architecture existed in the known world.

Myriad stars shimmered bright in the night sky when the attendants finished and left them. The emperor's head rested against the throne, his eyes closed, his breathing even. Not sleeping, but lost in a meditation state, serene and irritatingly beautiful.

"Do you wish me to accompany them to the stronghold?" Myac asked, amused by having a valid reason to interrupt.

The emperor opened his eyes. "No. I would rather not

risk you."

A flush of frustration burned Myac's skin. He couldn't sit in the palace and wait for the prince to make a move. Yiloch focused his limited ascard ability on enhancing physical combat. It would be satisfying to face him and show him how useless that training was.

Drawing upon more ascard energy, Myac infused his voice with it, using it to soothe and manipulate. "My lord, you cannot afford a mistake this time. I can ensure the success of this mission. If Yiloch is there, I will deal with him. The other creators and adepts can handle your personal safety for a short time."

"Maybe you are right, Myac." The emperor yielded easily to ascard influence. "I should send someone I can trust. This must be handled properly."

"I will make certain of it, my lord." Myac bowed his head.

"But Myac..." The emperor hesitated.

Myac waited, wondering at the troubled look in the emperor's eyes as he gazed through the crystal ceiling. The slightest shimmer of tears rose in them.

"Make it quick. He has earned that much."

He said quick, not painless. An oversight Myac wasn't about to point out. He smiled, cheerful. "As you wish, my lord."

* * *

Yiloch and Dalce circled each other, their breath coming in white wisps. Yiloch lunged with his blade high, then feinted away from Dalce's attempted parry and brought his sword around low, striking the other man across the ribs with the flat of the blade. Dalce recoiled with a pained grunt as Yiloch sprang out of range.

"Getting slow, Dalce," he taunted. "I'll have to find a new

commander soon."

Dalce smirked. "And who among our raw young companions has my mastery of strategy?"

Hax, leaning on the fence at the edge of the sparring circle, barked a laugh, suggesting that Dalce overstated his value.

Yiloch smiled. It felt good to fight, even mock battle with a blunted sword. The familiar routine of sparring with his captains allowed him to burn off the last of the ill temper built up during his imprisonment. He spent part of each day in the sparring ring, refreshing skills that went largely unused in those seven months. It also kept his mind off the anticipated reply from King Jerrin.

The Caithin king could turn to Emperor Rylan with the offer Yiloch made, hoping to smooth things over. It was unlikely, though, given Caithin's might and the insult Rylan paid them by snubbing the trade agreement. King Jerrin was no fool. Rylan's rule crippled Lyra, while Caithin grew in power and wealth, building relationships with countries on their other borders. Why bow to Rylan's madness when allying with Yiloch could end his reign at little cost to them?

While they waited for an answer, Ferin, the only adept among his top-ranking officers, was busy recruiting more ascard users to their cause. Paulin, Eris, and some lower-ranking officers paid visits to existing allies to ensure support now that Yiloch had returned. Throughout Lyra, mercenary forces and allied lords awaited his call to arms. Vital relationships that required constant nurturing.

Yiloch hated waiting.

With his mind wandering, he almost missed the next parry, recovering with a burst of ascard-enhanced speed.

"It would do you good to take a hit," Dalce grumbled.

"You'll have to get faster, old man." *Like the hound in the prison.*

The pain of that injury was gone. Indigo healed it well,

making it a memory that faded more each day while she persisted in his thoughts.

Dalce attacked with a series of fast strikes. Each successive blow came down stronger than the last, gaining momentum with every swing. Yiloch strained against the growing fatigue in his arms as he parried. In sheer strength, Dalce had him beat, but in dexterity, even without the ascard, he was the better. He caught Dalce's crossguard on his and jerked up, ducking under their blades and catching him with a foot to the chest. The burly man flew back, landing on frost-hardened ground with a heavy grunt.

Yiloch rested the tip of his blade against the soft, vulnerable flesh above Dalce's breastbone. "Commendable effort, but I bested you without ascard."

He moved the blade, offering a hand to help his second stand.

"That must be why you're in charge," Dalce muttered.

"Could be the royal lineage." Hax offered a teasing wink.

"That too," Dalce conceded. "You try to kill him. I'm exhausted."

Movement behind Hax caught Yiloch's eye. Adran strode around the corner of the stronghold, the messenger they sent to King Jerrin trotting behind him, his nose red with the chill.

Yiloch racked his sword and picked up a cloth to dry his face. Even in the crisp air, he worked up a sweat sparring, and it cooled fast. He tossed the cloth to Dalce and stepped out of the ring. Hax glanced over her shoulder, then flanked Yiloch. Dalce wiped his face and stepped up on Yiloch's other side. Adran moved to one side as the messenger bowed.

"I bring a missive from King Jerrin of Caithin, Your Highness."

The messenger held out the scroll, and Yiloch stepped back, remembering the one Renkle had given him that transported him into the prison.

Adran intervened, taking the scroll and breaking the seal

to unroll it.

"It's created," he commented with a note of surprise.

Yiloch nodded. The Caithin king did have creators.

Adran turned the parchment to him, and words appeared on it.

Your Highness, Prince Yiloch of Lyra,

Your missive arrives at an opportune time, as I am sure you realize. I find myself of a mind to entertain. You and your retinue would be most welcome in Demin. I invite you to join us for our Wakening Festival, if you are so inclined, or at your earliest convenience thereafter.

I look forward to our meeting.
Honorable King Jerrin of Caithin

For something so brief, it held considerable meaning. The respectful address and choice of words suggested the king was fed up with Rylan's antics and not only receptive to, but interested in, other options. The Wakening Festival, their celebration of spring, was coming soon, implying a desire for expedience.

Yiloch addressed the messenger. "Remain ready. I will have a response to send back within the hour."

"Yes, Your Highness."

When the messenger disappeared around the side of the stronghold, he read the message to the others, then met Adran's eyes.

"Prepare for a journey, my friend. We have a festival to attend."

Dalce nodded. "It sounds as if an alliance is almost certain. Perhaps we needn't send you, my lord."

"I am going to Caithin. I spent seven months in a miserably hot prison. The chill here is driving me mad."

"That's odd," Adran commented. "You've always done cold so well."

"I can take someone else," Yiloch warned.

"You could, but you would miss me."

Hax stifled a laugh.

Yiloch let it go. There was too much truth in it to argue. "Commander Dalce, I need my escort ready to leave at dawn. Captain Hax, send someone trustworthy ahead to arrange for twelve casks of the best Lyran wine and to secure passage from the port of Tunsdal. That should be far enough north of the capital that we won't draw attention. Captain Adran, find Ian and send him to my study."

His officers hurried off, each of them focused on their given task. Yiloch smiled as he watched them go. Tomorrow, he would take another step toward destroying his father.

CHAPTER THIRTEEN

Yiloch rose before dawn and pulled on the clothes laid out for him the night before. Then he dug into a dresser drawer and drew out a silver chain. On it hung a red stone pendant, a gift from his late brother, Delsan. Yiloch had never worn it. The stone supposedly brought its wearer good luck. He relied on skill and intellect, not luck.

He held it up, letting the early light illuminate the stone. "Perhaps you should have kept this for yourself, Brother."

He unclasped the chain, letting the stone slide off onto a bed of clothing, and shut the drawer. The stone forgotten, he walked to his sword stand and slipped Indigo's ring onto the chain. Then he clasped it around his neck and tucked it under his shirt seconds before Adran swept through the door.

"Let's go!" His grin faded to disappointment when he saw Yiloch awake, dressed, and ready to depart.

Yiloch scowled, pretending displeasure, and strapped on his sword belt. "Where's your sword, Captain Adran?" In the reflective surface of his blade, he saw Adran put his hands on his own waist.

"In my room." He sounded somewhat surprised.

Yiloch swallowed a laugh. "I'll see you in the courtyard." He sheathed his sword and strode past Adran into the hallway.

In his armory, Yiloch strapped another sheath to his thigh that held two daggers and fitted a third dagger to one boot. Satisfied, he proceeded to the rear courtyard, where twenty-five mounted soldiers and Ian waited. Three extra horses carried supplies for the trip to Tunsdal, and another four carried items for their stay in Demin. His dapple-gray stallion, Tantrum, stood saddled and waiting next to the well-mannered bay gelding Adran rode. Dalce was near the front of the group, talking with some soldiers.

Beyond the courtyard wall, the snowcapped peak of Mount Serst, the highest peak in the range, loomed over them, ominous and magnificent. Yiloch admired the fierce beauty and inhaled crisp mountain air. Now, when he finally started appreciating the majesty of this place again, when he finally started sleeping through the night without the prison haunting his dreams, he was leaving. Perhaps he didn't need to go, but King Jerrin would appreciate the respect implied by the effort. That alone could prove pivotal in securing an alliance.

And what of Indigo?

Ignoring the thought, he walked over to Dalce.

"Prince Yiloch." Dalce and the selected soldiers bowed.

Yiloch nodded acknowledgement. "Commander Dalce, is everything in order?"

"We're only waiting on Lord Adran now."

As if on cue, Adran came through the door. His long strides and straight posture suggested bold confidence. Only someone who knew him as well as Yiloch did would catch the flicker of self-consciousness in his eyes at being the last to arrive. He wore his sword with the self-assurance of a man possessing considerable combat skill.

Adran met his eyes and smiled. Then his gaze wandered to Ian, and the smile disintegrated.

"What's he doing here?"

"I requested that he accompany us to mask our identities when necessary," Yiloch replied. Adran might be Ian's cousin and Yiloch's closest friend, but neither relationship would help him win the battle he was starting.

"He's too inexperienced. The real world is a story in a book to him," Adran argued.

An undignified choking noise came from Ian, who might have come to his own defense, but Yiloch spoke first. "If he is to be of any use, he needs to gain experience. That will not happen hiding here behind his cousins. He goes, or he is no longer welcome in this stronghold."

"I would much prefer to go if…" Ian trailed off before a sharp look from Adran.

"You would never send him away," Adran countered, though he averted his eyes and his shoulders sank a touch, little indications of expected defeat that someone else might have missed.

"Try me."

Ian cleared his throat. "Prince Yiloch requested my services, Cousin. It's my responsibility and privilege to honor his request. I don't believe you have a say in the matter."

Yiloch smirked, enjoying the startled look Adran gave the young creator, though the show of spirit surprised him too. An adventure might bring out some backbone in the youth. If not, Yiloch would deal with the consequences when the time came.

"Let us be off then." Yiloch took Tantrum's reins and swung into the saddle.

Adran shook his head, muttering under his breath. He swung up onto his gelding, squared himself in the saddle, and stared hard ahead.

"Commander Dalce, I trust you to handle things. We will return as soon as we have secured an alliance and start this war."

"I look forward to it, my lord."

Dalce patted Tantrum's neck. The stallion ignored the rough gesture and swiveled his ears toward Yiloch.

When Dalce stepped back out of the way, Yiloch urged

Tantrum forward with a light squeeze of his legs. The rest of the retinue started moving, the guards positioning themselves before and behind Yiloch, Adran, and Ian. Outside the courtyard, the mountain path forced them to travel two abreast, squeezing them into a long line.

Ian maneuvered up beside Tantrum when Adran didn't claim the position.

"My lord?"

"Creator Ian."

"What sort of disguise did you have in mind?"

"A traveling merchant or a lord with private guards. Something close to reality. You will need to maintain it for a while. The simpler, the better."

"Yes, my lord."

"We should not require that service until we are past the second river crossing."

"Yes, my lord," Ian repeated.

The creator slowed his mount, falling back beside Adran again. The route was narrow and steep, but faster than the wide track that wound down the other side. Tantrum had an overabundance of energy, apparent in his tight prancing steps and the tossing of his head. Yiloch stroked his neck, soothing the stallion while he admired the towering cliffs of the Leras range. The mountains were steep and dangerous, piercing the sky with jagged peaks. Only the boldest winter hawks soared high enough to know those snowcapped summits.

The incline lessened, and the path joined a wider track where they could ride five abreast, creating a buffer on all sides between Yiloch and any threats. He increased the pace, moving the retinue up to a swift trot until they stopped mid-afternoon at the first river crossing to refresh the horses and themselves. The river ran high and strong with snowmelt, frigid water pulling at the horses' legs when they forded the crossing. After they crossed the winding river a second time, Yiloch glanced back at Ian, who met his eyes and nodded. The creator's expression turned distant, and the ascard in the surrounding air reformed, masking their identity.

Yiloch waved Adran closer. "Keep watch over Ian. If he shows signs of fatigue, I need to know."

"I still don't think he should be here. He isn't ready."

Tantrum pawed the ground, sensitive to Yiloch's rising irritation. "Think what you want, but this reduces our risk. Your precious cousin will earn his keep."

Adran's gaze drifted to the young creator. "I worry about him."

"You care more than you should," Yiloch snapped. "We will all sell ourselves for the right price. Ian's price is adventure and recognition. He's cheaper than most."

Turning his back on the dismay in Adran's eyes, he motioned the group onward.

* * *

Yiloch had them back on the road before dawn the next day. They kept up an easy trot through the morning, breaking at a meadow around midday to refresh and let the horses graze. They had just mounted up again when three men entered the far side of the clearing, one mounted and two on foot bearing the imperial crest on their surcoats.

Imperial soldiers rarely patrolled this far from the capital. They might be a rogue group. Regardless, three soldiers weren't likely to stir up trouble with a party this size.

Yiloch ordered the retinue to walk and closed the distance until they were a few yards apart. He recognized the mounted one. Garn, an unpleasant sort who fancied himself a great warrior and ladies' man.

Garn held up a hand. "Halt!"

They obliged, waiting while the man looked them over

and settled his haughty gaze on Yiloch. So much arrogance in the face of a large armed group meant he was either a fool, or he had some hidden advantage. Hope for a peaceful encounter faded.

"For what market are you bound, good merchant?" Garn asked pleasantly enough.

"My lord, I carry goods to Aldis and Tunsdal." The respectful address tasted like bile on Yiloch's tongue.

"A long road." Garn scanned their weapons. "We have been long on the road as well. Perhaps you would spare food and drink for the emperor's men."

"We have naught to spare."

"I think you have plenty," Garn countered.

More imperial soldiers emerged from the trees on both sides. Yiloch lowered his hand to his sword. His soldiers mirrored the movement, and Garn narrowed his eyes at the synchronized response that came from considerable training.

"I advise you to let us pass," Yiloch warned.

"We do this the hard way then." Garn drew his sword.

The imperial soldiers drew weapons and charged them. Dalce had chosen Yiloch's guard carefully, selecting the best the stronghold could offer, and they showed it now. They spun their mounts into the oncoming attackers, swords swinging with lethal precision. Still, Garn had an advantage, with two men for every one of his.

An imperial soldier staggered back, his blade bouncing off the air around one of Yiloch's men. Yiloch scowled, anger burning in his blood. Ian had created shields for them. The shields would rapidly deplete the creator, but he had other problems to deal with first.

Tantrum lunged on Yiloch's cue, ramming his shoulder into Garn's horse. The other animal went down, and Garn rolled clear, jumping to his feet. Swinging off Tantrum, Yiloch closed with him. He sped his attacks with ascard, crippling

Garn with a strike to the thigh and another to the shoulder of his sword arm. Then he parried a clumsy attack and drove a dagger home through the man's throat. Pulling the dagger free, he spun and thrust his sword into the back of an imperial soldier fighting another of his men.

He felt an abrupt change in the ascard when Ian passed out from strain. The shields and their illusions fell away. Only a few imperial soldiers still stood, fighting against much altered odds.

"The Blood Prince!"

Yiloch turned. On the outskirts of the battle, an imperial soldier stared at him in wide-eyed recognition now that the illusion was gone. The man turned and ran.

Drawing on more power, Yiloch swapped himself with the ascard in the air in front of the fleeing soldier. He grabbed the soldier's tunic, pulled him close, and swept his blade across the man's neck. The gurgling man dropped when he let go. All Garn's soldiers lay dead or dying, their blood soaking into the trampled ground around the roadway. Yiloch stalked back to the retinue, his soldiers clearing from his path.

Adran was helping Ian to his feet. Yiloch shoved him aside, took the front of Ian's shirt in his fist, and hauled the young man close enough that their noses almost touched.

"If you ever push yourself to the point of passing out again, I will kill you where you fall."

"My lord." Ian's eyes grew wide. "I was only trying—"

"Trying to help? Your sole responsibility is to ensure that I am not recognized. See to that before all else."

He shoved Ian away. The youth reeled and fell, landing hard on his tailbone.

Yiloch turned to Adran, who looked ready to strike him. He plowed through the other man's anger. "Captain Adran, find a secluded spot away from the road for this fool to rest."

He turned his back on them both and went to Tantrum,

still waiting beside Garn's body. A bright streak of red colored the stallion's right foreleg. He grabbed his waterskin and pulled the leg up, resting the hoof on his knee so he could clean and inspect the wound. A shallow cut. It wouldn't affect the animal's performance.

Indigo invaded his thoughts again. The feel of her gentle hands on his arm as she healed his cut, or pressed against his ribs, restoring broken bone and injured muscle.

How beneficial it would be to have a healer in his retinue. But why stop there? Imagine the power of the Lyran army with a troop of healers ready to tend minor injuries and get soldiers back out on the battlefield. If King Jerrin were at all receptive to the idea, it would be worth negotiating for.

He set down Tantrum's hoof and glanced around at the bodies his soldiers were busy searching and moving into the trees. Such a large patrol shouldn't be this far from the capital unless they were looking for something. Him perhaps? No matter the reason, they were venturing too close to the stronghold.

He caught the attention of the nearest soldier.

"Ride back and tell Commander Dalce what happened here. Tell him to increase the watch and send out scouts to look for more patrols. I want him to send word to the other officers as well. This may have been a rogue band, but if they know I have escaped, it could mean trouble."

"Yes, my lord."

The man swung up onto his mount and galloped back the way they had come.

A waste of good men. His father's erratic behavior had driven many troops rogue, even to the point of attacking other imperial patrols. Admittedly, some of those groups received discreet compensation from Yiloch's coffers. In those cases, the soldiers' discontent worked for him, helping him undermine Emperor Rylan's control, but it was one more thing he would have to fix when he took over.

Yiloch leaned on Tantrum. His final move with the ascard, transferring himself in front of the fleeing soldier, sapped his energy. When they found a place for Ian to recover, he would also need rest.

He led Tantrum back to where Ian waited, hunched alone and miserable in his saddle. "Do you understand what you did wrong?"

"I..." Ian trailed off, dejected and undoubtedly wary of incurring more wrath.

"Your intentions were good," Yiloch explained, his temper cooler now. "But you are here for a specific purpose. We don't want Rylan to know I have escaped. But even if he already knows, we cannot risk him learning my plans. The lives of my soldiers hang on my decisions. I do not make them lightly. Neither should you. Do you understand?"

"Yes, my lord," Ian mumbled.

"Good."

Adran emerged from the trees and scowled at him.

Hiding his own fatigue, Yiloch mounted and watched the soldiers finish their cleanup. Behind him, he heard Adran speaking to the creator.

"What did he say to you?"

"What I needed to hear," Ian replied.

Yiloch nodded to himself. The youth was no fool. He would learn.

CHAPTER FOURTEEN

Sunlight shone bright and warm on the front courtyard of the Caithin Healers' Academy, where Indigo and Andrea were finishing their afternoon meal. Spring blooms on trees and bushes were a balm to daily stresses, soothing with sweet perfumes and cheerful colors. Other students out enjoying the day occupied every stone bench and open patch of grass between winding paths.

Andrea tilted her hand this way and that, playing with the reflections of light on the brilliant center stone of the engagement ring Caplin had given her. Indigo thought it less attractive than the ring she had left in the prison, but would never say as much, especially now that the subject of her mysterious disappearance had ceased to be Andrea's favorite topic of conversation. Jayce had replaced Indigo's lost ring with a less expensive one bearing only a single blue stone centered on a simple band. He said the downgrade would remind her that such things were expensive.

The new ring weighed heavily on her finger, a tiny shackle.

Andrea set her hand in her lap. "Is something wrong?"

"I'm just tired from the long days."

Andrea scrunched her face into a sour grimace. "When will they give up? The sessions are obviously not helping."

A flutter of tremulous excitement rose in Indigo's chest in anticipation of her afternoon training with Headmaster Serivar. She could do much with ascard now that she never would have thought possible. Even Serivar seemed impressed with her accomplishments. A vast store of knowledge had opened up that she might never have discovered if she hadn't gone into the prison with her handsome Lyran revolutionary.

She breathed a sigh. "They think Lyran slaves were involved. They might never give up."

"Well, those beasts should be kept in line." Andrea's expression turned ugly with the harsh words.

Indigo recoiled from her.

"I know you sympathize with them, though I'm surprised this experience hasn't changed that, but I can't help my upbringing." Indigo would have disagreed, but Andrea rushed ahead, dodging the looming argument. "Have you remembered anything?"

How she longed to have a friend she could tell the truth. Just one person with whom she could share her fears and accomplishments. Was that so much to ask?

"No, nothing."

Andrea set a comforting hand on Indigo's arm. It was hard not to pull away. "I wish they hadn't rearranged your schedule. Classes aren't as fun without you."

So many lies were building a wall between them. At least Andrea now had wedding plans to occupy the time they once spent together after classes.

Indigo faked an encouraging smile. "They have to give up someday."

The academy bell tolled, somber tones signaling an end to the break and the awkward conversation.

Indigo grabbed her things and hopped to her feet, giving Andrea a quick wave as she hurried away. "See you tomorrow."

She hated conversing with anyone of late. The more she learned, the more she wanted to learn, and the more she wanted to tell someone about it. The inability to share this vital part of her life walled her off from everyone except the headmaster.

Andrea was too excited about her engagement to Caplin to notice the growing distance between them. Jayce was worse. At first, he complained about her time spent studying to keep up in accelerated classes. Then one of his peers convinced him to join an archery guild. Now he spent most evenings with that group, either practicing or, more often, drinking. At least it got him out of her way and, if she allowed him to do as he pleased with her when he stumbled in drunk late at night, he didn't seem to care if she distanced herself emotionally.

Today, for the first time, she faced a closed door at the headmaster's office. She raised a hand to knock when it swung open and Caplin nearly fell over her on his way out. He caught himself with a hand on her shoulder and offered a generic apology before recognition kicked in. Then his charming smile sparkled to life, rising into his eyes.

"Indigo. I mean...Lady Indigo," he amended with a slight flush.

"Lord Caplin." She smiled at his discomfiture. "What brings you here?"

"High Council business." He nodded to the headmaster, whose intent gaze had locked onto them. "And you?"

Her mind went blank. What could she say?

"I was told you wished to discuss your therapy sessions," Serivar offered.

She caught his eye for a second, grateful. "Yes. They're interfering with my studies."

Caplin cast the headmaster a meaningful look. "I am certain Lord Serivar will find a way to help. Have a lovely afternoon, my lady."

He offered an appropriate bow for the sake of their audience, and she reciprocated with a curtsy as he stepped around her and strode down the hall.

"Wait. Lord Caplin."

He spun, smiling at her. He had a most charming smile. "Yes."

"Might I borrow one of your horses tomorrow?"

"Certainly. I have several who need exercise. Will Lord Jayce be riding with you?"

"No." Too fast. Too curt. She winced inwardly.

His smile faltered.

Warming her tone, she said, "He has an archery tournament. I thought I might go out alone."

Caplin's nod was hesitant. "I will let Terun know you are coming."

"Thank you."

He nodded again, without conviction, and continued on his way.

She stepped into Serivar's office to confront the headmaster's curious regard.

"I know your uncle is important to King Jerrin, but I did not realize you and the king's nephew were close."

"We've been friends for years. Why?" She bumped the door shut with her heel. "Is he involved in the King's Order?"

"No, very few council members are." He shrugged, dismissing the subject, but the way he scowled at the papers on his desk made her uncomfortable. "Why ride alone?"

Frustration bubbled up. "Whenever I'm not training, I'm busy lying to everyone about what I'm doing when I am. I could use some time free of guilt and stress."

His gaze was steady. "I never said this would be easy."

"No. You didn't." The bluntness and truth in his words ground away at her failing composure. "Do you have a family, Master Serivar?"

His expression darkened. He stood and stalked to the back of the room to open the hidden door. The shadowed hallway beckoned. He glanced in her direction, not quite looking at her.

"More of one than you have."

She flinched at the rancor in his voice.

"Shall we?" He gestured brusquely down the hall.

Anger pulsed through her, both for the implication that lying was somehow worse for him and for his callousness toward the loss of her parents. Taking a deep breath, she plucked a candle off his desk, spilling wax on the wood, and stomped past him. When the long student's robes caught on a rough edge of the doorway, she grabbed a handful of material and yanked. The sound of fabric tearing answered her efforts, and she stormed down the hall even more frustrated. Time would have to be wasted repairing that later.

At the far end, she shoved open the door and stepped into the training room. Drawing from ascard in the candle flame, she reached out to the candles around the room. All twelve lit simultaneously, and despite her irritation, pride swelled.

"You have mastered that." Serivar slammed the bolt into place hard enough to make her jump.

She saw what was in the room then, and her pleasure faded.

A body lay on a table in the center. She had worked on human bodies in healing classes, but the corpse was more disquieting in this setting.

"What's that for?"

"What do you usually use them for?" He strode to the table, gesturing for her to follow.

"To learn human anatomy so we can heal it. Sometimes we also use them to practice mending damaged tissues." She stopped across the table from him.

The individual was a young woman, close to her own age. A swollen, discolored split on the side of her skull offered an apparent cause of death, and a cursory examination with the ascard confirmed that. She had been pretty, though much too thin. Her long brunette hair matted with dirt and blood, painted fingernails broken and torn, grime built up beneath them as if she had tried to claw her way through mud.

"She was a whore." His callous tone implied that her occupation made her fate less tragic. "The Watchmen found her by the river this morning."

Indigo gave him a sharp look, hoping he would take the hint and spare her further insight. When he started speaking again, she cut him off. "I would rather not know her history."

"Did I ask what you wanted?" he snapped.

She narrowed her eyes. "Does someone need a nap?"

Serivar sucked in a deep, trembling breath. The ascard around them thickened as if responding to his temper. A sword fell from a shelf behind him with a loud clatter, and she hopped back from the table in surprise. Serivar glared daggers through her, and she cringed, realizing how little she knew about his ascard ability.

"I would love nothing more than to send you home right now with a bruise across your backside from the flat of that sword." His scowl was enough to convince her he would do it. "However, we have this body today, so we will do this today."

"Right." Indigo stared at the body. A whore. A woman no one would miss, cursed by her low birth to a brief life of struggle and obscurity. "Can I ask something?"

He was silent.

"Would you have invited me to join the Order if I were lowborn?"

"Of course not."

"Why? Potential is potential."

He tapped his fingers on the table. "A peasant would have to become a ward of the crown to elevate their status before they could join the Order. That is not a reasonable precedent to set. Besides, the lowborn tend to have little or no viable connection to the ascard. An effect of poor nutrition in the womb, I believe."

"What would you have done with me if I had been lowborn?"

His hands clenched the side of the table, an ominous thickening in the ascard around them again. "If you intend to ask theoretical questions all session, I would rather go home to the family you think so little of."

She bit back a nasty retort, wary of driving him to act out his threat against her backside. "What do you want me to do?"

He took a minute to collect his thoughts, then gestured to the body between them. "I want you to do the opposite of what you have been taught. Rather than heal, I want you to inflict injury. We will start with something easy, perhaps with a cut in the skin. Before we leave today, I would like you to be able to shatter a bone without damaging the surrounding tissues. You will stand no less than five feet away to avoid the temptation to touch. Anyone you need to use these skills against will not let you get that close."

She stared at the dead woman. Healing damage someone else inflicted on a body felt like a positive thing, even if it did no good for the deceased. What Headmaster Serivar was asking her to do felt more than disrespectful. It felt immoral.

"Why must I know how to do this?"

He closed his eyes and clenched his teeth, his patience worn thin as fine silk. When he opened his eyes again, he said, "Some tasks you might be asked to complete could put you in danger. You have no weapons training, so you must have other defenses. Healing and wounding are two sides of the same skill. Because you can heal well and your connection is as strong as it is, you should be able to do the opposite with little effort. Shall we start, or shall I call in someone to erase your memory?"

For defense? Was that the only reason? Did it even matter? She would rather die than give up everything she had learned. But how far would she go for this knowledge? How far was too far? "Can we at least cover her face?"

He answered with a frosty look. "Start simple. A cut to the thigh."

She backed away from the table and focused her inner aspect on the ascard in the woman's skin, narrowing on her left thigh. The leg jerked, and she jumped, a squeal of surprise escaping her lips. The next six attempts were the same. It wasn't that she couldn't do it. The power was there, and the training to figure it out, but she didn't want to, and reluctance defeated her.

Serivar looked on with an impatient glower. There was no getting out of this.

She clenched her teeth and took a deep breath, realizing as she did so that the body had no stench. Suppressed with ascard? Her instructor's expression made it clear now wasn't the time to ask.

It's only for self-defense.

She walked through healing a deep cut in her mind, then reversed the process. A split opened in the thigh, and she choked on bile that rushed up the back of her throat.

Serivar smiled. "Well done. I knew this would be easy for you." He ignored her appalled look. "Try a torn ligament in the right knee."

She waited for her stomach to settle before complying.

They progressed through a complex series of exercises, culminating late in the evening with shattering a bone and sealing an artery in the heart. He inspected her work using ascard, grinning like a mud-covered boy by the time they finished. In contrast, she ended the session feeling drained, her stomach bound with more knots than a fisherman's net.

"Exceptional work today, Indigo. Very few mistakes. You are unusually versatile. Few people can master both healing and inflicting injury."

"You said they are two sides of the same skill." She spoke slowly, afraid her earlier meal might rush the opening.

"They are, but those with the temperament for healing rarely have the mental flexibility to accomplish the other."

She followed him to his office and hurried to the door, not in the mood to exchange pleasantries or discuss the lesson.

"Indigo." She stopped with her hand on the lever. "I apologize for my short temper earlier."

She only nodded and ducked out.

The residence was quiet when she arrived—Jayce either still out with his drinking companions or opting to sleep at home. Either way, she was too tired and unsettled to bother with dinner. She tossed her student robes onto a chair on the way to the bedroom. When she opened the door, a candle flickered on one bedstand, and there, in the center of the bed, were Eldrian's boots.

Her heart dropped into her stomach.

A hand grabbed her arm and spun her around, slamming her back into the wall beside the door. Jayce's face appeared in her swimming vision, his breath stinking of alcohol. He took her shoulders and pressed her against the wall.

"Who is he?"

Disorientation from the impact and rising terror jumbled her thoughts. "He? The boots? I... I don't know."

His hand caught her across the cheek. She tasted blood in her mouth. The strike cleared her head and ignited her rage.

"Don't lie to me. Who is he?"

She grasped for calm. "I was wearing the boots when they found me. They left them with me, hoping they would help me remember what happened."

"I said not to lie to me." His hand wrapped around her throat and squeezed. "Whore. I'll make you beg forgiveness from the Divine in person."

Blood began pounding in her skull. She couldn't get a breath. Her hands grabbed his wrist, trying to pull him away, but he held fast. His face, red with rage and too much drink, filled her vision, his eyes wild and bloodshot. She reached for her inner aspect, feeling the torrent of power waiting, a caged beast eager to burst forth.

She stared into his eyes. Her head felt as if it were swelling from the pressure. His fingers bit into her throat. She took a tendril of power and reached out, creating an invisible line of ascard through the skin of his throat. Life pulsed beneath that soft surface. It would be so easy.

I could kill you. A single thought and your throat would split open like rotten fruit.

All at once, she released her connection, pushing the power away.

I am no murderer.

Tears spilled from her eyes. She let go of his wrists, stopping the fight and going limp in his grasp. His hand loosened, letting blood flow into her pounding head. He kissed her hard, not caring that she didn't respond, and threw her on the bed, tearing at her dress. She let him take her there, his efforts clumsy and painful. Eldrian's boots pressing into her lower back.

That night, she wept for a long time while Jayce snored, hating him for the way he treated her. She was alone and afraid. Disgusted by the things she had done to the corpse and horrified by what she had almost done to him.

She could never do such things to a living person. It was cruel and far too easy. She had signed up for this training, but no one had given her a curriculum beforehand. More than ever, she longed for someone to talk to, someone to reassure her.

She curled in on herself and trembled, trying to remember the feeling of Eldrian's arms around her. The longing remained, but the memories faded, and with them, the comfort of believing she had made the right decision.

CHAPTER FIFTEEN

Jayce woke early for the archery tournament. When he asked her to join him, flashing a charming smile as if nothing had happened the night before, Indigo begged off, insisting she needed the quiet time to rest. After last night, she felt no guilt adding one more to the stack of lies building between them, rising out of the foundation he laid when he struck her that day over a month ago now. She faked a smile and suffered a quick kiss before he walked out the door. He took the boots with him, stating that he was going to get rid of the old things. She didn't stop him. Eldrian was in her head and heart. The boots were only boots.

Nerves that were on heightened alert around him relaxed, leaving her drained. Fifteen minutes later, after hiding bruises on her cheek and neck with a smidge of healing and some powder, she headed for the Duvox family residence in the Palace District.

The Duvox house stood alongside the high, spear-tipped iron fence that marked the edge of the palace grounds. A towering structure boasted attractive russet woodwork and black iron accents that incorporated the palace fence into the décor. The rich, dark gold of the main building absorbed the morning light, imbuing it with a welcoming glow that beckoned her. Caplin's ready smile and his mother's unfailing warm embrace waited within. His father, a typically gruff man, always found a quick, paternal smile for her.

She hesitated in the courtyard. A cloud passed over,

stealing away the warmth.

Going inside would lead to more evasion and lies. Today she meant to escape all the deception and pressure of training.

She angled toward the stable to the right of the house. An elderly man, whose purpose was to keep watch over slaves working in the stable, welcomed her and directed her to where Terun was preparing a fine-boned black mare named Velvet for her. With a flush of shame, she realized that, despite lofty claims to see Lyran people as equals, she had never acknowledged Terun's presence any of the times he had prepared mounts for her.

Comforting smells of hay and horses and the rustle of the animals moving in their stalls surrounded her while she watched Terun handle the mare. He was healthy and well-dressed, as were all the Duvox family's slaves. Smooth, pale skin, white hair, and the palest green eyes marked him as a lesser man in the eyes of most Caithin people. In his native country, those same traits were desirable indicators of a pure bloodline. Although his features were a bit too sharp and narrow for her taste, he was rather handsome. Not Lord Eldrian's level of devastating handsomeness, but far better than average.

The mare danced away from him a few times, but he corrected her, speaking Lyran commands in a patient but firm tone. The elegant aristocratic dialect he used while speaking to the animal brought Eldrian to mind with a fierce pang of longing.

He finished by dusting off the saddle seat, then bowed and held the reins out to her.

She accepted them with a gracious nod. "Thank you." She spoke Lyran although she knew he had a fine mastery of Caithin, meaning it as a courtesy.

His bow deepened a fraction.

Once mounted, she left the stable and the man who made her think of Eldrian behind, navigating to the south city gates. Merchants setting up in the market were almost all Caithin. With relations between the two countries on edge, fewer and fewer Lyran merchants traveled beyond the docks in Kilty. Even the representative from Lyra, who had formerly resided in the palace, returned to his home country. Palace officials said the king sent him away for his own safety, but their statements often benefited the king. Gossip suggested it hadn't been that congenial a separation.

The gate guards allowed her passage on her word that she was riding to one of the large manors that butted up against the city walls. Incoming farmers seeking to sell crops or livestock at market kept them too busy to question her in depth.

She trotted the mare away from the busy gate and turned down the river road. A peaceful ride to a riverside meadow would be the perfect way to unwind. There she could sit by the water and exist for a time without obligation. After yesterday, she needed such peace.

She urged the mare into an extended trot, enjoying the light breeze that passed around them. A fat morning sun, rising over distant hills, already baked the chill from the air. The wide swath of trees flanking the river closed in on her right, and vast fields of crops spread out on her left.

Two men were working just off the side of the road ahead. Not wanting to be rude, she eased the mare down to a walk to pass them. One man, a Lyran slave, was digging an irrigation trench. His hands and face were gaunt—his clothes dirty, tattered things that hung on his frame. The stocky, bronze-skinned man overseeing the work held a coiled whip in his meaty hands. He glanced in her direction, his dark eyes sliding past in disinterest.

There was nothing uncommon about the sight, but the

scathing comments her father used to make about such men predisposed her to instant disgust. Her jaw clenched with the effort of keeping her thoughts to herself, and she urged Velvet up to a faster walk. A sudden loud crack sent the mare bounding sideways. She reined her in hard, spinning her towards the noise, her heart pounding.

"Worthless fool," the stocky man bellowed at the slave, who now cringed over the remains of the snapped shovel handle.

He lashed out with his whip, and Velvet danced away. The slave fell to his knees, cowering. The man continued cracking the whip, hailing lashes down with all the mercy of an enraged wasp.

Fury boiled in Indigo. Velvet danced about, terrified of the sharp popping noise. Every successive crack made them both flinch and fed the fire building inside her. This was what her father had fought to stop. This was what Hadris had suffered before he freed her. People she loved, destroyed by such men as this.

Cruel men... like Jayce.

Cold, calm rage stole over her. Connecting to her inner aspect, she turned some of the ascard to calming the mare the way she would a panicking patient. Then she focused on the man with the whip and made a precise tear in the muscles of his forearm. He clutched the arm with a cry, and the whip dropped, the handle sliding down into the ditch, dragging the rest after it like a snake.

She took a few deep, trembling breaths and urged Velvet over to them.

"Are you all right, good sir?" She hid loathing behind false concern.

"I'm fine, lass. Just me arm." He grimaced, still clutching the afflicted appendage.

"You should have that looked at by a healer."

"I can't afford no healers."

Shame started twisting in her gut until she met the eyes of the slave. Pale depths glazed over with pain and despair she couldn't hope to comprehend. Stripes of blood marked his arms and hands where he had used them to shield his face from the whip. She could do nothing for him without drawing the wrong kind of attention. Helpless frustration brought the sting of tears to her eyes.

"Would you be so kind as to assist him back to the house?"

"Yes, my lady." The reply was little more than a whisper.

A tear slipped free when the slave turned to support his ailing master. The torn back of his shirt bore rust-colored stains from prior lashings. It took considerable will not to inflict more damage on the Caithin man. Watching them walk away, she felt another tear track down her cheek. Brushing it away, she turned the mare and kicked her up to a canter.

Anger and sorrow gave way to panic. What if an Ascard Watchman had been close enough to sense her? The craft of masking her workings eluded her still, and she had done something forbidden. She had used her ability to injure someone, a concept that sickened her to tears the day before. Serivar insisted the Watchmen wouldn't trouble her, but was that immunity unconditional?

A furtive glance around found a few wagons heading toward the city and a trio of riders walking away from the city farther back. She kicked the mare harder, trying to outrun fear and the persistent rage that strove to justify her actions.

They barreled along the roadway and rounded a bend. A familiar figure loitered on his mount to one side. Caplin's eyes widened when they charged around the trees. She suspected the surprise had more to do with her speed than her arrival. She sat up, her seat secure, and eased the mare down. The gradual slowing took them past him, and his gelding snorted, tossing his head against Caplin's hold.

She spun the mare and walked her back to Caplin. When she met his eyes, fresh anger threatened. "Why do I get the feeling this is more than a chance encounter?"

His sheepish grin brought out the ungainly boy he had been when they first met. "Sorry to intrude, but I couldn't resist the chance to see you alone, like old times. I can go."

"Caplin..." The angry retort caught on her tongue and melted away, his grin infecting her until she shook her head and laughed. "I should be angry with you, but maybe time alone isn't what I needed after all. Shall we?" She gestured down the road.

He moved his gelding into step with Velvet, and they continued at a calmer pace. Velvet's sides heaved, a layer of sweat slicking her black coat.

He glanced at the mare with raised brows. "I see you took me seriously about getting her some exercise."

"We were burning off energy." She stared ahead, muscles in her jaw tightening for a second, but she kept her tone conversational. "She seemed amenable. Where's Andrea?"

"With Mother, planning the wedding. It's safer to stay out of their way."

His chuckle was a balm to her soul, and she relaxed in the saddle, feeling the tension of recent events fading into the background. "I can imagine. At least she's no longer trying to plan my wedding."

They turned off the road together, acting with the unspoken accord of longtime familiarity, and wove through the trees. In the meadow by the river, they dismounted and left the horses to graze on the lush grass. At the river's edge, she pulled off her boots and sat on the bank, dipping bare feet into the cool water. The crisp scent of the river and the bright fragrance of the myriad wildflowers—yellow, white, and violet—carpeting the meadow, was invigorating. Some early summer blooms poked up amidst the spring blossoms.

Caplin sank down next to her, and they gazed out over the river, each lost in their own thoughts. A comfortable silence she rarely found in the company of others. She plucked a yellow flower and twirled the stem between her fingers, watching it spin. For a time, the only sounds were birdsong and the gurgle of water.

"What's the news from the High Council?"

He glanced sideways at her, his easygoing smile scampering away. "Why do you ask?"

"Serivar was rather short-tempered yesterday. I thought it might have something to do with that."

"Serivar?"

"Headmaster Serivar," she amended.

He leaned forward, his gaze inquisitive, and she looked down at the ripples playing around her feet in the river. She twisted the flower in her fingers. The temptation to tell him about her training was close to boiling over, but the potential repercussions of that simple act could be monumental. She clasped her hands around the now-mangled flower in her lap and held her tongue.

Caplin plucked at the grass and gazed out over the river again.

"We are considering forming an alliance to overthrow Emperor Rylan."

Her heart stuttered in her chest. *Eldrian. Could it be?*

"You can't tell anyone I told you," he added when she gaped at him.

"I'm quite competent at keeping secrets." Bitterness at how often it was necessary to do so put a sharp edge on the words.

His smile was disarming. "I trust you. King Jerrin has granted Prince Yiloch an audience to discuss a possible alliance."

Disappointment knotted her gut. "The Blood Prince?

How is he any better than his father?"

"Given the emperor's erratic behavior, the council thinks it might be time to entertain other options. Emperor Rylan banished Prince Yiloch three years ago. He's used that time to plan his takeover. We could stand to gain a lot by helping him."

She wanted to tell him that there were other options. So many secrets. Frustration added venom to her tone. "The prince burned two villages to the ground and slaughtered the people to punish one man. He massacred entire families. He's a vile beast."

Caplin's expression vacillated between amusement and shock. "He did it to find the man who murdered his mother in front of him. I don't excuse his actions, but you can imagine the grief and rage he was feeling at the time. Besides, it was Emperor Rylan who ordered the attacks."

"Prince Yiloch led them," she argued.

Caplin stared at her. "I'm amazed that you, of all people, would judge so harshly with only hearsay to go on."

She winced and averted her gaze.

"If Prince Yiloch gets Emperor Rylan off the throne, we can decide what to do with him later. The Lyran Empire is not as strong as it once was, and this upheaval will further weaken it. It's an opportunity to put them in our debt."

She tossed the flower into the river, watching it drift helplessly downstream. "What if he turns out to be worse than his father? What if you're trading a madman for an evil one?"

"King Jerrin has only granted him an audience at this point. Nothing is decided." He kicked the water with the heel of one boot, and she wondered how convinced he was by his own arguments.

Who would you put on the throne, Lord Eldrian? I never asked you that, did I?

Would he support someone like Prince Yiloch?

"I hope the Blood Prince turns out to be the better option." A cloud blocked the sunlight as she spoke, bringing a dark chill to the meadow before it passed on. An ill omen, or nature going about as usual?

Caplin cracked a grin. "It's a shame you're not on the High Council. We could use a woman's practical sensibility."

She started to laugh, but the sound died when she met his eyes. The respect in his regard caused a flutter in her chest. She looked away.

"Why tell me about this?"

He pulled his feet in and sat cross-legged. "I don't know. We used to talk about politics often, as I recall. It's nice talking to someone I can trust who isn't directly involved. It helps me get perspective."

If only she could afford the same risk. "Why me? I know you used to tell me things before, but never anything of this magnitude. Why risk the king's wrath?"

She glanced at him and turned away again from the affection in his smile.

"You're easy to talk to, Indigo. You're intelligent. Oh, and you did ask."

"I'm flattered you think I'm all that, though I question your judgment." She forced a playful grin.

"You are intelligent," he pressed. "I admire that you have an interest in more than fashion and gossip."

He was comparing her to Andrea. Uneasy silence fell between them. She let her mind drift, listening again to the simple sounds of water flowing and the chatter of birds.

"How are you and Jayce?"

She drew her feet out of the water and hugged her knees to her chest. "Well enough."

"You seem distant lately. I thought it might be a relationship problem, though Jayce has been rather cheerful the last few times I've seen him around."

"He is usually at his happiest when I am not," she

snapped. Her back stiffened, and her hand flew to her lips, wishing she could catch the words and put them back. "I didn't mean that."

"Yes, you did."

She shoved her damp feet into her boots and stood, starting toward the horses. "We should get back."

He stood behind her and placed a hand on her shoulder to stall her. "I know you're strong, Indigo, but you don't have to keep everything locked away. It's all right to let someone else support you once in a while."

Her throat constricted, the ache where Jayce's fingers dug in reminding her exactly how good things weren't between them. "Please, let's go."

"No. Jayce is an acquaintance of mine only because of you. You're the one who matters to me. If you are unhappy..."

She hung her head, trembling beneath his touch. With gentle pressure, he turned her and drew her into his embrace. Tears broke free unbidden, the strength of her sorrow turning her weak in his arms. He held her close until the tears ceased, then pushed her back and held her at arm's length, looking into her eyes.

"I understand the expectations and politics of high society better than most, but an engagement should not be a prison. I'm the king's nephew, I could—"

"No!" She softened her response with an apologetic smile. "Not now. I appreciate the offer, but terminating my engagement would make my life harder right now."

He frowned, searching her face for an explanation, but he didn't press. "The offer remains open."

She stepped back out of his grasp. "Thank you."

They collected the horses, and he let her direct their conversation to lighthearted chatter about the upcoming Wakening Festival and how spectacular the ball at the palace would be this year. The king never missed an opportunity to celebrate, and the expectation of the prince's arrival would drive him to heighten the extravagance.

"You will attend, won't you? Your beauty brightens a room."

She gave him a reproving look. "Wouldn't you consider such compliments inappropriate under the circumstances?"

His grin oozed mischief. "If it were a compliment, I might, but it was merely an observation of fact."

"Fine. Thank you." She yielded. "Regardless of what my *beauty* might or might not do to a room, I'm not fond of the idea of exchanging pleasantries with a man of Prince Yiloch's reputation. However, since Jayce wouldn't dare miss an opportunity to posture amongst his peers, I'll undoubtedly be there."

"Splendid. I'll introduce you to the prince."

She gave him a sour look. A shudder ran through her, and she nudged Velvet into a trot. What good could come of allying with such a man?

CHAPTER SIXTEEN

The seaward streets of Tunsdal were muddy and thick with human and animal waste. Even several blocks inland from the docks, the stench of rotting fish edged up underneath other questionable smells creeping out from the slums. Vessels didn't dock long, and no merchant lingered after passing on his wares, but it remained the second busiest port on the Lyran coast because the scarcity of imperial troops made it a prime dock for smugglers.

Hax arranged for them to meet Cadmar at an inn called The Weary Trader on the outskirts of town. If he had done his job, they should have a vessel secured for the trip across the Gilded Strait, and the wine casks already loaded. They could leave the miserable city behind almost as soon as they arrived.

Yiloch ignored the measuring looks as they rode into town. Locals were used to merchants of all classes visiting the city, but more than a few thieves looking for easy targets and dishonest traders hoping for gullible patrons roamed the streets. Rather than try to puzzle out who among their watchers might be a threat, he marked them all as suspect.

He sent Adran and Ian into the inn and waited outside with the retinue. Ian could maintain the existing disguise without having to see the entire group within a certain range, but he needed to see Cadmar in order to allow the warrior to see through it.

While they waited, Yiloch dismounted and scratched

Tantrum's forehead to hide his impatience. The big stallion's eyelids drooped in contentment.

Adran and Ian emerged several minutes later with the imposing warrior between them. Cadmar looked almost pure Kudaness with his dark skin, broad shoulders, and thick musculature. His trace of Lyran blood revealed itself in the unusual contrast of striking pale green eyes. Black hair, braided into thick ropes along his scalp, stretched to his lower back, even with the ornamental bone clasp that pulled it in at the base of his neck. The pommel of his long sword, a hissing snake head, peered over one shoulder, perfecting his menacing presence. Hax used him for critical assignments because his intimidating appearance often precluded the need to prove his skill. In a place like Tunsdal, that was an invaluable asset.

The dark warrior met Yiloch's eyes. "We sail on the *Maricelle* when the crew's done loading cargo. They loaded the wine this morning." His deep voice rounded out the daunting image.

Yiloch smiled, pleased they would not have to linger in the city. "Have you ever been to Caithin, Cadmar?"

"Never."

Cadmar's Kudaness appearance might remind King Jerrin that Yiloch had other options for building an alliance, and the dark man flanking him would create a striking contrast, making them each stand out even more than they did alone. "Would you care to?"

The warrior grinned, an almost feral expression that drew attention to an old scar pulling down his left cheek. "I would, Prince Yiloch, but Hax expects my return."

"I'll send someone to let her know I appropriated you." He mounted and turned to the nearest soldier. "Return to the stronghold. Inform Dalce that we reached Tunsdal and that Cadmar will make the crossing with us."

"Yes, my lord." The woman bowed her head and spun

her mount, kicking it up to a canter.

Cadmar led them to the docks, slogging through filthy mud on foot ahead of their horses. The reek of the streets made the prospect of open water appealing, despite Yiloch's distaste for boats. He preferred to keep solid ground under his feet, but the outcome of this journey promised to be worth a little discomfort.

Men swarmed the docks like ants. Workers loaded and unloaded shipments, hawkers called to passersby trying to sell everything from fish to jewelry, crewmen gathered supplies for their next voyage, and various traders and merchants finalized transactions for the import or export of goods. Moving through the throng behind Cadmar, Yiloch was vigilant. His soldiers kept hands near their weapons, ready to react in an instant. Their obvious weaponry and alert manner kept opportunists at bay. No thief gave them more than a second wistful glance before moving on.

They reined in their horses alongside the gangplank to a merchant vessel with *Maricelle* painted in fading red letters near the bow. A Kudaness man standing on deck spotted Cadmar, dark eyes flickering with recognition. The man was tall and lean, his black hair braided in ropes that cut off above the shoulder. Dark tattoos on either side of his face declared his tribe and trade.

Yiloch dismounted with Cadmar and motioned to Ian to follow. "Captain Adran, keep an eye on things here. We don't need trouble."

Adran settled into his saddle while Cadmar led Yiloch and Ian up the plank to where the ship's captain waited.

"*Nhia, Sen Markhia,*" Cadmar greeted, holding a fist over his chest.

Captain Markhai mirrored the gesture. "*Nhia, Cadmar. Shes Yiloch khuelgan?*"

Yiloch gestured to Ian. "Let Sen Markhai see us."

Ian nodded. A few seconds later, Captain Markhai's eyes narrowed. He offered Yiloch a stiff bow and glowered at Ian with open animosity.

"Your Highness, I mean no disrespect, but I risk the wrath of the gods by allowing you on my ship. I will not have a creator on board." The captain's thick accent made the Lyran trade dialect almost unintelligible.

Yiloch nodded. He knew and respected their beliefs, but he wasn't going without Ian. "I understand your displeasure, Sen Markhai, but the creator reduces risk for all of us. Should an imperial vessel hail us, he can disguise my men and our cargo."

Markhai's frown deepened. His eyes moved from Yiloch to Ian and back. Turning to Cadmar, he spoke fast in his native tongue, perhaps assuming that Yiloch would be unable to follow the exchange. He pointed at Ian, making the source of his aggravation obvious, and the young creator dropped his gaze to his shifting feet. The youth was fortunate he didn't understand Kudaness, or his cheeks might burn twice as bright at the captain's expressive tirade against ascard users in general, and Ian in particular, for their blasphemous use of the gods' powers. He continued, cursing Cadmar for trying to bring misfortune to his vessel and threatened to unload the wine.

"We won't be unloading the wine," Yiloch interrupted, stepping close to the captain. "We can do this politely, and I'll pay you an extra 1000 fven for your trouble, or I can order my soldiers to seize control of your ship, and we can dump you overboard halfway across the Gilded Strait. I'm confident you'll find the first option more agreeable."

Markhai's eyes flashed with outrage, and Yiloch thought he might test the threat. Then he gave a sharp nod. "The Blood Prince is bold, and his reputation formidable. I take an extra 2000 fven and you guarantee the safety of my crew.

Your creator has no contact with my men. None." He emphasized the last with a sharp cutting motion.

"1500 fven," Yiloch countered.

"Agreed." Markhai offered a hand to seal the bargain.

Yiloch accepted it in a firm grip. With the dispute resolved, he left Cadmar to handle the captain from there and nodded down to Adran.

Adran dismounted and started barking orders to the retinue. Twenty-three soldiers hastened about their assigned duties. Two men arranged horse lines. They would lead the horses south to a smaller port where Yiloch's party planned to dock upon their return. The rest moved supplies from pack animals onto the ship. Markhai's first mate called out orders to them, directing them to where their supplies were to be stored.

Yiloch turned to Ian, who swayed unsteadily with the rocking of the ship. "Go below and rest. You can release the illusion when we're clear of the port. Avoid interacting with the crew."

Ian nodded, listless, and wove a weary path to the steps.

Confident in the arrangements, Yiloch walked to the starboard railing where a strong breeze blew the stench of the docks inland. Adran joined him several minutes later.

"We're loaded. Captain Markhai has one more shipment to bring aboard before we cast off."

Yiloch nodded.

"Where's Ian?"

"I sent him below. He's been working ascard nonstop for days. He needs rest. Someone should stay with him. His ability makes him unwelcome here."

Adran waved a soldier over and assigned him to guard the creator. Then he leaned on the railing and gazed out at the strait.

The cool breeze caressed Yiloch's skin, and he closed his

eyes, imagining their destination. Indigo was there somewhere.

"Do you hope to see her?"

He opened his eyes, his gaze moving to Adran for a second before drifting back out over the open water. He didn't want to talk about her. She needed to get out of his head.

Silence stretched between them. The lap of waves and the thud of booted feet on deck filled the gap.

"You were right," Adran said eventually.

"I usually am." Yiloch set aside troubling thoughts in favor of a teasing smile.

Adran gave him a cross look. "Don't be obnoxious."

Yiloch chuckled. "Right about what?"

"Bringing Ian. It spared us considerable risk, and he's thrilled to have the opportunity, but I didn't want him to get hurt. You can be careless with those who serve you." An edge of personal hurt sharpened the comment.

"I understand you care about him, but he needs to test himself. It will give him much-needed confidence to realize how useful he can be."

Adran nodded and stared out over the water, brooding. Content to let him brood in silence, Yiloch stood watching the waves and wondered what Indigo was doing now.

CHAPTER SEVENTEEN

In the deep dark, several hours before dawn, the *Maricelle* pulled into the Kilty docks. Numerous ships moored there, diverse in size and purpose, rocking on gentle waves. A lone seabird called out, its childlike cry piercing the dark. An eerie stillness embraced a harbor full of ghost ships until another vessel began unloading cargo. A sliver moon sank on the horizon, its light barely brightening the inky night sky.

Darkness helped hide them from unwanted attention, taking some of the burden off Ian. One of Yiloch's men had gone ashore to speak with a guardsman in royal livery who had been watching the docks. Now the guard followed the king's representative out to them. At Yiloch's nod, Ian allowed the two men approaching to see past their disguise, changing the ascard around them.

Protocol dictated that they await the host's welcome before setting foot upon their soil, so Yiloch took this opportunity to assess the young man bedecked in noble finery, flanked by the royal guardsman. His square-cut jacket sported elaborate embroidery, and his dark hair appeared intentionally mussed in a manner that suggested a distinct awareness of his youthful good looks. A sword belt rested comfortably on his hip and, though a slight swagger hinted at arrogance, something in his relaxed bearing suggested the confidence might be justified.

Adran leaned close and whispered, "At least they sent

someone easy on the eyes. I'd sleep with him."

Yiloch flashed an amused smile. "Attractive or not, I recommend against making advances."

"Too bad." Adran shrugged and stepped back to flank him opposite Cadmar, who stood cross-armed and scowling at his left shoulder.

His soldiers lined up in two neat rows behind them, and Ian hovered behind Adran, drawing as little attention as possible. A heavy door slid open on the building behind the approaching men. Five coaches and two enclosed wagons rolled out, lining up in front of the building, along with a team of mounted royal guards who moved into position around the column.

When the two men reached them, both bowed, though the young lord did so with more refinement and respect.

"Prince Yiloch, I am Lord Caplin Duvox. I welcome you on behalf of King Jerrin."

Caplin Duvox, the king's nephew. Sending a member of the royal family on this clandestine endeavor was a show of high regard from the king, and the young lord's courteous manner earned him quick favor. Yiloch reciprocated with a respectful nod and introduced Adran as his ranking captain. Combined with his age and meek bearing, Ian's lack of introduction would encourage the assumption that he was a mere attendant.

Caplin gave Adran a respectful nod, which he returned, and said, "My men will assist with the transfer of your supplies."

Yiloch turned to Cadmar. "Take four men below and ensure everything is ready to be moved."

With a look that vacillated between alarm and awe, Caplin watched the big warrior disappear below deck. He dragged his attention back to Yiloch. "If you care to join me, Your Highness, I have wine waiting in my carriage. You could rest and refresh while your cargo is moved."

"I would be pleased to do so, Lord Caplin. If you will allow me a moment to settle with Sen Markhai."

Caplin looked puzzled, but he nodded graciously.

The ship's captain was overseeing the unloading of his other cargo. Under different circumstances, Yiloch would have had Adran close the transaction, which was likely what confused the young lord, but Adran didn't speak the language as fluently.

Getting the captain's attention, he restated their agreement in Kudaness and counted out the settled upon sum.

Markhai accepted the payment. "Our contract is satisfied."

"It is. *Iysweyr Silgand*," Yiloch said, offering a customary parting, meaning 'go with Silgand,' the Kudaness water God.

"*Silgand fvern tulahnd, Shes Yiloch*," Markhai answered, completing the parting with Silgand's blessing.

Yiloch returned to the others and set Adran to supervising the unloading. At his nod, Caplin led the way down the gangplank. The first hints of dawn brought a soft glow to the dark sky, and increased activity began animating the sleepy docks.

"I brought my new carriage for us. It offers a smooth ride, even on rougher roadways. I hope you'll forgive me for using this opportunity to show it off." Caplin gestured with an exaggerated flourish to an elegant carriage near the front of the line.

The deep red lacquer finish darkened to black at all edges with tasteful gold inlay accents that glittered in the flickering lamplight. Two fine-boned blood bay geldings pulled the carriage, their elegance complementing the expensive finish. It was the conveyance of a nobleman with refined tastes.

"Impressive, Lord Caplin," Yiloch commented as they climbed in and sank into soft seats upholstered in dark red velvet. He positioned himself by one window so he might view Demin as they approached.

"Thank you, Prince Yiloch. I am embarrassed to admit that I commissioned it with a mind to woo a lady."

Yiloch chuckled, falling into the casual comfort of the other man's friendly demeanor. "From your tone, I gather it did not work as planned."

"She was indifferent, although we are now engaged. It is the decision to woo her I am questioning." His jaw tightened with thinly veiled frustration. "But you aren't here to listen to my relationship woes. Would you care for some wine?"

"Please."

Caplin poured two glasses and handed him one. "I hope your journey was not too arduous?"

Despite the attempt at polite conversation, frustration persisted in the young lord's eyes. His engagement troubled him. The opportunity to build his trust now would be worth the effort in the coming days, so Yiloch disregarded the attempted change of subject.

"She has changed, or you have?"

Caplin's regard was calculating, fully cognizant of the situation. If he let the conversation delve into personal matters, it would be a deliberate choice.

The carriage started moving.

Caplin gazed out the window. "Father advised me to find a woman who would dazzle my peers with her beauty and charm. She certainly does those things. She can also gossip with the best courtiers."

"But?"

"But we have little in common. My mother warned me to find a woman who shared my interests, or I would grow bored with her beauty. I begin to wonder if hers was not the wiser advice."

"I suspect they were both right. If you were Lyran, I

might suggest you find a mistress to fill the void, but I under-stand your culture disapproves of such behavior."

Caplin chuckled. "So they say. Considering how many noblemen I know who have *secret* mistresses, I would say the evidence supports your approach."

"Perhaps."

"Do you have someone special in your life? A future Lyran Empress?"

He appreciated Caplin's willingness to acknowledge his ambitions. If only Indigo's face were not the first to come to mind. "No, not yet. I have been far too busy to court a lady."

"I imagine. Planning a war can be so time-consuming." His sudden, candid smile was infectious. "I am glad you are here. I can move into my rooms at the palace for a while. That will be glorious after a few days at the Kilty docks."

Yiloch smiled, willing to reciprocate the cordial manner for now. "Your efforts are appreciated. I am sure King Jerrin knows it is an honor to be greeted by a member of the royal family in these circumstances."

"He does nothing by accident. If he spent less time on celebrations and more on politics, he would be an incredibly powerful man, though he seems content with the rule he has."

It disconcerted Yiloch that this man spoke to him more like an old friend than the disfavored heir of a race his people used as slaves. "You are rather forthright considering you do not know where my long-term ambitions lie."

Caplin sipped his wine and shrugged. "I've always been quick to trust, but it has never played me wrong. In my experience, the differences that matter are rarely as simple as the color of a man's skin."

Caplin's unguarded gaze confirmed the sincerity of his words. There was something in his manner that made Yiloch want to believe him. Still, he had learned the danger of trusting too easily. He needed to remain wary of Caithin's superior might in the current circumstances. King Jerrin didn't need to ally with him, but this alliance could save Caithin the cost of a full-scale war with Lyra the way things were going. He had some bargaining advantage in that.

Yiloch traced the rim of his glass with one finger. "Kudaness prophets believe physical diversity in men is akin to the varied colors of horses. Merely ornamental. Rather than dividing men by race, they use a hierarchy of moral qualities to categorize people. Though the prophets themselves are the only ones who seem to practice that philosophy," he added with a wry smile.

"And you speak Kudaness fluently."

"Lyra values its peaceful relationship with Kudan." Yiloch refrained from pointing out that Caithin's prejudice toward the Kudaness reinforced that relationship. "Making the effort to learn their language demonstrates respect."

"The man you called Cadmar, he is Kudaness, is he not?"

"He has some Lyran in him."

"That explains his eyes. He is an intimidating figure, and I don't imagine I have to tell you how spectacularly you two contrast one another."

Yiloch smirked and took a drink of the wine, a poor substitute for a good Lyran blend.

"King Jerrin will love it," Caplin continued. "He has a penchant for the dramatic. If you are up for it after your travels, I might get you an audience with him this afternoon."

"I find sitting still more exhausting than travel, Lord Caplin. It would please me to meet with King Jerrin this afternoon."

"I am inclined to agree. I get into far less trouble when I'm traveling. Quarters have been prepared for you in the palace, with attendants if you so desire. There are adjacent rooms ready, should you wish to keep some of your men on hand. There was concern of conflict with Caithin soldiers, so we arranged a section of barracks for the dedicated use of your soldiers."

"I have no misconceptions of Lyran status among your people, and I appreciate such matters being taken into consideration." Yiloch kept his tone pleasant despite the flash of loathing that burned through him. The slave trade negatively influenced Caithin attitudes toward his people. It would end, but he wasn't here to end it now.

The escort slowed to a walk upon entering Demin. In the soft amber light of early morning, the Caithin people started their day. How strange to see so many bronze-skinned people in one place. Few Caithin traveled in Lyra, though it had been different once, before the slave trade.

Pale red and tan stone cobbles paved the inner streets, a striking divergence from the gray and blue that paved the streets of Yiroth. Buildings painted in shades of tan and brown pulled in the light of sunrise, generating a golden glow, and the air grew warm despite the early hour. In the distance, down one side street, the sun lit two gold spires rising high above the rooftops.

"What is the building with the spires?"

"The Caithin Healers Academy. One of the great prides of the city."

Indigo. "I have heard great things about your healers."

"They are not so extraordinary next to your assortment of creators and adepts, but their skills are always in demand. My fiancé is a student there, which reminds me." Caplin's changed tone drew Yiloch's attention back from the distant spires. "The king hoped you would attend the Wakening Festival feast and ball."

"I had planned to do so, hence the wine casks."

Caplin grinned. "Brave man. You will get to meet the best and worst Caithin nobility has to offer. I don't suppose you're familiar with our dances?"

"Enough to manage."

Caplin pointed out other spots of interest as they passed through the city, including the marketplace and the ornate ironwork gates marking the entrance to the education district. The palace looked more like a confused grand manor. Steep rooflines and sharp pinnacles intermixed haphazardly with the odd square tower. The number of peaks suggested a sizeable structure, but one that would still fit inside the massive palace in Yiroth.

The carriage entered a circular courtyard. A covered walkway lined with stone columns led to the main entrance. Two smaller pathways led out through manicured gardens on either side of the rambling structure.

Yiloch and Caplin stepped out of the carriage and waited while the rest of his retinue joined them. Countless decorative flowers burst with color amidst lush greenery, enriching the garden with rich perfumes. It created an enchanting presentation to welcome visitors, though his father would consider it frivolous. Perhaps he would have a similar garden added to the palace in Yiroth once it was his.

"Prince Yiloch, if it pleases you, I will show you where your men will be staying."

Yiloch nodded and motioned for the retinue to follow. Caplin guided them along a side path through more remarkable gardens. Beyond the gardens, they came to a series of long, low buildings with a sparring circle and archery targets outside each. The first building stood silent. Beyond that, royal soldiers trained, several of whom stopped to watch them.

Ignoring their audience, Caplin led them inside the first building. A row of cots lined both sides of the long main room, every bed area furnished with a chest for storage and a bedstand with a candleholder. Several battered wooden dummies sagged along the rear wall on either side of a fireplace.

"Will this serve?"

Yiloch deferred to Adran with a glance, and Adran inspected the bedding on the nearest cot. "Do they have permission to use the practice facilities outside?"

"Yes," Caplin answered. "We only ask that there be no competition with Caithin troops at this time, friendly or otherwise. Our soldiers have been warned against provoking your men. They will have two dedicated servants to see to their needs."

Adran nodded approval. "This should be sufficient."

"Then I will show you to the rooms inside the palace."

Adran set the soldiers to settling into the barracks. Then he, Ian, and Cadmar followed Yiloch and Caplin out. A few Caithin soldiers resumed sparring while they walked past. Yiloch's hand drifted absently to the hilt of his sword.

"Lord Caplin, you wear your weapon comfortably. If you are willing, perhaps we could cross swords during our stay."

Caplin flashed him an enthusiastic grin. "I would be. I am curious how your styles differ from ours."

"Be careful. Rarely a day goes by that he doesn't practice," Adran warned good-naturedly, also sinking into the comfort of Caplin's friendly manner.

Caplin chuckled. "Remember, killing the king's nephew is bad for relations."

Yiloch tapped his sword hilt. "I will take that under advisement."

After showing them the opulent second-floor sitting area and the adjacent rooms they would use during their stay, Caplin excused himself to arrange an audience with the king. By the time he returned, they had settled and were lounging in chairs on the attached veranda overlooking a courtyard garden, all except Cadmar, who stood tapping his fingers on the railing. The dark warrior had declared himself uncomfortable with so much comfort.

"King Jerrin is concluding a land dispute between two lords," Caplin announced. "I don't know why he bothers. Those two find a new reason to fight every few months. I think he should strip them of their titles and put them to work cleaning back alleys. Teach them both some humility."

"A sound judgment. My father would sell them off as slaves." Yiloch let bitterness come through this time to see how Caplin would react.

"There are always those driven more by riches than reason."

A cautious and tactful reply. "As there always will be."

"Come. I will show you to the throne room."

They followed Caplin through the palace to a set of imposing wood and iron doors flanked by two guards who bowed and pulled the doors open. At the far end of a room similar in size to the council hall in Yiloch's stronghold, but much less brightly lit, a raised dais supported a throne flanked by several more guards bristling with weaponry. The gilded, gem-encrusted throne was the first truly gaudy thing he had seen in the palace, other than the man sitting on it.

King Jerrin was heavyset, with a thick head of graying brown hair and a full beard hiding most of his face, giving the impression of a dying bush set atop the fur-trimmed red velvet robes he wore. Yiloch counted no less than three heavy rings per hand and two gold, jeweled amulets around his neck. He cringed at the excess as he and his entourage bowed before the throne.

When Yiloch straightened, King Jerrin was grinning, his dark eyes peering out at them over a thick nose. With that simple expression, his entire bearing morphed from arrogant and excessive to merry, if perhaps a bit eccentric.

Jerrin stood, coming down from the dais to greet them.

Any intimidation he might have possessed through rank and bulk vanished behind a delighted grin. The king clasped Yiloch's hand as a warrior might greet his equal in battle, and Yiloch noted the firmness of the sovereign's grip. A soft sigh from Caplin forced him to suck back a grin.

"Prince Yiloch," the king greeted. "It is an honor. I have heard a great deal about you."

Yiloch dared a touch of humor. "None of it good, I am sure."

"Not a bit." The king chuckled and turned to Cadmar. His eyes lit up like a child discovering a new toy. "And who is this rather imposing gentleman?"

"Cadmar is a personal guard," Yiloch answered.

The king grasped Cadmar's hand as well, ignoring the big man's mystified expression. "You are nearly as striking a figure as your prince, good sir. It is my pleasure to welcome you here."

The king greeted Adran and then Ian, who turned a light shade of green when the jovial monarch took his hand. This unconventional man wasn't what Yiloch expected. He would have preferred someone more kingly, but it could be far worse.

"I thank you for the wine, Prince Yiloch. Emperor Rylan cut our imports, and local varieties are a poor substitute. I would have liked my wife and son to meet you. Alas, her sister is ill, and they have gone to her manor in Innid to be with her."

"So does life continue regardless of our plans."

"Indeed," the king agreed. "Come, let us meet in the council room where we can all sit."

An attendant stepped out from the shadows of a corner and trotted to one side of the room, opening a door into a round room with a massive circular table consuming most of the space. This room had more windows set high in the walls, making it brighter than the throne room and illuminating an array of maps hung around the perimeter. Yiloch longed to examine them.

"This is the High Council meeting room," Caplin offered.

Ian and Cadmar stood back from the table, separating themselves from the discussion as appropriate to their stations. The king's guardsmen positioned themselves around the room. Yiloch and Adran accepted the seats offered, several chairs to the king's right, and Caplin sat across from them.

The king's expression turned grave when the door clicked shut. "As I am sure you are aware, Emperor Rylan has violated nearly every condition of our trade agreement over the last few years. I believe that agreement has outlived its usefulness. However, as you currently have no empire, I would venture you are looking to negotiate more than a trade agreement."

"I believe my father has outlived his usefulness," Yiloch said, using the king's phrasing and emphasizing the sentiment with a healthy dose of disgust. "I seek a military alliance to overthrow him. Specifically, I want naval support to provide a distraction while I move my army in on the landward side. I also want healers to support my army." Both Caplin and the king stiffened in their seats at the mention of healers. That subject would require careful negotiation. "There will be benefits for Caithin, of course. Once the empire is mine, I will open trade again, removing restrictions on many of your exports and on those now blocking the import of most Lyran goods, including our wine."

"What do you believe your chances of success are?" Caplin asked, offering a quick look of apology to the king for speaking out.

Yiloch waited for Jerrin's nod before answering. "Rylan has lost the backing of more than half the noble families in Lyra. Many of those families have agreed to send troops to support my efforts. Others have at least consented to staying out of the fight. With your support, we would be certain to win." Yiloch held back the fact that he had assistance inside Yiroth for the sake of protecting Lyric, since Jerrin could still choose to take this information to Rylan to use as a bargaining chip.

"I am interested in discussing this further, Prince Yiloch, but I must ask, what are your intentions regarding the slave trade? Caithin's aristocracy has grown accustomed to their conveniences." The king tapped his fingers on the table as he spoke.

Adran, ever hopeful, nudged Yiloch's foot under the table, but trying to stop the slave trade now could kill the alliance.

"There will always be criminals, Your Majesty, and a need to control the people."

The king's smile returned. "Prince Yiloch, I believe we're going to work well together."

CHAPTER EIGHTEEN

Dalce gripped the edge of the embrasure and stared out beyond the wall. The stone was coarse, grinding into his flesh, not smoothed over with creation as it was on the palace walls in Yiroth. Reality. It pressed into his skin, harsh and unyielding, reminding him of a simpler time and the circumstances that brought him to this moment. He had made his choices, and he didn't regret them. Now, his journey appeared to be rushing to its end.

Imperial soldiers gathered outside the rear gate of the stronghold. They were assembling around the front gate as well. The total force was perhaps two hundred strong, and he counted no less than ten without weapons. Those would be creators or adepts, which meant they would soon be inside the walls.

Upon receiving word of the troop Yiloch's party had encountered, Dalce sent out scouts to search for other signs of imperial activity in the area. Thanks to one of those scouts, they had some warning of the coming attack. The small force residing at the stronghold had time to retreat to a sheltered valley higher in the mountains, the evidence of their passing obscured by Ferin and the few other adepts in residence. They took all the horses and arms they could transport with them. Better to hide today and be ready to fight when Yiloch needed them.

Dalce stayed behind with the steward, Galen, to destroy evidence of their plans and their numbers before imperial soldiers arrived. An unfortunate but necessary process that took more time than they had.

Outside the rear gate, a familiar figure with the pale skin and fine-boned features of pure Lyran lineage, contrasted by hair and eyes blacker than obsidian, rode up through the middle of the imperial ranks. Dalce raised his lip in a silent snarl.

When he left Yiroth, Myac had been gaining favor and influence with Emperor Rylan through his substantial power and growing skill. Judging from the way the soldiers parted before him, he had continued that climb. Any hope of making it out alive fled with Myac's arrival.

Dalce started down the staircase, his steps heavy.

He loved the young prince. Not the way Adran did. Not with passion or desire, but with complete dedication. He had served Yiloch's father, the emperor, and hated the man for the callous way he used his sons and disrespected his people. For all their similarities, Yiloch was not his father. The prince respected his officers and would never send his soldiers needlessly to their deaths. His regard for the peasantry might be less than ideal, but he at least recognized his need for them, and Dalce believed he would be a better ruler to them than Emperor Rylan had ever been.

If things went as planned, Yiloch's retinue should be in Demin now. Another man might resent facing this attack in the prince's stead, but Dalce didn't. The proud prince might have hesitated at abandoning the stronghold to his father's soldiers had he known they were coming. Against this force, limited as their defenses were, that could have been the end of their hopes. He had made the choice to stay behind with Galen to safeguard the prince's chances for victory and prevent another dire setback. He was the only one he trusted to do what was necessary now.

Heading inside, he found Galen in Yiloch's study, seated

behind the prince's ransacked desk, scanning a document. A deep iron pot sat on the floor, papers burning within it. He looked up when Dalce entered and tossed the document into the fire, watching the flames consume it.

"Are we finished?" Dalce asked.

Galen nodded. "That was the last. I have destroyed all of it. There's nothing for them to find."

"Good. They're here."

"I know."

If only they had more time. An hour more. But such thoughts served no purpose. "There is still evidence we must destroy."

Galen swallowed hard. "I know."

Though fear filled Galen's eyes, his voice held complete acceptance of his fate. Dalce was impressed. For a steward untrained in war, he showed remarkable courage. Perhaps the man could have done this by himself, but it was a lot to ask of a man alone.

When your enemy had powerful adepts at their disposal and capture became inevitable, there were only two ways to avoid betrayal—true ignorance or death. For the two of them, only one of those options remained. Dalce drew his sword and walked around the desk. Galen sat rigid when Dalce placed a hand on his shoulder. He drew the sword back, aiming it at the steward's chest. Galen met his eyes, refusing to look at the blade.

"Peace, good sir," Dalce said.

"Peace," Galen echoed, the tremor in his voice betraying his fear.

Dalce appreciated his own strength now more than ever. The steward had earned a quick death. With one mighty thrust, he sent the weapon into Galen's chest and out through his back, pinning him to the chair. Blood flowed from the wound, running from his mouth as he choked, his jaw working as if trying to form words. In seconds, the pain and terror in his pale eyes faded to lifeless emptiness.

Dalce drew the dagger from his belt and sat in the chair across from Galen. He picked up the wine the steward had been drinking and raised the cup in tribute to the other man before taking a last swallow. Setting the cup down, he held the wine in his mouth, savoring it before letting it slide down his throat. The will to finish this was harder to find than he expected, but it was there, meshed deep within his love for his prince, growing stronger the more he thought about Yiloch and the dream they all shared.

The dagger was sharp, with a good point and a wide base. He opened his shirt and positioned the blade under his sternum. Taking a deep breath, he wrapped both hands around the hilt and shoved up into his chest with all his might. His arms jerked, tearing the blade back out and allowing blood to drain faster. The agony, excruciating though it was, paled before the certainty that he would never betray his prince.

* * *

Myac sat upon his mount and manipulated the ascard in the heavy iron and wood gate, creating flaws throughout the structure. Then he made an invisible barrier across the outside of the gate and shoved. The gate burst inward, throwing splintered wood and shards of iron throughout the courtyard. His horse flinched but remained in its place while several others attempted to wheel about and flee. Myac patted the animal's neck and urged it forward with the first line of soldiers, disappointed, but not surprised that no one had been in the courtyard when the door burst. More soldiers flooded in and dismounted, flowing in units to the barracks, stables, and other outbuildings.

Myac dismounted and walked up the steps to the rear

doors of the stronghold. For the simple amusement of it, he used the ascard to throw open the large double doors. Imperial soldiers streamed in ahead of him, moving with weapons held ready.

Stretching ascard energy through the stronghold and grounds, he searched for signs of life, becoming distracted by an anxious presence directly behind him. He glanced over one shoulder at the young soldier, Leryc, who stood staring into the stronghold. Leryc trained extensively with Yiloch before the prince's banishment, but he wouldn't talk to Myac about that time. His smooth, pale brow under a head of light blond hair furrowed with worry. The concern in his pale eyes disagreed with the permanent smirk caused by a scar that lifted one corner of his mouth.

Was the tension Myac sensed in the youth from fear of him, or did he also fear the wrath of his old mentor? Did he still feel some loyalty to the prince and worry that an encounter would test that? He was difficult to read.

Myac gestured for the youth to follow him, sensing the answering chill of dread through his ascard ability when Leryc moved to comply. The youth earned a glimmer of respect for not allowing his emotions to show.

The cold colors Lyran nobility favored appeared sparingly in the scanty furnishings. In the palace, delicate silver and created crystal ornamentation enhanced the icy blues and grays. Here, the prince hadn't wasted effort on such frivolity. It wasn't opulent, like the Imperial Palace, but it showed an elegant trace of that influence in every room, layered over a rugged and functional base. The exiled prince might be practical, but he was still royalty.

Appreciation emanated from Leryc, and Myac glanced over his shoulder again. The youth ran his fingers over a simple, elegant table pushed up against the wall. The hint of a smile balanced his expression, bringing out the Lyran beauty of his pure blood. His build was slight, better suited to his pretty violet eyes, but otherwise he was the exact image of his father, Rylan's captain of the guard. His uncle had deserted with Yiloch only to meet his death when he appeared in the prison with the prince. Where did Leryc's loyalty lie?

Noticing Myac's scrutinizing gaze, Leryc jerked his hand back.

A soldier came jogging toward them. "Adept Myac."

"What is it?"

"I think you should see this."

Myac nodded, gesturing again for Leryc to follow as the soldier led them down a side hall. They entered a study, decorated most recently with the blood of the two men within. One sat pinned to a chair with a sword through his chest. The other lay face down on the floor. The soldier rolled him over with one foot. A dagger lay on the floor beneath the dead man. He had a hole punched deep into his chest. The man in the chair was unfamiliar, but the one on the floor, a satisfied smile frozen on his still warm lips, was a ranking defector from the emperor's army.

Choking behind him preceded the sound of retching and the unwelcome, sour stench of vomit. He glared back at Leryc, who straightened again, his eyes riveted on Dalce with unmistakable recognition while he wiped the back of one hand across his mouth. The young soldier's pale skin had a slight greenish cast to it, and his stark anguish pierced Myac's extended ability.

"You're supposed to be a soldier," Myac snapped. Anger swelled, along with disappointment. There would be no putting the prince in his place, not today.

He knelt by the man on the floor and turned his head to get a better look at his expression. A smile?

Captain Dalce, were you actually happy to die for him?

How did such a man inspire that kind of loyalty? Perhaps

he had underestimated the threat Yiloch posed. If he held this much sway over his followers, getting him off the throne might prove complicated. Somehow, he had to keep the prince from getting that far, but how could he do so with a partially mad emperor whose influence weakened with every passing day? Even if he controlled Emperor Rylan, he didn't know enough to wage war from behind the throne.

Myac set his jaw. He would find a way.

He stood and turned to the soldier. "We'll find nothing here. They knew we were coming. Get someone to help drag these bodies outside. I want to leave a message in case someone returns."

"Yes, my lord." The soldier hurried off.

Myac walked to the dead man pinned in the chair. "I imagine this fine blade was yours, Dalce."

He knew he couldn't pull the blade out with sheer strength. The physical power and weapon skill of the man who had put it there were well beyond his own. Using ascard to push away fabric, flesh, and bone around the blade, he eased it out. In his life, he had handled a sword only a few times. He had no need for weapons of steel. The sword hung heavy and awkward in his grasp, but he didn't intend to hold on to it for long.

"Wait here and help move the bodies," he ordered Leryc.

The youth nodded, still transfixed by the body on the floor.

Myac walked to the double doors at the end of the hall, behind which he suspected he would find the prince's chambers. Blood dripped from the blade, leaving a trail of red splotches along his path.

Where most of the rooms were functionally furnished, the prince's spacious chambers boasted a tasteful touch of luxury. Everything was in varied shades of blue and gray, with silver and ivory worked through. Furniture constructed of pale wood, accented with silver inlay, and windows of flawless ascard-created glass brought the palace to mind. The bed stood on a raised dais with a chaise lounge at the foot. It all reeked of the prince's annoying refinement.

Myac strode to the bed and lifted the dripping blade over the pillow where he imagined Yiloch laid his head to sleep. With an extra push of ascard, he shoved the blade down through the pillow and deep into the mattress. Smeared blood stood out brightly against the fine fabric. From a pocket in his cloak, he drew a blue stone pendant engraved with the imperial family crest and hung it on the crossguard. He had taken it from Prince Delsan before his death, hoping to taunt Yiloch with it someday. If Yiloch returned to the stronghold, it would serve its purpose.

A trap worked into the display would be too obvious, and he needed to save energy for his other plans, so he swept from the room, slamming the door behind him. On his way out, he caught up with the men moving the bodies.

"Drop them here. I need only the heads."

The soldiers dropped the bodies and prepared to do his bidding. Leryc vanished into a neighboring room. He didn't stop the youth. As much as he might enjoy making Leryc suffer, he wasn't enthusiastic about him vomiting again.

It took two strikes to remove the head of the unfamiliar man. For Dalce, it took four. He might have helped with ascard, but he enjoyed seeing Yiloch's men mutilated. The soldiers followed him out with their grisly trophies. In the courtyard, Myac used ascard to reform splinters of iron and wood from the gate into two small cages. On his orders, the soldiers placed the heads in them and hung them on either side of the courtyard entrance.

The many ascard exertions were sapping his strength, but Myac took time to work a trap into each cage so they would explode in a violent spray if anyone tried to open them.

Weary, he settled on the stairs leading into the stronghold, content to rest while his soldiers searched for supplies and information.

CHAPTER NINETEEN

Several days ground by. The High Council spent mornings in laborious discussion with Prince Yiloch. Each afternoon, the king and High Council reconvened for private discussion. Today was different. They called Yiloch and Adran back after only an hour in their private session. The time for open debate was ending. King Jerrin was nearing his decision.

The majority, including Caplin and his father, supported the alliance and were open to providing healers with explicit stipulations. Unless Caplin misread him, the king leaned in that direction as well. Lord Serivar, acting predominately as headmaster of the Healer's Academy, was a staunch opponent, especially to the request for healers. Arguably, he was the most qualified to advise on that subject, but the final decision was King Jerrin's to make. Despite the headmaster's outward calm, Caplin sat close enough to see the way he wrung his hands under the table every time he spoke against the idea and the prince's icy gaze settled on him.

Caplin watched the prince. A certain calculated coldness beneath that perfect exterior made it easier to believe him capable of the cruel acts that earned him his reputation as the Blood Prince. Yiloch managed that aspect of himself well, though. As the prince's appointed escort, Caplin spent more time around him than most and was growing to like him despite what secrets might lurk beneath the surface. He yearned to ask about the massacre, to learn the truth behind it, but he got the feeling that subject was one the prince preferred to avoid.

Adran appeared to hold a special place in Yiloch's regard. If he could catch the captain alone, he might learn something from him, but the man was rarely away from his prince's side long enough for Caplin to get beyond exchanging formal pleasantries.

When he first met Yiloch, his hackles had gone up, but he recognized the reaction for what it was. The man was remarkable—extraordinary in appearance and powerful in presence. Could any man help the instinctive territorial defensiveness that came with feeling so outclassed? The Divine help them all when the prince got his chance to charm noble women at the feast. Caplin hoped that visceral reaction wouldn't lead to trouble. Maybe they could talk the prince into dressing down for the occasion.

Not likely. Caplin held back a grin. *Might as well ask a falcon to clip its own wings.*

Yiloch glanced at him, and a flicker of amusement lit those icy blue eyes as if he were privy to Caplin's thoughts. Then his gaze returned to Lord Cardess who was making a statement supporting the alliance.

Another fresh convert to the prince's cause.

From the start, Yiloch set out his plans and expectations in precise detail and with confidence that bordered on arrogance. He made it clear what he wanted and what he offered in return. The council faltered before his straightforward approach, as if they had expected deception. Whatever they anticipated based on his reputation was not what they got, and it left them scrambling. Yiloch forged ahead without hesitation from the start while they raced to catch up.

"And the slave trade?" Lord Davrick asked in a moment of silence.

"We have agreed that the slave trade will continue, Lord

Davrick." A hint of a growl came through in the king's deep voice.

"I would like to hear the prince say it," Davrick pressed.

Caplin watched for a crack in Yiloch's impeccable emotional armor as his pale eyes locked on the older lord. His expression remained calm, but a chill spread through the room like a wave of cold water. King Jerrin opened his mouth to speak but fell silent when the prince lifted a hand. The reaction was so automatic, Caplin wondered if the king even realized he had done it. Yiloch gave the small show of deference no notice either. Perhaps he was so accustomed to obedience that the possibility of a different reaction never occurred to him.

Yiloch held Davrick captive with his eyes. "The slave trade serves a purpose and, as I have stated here more than once, is not part of these negotiations."

Beside the prince, Adran's eyes narrowed, his jaw tightening the way it always did when the subject of the slave trade came up. That they disagreed on the subject was evident, but he wouldn't speak up against Yiloch, at least not openly. What happened behind closed doors remained a well-kept secret, but in public, his deference was absolute.

Lord Davrick gave a nod and broke away from Yiloch's intense gaze.

"Good," King Jerrin rumbled. "If you are through being rude to our guest…" Lord Davrick shifted in his chair, then he nodded again in the weighty silence that followed. The king's dark eyes swept the table. "Based on our discussions, I have decided that we will offer an alliance to Prince Yiloch. Tomorrow is the Wakening Festival. The day after, we shall reconvene and sort out the details of that alliance. If we are all in accord…"

Another heavy silence. The words implied an opening for further discussion, but the king's tone warned that it had best be the most compelling of arguments. No one spoke, and the whisper of a smile curved Yiloch's lips.

"Very well. I am adjourning this session. Lord Caplin, if you would be so kind as to see to Prince Yiloch and his companions."

Caplin stood and bowed. "Yes, Your Majesty."

"Lord Serivar. Lord Gavin. I would like you to remain."

Caplin rose, and the rest of the table, except for the king and the two men he had singled out, rose with him. Though not everyone appeared pleased with the decision, they were content to adjourn early. After a few appropriate parting words, Caplin led his charges from the room. When they were clear of other council members, he stopped and regarded Yiloch.

"My lord, on your first day here you expressed an interest in sparring. I wondered if..." He trailed off. Yiloch's eager grin was all the answer he needed.

"Nothing like politics to awaken those aggressive urges," Yiloch commented, a faint predatory gleam in his eyes.

"Do you mind if I retire to my room, my lord?" Adran asked.

Yiloch turned to his captain, a flicker of comforting concern warming his cold eyes, the first solid evidence that the two men were closer than their official relationship required. "Are you well?"

Adran nodded, his lips curving in a tired smile. "Yes, my lord. Merely weary of debate. I choose to unwind in other ways."

The momentary tightness in Yiloch's shoulders eased. "Go then." His gentle tone also hinted at a softer side.

Oh, to be privy to their private conversations.

Adran started walking away, then he paused, glancing back at them. "Promise not to damage one another while I'm gone."

Caplin met Yiloch's eyes. They both grinned.

Adran shook his head and walked away.

"This way." Caplin led the way to a practice ring around behind the palace, his nerves dancing with anticipation and a touch of dread. Gossip painted the prince as an exceptional swordsman. He might be sorely outmatched. "We are less likely to draw attention back here. I don't want to be accused of encouraging competition between Lyran and Caithin soldiers."

Yiloch nodded in agreement.

"You and Captain Adran seem rather close," Caplin commented, keeping his tone casual.

Yiloch glanced sideways at him, a thin veil of frost rising between them for an instant. The question was born of honest curiosity, and while it might be strategically beneficial to understand their relationship, there wasn't any malicious intent behind it. Caplin kept his expression open and friendly before that wary regard and, after a few seconds, the cold faded.

"Adran has always been with me. His father was a favored captain of the guard and a good friend to my father when we were children. He and his sister often stayed in the palace and attended lessons with my brother and me. Adran is perhaps a little sensitive for politics, but he is a good fighter and one of very few people I would trust with my life."

"A rare thing indeed. Your father doesn't sound like he was always so bad," Caplin prompted.

Tension rippled through the prince. When he spoke, there was loathing in his voice. "My father is no longer that man."

"Yes. It would seem not. We received news not long ago that he had your brother put to death. You have my condolences for that loss."

Yiloch shrugged. "We were never close."

The dismissive tone chilled Caplin. "There was also a

rumor that you were dead for a time, but that would appear erroneous given current evidence to the contrary."

They reached the practice ring, a sandy circle devoted to combat tucked away in a vibrant garden of bright, sweet-smelling flowers and decorative trees that evoked thoughts of lazing in the shade on such a warm day.

Yiloch smirked at the setting as he walked to the rack by the palace wall where a selection of practice swords waited. He tried several swords, his swings easy and confident, before selecting one and walking into the ring. Caplin took his preferred weapon, a sword he had marked with a red X on the pommel, so he didn't have to test them all each time, and moved out to face the prince. Apprehension rose, sparking in his nerves and bringing a faint metallic taste to his tongue.

"If those rumors are true, I think you will find me a rather lively opponent for a dead man." Yiloch smiled slyly.

Caplin grinned, though the expression didn't come quite as easily this time.

Setting aside other thoughts, he took measure of the man facing him. Yiloch was taller, which meant he had greater reach, but not enough to make a difference if their skills were comparable. Still, Caplin had a feeling he was outclassed in this case, a feeling strengthened by the catlike grace with which the prince moved and the easy way he held the unfamiliar double-edged blade, a weapon much different from the curved single-edged weapons his people favored.

Yiloch spun the sword in his grip, then shifted into an aggressive stance, every motion fluid as flowing water. Caplin adjusted his position as well, noting differences in their postures and the way they held their weapons. Yiloch advanced, and they exchanged a few testing strikes, parrying one another effortlessly.

The first several engagements were straightforward, almost polite. Then they became more aggressive. Soon practice swords were clashing with jarring force, and Yiloch began exploiting flaws in Caplin's techniques. He pressed in hard with swift and varied attacks, not giving Caplin time to look for openings. Then he caught Caplin's blade with his own and twisted it neatly from his grasp.

Caplin's muscles trembled. He was almost relieved to surrender and have a moment to rest.

"You are quite capable," Yiloch commented.

Caplin took a few seconds to catch his breath, pleased that the prince sounded a little winded. "That must be why I couldn't get an attack in."

"It would have surprised me if you had."

Something in his tone gave Caplin pause, and he gave Yiloch a shrewd look. "You're not an adept, are you?"

Yiloch gave him a long, calculating look, then picked up Caplin's practice sword and handed it back to him hilt first. "I am, but I wasn't using ascard."

That answer didn't comfort. "We were told there might be a creator in your group. It's not you, is it?"

"I am no creator," the prince answered, neither confirming nor denying the creator's presence in his retinue, which was confirmation enough.

"Then who?" Caplin asked, though he knew better than to expect a straight answer.

"I would prefer not to single out any of my men for special attention. Having a creator along makes it easier to travel undetected, something that was rather necessary given the circumstances."

Knowing the Lyran retinue had a creator and at least one adept among them made Caplin nervous, but it was something the prince would give little thought to. For him, it was normal to always have that unrestricted power around.

He forced himself to relax. "Will you at least tell me what kind of adept you are?"

Yiloch responded with an enigmatic smile and moved

into a fighting stance. Recognizing that for the refusal it was, Caplin altered his own position, adjusting for the style of combat he now expected. When they clashed this time, he got in some attacks, gaining ground if only for a few strikes. Then Yiloch changed his approach, going from a fast, aggressive style to an even swifter, more evasive technique that was dancelike in its fluidity. Without warning, he dipped down and swept Caplin's legs out from under him. Caplin hit the ground hard, clinging to his sword as breath burst from him on impact, leaving him dazed.

Yiloch stepped back, giving him room to recover.

Caplin sat and squinted at the prince, who stood haloed by the light of the sinking sun, his silver hair glowing in brilliant light. "You aren't much good for my ego."

Yiloch laughed and offered him a hand up, which Caplin accepted, letting the prince do most of the work to get a feel for the considerable strength in the Lyran's lean frame.

"I learned to wield a sword almost before I could walk," Yiloch offered in consolation. "I have training in six Lyran styles and three Kudaness ones, along with less formal experience in several others. The sword is my weapon of choice and my preferred pastime. You are one of the more challenging opponents I have had in a while outside of my top officers, so don't underrate yourself. You adapted well enough to the style I used in our first round that I found it prudent to change things up. That is admirable in itself."

Caplin searched his face and found nothing to suggest that he was anything less than sincere in his comments. He swallowed his pride. It wasn't as bitter as he would have expected. "I don't suppose you would teach me a few things?"

Yiloch grinned. "It would be my pleasure. Shall we?"

At his gesture, they moved to the center of the ring again, and Yiloch began working Caplin through moves in the most common Lyran style. The more they worked, the more Caplin realized that this man would be a very dangerous enemy indeed.

Were they fools to help him gain power?

Only time would tell, but odd as it was, the growing respect in the prince's eyes made him giddy with pride.

CHAPTER TWENTY

Indigo sagged into a chair in the headmaster's office. Long days of training and the effort of balancing lies with forced shows of affection to appease Jayce left her exhausted in every way.

In a few hours, the Wakening Festival feast at the palace would start. There was no mention of the visiting prince in the invitations, though rumors had leaked of a Lyran dignitary staying in the palace, spread, no doubt, by palace staff. Those with too much time on their hands spent long hours speculating over who it might be and why he was visiting. She knew who he was. Interestingly, that knowledge didn't come only from Caplin. Serivar divulged the prince's presence to her earlier in the week for reasons yet to be revealed.

This morning, he sent a messenger requesting her presence in his office. She sat across from him now, trying not to let irritation at her interrupted day dictate her behavior. That he had yet to look up from the document he was reading to acknowledge her didn't help her mood.

She coughed lightly. "Serivar."

He glanced up.

"You wished to see me?"

"When did I give you permission to address me informally?"

"When did you ever address me formally?"

"Valid point, but I am the instructor, am I not?"

She said nothing.

He adjusted some items on his desk. His hands were slender, almost feminine, his nails neatly trimmed. In the beginning, his rank had intimidated her enough that she hadn't noticed such details. The knowledge that her ascard connection was stronger than his reduced the sense of awe and increased her concern. Was he even capable of teaching her to control her ability?

"Perhaps I have been working you too hard." He gave her a scrutinizing look, which she responded to with a bitter smirk. Unruffled, he continued. "You are attending the feast this evening, I presume?"

"Yes."

"I have a test for you then. The Watchmen believe Prince Yiloch has a creator with him." She shivered at the thought, but the reaction went unnoticed or ignored. "The best adept I have for assessing the inner aspect of others is out of the city on assignment, and my skill in that area is lacking. We have worked on your sensitivity to others a great deal, and you are quite capable with your masking. I want you to investigate the prince's men at the feast."

"Why can't a Watchman handle it?"

He gave her an indulgent look. "You know Watchmen only sense ascard manipulation. Determining the strength and trained purpose of someone's inner aspect is a separate skill. I need your ability, Indigo."

"When I finally have a chance to enjoy myself, you're putting me to work?"

"I am sorry." His biting tone and stern look negated the apology. "You are in our service now. It should not take long for you to investigate the prince's group. We know it's not one of his soldiers in the barracks. That narrows it down to four possibilities: his captain, his Kudaness guard, his young attendant, or the prince himself. Supper would be an ideal time to investigate them discreetly."

She rubbed her temples, fighting a threatening headache. "You're right. I agreed to this."

"You might take a nap before the feast. You seem tired."

"Surprising. Perhaps I'm not getting much rest lately," she snapped. He met her eyes, and she lowered her gaze to her hands. "I'll try to do that. Is that all?"

"It is. I will see you this evening, Indigo."

She nodded and left.

At least Jayce was out, which meant she could take the nap Serivar suggested and perhaps even visit the residence bathhouse before dressing for the feast. A lady's maid, compliments of Caplin's mother, was going to help Andrea prepare for the evening, and she had offered the woman's services to Indigo as well. That would take the stress out of the process.

* * *

Andrea wore a green gown with a pale skirt and a dark green velvet bodice. It had a square neckline and fitted waist, trimmed in dark green with gold accents. The maid had wrapped her red hair into an elaborate bun, held in place by gold pins tipped with jeweled butterflies. A gold necklace with a large emerald pendant completed the ensemble.

"You look stunning," Indigo commented as Andrea did a slow spin to show the finished product.

Andrea blushed, beaming. "Your turn!"

The maid helped Indigo into a gown with a deep V-waist. It had a deep blue overskirt wrapped around the back and sides, split in front to reveal a pale gold underskirt. The bodice, also deep blue, had a low neckline mirroring the V of the waist. Braided gold cord accented both the neckline and waist and crisscrossed down the sides of the snug bodice. Fitted sleeves started below the shoulder, leaving her upper back and shoulders exposed. More gold braiding banded tapered wrists. The maid pulled part of her hair up, adding sapphire-studded clips that matched her necklace to hold it in place, leaving the back loose to fall over her shoulders in thick waves.

Indigo smiled at her transformed reflection. Then the smile faded. She had only Jayce to look this good for.

"You look spectacular." Andrea's face appeared over her shoulder in the mirror. "We're going to stun the entire place silent."

Her delighted laugh was contagious, and Indigo smiled again. "We will, won't we?"

"Absolutely!"

Andrea embraced her, and she savored the sense of normalcy the occasion allowed. The simple process of preparing for a royal feast required no lies or deception.

Jayce arrived in a fine black suit with elaborate gold embroidery. Clean-shaven and trimmed, he stopped inside the doorway and stared at her with wide eyes. A slow smile curved his lips. She walked over and gave him a quick kiss.

"You look incredible. I'm not sure I want anyone to see you like this."

"Thank you." Let him think her blush was embarrassment rather than distress over his possessive comment.

He looked past her. "You look fantastic, Andrea."

"Thank you, Jayce. You look splendid yourself."

"Caplin sent his carriage, but he couldn't join us. Apparently, he's acting as escort to some Lyran dignitary. From the message, it sounds like he's enjoying himself."

Indigo frowned. "I wouldn't have expected Caplin to appreciate such a man."

Jayce gave her a puzzled look. "And I wouldn't have expected you to judge someone for their race."

She gave herself a mental kick. They didn't know who the Lyran dignitary was. The most widespread gossip suggested he was an ambassador from Emperor Rylan, sent to renegotiate the trade agreement.

"You're right. I shouldn't judge."

He shrugged it off and offered her his arm.

* * *

A gentleman usher announced them when they entered the palace ballroom. Guests milled about like frolicking butter-flies in their formal attire. Myriad draperies and streamers in rich red and gold could have been flower petals in a giant garden. Massive crystal and gold chandeliers added a warm glow to the fading daylight streaming in through many arched windows along the outside wall of the ballroom. Rich aromas wafted from the kitchens beyond the feast hall, making her mouth water.

"Lady Indigo."

She turned. Serivar and his wife had entered behind them.

"Headmaster Serivar," she greeted with a formal curtsy. "This must be your lovely wife, Lady Vera?"

Vera, a strong-featured woman with steely eyes and a cutting smile, looked Indigo over as though appraising a cut of meat at market. "You're the girl who has my husband staying late so many nights. I see what must keep him."

Serivar's eyes popped wide. He took Vera by the shoul-ders, whispering in her ear while he steered her away. Indigo stared after them, aware that her mouth hung open in shock. She turned back to the solace of her companions only to have her world flipped on its head again.

Caplin was there now, introducing Andrea and Jayce to two men, one of whom haunted her sweetest dreams. A man she wasn't supposed to see ever again. The third man with them had dusty blond hair and pale eyes, a trace of stubble betraying mixed blood. Lyran royalty was always of pure descent, which meant that her Lord Eldrian *was* the Blood Prince. His regal bearing and the way his companion always stayed a half-step behind him left little room for doubt.

How exquisite he looked in black pants and high boots. His black fitted jacket had tails that hung to mid-thigh in the back over a pearlescent white vest with elegant embroidery in gold and deep blue. Under the vest was a decorative white shirt worked through with threads of pearlescent white. His jacket also had stylish accents of gold and blue thread on the lapels. His long, silver hair added a touch of over-the-top magnificence to the overall image.

Rage burned through her, along with dizzying elation. Her heart had barely started beating again when Caplin turned to her.

"And this is Lord Jayce's fiancée, Lady Indigo. My lady, may I introduce Lord Eldrian and Lord Kasyn."

Lord Eldrian? He must be using a false name to avoid unwanted attention and drama. Allowing the nobility to go on assuming he was merely a dignitary. But did he have to use that name?

A well of composure deep within came to her rescue, and she executed a graceful curtsy, offering her hand to the prince.

"My lord."

When he took her hand and kissed it, her pulse quickened, and she consciously slowed her breathing to hide the thrill that coursed through her. As she rose from the curtsy, she caught the infuriating shine of amusement in his pale eyes. If only she dared to slap him. It would almost be worth the ensuing chaos to see the humor struck from his handsome face.

She forced a tight smile.

"Truly a pleasure," he murmured.

He eased his hold on her hand, letting her slide it free, and Jayce moved closer. Yiloch stepped to one side, watching her while the man introduced as Lord Kasyn came forward. She curtsied to him as well. When she met his eyes, she saw curious interest there. Had the prince told him about her? Warmth blossomed in her chest at the thought.

"It is a pleasure to meet you, my lord."

"Likewise, Lady Indigo."

When he moved away, Caplin stepped around beside her and rested a hand on her shoulder in an absentminded familiarity, drawing dark looks from Jayce and Andrea. He didn't appear to notice the effect the action had. He was looking at the prince. She longed to flee like a mouse that had walked unsuspectingly into a room full of cats, but pulling away would draw more attention. She waited the moment out, doing her best to act as if nothing at all were amiss.

"Make yourselves comfortable. Supper will be served soon. I must introduce our guests to a few more people." Caplin was already scanning the room for those people.

Yiloch gave Indigo a small, clandestine smile before moving on. A tall young man followed them, staring intently at Lord Kasyn's back—the attendant Serivar had mentioned—and an imposing dark-skinned Kudaness warrior flanked the group.

Indigo stared after them, struggling for inner balance.

Jayce grabbed her arm, his fingers pinching skin. "Be careful of that Lord Eldrian. He seemed much too interested in you."

"Did he? I didn't notice." She twisted free and trotted after Andrea, who was stalking away. "Andrea."

The other woman stopped and whipped around, scowling past her to where Caplin had vanished into the crowd.

"When did you and Caplin get so friendly?"

"Andrea, we've been friends for years." Indigo kept her

tone light, suppressing a burst of irritation. "He's distracted right now. I could have been a table for all the notice he gave me."

Andrea maintained her stubborn scowl for a second or two more, then relented. "You're right. I'm being sensitive." She smiled and leaned close, abandoning anger with dizzying speed. "I never thought I would say this about a Lyran, but that Lord Eldrian is something to behold. He even made my heart skip a beat. I guess breeding does make a difference."

A wave of nausea swept through Indigo as she recalled the lies he had fed her. *I was so willing to believe.* "He *is* something else."

Jayce's hand slipped under her hair and tightened on the back of her neck, letting her know her evasion hadn't pleased him. "It isn't polite to gossip, ladies."

The call to supper rescued her. Andrea hurried toward the head of the table to sit with Caplin. Attendants guided Indigo and Jayce to places further down one side. She avoided staring at Yiloch, though many people were less considerate, gawking at the Lyran prince with unabashed curiosity.

When the courses came, dish after dish—succulent, savory, and sweet offerings for the refined palate—she barely tasted the extraordinary selection. The wine, however, helped soothe her nerves, and she took advantage of the generous servers.

She needed to ignore the prince. Jayce was already upset. Her heart, however, wouldn't let it go. Despite being enraged by his lies and saddened by the truth, seeing him again thrilled her. How long could she sit still and pretend to be content?

A light touch on her arm made her turn, but neither Jayce nor the man on her other side was paying any attention to her. She spotted Serivar at the opposite table. He lifted his cup and smiled, a reminder of her duty. She gave a small nod, happy now to have a task to distract her.

With a quick glance around the room, she located Yiloch's three companions. Even with careful masking and Serivar's assurance of immunity, connecting to her inner aspect with Watchmen in the room required an act of extreme will. She needed to face that fear.

Taking a swallow of wine, she steeled herself and reached out to the Kudaness man first. He was the least likely to be a creator, considering Kudaness beliefs regarding ascard use. As expected, she found nothing out of the ordinary about him, aside from his menacing appearance.

Satisfied, she sought out the young attendant sitting at the lowest table. When she touched him with her ability, his head snapped up. He looked around the room. His inner aspect was powerful, and ascard around him fluxed, bending to his will the instant he connected to it. She drew back, taking a sip of wine to hide her alarm. Clever of the prince to let his creator appear to be the lowest of his men.

For curiosity's sake, she inspected the captain, but he had no notable connection. She reached out to Yiloch then, and the ascard around him changed, forming a barrier that deflected her inquest.

Was that his doing or his creator's?

She drew back into herself.

The prince continued talking with the king's brother, Gavin, giving no outward indication that he had noticed her activities. When Gavin turned to say something to Caplin, however, Yiloch looked at her and smiled. She averted her gaze.

Had he felt her touch after all? If so, how had he known it was her? Or had he looked her way for another reason?

She took a long drink of her wine to quell the fluttering in her stomach.

I must learn to mask my ability better.

An ascard sweep of the room picked out many Watchmen among the guards and a few other notable connections, including Serivar. The rest were undoubtedly healers, though some might also be members of the King's Order. A visual sweep brought her attention to the lack of Lyran slaves among the servers and attendants. Polite of the king to make such an effort, though she suspected it also avoided the risk of one of them recognizing and calling out the prince for who he truly was.

She sipped more wine and nibbled at her meal until people began wandering out to the ballroom, lured by the king's musicians. Hoping to avoid angering Jayce more, she asked him to dance.

He smiled, his cheeks flushed with wine. "Certainly."

Taking her arm, he escorted her onto the floor. He was a decent dancer, but he didn't have the patience to keep it up for long. After two songs, she found herself shadowing him around the room so he could chat with his archery companions until she excused herself to search for Andrea, who might have something more interesting to discuss than the aerodynamic benefits of different fletching materials.

Yiloch had taken to the floor several times with various simpering ladies, executing Caithin dances as if he had grown up with them. The sting of jealousy refreshed her frustration, and she abandoned her quest for Andrea to secure another glass of the Lyran wine set out on a long table in the dining hall. With her back to the scene in the ballroom, she choked down one large swallow for the butterflies in her stomach and another for the tremble in her hands.

In the brief pause between two songs, someone spoke behind her.

"Might I have this dance?"

When she spun around, Prince Yiloch offered her his arm.

CHAPTER TWENTY-ONE

Indigo couldn't find her voice.

Yiloch plucked the glass from her hand and set it on the table half-empty, then offered his arm again. Lacking any practical escape, she placed her hand on his arm and let him lead her onto the dance floor through a sea of extravagantly dressed aristocracy. He swept her around to face him, his right hand sliding into place over her shoulder blade. Explicit memories of their time in the prison further warmed the wine flush in her cheeks.

Keeping her voice low as he led her into the dance, she said, "You lied to me, Prince Yiloch."

He matched her volume. "I wasn't sure you would help me if I told you the truth."

Would she have? Even with her attraction to him, knowing who he was might have been enough to drive her from the prison. He had made the right choice for his situation. That didn't mean she had to like it. Although she did like it. Not the lies, but feeling his touch again. Even this restricted contact revitalized her.

While she gathered her thoughts, he led her through the dance so perfectly that she need not have known the steps at all. Was there anything he did poorly?

"You looked into Caithin's ascard use."

She stiffened, throwing them both off. He recovered within a beat, drawing her back into step with him.

"What do you mean?"

"At supper, you were investigating my men with ascard. What are they teaching you?"

"I'm not telling you anything."

His chuckle infuriated her. "But you already have. Now I know they are teaching more than healing, and whatever they're teaching, they don't want people knowing about it."

She grasped for something to divert him. "I almost died after you left me. One of those hounds followed us."

His hands tightened, the humor in his eyes flickering out. Perhaps there had been more to his affection than convenience.

"I am sorry. I didn't want you hurt."

"But it was a risk you were willing to take." She bit her lip. She needed to keep her voice down.

"Indigo…"

The gentle way he spoke her name brought delicious longing to the fore. She scowled, resisting. "Do not address me so informally, Lord Eldrian."

The song ended.

"Another dance," he pressed.

Before she could answer, his companion, the man introduced as Lord Kasyn, walked up to them.

"Lady Indigo, this is Lord Captain Adran," Yiloch said in a hushed voice.

Adran nodded in distracted greeting, his gaze sweeping for anyone within earshot. "My lady, I believe your fiancé is displeased."

She spotted Jayce watching them from the entrance to the dining hall, his face a reddening cloud of anger. "Do you think so?" She became aware of Yiloch's hand still holding hers and jerked away.

Rather than taking offense at her flippancy, Adran's eyes lit with amusement. He grinned.

Yiloch glanced at Jayce. "Adran, perhaps you could inform Lord Jayce that I am merely dancing with her. I'm not looking to get engaged."

"I could take her place." Adran gave him a suggestive wink.

Indigo choked back a startled laugh. "You seem a decent man, my lord. Be wary of associating with Lord Eldrian overmuch, lest he sully your name irreparably."

Adran chuckled. "I like her, my lord. Perhaps we should take her home with us."

Yiloch frowned at him. "Lord Jayce."

"Yes." Adran smiled with the patience of an old friend. "Perhaps he would appreciate more wine."

"I am certain he would," Yiloch replied.

As Adran walked away, Yiloch looked down at her with his arresting silver-blue eyes. "About that second dance?"

She almost turned away, but to touch him again, even for a few moments...

She nodded, trying to ignore the vague sense of doom that accompanied the gesture. This time they simply danced and neither spoke. The urge to run her fingers through his hair, to step close and savor his warmth, plagued her. His eyes reflected her longing, and it comforted her to know she didn't face that torment alone. He squeezed her hand, his other one warm against her shoulder blade, and she closed her eyes, following his lead while recalling the first time she had seen him. When she opened her eyes, his smile made her pulse quicken. The dance was sweet suffering. It lasted too long and ended too soon.

When they stopped, he leaned close. "You look magnificent."

She made herself step away. "You should find someone else to dance with."

"Yes."

Every fiber of her being objected when she walked away.

Once clear of the dance floor, she stopped and scanned for Jayce. No good could come of giving him time to get more upset.

Someone held a glass of wine up beside her in offering. Turning, she met Lord Adran's eyes and accepted it with a grateful smile.

"Thank you, my lord. What have you done with my fiancé?"

He gazed out at the dance floor, brows pinching together. "I had Ian make a special drink for him. He'll sleep it off by morning."

Her stomach did a flip. "Ian? He's the creator?"

Adran stared at her. "Yilo…" He caught himself. "Lord Eldrian didn't tell me you could do more than heal," he whispered, confirming that Yiloch had spoken of her.

She bit the inside of her lip. She wasn't managing secrecy well. The evening had disrupted her composure, and all she could focus on was the heady sensation of knowing Yiloch had told someone about her. He hadn't left and forgotten her.

"Thank you for handling Jayce." Whatever they had done to him, she could only hope she wouldn't pay for it later.

Adran inclined his head. "You're welcome, my lady."

She sipped her wine and watched Yiloch lead another partner onto the floor. The woman blushed profusely, grinning like a fool. For all the prejudices they had against his people, the hypocritical vixens were happy to dance and flirt with a handsome Lyran nobleman.

"He does make a stir among the ladies," she commented, unable to hide her irritation.

"Predictably. His is the purest Lyran blood. He is far more beautiful than any Caithin man could ever hope to be."

"Oh?" She arched an eyebrow.

"Come view the wildlife with me." He offered her his arm.

With a giggle at his choice of words, she accepted, letting

him lead her around the perimeter of the room. She enjoyed his manner, and the way he started to use the prince's name so casually hinted at a close relationship, which intrigued her. They went to a half circle of plush chairs in one corner of the ballroom and sat so they had a clear view of the dancers, especially Yiloch and the woman he swirled about with almost unnatural grace.

"Look at the other men here." Adran leaned close and gestured to the dancers with a finger. "Do any of them come close to him in elegance? In presence?"

Obliging him, she scanned the room. Caplin, one of the more handsome men there, had a captivating presence, but the prince even overshadowed him. She shook her head.

"A pure-blooded Lyran man, especially of royal lineage, is like a peacock; beautiful, bold, and in this setting, exotic as well. No other man stands a chance."

She watched Yiloch. Beautiful without question, but masculine power and self-assurance made it acceptable for him to be beautiful. The prince, truly a peacock among jays, appeared entirely at ease with the contrast. Perhaps he even thrived on such disparity, considering the Kudaness guard with whom he traveled.

She realized a fond smile had stolen across her lips and glanced at Adran to see if he noticed. He was watching her with an unreadable expression. She stared into her wine, mortified by her lack of self-control.

Attempting to shrug off the candid moment, she asked, "How do you put up with him?"

Adran shrugged and leaned back in the chair. "Me? I have been hopelessly in love with him for most of my life."

Adoration weighted his words. Did he mean brotherly love? She would stick to that assumption. "What about the things he's done?"

"You are referring to his nickname, the Blood Prince?"

She nodded.

Sorrow filled his eyes. "He didn't do those things alone."

She turned away. No, the prince hadn't done them alone. A full force of soldiers and adepts followed him, one of whom sat with her now. Adran's eyes said he shared the guilt of those atrocities and suffered for it. He didn't seem like a monster.

He leaned closer again, lowering his voice. "His mother was everything to him. When she was murdered, he became irrational for a while. He would stop at nothing to avenge her death, and those of us who followed him would do anything to ease his pain. The emperor took advantage of that, using it to serve his own ends until Yiloch came to his senses and turned against him."

Caplin approached them, saving her from responding. He gestured to a seat. "May I?"

"Please," they answered in unison.

Caplin sank into the chair. He looked tired but satisfied.

"Where's Andrea?" Indigo asked.

He shrugged. "I am not sure. She's at my side one moment and the next she is off gossiping with someone's wife. I can't keep track. Where's Jayce?"

She shrugged in turn. She didn't know where Adran and the creator had left her fiancé. "He seems to have vanished."

Caplin considered Adran. "Are you enjoying yourself, Lord Kasyn?"

"Yes, though perhaps not as much as he is." Adran nodded toward the dance floor.

Caplin glanced at Yiloch, who had charmed yet another woman onto the floor. "He has danced with every willing woman in the place, to the distress of many husbands and fathers, I think. Yet you have attracted the most enchanting one."

"A highly inappropriate comment, Lord Caplin," she

admonished.

"But not untrue," Adran argued.

Her cheeks burned. "You are not helping."

They chuckled at her embarrassment, and she averted her gaze, relieved to spot Andrea walking toward them. "Finally, another woman to talk to."

Andrea settled next to Caplin. "What are we all chatting about?"

He took her hand. "I was wondering where I had lost you."

Yiloch also joined them then, gesturing to a chair beside Indigo. "May I?"

"Certainly, my lord." His presence lit her nerves on fire, but what else could she say?

Caplin turned to him. "Lord Eldrian, did you run out of women to seduce already?"

The familiar bantering tone he took with the prince surprised her. Apparently, Yiloch's charms worked for more than enthralling unsuspecting women.

Yiloch's smile was friendly. "There are more, but the best ones were over here."

Caplin grinned at Indigo, and she caught herself before sticking her tongue out at him, as she would have when they were younger.

"You *are* charming." Andrea batted her lashes at Yiloch, her default response to flattery. "How long will you be here for?"

"Only a few more days." Yiloch met Caplin's eyes.

Caplin nodded. "You should come watch Lord Eldrian vanquish me in the practice ring."

The prince gave a self-effacing smile, an expression that somehow made him even more captivating. "He is exaggerating."

Caplin negated the comment with a quick shake of his

head. "I thought myself a skilled swordsman. This man has taught me humility."

"I doubt that," Andrea teased.

A small laugh escaped Indigo, drawing Andrea's attention. Her expression turned thoughtful, her eyes jumping from Indigo to Yiloch and back. "The embroidery on Lord Eldrian's jacket and vest matches your gown almost perfectly?" She gave an approving nod to him for his stylish selection.

All eyes considered them, and Indigo yearned to melt into the chair.

"You two do almost look like you dressed to match," Caplin observed.

"Isn't that odd?" Something in Yiloch's tone made her wonder how odd it really was. He might have guessed she would choose a blue to complement her eyes, and Caithin nobility favored gold accents in formal attire. "Perhaps, since we are so well matched, we should share another dance. My lady?" He stood and offered her his hand.

The sweet, sultry string notes of a popular romantic ballad rose into the air, and her stomach knotted.

"It is getting late, my lord, you must be weary of dancing."

"Never." His eyes sparkled with delight. He knew, at least in part, how much his presence tormented her.

"Yes, let's dance." Andrea got up, drawing Caplin with her.

Indigo glanced at Adran, who smirked unhelpfully. Resigned, she let Yiloch lead her onto the floor. He drew her out to the center and turned her to face him, his hand sliding back into place comfortably on her shoulder blade.

"You truly are the most remarkable woman in the room."

"I guess we are the perfect pair then," she replied.

He smiled. "Thank you."

Her cheeks burned with the unintended compliment, not that it was untrue. She let him sweep her about, her heart catching flight whenever she met his eyes. The torture of being so close when she knew it would end soon made each moment almost as bitter as it was sweet.

Let it never end.

When the music changed, they returned to the chairs, but rather than sit, she turned to Adran, seeking escape from the merciless fire Yiloch set within her. "You said you saw Lord Jayce earlier?"

"He retired to a room in the east wing. Third door down on the left, if I recall. He said he wasn't feeling well."

Liar. "I had best go check on him."

Caplin stood.

"I don't need an escort, my lord."

"I would hate for you to get lost in the palace," he said, but the concern in his eyes belied the words. He worried because he knew she and Jayce were having difficulties. The gesture was sweet, but she had a feeling Jayce would still be unconscious.

"I will be fine."

Caplin sank back down. "You are welcome to keep the room for the night."

"Thank you. Good evening." She excused herself politely, avoiding Yiloch's gaze, and hurried away.

Jayce lay stretched across the bed in the room Adran had indicated. He didn't stir when she shook his shoulder. His breathing was slow and steady, so she sank into a chair and watched him sleep, feeling nothing for him, aside from a vague sense of regret.

When the palace grew quiet, she crept from the room, leaving her shoes behind so her footsteps wouldn't disturb anyone. She made her way around an inner garden courtyard, enjoying the brisk, refreshing evening air. Bright stars lured her up a set of stairs onto a veranda. She leaned on the railing, turning her face to the sky. The stars blinked at her, brilliant and unattainable. Lingering warmth from too much wine kept the night's chill at bay.

Footsteps approached. A light ascard touch identified Yiloch, sparking her nerves to life yet again. She waited, letting him come up behind her. His fingertips touched the rose tattoo on her back, and she shivered. Then he stepped close, sliding his hands down her arms and wrapping his arms around her. She leaned into the embrace.

If this was so wrong, why did it feel right?

He kissed her neck, then turned her and kissed her lips. She closed her eyes, returning the kiss while he caressed her neck with light fingers, sending delicious shivers coursing through her.

"Come with me," he murmured.

She tried to shake off the fog of wine and the heat of desire. "I'm engaged."

"But you are not in love."

Such arrogance! She drew back. "Am I not?"

He smiled, leaning close enough that their lips almost touched. "Not with him."

In the unreal environment of the prison, it felt like cheating on Jayce in a dream. This was different. She met his eyes, remembering the first time she had sunk into those icy depths like a ship broken on the rocks. Perhaps she was broken.

She offered no argument when he took her hand and led her to a room with a private entrance to the veranda. He guided her to a canopied bed and began undressing her, kissing her skin as he exposed it. She unlaced his shirt, pushing away when she exposed the ring hanging on a chain around his neck.

Indignation warred with a surge of absurd pleasure

within her. "You thief. You stole my ring."

His fingers brushed her cheek, and she almost pulled away, but the sudden warmth and sorrow in his gaze ensnared her. "I would have stolen you instead, if I could have."

With his words, she was back in the prison, her head pressed to the stone pillar, wishing she could follow where he had gone. He had told Adran about her, and he wore her ring around his neck, having no way of knowing if he would see her here. He carried her with him as much as she had carried him over the many months since the prison.

All apprehension disappeared. She moved close and kissed him. Her fingers resumed undoing his shirt.

CHAPTER TWENTY-TWO

Cool predawn light trickled in the windows, a warning that sunrise threatened. It was reckless for Indigo to still be with him. Yet, though her presence could ruin everything, he had no desire to see her go.

Rising on one elbow, he gazed down at her.

She looked up with a drowsy smile and lifted the ring hanging around his neck, turning it so the light of the candles, burned down to almost nothing, reflected in the blue stone.

He reached up to unclasp the chain. "This belongs to you."

"No." She pressed the ring to his chest. "I like the idea of it touching your skin when I cannot."

He left the chain in place and took her hand, kissing delicate fingers. "Come with me."

She pulled away. "Don't. I cannot, I will not, and I don't need you making my life more difficult by placing ridiculous ideas in my head."

She was right, but... "Indigo."

"No." She rose from the bed. "I'm leaving."

He helped her into her gown, then turned her and kissed her. She pressed against him for a moment, giving rise to fresh desire before pulling away and giving him a stern look.

"I must get back before Jayce wakes. As it is, I'll be dodging servants all the way."

He gave a grudging nod. "I have never been this unhappy to see the sunrise."

She touched his face and kissed him again before slipping from the room without a backward glance.

He stared at the door for several minutes, lost in wonder at the yearning she evoked in him. No past lovers affected him the way she did, and seeing her again, touching her again, only made it worse. He exhaled. With a shake of his head, he climbed back into the bed, the smell of her enfolding him.

Sometime later, a knock on the door jerked him up from sleep. Clenching his teeth, he rolled over and put his back to the door. After a few more knocks, the door opened and shut. Only a few people would be that bold.

"Still sleeping?" Adran asked. He came around and sat on the edge of the bed.

A heavy silence fell while Yiloch drifted on the edge of sleep.

"You had company."

"Does it matter?" He didn't open his eyes.

"It was her, wasn't it? The distinctly promised Lady Indigo?"

Yiloch rolled over again, putting his back to Adran this time.

"I find it hard to believe you would risk this alliance for one night of sex with a woman you'll never see again."

Sometimes, if you ignored things, they would go away. This clearly wasn't one of those times. "I didn't think I would see her again after the last time," he muttered, wishing Adran would let him sleep. "You're jealous."

Adran was silent long enough that Yiloch almost fell asleep again. Then he said, "You're supposed to meet the High Council to finalize the details of the alliance today."

Rolling onto his back, Yiloch rubbed his eyes. Adran's jaw looked tight enough to crack teeth.

"When?"

"A little after noon."

He closed his eyes. "Wake me a little before noon, then."

The door slammed, and Yiloch winced with a sting of guilt. They had been friends practically since birth, but Adran's persistent jealousy irritated him, perhaps more than it should. It had been a foolish risk, taking a promised woman to his room while forming an alliance. When he saw her leaning on the veranda railing, no more able to sleep than he was, sense had ceased to play a part.

How could she be a liability? She completed him.

* * *

The nip of night air fled before the sun, and wispy clouds of morning burned away, promising a bright, warm day. The city streets the carriage traveled already bustled with the activity of everyday life. Nobles who had spent the night in luxurious palace accommodations made their way back to their own homes, while the less fortunate carried on with their arduous lives. Tradesmen prepared their shops to handle the day's business while slaves and servants went about their tasks, cleaning streets or completing errands for those they served.

These people make this city what it is.

A young woman cut off a Lyran slave carrying a sack, something heavy judging by the bulge in his muscles and the sweat on his brow. She offered no apology, nor even glanced his way as he struggled to manage his load without bumping into her. Myriad such disrespects occurred every day, and few took notice. It wasn't even that no one cared, though admittedly plenty didn't. Some more privileged citizens treated them well enough, though even she had to admit that having this as the standard most of her life made her less aware.

Was it her time with Yiloch that made her so cognizant of them now? Did the Lyran prince notice the slaves, or was he too enmeshed in his own goals to care? She had wanted to ask him, but when the opportunity arose, such things had been far from her mind.

Very far.

The heat of remembered passion warmed her as their coupling played back in her head until a groan next to her made her cringe. Whatever they gave Jayce, it had much the same effect as too much alcohol. She hoped he wouldn't get sick in the carriage.

Anxiety spread through her chest like a blossom of thorns as he recovered. His fierce pride wouldn't accept early retirement from the festivities easily, and he wasn't likely to accept blame for it either. She was the only other person around to lay blame on, and she dreaded that fight.

"I don't recall drinking this much." He moaned.

"The Lyran wine Lord Eldrian brought seemed stronger than usual." A desperate stretch that wasn't likely to appease.

Jayce placed a hand on his head and grimaced.

He deserves this suffering for ever striking me.

The attempted justification held no weight. Their relationship had become an empty thing, a lifeless parody of love. Was that entirely his fault, or was she partly responsible? With Yiloch fresh in her mind, guilt rushed in, twisting in her gut, but the relationship had begun crumbling long before she first saw the prince by the fountain.

Jayce stumbled upstairs at the residence, leaving her to dismiss the carriage driver. With an unshakable sense of walking to her ruin, she plodded upstairs after him.

The Divine willing, he would go to sleep it off.

The front door stood open—the hungry maw of a beast waiting to devour her. Easing it closed behind her, she crept inside. Jayce was in the bedroom gazing out the window, muscles in his neck and jaw tight bands of iron tension. Warned by his brooding look, she turned in the doorway, intending to leave him alone, but then he murmured something and she walked closer to hear him, every nerve firing in warning.

"What was that?"

"Did you enjoy the dance?"

The question sounded innocent, but his hostile tone made her heart race. "It was fine."

"And Lord Eldrian?" Jayce looked at her now, lips twisting in a bitter sneer. "Did you flirt with him after I was gone? He certainly seemed interested."

She ignored the bait. "There's no point in this, Jayce. We can talk about it when you're feeling better." She walked away, holding her breath. His footsteps followed, and she stopped in the doorway when he put a hand on her shoulder. Turning, she said, "I—"

His fist struck her jaw, sending her staggering back. A flash of white blasted across her vision. In panic, she opened herself fully to her inner aspect and reeled with the shock of so much power all at once. Jayce shoved her down. Her shoulder struck the corner of a small table. Skin tore against the edge, adding sharp pain to the rising chaos.

"How could you let me make"—he kicked her side—"such a fool"—another kick, harder this time—"of myself?"

He kicked her again, and the extraordinary pain of a rib cracking struck a brutal clarity in her. He wouldn't stop now that he had crossed the threshold into frenzied violence. The slave owner popped into her head, clutching the arm she had injured. She could do the same or worse to Jayce. It would be easy to hurt him. To take out her pain and anger on him. She could be just like him, only far more dangerous.

Struggling to focus beyond the pain, she reached into him with ascard and put him to sleep the way she would an unmanageable patient. He dropped like a rock, and she winced, hoping Andrea wasn't home downstairs to hear the thud.

Pain speared her side with every frantic gasp. She stayed

on the floor, focusing her ability to heal the cracked rib, some-how having the presence of mind to mask her working. Tears poured from her eyes, both from pain and from the after-effects of terror now that she had neutralized the threat.

She glared at Jayce, where he lay locked in forced slumber. He might have killed her if she hadn't had the means to stop him.

And I could have killed him.

She finished healing her ribs and rolled onto her hands and knees. When a wave of dizziness passed, she rose un-steadily to her feet. Pressing a cloth over her injured shoulder to stop the bleeding, she stepped over Jayce and walked to the vanity. The mirror showed a dark bruise developing along her jaw. She could style her hair to hide it, so she ignored it for now, conserving energy. She dried her eyes, then wrestled her way out of the ball gown and into one of the form-fitting summer dresses Jayce hated. A few minutes spent brushing her hair did nothing to calm her. She went to where he lay and stared at him, trembling with the urge to do worse than sedate him.

If what Serivar said were true, the Ascard Watchmen wouldn't come calling, even if they sensed her masked work-ing. If they did come, she was going to have a hard time explaining this.

What have I done?

A knock on the door made her jump. Light shining in the window showed that morning had come and gone. It was mid-afternoon. At some point, she had gone from standing over Jayce to sitting on the bed. She dragged her sedated fiancé into the bedroom and left him, shutting the door behind her. The knock came again, more insistent. She went to the door and took a few deep, calming breaths to test the healed rib.

"Indigo?"

Andrea. Relief flooded her. Andrea, she could handle. She steeled herself, opened the door, and smiled a welcome.

"Indigo. I thought you might not be home. I'm going to the palace to see Caplin. Would you like to come with me?" She scanned the room. "Where's Jayce?"

"He's resting. He wasn't feeling well."

"Oh." Andrea put a foot over the threshold and leaned in, peering toward the bedroom. "Poor thing."

Before she could get any foolish ideas in her head about visiting him, Indigo stepped forward, driving her back into the hall. "I was about to take a walk so he could have some peace and quiet. I would be happy to join you instead."

Andrea allowed Indigo to usher her down the stairs and out into the harsh sunlight. She brushed her hair forward when she climbed into the waiting carriage to be sure it hid the bruise. Settling into the middle of the seat, she leaned back, avoiding the sunlight that crept into the dark interior. Andrea settled into the opposite seat and gave her a curious look but said nothing.

Leaving Jayce unconscious in the residence was risky, but she couldn't wake him yet, not until she had time to think. She had a lot to think about. That kind of rage was dangerous. Caplin could get the engagement nullified, but she still had to finish training at the academy. The idea of skulking around back streets to avoid Jayce didn't appeal. Laws protecting women from such mistreatment were inadequate at best. Even with Caplin's backing, Jayce wouldn't suffer much for it, not as much as she would as his victim. The ending of their engagement would also put her future on shaky ground, and the respect she would lose if people learned of the abuse would only make that worse. Serivar might even remove her from the King's Order, a possibility with numerous unpleasant repercussions.

"Indigo, are you all right?" Grooves of worry etched

Andrea's brow.

I don't want to lie anymore. "Yes. I'm tired after last night."

"The feast was marvelous, and Lord Eldrian took quite a fancy to you." Andrea winked.

"Who?" Indigo shook her head, finding it hard to keep up in her frazzled state.

"The Lyran lord. The one you danced with at least three times. I'm amazed you could forget him so easily. You *must* be tired."

Yes, tired and scared. Perhaps accompanying Andrea had been a mistake. In her current state, she might say something she shouldn't.

She began picking at her fingernails. "You're right. I couldn't forget him so easily."

Andrea brightened. "That's more like it. He'll be at the palace. He and Caplin have been sparring, and Caplin invited me to watch. I thought you might enjoy watching too."

Indigo sighed. *Out of one mess and into another.*

CHAPTER TWENTY-THREE

Adran had woken Yiloch again before noon. Whatever the High Council planned to put before him, he was ready. He smiled now, sitting on the veranda with Adran and Cadmar, basking in the warmth of another beautiful day that held much promise.

Cadmar sat in the chair next to him. His substantial sword rested beside him, contradicting the ease with which he lounged there. The dark warrior had already adjusted to the relaxed setting despite his claim that such things didn't suit him.

Yiloch rested a hand on the hilt of his own sword where it leaned against the chair. Like Cadmar, he couldn't relax without a weapon in reach.

"You seem pleased." Adran's tone suggested that he didn't share the feeling.

"I was thinking about revenge."

"Ah, good." Adran took some bread from the tray of food brought up for them. "I feared you might be thinking about women again."

Yiloch ignored the comment. "You should shave."

Adran answered with a scowl, though he brought a hand up to feel the stubble of beard, that constant reminder of the impurity of his blood.

Ian staggered from his room, a hand pressed to his forehead.

"Too much wine?" Yiloch couldn't decide whether to

find the youth's state amusing or irritating.

"No. I couldn't sleep. That woman you had in your room..."

Yiloch scowled a warning.

Ian held up his hands as if to ward off an attack and melted into an empty chair. "I wasn't eavesdropping. Her inner aspect is so strong, it was like having a cyclone in my head."

Yiloch leaned forward. "Lady Indigo?"

"Yes. She was the one poking around at supper. The reason I shielded your inner aspect. She had masking in place. It took most of the evening to figure out that all that power was coming from her. Couldn't you feel it, my lord?"

"No, but few people are as sensitive as you." He rested his elbows on his knees and stared at the creator. "You say she's strong. How strong?"

"Frighteningly." Ian leaned back and closed his eyes. "I've never felt anything like it."

Adran was watching Ian with a pensive frown. Was he thinking the same thing? If Indigo was that strong and they were training her to do more than heal, she might make a valuable addition to his army. But he didn't dare ask for her by name.

"Did you notice anyone else with that kind of power?"

Ian shook his head. "The king had a low creator with him. The Healer's Academy headmaster is an adept, but not as strong as Ferin. There were several healers and Ascard Watchmen and a few other adepts with specialized skills. Nothing else extraordinary."

Caplin strode out to the veranda in his usual confident-bordering-on-arrogant manner, his arrival ending the conversation. "Prince Yiloch. Lord Adran." He nodded to each of them. "The High Council is ready for you."

Ian sank deeper into the chair, closing his eyes as Yiloch

and Adran stood. Caplin led them through the halls, his pace businesslike, but his smile affable as always.

"Would you care to spar after the meeting?" He cast a hopeful glance at Yiloch.

"I would."

"Excellent. I invited Andrea to watch. It would have been awkward if you had refused."

Yiloch grinned. "I imagine so. You would have had to spar with yourself."

Caplin laughed. "And I probably still would have lost."

When they entered the council room, the High Council members stood. Caplin walked to his place, leaving Yiloch and Adran to the chairs left open for them. A servant waiting inside the door stepped out and shut them in to signal the start of the session. They sat at the king's bidding, and formal greetings went around the table. Then King Jerrin cleared his throat and glowered at Lord Serivar before speaking.

"Prince Yiloch, Lord Serivar still has reservations about sending healers to assist your army," he stated.

Yiloch met the king's eyes. They had argued over the subject enough. Most of the men around the table, and the king in particular, wanted this alliance. Time to find out how badly they wanted it. "I have reservations about removing import restrictions, Your Majesty, but we must all make concessions."

Several members muttered and shifted in their seats, but the king nodded. A price had been set. "The majority agree you should be granted healers with some caveats. Lord Serivar, I am afraid you have been overruled."

Serivar's face pinched with displeasure, but he gave a curt nod.

"Very well, Prince Yiloch," the king continued. "In addition to the ships offered, the High Council has agreed, almost unanimously"—he glanced at Serivar, who appeared to be trying to glare holes through the table—"to send fifty healers to accompany your force. Those healers come with five hundred Caithin soldiers whose primary purpose will be to safeguard them and see that you do not misuse their services. Those soldiers will be available to you in battle at the discretion of their captain, Lord Caplin, who has graciously offered to select and lead that troop."

Yiloch inclined his head. "Your Majesty is most generous. This will allow for quick and decisive action."

"That is our expectation. Be aware that the council has given Lord Caplin the right to act independently in pulling our healers out if he feels they are at undue risk or their services are being abused in any manner."

"I would expect no less." Yiloch struggled not to smile. Their chances of a swift victory had improved significantly.

The rest of the session went to writing the treaty and refining details of the assault on Yiroth. They settled on the timing and location for the rendezvous between Yiloch's army and Caplin's force. Yiloch would arrange for supply wagons to meet the healers and soldiers when they arrived on Lyran shores. He agreed to leave Cadmar behind to guide them to the rendezvous. The Kudaness warrior knew that territory well and would get over any irritation at being committed without being given a say in time.

After three hours of tedious and irritating nitpicking, they adjourned. Yiloch got almost everything he wanted from the arrangement. The sparring match with Caplin would help to burn off pent-up energy. It would also be his last opportunity to build influence with the man before they met again at the rendezvous.

"Prince Yiloch, it feels like you got an exceptional deal in our negotiations. Or maybe that's just my perception of it." Caplin's tone remained light despite the uneasy weight in his words.

"Time will tell," Yiloch replied, noncommittal. Caithin

anger toward Emperor Rylan had given him even more of an advantage than he expected. He would have to thank his father for that before he cut his head off.

"It's unfortunate you're leaving so soon. I have learned a great deal from sparring words and swords with you."

"Is that why you volunteered to lead the troop?" Yiloch selected a sword from the rack, and Adran sauntered off to lean against a tree and watch.

Caplin wandered into the ring, set his chosen sword point down in the dirt, and leaned on it. "I'm not sure, really. Part of it is the wedding and wanting to get away from the city for a while, but I think it's mostly curiosity and, if you will pardon the conceit, the feeling that I am the most qualified for the job."

Yiloch stepped into the ring and positioned himself four feet in front of Caplin. "Since I have met few of your captains, I cannot disagree, and I doubt I would."

A hint of pleasure in the young lord's smile as he moved into a fighting stance rewarded the comment. Consciously or not, Caplin had accepted him as a mentor, so his words held weight. Yiloch enjoyed the arrangement. He hadn't worked with anyone like this since he mentored Leryc before his departure from Yiroth, and he appreciated the practice.

They engaged. Despite his overconfident bearing, Caplin was aware of his limitations and eager to learn. He improved each time, adapting with admirable ease to the Lyran and Kudaness styles Yiloch brought to the ring.

They focused on each other, occupied in their preferred form of dance with such intensity that Yiloch almost didn't notice the two women outside the ring. Bright sun glinting off gold highlights in Indigo's long dark hair, hanging loose to frame her face in soft waves, caught his eye. She was lovelier in her simple summer dress, standing in the sunshine, than she had been in her gown the night before, and he burned to touch her.

He wrestled his attention back to the match. When he glanced up again a few moments later, Andrea stood alone. Indigo had walked around the ring and was talking with Adran. The tension in her bearing that hadn't been there the night before. It might just be the dearth of wine to ease her nerves, but the sorrow in her eyes and the willful set of her jaw spoke to something more complex.

Impatient, Yiloch slipped in a new move to disarm Caplin, sending his practice blade skittering to one side.

Andrea applauded. "Impressive!"

Smiling good-naturedly, Caplin walked to Andrea and leaned in to kiss her.

She stepped back with a grimace. "You're all sweaty."

He laughed. "It's hot." His expression turned serious, and he glanced toward Yiloch. His gaze drifted to Indigo and lingered there perhaps a moment longer than appropriate. "Excuse us for a moment. I must speak with my fiancé alone."

Andrea's smile crumpled as Caplin led her around the corner of the building, and Yiloch seized the opportunity to join Indigo and Adran.

"Is the king giving you what you wanted to fight your war?" Indigo said, staring after Caplin and Andrea with disturbing intensity.

His answering silence got her to look at him, her deep blue eyes demanding an answer.

Adran shook his head. A warning.

Yiloch glanced away, unsettled by the cold calculation in her gaze. What had happened since he last saw her? "The king is providing naval support. He's also sending a troop of five hundred soldiers and fifty healers. Lord Caplin will lead them."

"They are giving you healers?"

He faced her. "I would take you, given my choice."

Her gaze pierced him, cutting into his soul. "You would put me in danger again?"

Those words yanked the ground out from under him. He had no answer.

"I think I understand you now, my prince. You are all ambition. You cannot see the sun past the fire that burns so bright within you."

The lack of anger in her rather accurate assessment surprised him. Only sorrowful adoration showed in her eyes. Everything around them ceased to exist. He brought a hand up to touch her face, and she pulled back, catching his wrist with one hand. She searched his eyes for a long moment, then nodded and released him. Turning away, she walked toward Caplin and a teary-eyed Andrea returning from their talk. Yiloch stared after her, feeling like a man who had fallen down a bottomless pit.

Indigo embraced the other woman.

"I'll never be married," Andrea sobbed, burying her face against Indigo's shoulder.

Caplin, looking deflated, trudged over to join Yiloch and Adran. They looked on in silence while Indigo stroked the other woman's hair to comfort her.

"It'll be all right, Andrea. My wedding is postponed as well."

"Yes, but Jayce isn't going to war," Andrea wailed and sobbed harder.

Indigo turned her head, pinning Caplin with her gaze. Fierce determination blazed in her blue eyes. "No, *he* isn't."

Unspoken volumes passed between the two in that look. Caplin didn't appear pleased. He and Indigo shared a far deeper relationship than Yiloch had first thought. How had he missed it, and how deep did it go?

Indigo gently pushed Andrea away. "Go inside and have some tea brought. I would like to have a word with your fiancé."

Andrea nodded, giving Indigo a grateful look that assumed she would somehow fix things. Indigo watched her vanish into the castle. With dragging strides, Caplin walked over to her, and she turned, meeting Yiloch's eyes for a long moment. He thought she might ask them to leave, but defiance flashed in her eyes and she faced Caplin. The stubborn set of her jaw made him feel a twinge of sympathy for the young lord.

"I want to be on the list of healers."

Caplin gave them both cross looks, correctly blaming them for her knowledge.

Yiloch shrugged.

Caplin assumed an indulgent tone. "Indigo, even if you were a full healer, I wouldn't want you in the middle of a war, but you're not. You're still in training. They might let me take some third-year students, but I can guarantee they won't let me recruit second years."

She didn't back down. "The headmaster has me taking advanced classes. He says I am skilled enough to be working in the field now. Figure something out and put me on that list."

"Indigo, it's not..."

She stepped closer to him, cutting him off with a severe look. Yiloch admired Caplin for standing his ground. Then she drew back her hair, showing a dark bruise along the edge of her jaw.

Rage coiled in Yiloch, a deadly viper eager to strike, but this wasn't the time or place to act on emotion. That same rage rose in Caplin's eyes.

"This is the fastest way to get me away from Jayce before one of us kills the other." She lowered her voice enough that Yiloch had to strain to hear. Then she let her hair fall over the bruise and stepped back, her gaze now beseeching. She knew how to play him.

"I will do what I can." Caplin's voice was thick with fury.

"Thank you."

Her eyes met Yiloch's for a second, but her expression was unreadable. When she walked away, he and Adran went to Caplin. A swirling breeze lifted a spiral of dust in the sparring ring as the door thumped shut behind her.

Caplin shifted his feet. "I don't know what to do about her."

His phrasing didn't ask for an answer, but Yiloch responded anyway. "In what way?"

"She wants to be among the fifty healers. Ignoring the other complications of putting her on the list, such as the fact that she hasn't graduated yet, I would opt to keep her out of harm's way, not drag her into it." Caplin still stared at the door through which she had departed.

Some things were too easy.

"It looks to me as if she's already in harm's way."

Caplin's jaw tightened. He nodded. "I suppose she is."

CHAPTER TWENTY-FOUR

Yiloch strode to the bow of the ship. Ian and Adran lingered by the port-side rail, looking back at Caplin and Cadmar, who watched from the dock. Hax would not be happy about the latter, but Cadmar knew the territory coming up from the northern edge of Kudan. He was the sensible choice to lead Caplin's force to the rendezvous.

A chill south wind blew through the Gilded Strait, catching his hair and sweeping it back from his face. It brought with it the salty smell of the sea. The wind would slow early progress, but the winds changed often on the strait. They would make up time later. The ship Caplin secured for their return was small, built more for speed than carrying capacity. Without the wine casks, they could travel faster.

He had the promise of a naval distraction and the healers he wanted. He would also have a powerful Caithin adept. Indigo had made her decision, and he didn't doubt she would find a way to get what she wanted. Her training might be incomplete, but that didn't matter. He could get her to divulge what they were teaching her, if not through willing disclosure, then through her actions.

He would have his war and his throne. The emperor commanded a powerful army, but his troops were running rogue and lords were deserting, fearing the emperor's growing unpredictability. If they didn't rally when Yiloch's army marched on the capital, he could contend with them after he secured the throne.

"I'm surprised they gave you healers." Adran leaned back against the rail next to him, his gaze still on the city falling behind them.

"I suspect Lord Caplin put in a word on my behalf." Yiloch watched the open water ahead.

"Befriending him was a clever political move."

A bird dove into the water, emerging with a fish in its claws.

"It was hard not to."

He wouldn't mind having Caplin watch his back. The man wasn't a master swordsman, but he learned fast and acted as though he didn't see their racial differences. He would select capable men and talented healers. If Yiloch read the situation right, he would also be an ally in getting Indigo added to that roster. Caplin's concern for her would drive him to keep her close rather than leave her in the hands of a man who was an obvious danger to her, a situation Yiloch would have liked to do something about, but the risk was too great, and Jayce would eventually pay if he pushed her too far. It seemed appropriate to leave her that option.

Ian still leaned on the port-side railing, staring back toward Kilty and Demin. Gesturing for Adran to wait, Yiloch walked to the young creator.

"One should learn from the past and look to the future," he said, quoting a childhood tutor.

"I am looking to the future, my lord."

"Meaning?"

Ian kept his voice low so Caithin crewmen wouldn't overhear. "Have you considered that if they have others like her, they have power as formidable as anything Lyra has?"

"Do you think they have more like her?"

"I don't know. I think she may be an anomaly, like Myac, but I can't *know* that." Ian's knuckles whitened from his strangling grip on the railing.

"And that scares you?"

"Shouldn't it?"

"Ian." The creator faced him, then glanced away, and Yiloch waited silently until his gaze shifted reluctantly back. "I have considered this and I have a plan, but first we take the throne."

"Yes, my lord."

Yiloch left him and returned to the bow where Adran stood in thoughtful contemplation.

"He's changing," Adran observed.

"Ian? He's still timid, but he is gaining confidence."

Adran nodded. "When you have your empire, what then?"

Yiloch waited until no one was within earshot. "Then, dear friend, we take our dignity back from Caithin. The slave trade will end, one way or another."

Adran smiled and turned to gaze out to sea.

* * *

With the authority the emperor granted him, Myac steered the troop southwest, angling away from the capital. Now he gazed down into a cloud-shaded valley, upon a grand manor and the verdant land surrounding it. The holding of Lord Terral, Emperor Rylan's nephew. A holding Myac would inherit if Terral acknowledged him as his son, something he only recently offered to do.

Too little offered much too late. Myac no longer wanted the property. Beautiful and secluded though it was, it was a flawed gem next to the magnificence of the imperial palace. Besides, time spent serving the emperor taught him that he preferred being in the thick of things.

Squeezing his legs, he urged his mount down the hillside. Two hundred soldiers followed.

As the company reached the valley floor, two soldiers from Terral's guard intercepted them. His military might was formidable when gathered, and a notable portion of that force now occupied the grounds. Terral expected to need his soldiers soon, which meant someone must have contacted him.

Reining in his mount, Myac waited for the soldiers to close the distance.

"Lord Myac." One of them bowed his head, recognizing him, and he felt a tremor of alarm ripple through them both as the other followed suit.

"I would speak with Lord Terral, and my soldiers need rest and refreshment."

They swept wide eyes over his followers, recognizing a company strong enough to challenge their current numbers. Their hands twitched tight on their reins, their mounts shifting restlessly in response.

They knew Myac had the emperor's favor, and they knew with whom Lord Terral had been treating of late. What they didn't know was that Myac knew of Lord Terral's alliance with Prince Yiloch. He had even encouraged it.

The first man gave a tense nod. "Please follow me, my lord."

Myac fell in beside the man. The second soldier galloped ahead to alert Lord Terral of his unexpected visitors. They knew very little. They didn't know he was their lord's son, and Terral hadn't ever intended for anyone to know. Once Myac had been naïve enough to think ties of blood would matter, but Terral wanted nothing to do with him. Terral also feared him, and now, with power and an elevated status in the palace, Myac held the advantage over his father. His lineage would be acknowledged, but on his terms.

Myac's company dropped back outside the courtyard of

the towering manor house to await further instruction or offer of hospitality. He dismounted within and handed his reins to the groom. The usher met him at the door with a glass of wine held out in offering. Myac accepted it and swept into the grand entry, a swirling sea of blue marble holding afloat twin spiral staircases that led to the second floor. He turned into a sitting room to the right of the entry, finding Terral with ascard, and tossed open the door with his power, leaving the usher fumbling along behind to belatedly announce him and shut the door.

Terral's arms draped over the arms of a deep chair. Pale gold hair hung long around a face that reminded Myac offensively of Prince Yiloch, if a touch less perfect for the sharpness of his nose and thicker brow. Pale gold eyes narrowed at Myac's abrupt entrance, but he presented a pleasant enough smile until the usher was gone.

"To what do I owe the pleasure of this visit?" An icy tone contradicted his polite words.

"Can't a son miss his father?"

"Keep your voice down," Terral hissed. "Someone might hear you."

"Please, Father." Myac relaxed into another chair, the light violet brocade fading with age. "Do you think me a fool?" He held up a hand. "Best if you don't answer that. I created a sound barrier on the way in. No one will hear a word we say."

Terral shifted in his seat and sipped from one of several glasses of wine sitting on the table next to him. "You make me nervous. You're too young and reckless to have such power at your disposal."

Myac shrugged off the comment. "I take it the prince is preparing to march?"

"They have advised me to be ready. He's up to something. Captain Paulin said it would be a few more weeks at most. You should have taken Yiloch out when you had him trapped rather than allowing them to go to war like this. It will be too costly."

Myac shook his head. The idea of war held a certain appeal. "It might work out in our favor. People are angry. The conflict between Rylan and his son will further destabilize the country and leave the populace starving for any leadership they can find. Besides, I'm curious to see who wins. Once one of them kills the other, I can arrange the death of the survivor in the aftermath."

"And what do I do?"

"Continue supporting the prince. He's the more popular of the two at this point. Even if he fails, supporting his cause may improve your standing with the majority. Just don't get killed."

Terral frowned into his wine, his unsteady gaze suggesting he had a fair amount already. "I don't want the throne."

Myac wrinkled his nose and sniffed the wine as if it, and not his father, triggered his disgust. "That is the difference between you and me. You are content to follow any fool who will leave you be. I would rather lead the fools."

Terral fussed with a rumpled cuff on his silk shirt. "What about Kudan?"

"They have no particular love for Rylan or his son, and until they stop killing each other, they pose little threat."

"Would you care for something to eat?"

"No, thank you." Myac gestured to the glasses on the table. "Do you have something there with more spice?"

Terral sniffed several glasses and traded him one.

Myac tasted this wine and nodded approval. "Did you ever love her?" He had long avoided asking that question because he feared losing his temper with the man and doing something he would regret, but he had more confidence in his control now.

Terral traced the rim of his glass with a finger. "Who?"

"Don't be an obtuse bastard," Myac snapped.

"I am not the bastard here."

The air thickened with the amount of ascard Myac drew on then.

Terral froze, blanching. He swallowed.

Myac barked a humorless laugh and released it. "My mother."

Terral's gaze turned inward, his face softening. "She was so sweet. A gentle woman. I wanted her love, but I was young and impatient. I took her body instead."

"That is an indirect no." If only he didn't need his father. "So you don't care that Rylan's greed and Yiloch's temper killed her? You don't care that they disfigured your only son?"

"Your scars are gone," Terral observed.

Are they?

As a naïve youth covered in seeping burns, with his home and mother destroyed, Myac had come here, hoping against hope that the man he had been told was his father, a man he had never met, would take pity on him. All he saw of Terral that day before the guards dragged him off the holding had been a disgusted sneer on his handsome face in a window—the window to this room, in fact. That day he swore he would come back and claim his birthright, but now he knew he was destined for more.

"Healed enough that I'm allowed in your home now, not that you could stop me." He smiled with false civility. "I suppose we should be on our way. It is a long ride to Yiroth from here."

Terral escorted Myac to the courtyard. His relief at seeing him go made Myac wonder, not for the first time, if his father might betray him. When it came down to it, though, Terral feared him far too much to betray him.

When they emerged, several of his soldiers were in the courtyard, chatting with some of Terral's officers. They snapped alert, saying quick farewells before hastening to their mounts. As Myac swung into the saddle, the words of one officer caught his attention.

"Good journey, Leryc, though I don't see how you can follow that abomination."

Myac turned his horse, and the officer met his gaze.

Leryc shook his head and sidled his mount out of the way.

Had the youth said something to provoke this disrespect? He wouldn't waste time investigating now, but he would keep it in mind.

Myac smiled at the offensive man, a grizzled officer who had likely seen enough conflict to believe he knew how to handle a fight. Moving his horse closer so he wouldn't have to raise his voice, he met the older man's eyes. "You have chosen the wrong enemy this time."

He created a thick bar of steel in the air, blazing red hot as if pulled from a forge, and plunged it through the officer's chest using a thrust of power. The man screamed, a long, agonized howl, and dropped to his knees, the stench of scorched flesh corrupting the air. Then he fell silent and toppled forward. The bar vanished, leaving behind a large, cauterized hole in the officer's torso.

Myac turned his mount to Terral, ignoring the tumultuous surge of emotions and startled stares around him. "Always a pleasure, Lord Terral."

Terral answered with silence and a stiff bow.

Myac spun his mount, catching Leryc's guarded expression as he left the courtyard. Imperial soldiers fell in behind him, leaving the valley at a swift trot.

Myac long ago repaired the disfigurement from the severe burns he suffered in his youth, but many still called him names—freak, monster, abomination—because of the odd color of his hair and eyes and the extraordinary strength of his inner aspect. Today, after his brief talk with his father, was the wrong day to do so.

Ten miles outside of Terral's valley, on the far side of a small village, Myac pulled up.

"Adept Ladon!"

The adept maneuvered his mount forward and inclined his head. His darker coloring betrayed some unfortunate Caithin or Kudaness lineage, but he was the strongest adept in the group after Myac himself.

"Yes, Lord Myac?"

"Ladon, did you come into Emperor Rylan's service before or after the prince's banishment?" Myac investigated the other man's ascard connection while he spoke.

Ladon's eyes narrowed in response to the invasion, but he made no outward complaint. "After."

"Can you mask your ability?"

Ladon's gaze turned distant, and Myac felt him constructing a barrier to hide his ability from outside prying. When he was done, Myac could barely sense the man's inner aspect. It would take someone much stronger than Ladon himself to detect the barrier without knowing it existed.

"Good. You will stay behind until the prince's army passes through. This is his easiest route outside of the main roads, and he will want to avoid those. Follow them. Let them catch you. Do whatever is required to convince them you're merely a scout and willing to change sides. Do not, under any circumstances, let them know you're an adept."

Ladon looked doubtful. "The prince is not reputed to be merciful."

"If you let him know you're an adept, he will kill you. As a scout, he won't consider you a threat. I'll create a link between us to alert me when you're nearing the capital to give the emperor advance warning of his son's approach."

Ladon eyed him uneasily but nodded.

"Good."

Punching through the other man's barrier, he fastened a tendril of his inner aspect to Ladon's, weaving it in so the other man couldn't break the connection. Ladon paled before the assault, disturbed perhaps by Myac breaking through his barrier so effortlessly.

Myac sneered. "Remember, Adept Ladon. Anyone with an inkling of ability is probably stronger than you in some skill. We each have our specialties. You should always expect to be surprised."

Ladon inclined his head. "You speak wisdom, my lord. I would do well to remember your words."

Myac hesitated. He hadn't expected such respectful deference. It tasted sweet. If Ladon survived, he would recommend him for a higher rank. Better yet, if all went according to plan, he would appoint the man to a higher position himself. *Emperor* Terral wouldn't dare argue with him.

"Follow me." He gestured to Ladon and rode back along the ranks until he found a soldier of similar build. "You will exchange clothing and equipment with Adept Ladon."

Under Myac's scowling regard, the man dismounted. The two men traded clothing and equipment as ordered. When they were through, Ladon appeared to be a soldier like any other. If his masking held, they wouldn't discover him before battle was engaged, at which point it would no longer matter.

"I'm counting on you, Adept Ladon. I don't expect you to disappoint. Until the prince passes this way, I suggest you work on perfecting your masking."

Myac motioned the rest of the soldiers onward, leaving the adept alongside the road in his disguise.

CHAPTER TWENTY-FIVE

Indigo glanced at Andrea's door on the way out. Her new schedule required her to arrive early and stay late, so they no longer walked to the academy together. She stepped into the cool morning street alone and spotted Caplin loitering conspicuously in the shadows of the next residence like a hopeless thief.

He motioned her over with a quick wave. "I've gone through the academy files and talked to your instructors. I have enough information to convince my uncle, but I don't know about the headmaster. King Jerrin is reviewing the list this afternoon. If I get his approval, I'll present it to Headmaster Serivar tomorrow."

His covert whispering and the nervous darting of his eyes brought a fond smile to her lips.

He frowned. "This isn't a game, Indigo."

She forced a more serious expression. "Can you let me know if the king approves the list before you take it to the headmaster?"

"Certainly."

"Good. If you take the list to Serivar at the end of the noon break tomorrow, I'll be there. I can help convince him."

"That might not be the best idea." His eyes swept the area, watching for anyone taking an interest in their conversation.

Her ascard senses would warn her long before he noticed anything, but she appreciated his caution. "Trust me. I have some leverage."

His brows pinched in confusion. "Whenever I think I have you figured out, you do or say something unexpected. You never cease to amaze me."

"If you only knew." She ignored his searching look. "Let me know what the king says."

"I will."

She placed a hand on his arm when he started to turn away. "Thank you."

"Of course." He took her hand and clasped it for a moment before walking off.

His voice and manner hinted at more than friendly concern. She shook her head. She had to be mistaken. Life had complications enough without that.

Attend to one thing at a time. She squared her shoulders and resumed her solitary trek.

* * *

Serivar snapped to attention when she entered his office. "I'm glad you're here. We need to discuss the feast. I almost brought you in yesterday after the prince departed, but I thought you might appreciate the longer break."

"Yes." She shut the door and sat across from him. "The youth, Ian. He was the creator, and an exceptionally strong one."

"He seemed young to be that skilled. A bit of a prodigy, perhaps." He smiled at her then, in a way that made her uneasy. "I didn't realize you were such a political asset."

"What do you mean?"

"You got on splendidly with Prince Yiloch and Captain Adran."

Deception, like many things, came easier with practice. "Lord Caplin is a friend. As he was acting escort to the prince, it makes sense that I would have spent time around them."

"Perhaps," he allowed, but his perplexing smile persisted. "Yet you are the only woman the prince danced with more than once. Not that I could blame him. You looked remarkable." He dropped his gaze and fidgeted with a scroll on the desk. "Something my wife was rather sensitive about. I apologize for that. We have had our rough spots lately."

"No harm done." Truthfully, Yiloch's appearance had banished the incident from her mind.

"Where did your fiancé vanish to during your dalliance with the Lyran prince?"

She tensed at his choice of words. "Jayce drank too much at supper and wasn't feeling well."

"And you weren't taking care of him?"

"Why should my evening suffer for his poor judgment?" Serivar frowned.

She matched his expression. "You should be happy to see my relationship failing. Imagine how much you could teach me without Jayce competing for my time?" She meant the comment to be sarcastic, but Serivar brightened. Before he could pursue whatever disturbing thoughts ripened behind that look, she said, "I have a question for you."

"You have not assuaged my curiosity yet." She gave him a severe look, and he conceded. "Very well, ask."

"I've been thinking about our lessons. Much of what you've taught me has obvious aggressive applications. I feel as if I'm becoming dangerous, and I don't like it. What are you training me for?"

His attempt at a disarming smile was unconvincing. "The strength of your connection determines how much of your inner aspect you can manipulate at one time, but the strength of your inner aspect itself determines your developmental potential. People with average strength can learn to do many things adequately or a few things very well.

"Take your friend Andrea." He gestured toward the door as if she might be standing outside it. "Her inner aspect is average, and she has a natural affinity for working with soft-tissue injuries. If she trains exclusively in those skills, she can become adept in that area of specialization. However, the inner aspect changes when trained for a specific purpose, so she won't be able to extend her ability for much else once her training is complete.

"With each new skill that is learned, a separation takes place in the inner aspect, molding a portion to that skill. If you continue to develop that skill, more inner aspect becomes allocated to it. Because of the unusual strength of your inner aspect, you may have the capacity to learn hundreds of skills, each with the potential to reach the adept level most people achieve with only a few skills."

He leaned back in his chair, steepling his fingers in front of him. "Another often-overlooked factor that limits an individual's ability is their acceptance of what is possible and what they can do. Some people harbor too much doubt, thereby unwittingly limiting themselves. Anytime I've told you that you can do something, you've tried and tried until you succeeded. That's a rare gift. I don't know your limits. This is a discovery process for me as much as for you, and yes, many things I'm teaching you have aggressive applications. That doesn't mean anyone will ask you to use them that way."

"It doesn't mean they won't."

"There's always a chance, but this is part of what you are now. If you don't wish to continue..."

She swallowed a surge of sour resentment. "No, I will continue with the lessons, but I'm afraid something bad could happen if I lost my temper."

"You must develop enough discipline to prevent that."

She hated him for putting responsibility on her, even though he was right, perhaps more so because he was. "I should get to class."

"This afternoon, then?"

"Yes." She stood.

"Tell me, what *did* you talk about with the prince?" Curiosity sparkled in his eyes. "I'd love to know."

"Dancing and customs. Trivial things."

He looked unconvinced.

She smiled and walked out. Let him regret the day he encouraged her to lie.

* * *

That afternoon they worked on her ability to sense his ascard use until she could detect it when he initiated the slightest connection. He then showed her how to block physical ascard attacks. Several hours passed with him making unannounced attacks while she reviewed earlier lessons. He blasted her out of her chair the first time. From that point forward, determined not to add to the bruises from that first strike, she sensed and blocked him with almost perfect accuracy.

When he gave up, sweat beaded on his brow, and his hands resting on the table trembled. It took effort not to gloat over how tired she wasn't. With each passing day, the hours spent controlling ascard took less and less out of her.

"Indigo, you are remarkable. It's unfortunate that you're also so stubborn."

"If I were any less stubborn, I wouldn't have gotten this far."

"Granted. After everything I've taught you, will you finally tell me what happened when you disappeared?"

"I don't remember." That was still the easiest lie of all.

A scowl started forming, then melted away. Perhaps he was too tired to be irritated with her. "Then tell me why the prince found you so fascinating?"

Her pulse quickened. Had he found some connection

between the two subjects? "His creator reacted to my investigation. Perhaps he mentioned it to Prince Yiloch."

He stiffened. "I hadn't thought of that. I should not have allowed you to attend. If he—"

"Or perhaps he likes attractive women. It doesn't matter now. In the future, it might help if I knew more about masking my ability, especially when poking around that of others."

"You're right. I should have focused time on that in your training instead of leaving you on your own. We will spend time on masking tomorrow. Today, I thought I might let you go early."

"Tired?" she teased.

"Don't become arrogant." His proud smile mitigated the warning in his tone. "Have a pleasant evening, Indigo."

"You as well, Serivar."

The focus on information gathering and defense, though an obvious ploy to ease her mind after their morning talk, served its purpose. A brighter mood lightened her steps on the walk home.

Outside the residence, Caplin and Jayce sat on the steps chatting in the fading light of evening. She forced a smile for Jayce, who remained wary and distant since their fight, and offered a polite nod to Caplin.

Caplin mirrored the gesture. "Lady Indigo, I was telling Jayce that the king signed off on my list of soldiers and healers for the coming campaign. Things are going smoothly, other than Andrea, who is still furious with me."

As far as the public was concerned, a unit of soldiers and healers was heading south to resolve fighting that had broken out over a territorial dispute. Such minor military actions were not uncommon, and the truth had to remain secret at least until the attack on Yiroth was underway.

She sat between them. "What happens now?"

Caplin's gaze dropped to his boots, and he dusted a spot

of dirt off one. "I'll present the list to Headmaster Serivar tomorrow afternoon for approval."

She allowed herself a private smile, knowing Jayce couldn't see it from his vantage.

Caplin looked out into the street and paled. She followed his gaze. It was near suppertime, and the evening streets experienced a lull in traffic. Among the few pedestrians, she spotted Andrea coming toward them.

Caplin rose to greet her, and she gave him a thin smile, turning her cheek to his kiss.

"How are you, my love?" He offered a sweet smile.

"I've been better." She took a step away from him.

"Andrea."

Her look was ice.

He clenched his teeth, then turned to Jayce and Indigo. "I'll see you both later." He spun and stalked away.

Indigo ached to comfort him, but she didn't dare follow. Andrea stormed into the building, tears welling in her eyes. Jayce sat for a few minutes more, then also went inside. Alone, Indigo drew up her knees, laid her arms across them and rested her head there.

So much had changed, and very little for the better. Her lessons were the best part; except she couldn't tell anyone about them. That and the unshakable feeling that she was becoming a weapon undermined her pride in her accomplishments. She had come to Demin to learn to heal. Now she knew how to destroy as well. Not only did she know how to do so, but she was good at it. It didn't feel right that they would give Serivar free rein to train her this way if she were as powerful as he believed.

If Caplin's interest in her were more than friendly, then Andrea's treatment of him could intensify that. It made her wary of joining his healers, but she couldn't stay here with Jayce. If he attacked her again, she would hurt or kill him to save her own life. There would be dire consequences for that, given the confidentiality of her lessons and her shaky social status. Going to Lyra would only postpone her problems, unless she died. They were joining a war, after all. If she survived, she would ask Caplin for help to nullify the engagement and contend with the consequences then.

What about Yiloch?

She would be lying if she tried to pretend he didn't influence her desire to go to Lyra, but being near him without being able to touch him might be worse than having him beyond reach.

What do you think of this mess, Father? Have I done anything right, or am I burying problems beneath bigger problems?

Melancholy outweighed hunger. She stayed on the steps and watched night creep in. Foot traffic increased after supper, the nightlife kicking into action. Some acquaintances from the academy stopped to exchange a few words. In time, the traffic lulled again. The stars and moon strolled across the sky. When the streets emptied and the cool night air had her shivering, she went inside.

When she crawled into bed, Jayce rolled over, putting his back to her. It was unlike him to turn away. It was also unlike him to leave her on the steps unsupervised for hours.

She turned her back to him and drifted to sleep.

In the morning, he didn't speak to her. She liked the silent treatment, even if she wasn't sure how she had earned it. It allowed her to brood in peace.

Andrea, who looked as if she hadn't slept at all, came out early and walked to school with her. They each held to their own council, as if the melancholy from the night before waited at the steps, embracing them as they passed. When they met at the noon break, bright sunshine contrasted the sullen mood, and wetness shimmered in Andrea's eyes.

Indigo relented, breaking the long silence. "He will come

back."

Andrea picked at her food. "Why must he go?"

"He's a captain in the Royal Army. This kind of thing is always possible. It's an honor for him to be entrusted with such a mission. You should be proud of him."

Andrea frowned, unconvinced. "Why now?"

"Politics have no care for love." She placed a comforting hand on her friend's shoulder. "It'll be fine. Wait for him."

"I'm sure you're right."

Indigo smiled, and Andrea managed a tremulous smile in return.

"I've got to go." She stood, waiting until Andrea looked up at her. "Would you rather send him to battle with the confidence of your love or this sorrow?"

A tear escaped down her cheek. She wiped it away and resumed picking at her food.

Indigo nodded to herself, satisfied she had at least given Andrea something to consider, and made her way to Serivar's office. She needed to arrive before Caplin, but not by too much, or Serivar would start her lesson before Caplin arrived. Down the hall from Serivar's office, she spotted Caplin chatting with a healer. She made a point of meeting his eyes before going in.

Serivar had a scroll unrolled on his desk. She shut the door and waited while he finished reading it. He had just looked up to acknowledge her when the knock came, and his gaze snapped to the door.

"Come in."

Caplin stepped in, offering a bow to each of them. "Lord Serivar, I apologize for interrupting. I have the list of healers King Jerrin approved. I need your endorsement."

Serivar snatched the scroll, smoothed it on his desk, and began skimming names.

"Apologies, Lady Indigo," Caplin said, supporting the

illusion that his timing was coincidental. "This should only take a moment."

Serivar looked up and stared at Indigo for a long moment before turning a cutting gaze on Caplin. "Lady Indigo should not be on this list. She isn't even a third year, and she certainly isn't ready for this kind of campaign."

"I tried not to add active students, but the available pool is limited given our timeline," Caplin explained, prepared for resistance. "We have summoned healers from outside the city to fill in for instructors and full healers we are taking from the academy, but we don't know who will come and when. We can't leave the city without skilled healers. I had eleven extra spots to fill, so I selected the most qualified students to fill them based on instructor recommendations and the information in your records." Serivar started shaking his head, and Caplin pressed on. "According to those resources, Indigo has excelled and is, I believe your exact words in the file were, 'advanced beyond the level of many journeyman healers'."

"I won't allow it." Serivar rolled the scroll.

Indigo drew a breath to calm her nerves. "Would you excuse us for a moment, Lord Caplin?"

Caplin's brows pinched, but he nodded. "If you wish, my lady."

"Please."

When he was gone, she turned a frosty glare on Serivar.

He met the glare, his jaw tight and his eyes equally cold.

"The king doesn't know about me, does he?"

Surprise slackened his expression for a second. Then he composed himself and waved a dismissive hand her way. "Don't be foolish. Of course he knows."

"For someone who touts the value of lying, you aren't very good at it."

He picked at a corner of the healer list, his jaw tight.

"Why haven't you told him? What are you hiding?"

He stood and walked around the desk, stopping in front of her. She almost backed away, remembering his superior experience, but she wasn't helpless anymore.

"Indigo, your strength is unequaled." He took hold of her arms, a feverish hunger in his eyes like a feral dog shown a slab of beef. "You have such potential. You can do things I have only theorized were possible. If I tell the council about you, they'll take you from me and force you to be the weapon you're so loath to become."

A cold lump settled in the pit of her stomach. To what end was he training her then? She should tell the king. That was the right thing to do.

"What do *you* intend to use me for?"

"I only want you to realize your full potential. You must understand—"

"No!"

He fell silent and stepped back from the force of her rejection.

She knew what was right, and she knew what she wanted. The two didn't exactly work together. "I don't want to understand. Not yet. Allow me to go with Caplin, and I won't tell King Jerrin what you're doing behind his back."

She felt him connect to his inner aspect and intercepted him, closing ascard in around him like a shield to block his ability. His eyes widened, and color drained from his face. Panic twisted her gut. This was madness, but she couldn't turn back now.

"Don't. I'm going to Lyra. This is what I want, and I need you to help me prepare. Show me how to mask my ability better and build my defenses. When I return, I will continue to work with you. No questions asked. Are we agreed?"

"Indigo." He was pleading now. Fear and desperation shone in his eyes, but also desire ignited by her offer. "You do not have the necessary control. Stay and allow me to teach you. Doing this now could be disastrous for you and for those around you."

"I'll manage. Sign the list."

He could only stare, disabled by the barrier she had placed around him. She felt him testing it and met his eyes, daring him to fight her.

He surrendered. "I will sign it, but you must promise to keep your full strength and what I have taught you hidden."

"I go only as a healer." She released him.

He trudged around behind his desk, dropped into his chair, and signed the scroll.

She opened the door and called Caplin in.

Serivar handed him the scroll. "You have your healers." He snarled the words.

Caplin snatched the scroll and stepped back, wary of his anger. "Thank you, Lord Serivar."

"Go."

Caplin bowed to each of them and hurried out.

Indigo bumped the door shut with her heel. "Shall we work on masking?"

CHAPTER TWENTY-SIX

A mile from the stronghold, Yiloch had Ian reach ahead with the ascard. He wanted no surprises, but what the creator found was indeed a surprise. There were only three people at the stronghold. One of them Ian could identify as Hax from her ascard signature.

Yiloch halted the retinue.

Adran moved his mount up alongside him. "What's wrong?"

They wouldn't have moved the rest of the stronghold without a good reason. He glanced at Ian. "Check again."

The creator's focus turned inward, and they waited several minutes before he shook his head. "There's no other signature of human life. I sense some horses in the stables."

Yiloch kicked Tantrum up to a canter. The soldiers sped after him, sweeping up the narrow cliff path until the stronghold rose before them, nestled snug into the craggy mountainside. They slowed to a stop again, a few yards from the wall.

The back gate was gone. Not standing open or busted in, but reduced to fragments. Piled splinters of wood and iron bordered two cleared paths to the rear door of the stronghold and the stables. A grisly display greeted them. Two heads hung in small cages on either side of the entrance, those of Galen and Dalce, both recognizable despite the work of scavenging birds.

Yiloch cursed, venting a tiny fraction of the rage and

anguish rising inside him.

Hax emerged from the nearest stable and marched up to his horse, resting a hand on the stallion's neck. She looked up at him for a moment, but the weight of misery in her red-rimmed eyes pulled her gaze down.

"What happened?"

"Your father sent two hundred soldiers to visit. We had enough warning to get everyone out, but Galen and Dalce stayed to destroy evidence of your plans." Her gaze flickered toward the gate and away. "They weren't able to get out in time."

Yiloch stared at Galen's disfigured face, a portion of lip torn away, eye sockets picked clean. "Were they questioned?"

"No. I watched from the cliff, hoping to see them leave." Her jaw tightened, and she fell silent, blinking at the moisture in her eyes.

Her grief helped him to leash his fury. They depended on his leadership. He couldn't afford to give in to his emotions the way he had after the murder of his mother. He wouldn't repeat past mistakes.

Hax sounded hoarse when she continued. "One of Ferin's adepts confirmed their deaths before the emperor's men entered."

His gaze settled on Dalce for a second, and fury rose again, a caustic surge threatening to melt through his precarious calm. "Why are those still up there?"

"We buried the bodies, but Myac created those cages. Ferin feared a trap. Myac left something in your chamber as well."

"Myac." The name left a foul taste on his tongue. He reached out with his inner aspect and inspected the cages, quickly giving up. His ability wasn't strong enough to detect something Myac wanted hidden. "Ian, do what you can about those, but be careful. I would rather leave them than lose you."

"Yes, my lord." Ian dismounted. He leaned on his mount, staring at the ground, and swallowed hard, then clenched his fists at his sides and approached the nearest cage.

"Do we have our alliance?" Hax's eyes shone with a desperate need for favorable news.

Yiloch gave a stiff nod, still fighting rage. Lashing out at one of his soldiers would serve no purpose. "We have our alliance with Caithin."

"We'll need them. Leryc didn't exaggerate in his reports. Myac appears to hold considerable status now. The imperial soldiers parted before him like water before the bow of a ship. We should be wary of him."

"Duly noted. I may have found what we need to deal with him, but that's a matter for later." He swung from the saddle, handing Tantrum's reins to a soldier. "Where are the others?"

Adran dismounted and followed them into the courtyard.

"We hid in the high valley until they left. After checking things over here, I sent the troops with Paulin and Eris to Lord Terral's manor."

He nodded approval. The manor would be the first gathering point for the heart of his army, and his cousin, Lord Terral, had long been an ally.

"I need a new commander." He glanced at Adran, who shook his head. No surprise there. He had turned away promotions before, preferring to stay in his current role at Yiloch's side, but he was only one of several solid options. "Consider yourself promoted, Commander Hax."

"My lord." She bowed. "You honor me."

"It's time to gather my army. Send word that we are marching out of Murvid in nine days. Everyone who can is to gather there. The rest should prepare to march to one of the other rendezvous points. Use soldiers from my retinue as messengers if you need them."

"Immediately, my lord." She turned and strode toward the stables, then stopped and spun back to face him. "Speaking of *your soldiers*, where is Cadmar?"

"I left him in Caithin. He will be guiding a troop of five hundred men and fifty healers to the southern rendezvous."

Hax's eyes lit with a spark of her usual ambition. "You got healers out of them?"

"It required some persuasion."

"Did we get a naval distraction?"

"We did."

Anger swelled in her eyes like a stormcloud about to burst. "Dalce was eager to go to war with you. I won't let him or you down."

"I know you won't." Her defiant tone and fresh anger over the loss of his second stoked his thirst for vengeance.

Hax spun and resumed her march to the stables. He watched her go. How would she measure up in the role Dalce held for so long? Adran continued to turn the position away and, because of the comfort he took from having his old friend at his side, he would never force him into the position. Hax had strength, determination, and leadership ability, but she didn't have the experience.

She will get it soon enough.

Adran flanked him into the stronghold. The invading force had touched very little. They came for a specific purpose and wasted no time on pointless destruction. The only act of senseless violence so far was the hanging of the heads by the gate, and that was Myac's handiwork. The adept had a reputation for brutality. Coming up empty-handed at the end of the long trek from the palace must have infuriated him. The opportunity to dishonor Yiloch's men and pay him back for that disappointment would have been too tempting to pass up.

In Yiloch's study, they found evidence of Dalce and Galen's deaths. Given the amount of blood, both men had died there.

I don't care how powerful Myac is, he will pay for this loss.

Adran stared at the bloodstained hole in the desk chair. "Your father obviously knows of your escape."

"My sympathies to whoever broke him the news. I suspect Myac left here with no more knowledge than he came with. Father knows I am free, but he doesn't know where I am or what I'm doing. Let that mystery drive him mad for a while." He smirked and traced the hole in the back of his chair with a finger. A sword blade made that hole, presumably Dalce's blade if they were dead before imperial soldiers reached them.

He looked at Adran. "We're going to stay a few hours to rest before we strike out for Murvid. Advise the soldiers to take advantage of the time."

"Consider it done."

After he left, Yiloch continued to his private rooms. Everything was as he had left it, with one unsettling exception. At the head of the bed, Dalce's sword stuck up like a grave marker, the blade shoved through his pillow and into the mattress. He approached the sinister display. Something was hanging around the hilt. A silver chain his brother had always worn, dangling a blue stone pendant engraved with their family crest.

Myac misjudged him if he sought to incite Yiloch's wrath over the death of his brother. He had shared his father's disdain for Delsan's weak disposition enough that he took Leryc under his wing in his brother's place. There wasn't enough love between them that he felt a need to mourn or seek vengeance for that loss. The sword was another matter. To have Dalce's sword used in an obvious threat against him insulted the man's memory, but he didn't dare remove it. Nothing Myac touched was worth the risk. If Ian solved the problem of the cages outside the gate, he would have him check this.

Turning his back on the sword and chain, he rummaged through his wardrobe, collecting various items he wanted. With a bundle of clothing in hand, he walked a few doors down to Adran's room. It would suffice for a brief rest before they moved on again. He set his things on a dresser inside the door.

Adran entered behind him. "This room looks strangely familiar, as if I might have been here before."

"It is the second nicest room in the stronghold, and there's no sword embedded in the pillow. I'm moving in for a few hours."

Adran grimaced. "The *something* Myac left you?"

Yiloch didn't answer. There had been enough talk of Myac for now.

"Do you mind if I also take my rest here?"

He shrugged. "It's your bed."

Hax bumped Adran into the room and stood in the doorway. "My lord."

"Yes."

"I sent riders out to our allies. I thought I would ride ahead to Murvid unless you need me here."

"Thank you, Hax." He took off his jacket and started unlacing his shirt. "It would be wise to ride ahead and warn Terral that we are coming."

Her eyes narrowed. She strode forward, her hand snaking out to snag the ring hanging around his neck and hold it up to the light. "This looks like a woman's ring."

Yiloch rubbed his forehead wearily. He had forgotten about the ring.

Adran glanced over and sighed theatrically. "Indeed, it

is. We lost his heart to a Caithin girl."

Yiloch glared at him.

Hax let the ring fall back against his chest and met his eyes. "You haven't fallen in love, have you?"

He scowled. "I don't have time for love."

"Since when did love care about time?" A weary smile tugged at the corners of her mouth. "Is she pretty?"

"For a woman." Adran grinned.

Yiloch exhaled and walked to the bed. The discussion was absurd, and he would have no further part in it. Without a word, he kicked off his boots, stripped off his sword belt, and reclined on the bed, closing his eyes to let them know he was ignoring them.

"A Caithin though?" Hax asked.

"Yes. A Caithin healer, no less." Adran used a suggestive tone meant to taunt him.

"I've got to give you credit, my lord, finding time to court a woman while arranging an alliance to destroy your father. That's talent."

He clenched his teeth when Hax laughed.

"Isn't it?"

The amusement in Adran's voice prompted him to open his eyes, glaring a warning at his old friend before turning his stony gaze on Hax. "I thought you were riding to Murvid."

"Indeed, my lord. I was merely catching up on court gossip." She winked and offered an exaggerated bow before turning to Adran. "Perhaps we can chat more in Murvid."

"I would love to." Adran gave her an exaggeratedly feminine wave.

"Oh. I almost forgot. Your armor is in Murvid. We took everything we could carry out before the attack." With that abrupt announcement, she left.

Adran flopped onto the bed next to him, still smirking.

"You don't believe the foolishness you were spouting, do

you?"

"Who knows you better than I do?"

Yiloch gave him a cross look. "What's that supposed to mean?"

Adran rolled over, putting his back to him.

With a shake of his head, Yiloch closed his eyes. At least they had found something to take their minds off recent losses for a short time. Too bad it wasn't something else.

* * *

Ian successfully deconstructed the created traps on the cages, and they buried the heads before departing. Upon his determination that Myac hadn't worked a trap into the display in Yiloch's rooms, Yiloch pocketed the pendant and wrapped the sword in a cloth that he strapped on his saddlebags.

He motioned Ian up beside him as they left the stronghold behind. "If you have the energy, an illusion to disguise at least myself and Adran would be useful. The fewer interruptions, the faster we get to Murvid."

Ian nodded, his gaze set on the path ahead. "I can handle it. Anything else, my lord?"

Yiloch watched the creator until Ian turned and met his eyes. "Thank you for working out the cages."

The youth bowed his head, muscles in his jaw jumping. "I had to. They deserved that much."

"They did." Yiloch faced forward, giving him privacy for his sorrow.

Ian stayed beside him this time instead of falling back with his cousin. Yiloch approved. The creator needed to be a partner more than a servant. With his skill in creation, the boy could be a valuable asset, but his timidity had driven Yiloch to dismiss him in the past. A mistake he would pay for through their lack of rapport in coming battles. He would do what he could to remedy that in the time they had.

* * *

They covered the last miles to the manor a few days later in a misty drizzle that soaked through their clothes. When they topped the last rise overlooking Terral's valley, Yiloch dreaded seeing an army in the making that would be obvious to any travelers. What he saw instead sent a spear of panic through him. They stopped at the top of the hill. The valley below, with its many outbuildings and massive manor house, was empty.

Yiloch opened his mouth to voice his alarm when Ian grinned. "Absolutely magnificent."

He suspected the comment wasn't born of an admiration for soggy farmland. "What is?"

"The illusion. I almost missed it. It's…" He trailed off before Yiloch's bewildered look. "Sorry, my lord. Here."

The young creator's brow furrowed, and Yiloch felt ascard around them changing. Suddenly the valley swarmed with people, tents poking up all over the muddied fields like some peculiar new crop. Despite the recompense he would owe Terral for damage done to his fields, Yiloch reveled in the scene. This was the start of his army. It would grow substantially before they moved on.

"Who created the illusion?"

Ian shook his head. Water dripped from his soaked hair. "I don't recognize the signature. It isn't strong, but it is well-masked. Any patrols riding by won't see anything unusual. If anyone rode down far enough to cross through it, I don't imagine they would ever ride out again."

A rider barreled towards them, bursting from the perimeter of the army with their horse stretched into full gallop. Yiloch grinned as she raced a mad dash up the hillside. The front soldiers backed their mounts out of the way. Eris reined her horse in at the last possible moment, skidding to a rough halt close enough that even Tantrum tossed his head, his hoof splatting on soaked ground in a stomp of irritation.

Adran shook his head at her reckless display, but Ian looked on in open admiration. The youth could find worse people to admire.

Eris gave Yiloch a measuring look. "It's about time you arrived. Ian, how was the trip?"

"Good. I—"

"And you two!" Eris cut him off, splitting a glare evenly between Yiloch and Adran. "You could have told me he was going with you."

"I do occasionally make decisions without consulting you," Yiloch stated.

Eris scowled, and Adran chuckled, earning another chastising glare from her.

"Is Ferin here?" Yiloch asked.

"Yes." She wiped a soggy strand of hair from her face. "His recruiting went well. Though he found no one as strong as our Ian." She added a proud smile for her cousin.

"I need to meet the recruits, but I must speak with Terral first. Adran, I want you with me. And Ian, I want your evaluation of Ferin's recruits."

A boyish grin cracked Ian's features. "Certainly, my lord."

Eris gave Yiloch an approving wink before turning her horse to accompany them.

How convenient that he could satisfy two captains by simply taking advantage of Ian's skills, and Ian's anxiety faded before his enthusiasm. It was working out better than he had expected.

When the retinue entered the valley through the veil of rain, soldiers began hailing Yiloch. By the time they reached the manor, a cry rose throughout the army amidst the banging of swords and shields, creating a thunderous roar. With the noise, the power of ascard rose around them. Though few of those soldiers had any notable ascard ability, the unified cry drew from their inner aspects, binding them together in their passion.

The horses danced into the courtyard amidst the racket. They dismounted and handed the animals over to a couple of stable hands. Yiloch turned to peer through the rain at his soldiers. They were here for him. It didn't matter if they believed in him or merely wanted anyone other than his father on the throne. What mattered was that they were here to follow him to war, and more were coming. The ascard energy generated by this display of unity would keep them loyal.

The doors to the manor house flew open, and Terral strode out, a long blue cloak with thick fur trim billowing behind him, his pale gold hair swept back long and loose like Yiloch's.

"I had some strange inkling you might have arrived, Cousin," Terral shouted with a wry glance at the men beyond the courtyard.

Yiloch returned a brief, partial embrace. "Well met, Lord Terral."

"Indeed! Come dry off. We can talk where it's not so deafening."

Yiloch nodded, but when Terral returned to the manor, he didn't follow. Standing in the rain, he listened to the din of his soldiers and smiled.

CHAPTER TWENTY-SEVEN

Indigo pulled on riding pants and a pair of tall boots. Her hands trembled as she put on a dark jacket over her simple laced shirt, then dragged the bundle she had packed a few days earlier out from under the bed. Caplin would arrive soon. They had kept her selection as one of his healers a secret from Andrea and Jayce. Now that the day of departure had come, she had only to escape Jayce without a fight.

She clutched the bundle to her chest, straining her ears for the sound of footsteps on the stairs. What she heard instead was familiar ones coming down the hall that froze her in place. The bedroom door swung open.

Jayce's gaze went straight to the bag. "What are you doing?"

She had no time left for games. "I'm one of the healers going with Caplin's force. We leave today."

"That's absurd." His mocking laugh faded when she didn't react, and he balled his hands into fists. "Why am I finding out about this now?"

Since Serivar had helped her improve her masking, she had taken to maintaining a constant connection to her inner aspect. She could respond instantly if he attacked.

"I thought you might try to stop me."

"You were right." He positioned himself in the doorway. "You're not going anywhere."

"Why don't we talk about this?"

He took a step closer. "It's a little late for that."

A rush of panic made her lightheaded, but she stood her ground. Reaching out with ascard, she borrowed from the flame of the bedside candle she had left burning. When he grabbed her arms, she transferred the borrowed flame to his palms.

He yanked his hands away with a yelp and backed several steps, holding them against his chest. "What did you do?"

Someone knocked on the front door.

"Come in," she called, her voice sounding shrill to her ears.

Jayce's lip rose in a snarl. He shifted his stance to glance toward the door, afraid to put his back to her. That must be like salt in a wound.

Caplin entered, and tension swelled. Jayce would suffer severe consequences if he assaulted the king's nephew, but she wasn't willing to test his self-control in the heat of the moment.

"Good morning, Jayce, Indigo," Caplin greeted, his tone soothing.

"Get out!"

Ignoring Jayce's demand, Caplin took another step. "I am afraid we haven't got time for this. We need to leave. Indigo?"

Jayce clenched his fists, winced, and unclenched them. Staring down at his burned palms, he pressed back against the wall.

"Go." He gestured brusquely towards the exit.

She drew upon ascard in the fire again and started past him.

"You will regret this."

Rage boiled in his eyes, and she trembled, from fear of killing him now as much as fear of him. He was flesh and blood, easily destroyed.

She met his eyes. "Possibly, Jayce, if I live that long."

Something shifted in his expression in recognition of the danger she might face. It wasn't concern, though. His callous sneer sent grief piercing through her chest, and the sting of tears caught her by surprise. She looked away, unwilling to give him the satisfaction of seeing her pain.

Caplin ushered her out and down the stairs to his carriage. Accepting a hand up, she settled onto the seat, and he sat across from her. When the carriage started moving, she exhaled a shaky breath.

"That could have gone worse," Caplin commented.

She bit her lip, fighting tears, and he moved over beside her, sliding an arm around her shoulders. The tears broke free, and she wept for a moment in the comfort of his embrace.

"I am sorry, Indigo."

"Don't be." She pulled free of him and sat back. "This was my choice."

"I don't know how you expect to go back after this."

She smoothed her shirt unnecessarily. "Let's survive going forward before we worry about going back."

His smile was warm and understanding. "A sound plan."

They rode in silence to where soldiers and healers gathered outside the city gates. She had never seen so many people in one place. Hundreds of soldiers milled about, the healers easily spotted among them. Those few not clustered together, seeking the familiarity of people they trained or worked with, she could pick out by the strength of their ascard connection.

They had paired up all the healers, giving them someone to work with and watch out for once fighting started. As the youngest, and as someone Serivar had a particular interest in, they had assigned her to Master Siddael, the senior healer in the group and the one who had tended her injuries after her return from Yiloch's prison.

The carriage pulled up next to Siddael, who smiled a

warm welcome when she stepped out. Yiloch's intimidating warrior, Cadmar, stood next to him, his nearly black skin making Siddael look like he had a dark tan by comparison. Cadmar stared at her, and she got the uncomfortable feeling he knew something about her relationship with his prince. She met his pale eyes and offered a polite nod.

"You can pack your things on Velvet." Caplin gestured to the black mare. "I thought you might appreciate having a familiar mount." He turned to Cadmar and switched to the Lyran trade dialect. "We are almost ready."

The big man replied in kind. "Prince Yiloch will be done with his war before we arrive."

Indigo laughed, and Caplin gave her a sharp look, undermined by the rogue smile tugging at the corners of his mouth.

Caplin turned back to Cadmar. "I'll be pleased to give you back to him as soon as possible." His cheerful tone made a light jest of the sentiment.

Within an hour, the company moved out, everyone on horseback to allow for better speed to Port Aaron. Because of the cost of transporting them, only a few of the animals would make the crossing. The remaining horses would return to Demin with the emptied supply wagons.

As they rode, Siddael quizzed the younger healers on triaging injuries in battle, stressing the importance of not over-extending their ascard ability for minor injuries. Less severe wounds they could tend without ascard until fighting ceased to allow for prompt treatment of more serious injuries.

By the time they set camp, her muscles ached from unaccustomed hours in the saddle, and her mind felt numb from Siddael's drilling. After eating, she sprawled wearily on her bedroll. Then a thought struck her, and she smiled. Out here, she didn't have to fear Jayce making demands of her. No matter what the bedroll lacked in comfort, it was hers alone.

* * *

Crippling stiffness the next morning from unfamiliar hours in the saddle came as a shock, but Indigo used a bit of healing to ease the pain going into another day of travel. Once the army was on the move again, Siddael initiated a discussion about mending broken bones.

She practiced while she listened, reaching out with ascard to touch methodically upon the inner aspect of each person and familiarize herself with their unique signature while paying close attention to see if anyone noticed the intrusion. Eventually she reached out further, seeking wildlife in the trees. She touched upon several birds, a family of rabbits, and a doe. Then she spotted Caplin working his way toward them through the ranks.

He guided his mount into step with hers. "Master Siddael."

"Lord Caplin, to what do we owe the pleasure of your company?"

"I had hoped to borrow Lady Indigo."

Siddael raised an inquisitive eyebrow. "As you have been charged with our protection, my lord, I will assume this interruption of her studies is in her best interest."

Caplin gave a wry smile. "I believe so. Thank you, Master Siddael."

Indigo followed him back up through the ranks, trying to ignore the suggestive looks they received from more than a few soldiers. Those who knew Caplin well were aware of their long-standing friendship, but that wouldn't stop rumors from spreading about the extra attention he was giving her. Seeing few alternatives, she smiled politely at anyone who met her eyes.

Caplin settled them into an easy pace near the front. "How are you holding up?"

She inhaled fresh air, thick with the fragrance of evergreens and wildflowers, and exhaled again before answering. "It seems like I should feel regretful or afraid, but I don't. I feel good. Better, in fact, the further we get from Demin. Is that wrong?"

"If it is, then I am also guilty." He rested his hands on the pommel of his saddle, appearing more at ease than she had seen him since he took his seat on the High Council. "No misgivings? You don't hate the discomfort of travel or have concerns about the coming conflict?"

"I have concerns, but dwelling on them won't change anything. As for discomfort, I am a healer. I can relieve my aches."

"Handy skill to have."

She grinned.

Caplin turned to the man riding on his left. "Deryk."

"Captain?"

"Continue to the meadow. I want to show Lady Indigo the viewpoint."

The man glanced at her, his expression guarded. "Yes, Captain."

Caplin, either oblivious to or undisturbed by the potential for gossip, turned to her. "Follow me."

They trotted their horses to where Cadmar rode. In Lyran, Caplin bade the warrior join them before steering his horse away from the column.

Cadmar smiled mysteriously at her and brought his mount over beside her. His presence would discourage rumors that would have resulted if they had gone off alone, but she still worried about what he might know of her relationship with Yiloch.

"How do you fare, Sir Cadmar?" She spoke to him in Lyran, since everyone else did.

"Cadmar, my lady. I claim no title. I will do better when

I am fighting with the prince."

Did he yearn to be there half as much as she did? "He must think highly of you to have given you this task."

Cadmar studied her, his unnerving pale eyes searching for something. She couldn't tell from his expression if he found what he was looking for before he faced forward again.

"Perhaps he believes I can protect that which is important to him, my lady."

She wanted to ask what he meant, but Caplin stopped some distance up the hill to wait for them. "You would think we were taking a stroll by the river at the pace you two travel."

A slow, roguish smile turned Cadmar's lips, and he glanced sideways at her. "Shall we catch up?"

It took a second to come to terms with the playfulness in the intimidating warrior's expression, but then a smile curved her lips. "We shall."

The horses danced in response to the changed mood and lunged forward together when they urged them on. Caplin's momentary wide-eyed surprise turned into a reckless grin, and he spun his mount, charging up the ridge ahead of them. Cadmar glanced at her as they raced after him, and the approval in his eyes gave her an absurd burst of pleasure.

Caplin finally slowed, and they walked the horses out onto a flat overlook where they could see down into a valley. At the near end, a waterfall cascaded down in several tiers, filling the air with its low rumble, its base shrouded in a cloud of mist. From there, a stream meandered across a meadow framed by towering trees and brightly spotted with cheery pink and yellow summer blooms, eventually passing under a rough timber bridge and on into the forest. Further out, beyond the distant tree line, the Gilded Strait blended seamlessly with the bright sky.

She smiled. "Beautiful."

Caplin turned to Cadmar with a challenging look. "Your

verdict?"

"It is beautiful, I give you that, Lord Caplin, but it is not Lyra."

Caplin laughed. "But it's beautiful."

They stayed there, each drifting with private thoughts, and gazed over the valley for a time. Leather creaked when the horses shifted, and the waterfall grumbled. A light breeze lifted Indigo's hair, sending a small shiver through her. The company began trickling into the valley below, and Caplin stirred, his movement unsettling the stillness.

"We should rejoin them." He turned his mount to depart.

Indigo followed him, and Cadmar came last with notable reluctance. He appeared to appreciate the beauty of the scenery more than he cared to admit.

They headed down at a swift walk, swinging around a blind corner in the path to surprise a black bear with two cubs. Indigo sucked in a startled gasp and jerked back on the reins. The mother bear rose on her hind legs and roared at them, making an impressive display of her large canines. Caplin's gelding reared and spun, crashing into Velvet. The mare squealed and staggered. Indigo swung off, fearful the animal would fall. Caplin rolled clear when his gelding went down, somehow keeping hold of the reins.

The bear belted out another roar, and Cadmar kicked his mount hard, lunging past them and drawing his sword. He let out a roar as impressive as the bear's and skidded to a stop a few feet shy of the startled animal, his sword raised in threat. The bear wheeled and chased her cubs into the trees.

Caplin got to his feet.

"Are you hurt?" Her voice shook.

"Dusty and bruised perhaps, but fine."

Cadmar dismounted, sword still drawn. "The mare is ruined."

She looked at him, seeing death in his eyes, then turned

to the mare. The animal held up one foreleg that bent along the cannon bone. Indigo grimaced, but put out a hand, stopping Cadmar with a touch. His intent, judging from the way he regarded the mare and hoisted his weapon, was to put the animal out of her misery. She didn't intend to let Velvet die today.

"Caplin, hold the other horses."

Caplin took Cadmar's reins without question while she pressed a hand to the trembling mare's forehead and drew on ascard. The mare relaxed and sank gracelessly down, rolling onto her side, her breathing becoming shallow and steady.

Indigo beckoned Cadmar with a wave of her hand. "Can you straighten the leg?"

Sheathing his sword, he knelt and took the injured leg in his hands. With unexpected care and skill, he felt the damage and manipulated the bones into place. The mare made small, heartrending sounds, but Indigo kept her too sedated to fight.

"Hold it steady." She set her hands upon the break.

Physical contact wasn't necessary anymore, but Caplin, who had watched healings before, would expect it. Drawing on more ascard, she checked the alignment of the bones then began mending the break and surrounding tissues. As with Yiloch in the prison, she had to heal more than she should in one session, but the mare would die if she couldn't continue. When the repair was strong enough, she moved back, waving Cadmar out of the way before relinquishing control of the mare.

The animal struggled to her feet, tentative and probably quite sore. Indigo exhaled, releasing tension built up through the process. She felt a hand on her shoulder and turned to see Caplin's worried face.

"Are you well?"

She nodded. "Just tired. We should lead her back."

"You can ride with me. Cadmar, can you lead the mare? I

need to make sure our weary healer doesn't fall off."

Cadmar eyed the healed leg with a thoughtful furrowing of his brow. "I see why the prince pressed so hard for healers."

Caplin mounted and gave Indigo a hand up behind him. She sagged against him, drained by so much healing after an entire morning spent practicing with ascard. She would have to remember not to waste energy like that once they entered a more hostile setting.

Siddael and Deryk fell upon them the instant they arrived, drawing a curious crowd.

"What happened?" Siddael gave Indigo a hand down, and she let him support most of her weight.

"A minor accident." Caplin dismounted and handed his reins to Deryk. "The mare broke a leg, but Indigo healed it."

Siddael handed her off to Caplin, who supported her with a gentle hand under her elbow, and walked over to the mare.

"Which leg?"

"Right front," Caplin answered.

Siddael laid his hands over the mended leg, inspecting her work. After a few minutes, he straightened and walked back to them.

"It's good. Another healing in the morning, and she might bear a light rider for short stretches, but Indigo will need a new mount."

Caplin nodded. "We'll take one from a supply wagon."

Cadmar stepped forward, his size and his deep voice commanding attention. "The wagons need those animals, and we need the wagons. I would offer mine instead. It is a good mount, and she has earned it. I can travel as swiftly on foot."

Caplin hesitated, and Indigo suspected he might be weighing the diplomacy of accepting the offer against their need for haste. She found the offer gratifying, not only because of who had made it, but because of the respect in his voice when he did so.

Caplin nodded. "We shall accept your gracious offer. Thank you, Cadmar."

Cadmar's eyes stayed on Indigo. "The offer was for her."

Her cheeks growing warm when they all looked at her, she inclined her head. "Thank you, Cadmar."

He returned the nod.

"It's settled then." Siddael placed a hand on her shoulder and turned her toward camp. "You need food and rest."

She leaned on him, exaggerating her exhaustion because he would expect it after such healing, not that she wasn't weary after using ascard all day. She needed to avoid drawing attention per her agreement with Serivar. However, limiting her ability to protect the headmaster's interests could force her to make hard choices when dealing with battle injuries. Did he honestly expect her to hide her strength when it might save someone's life?

"I hate to boost a student's ego too much, Indigo, but you saved that animal. The bones are nearly as good as new, and you tended to the surrounding tissue damage. Your work was thorough and attentive. You must be quite strong to have done that alone. I don't think you need my guidance as much as Lord Serivar implied, but I will enjoy watching you work."

The thrill of a master like Siddael recognizing and praising her healing ability made her giddy. After months of practicing skills she couldn't share, it felt wonderful to do something she could be openly proud of.

CHAPTER TWENTY-EIGHT

While Caplin oversaw the division of soldiers and supplies, Siddael split the healers among three mid-sized cargo ships to assist with seasickness and the calming of horses during the crossing. They had arrived at Port Aaron the previous evening. Loading and preparation stretched into morning because the small dock only accommodated one big cargo ship at a time. The crossing from Port Aaron would take between two and three days, depending on conditions in the strait.

Indigo stood at the bow of the third ship as they cast off. Already she found the wave motion pleasant, if disconcerting.

Cadmar had found a spot at the railing a few feet to her left.

Caplin came up on her right. "What do you think?"

"It's still an adventure to me. I've traveled very little. When we join the army, perhaps fear will outweigh novelty and freedom, but for now, I am content."

"It doesn't bother you knowing we're going to fight for the Blood Prince?"

She gazed out over the water. What did he want her to say?

"I'm sorry," he said, interrupting her silence. "I thought I should address the subject now. You did not seem to mind Prince Yiloch in person, but you had strong opinions about him prior to that. I need to know if that will be a problem."

"He wasn't..." she paused, struggling for the right words,

"the man I expected." Did Cadmar understand what they were saying?

"He was in a formal setting, striving to make a good impression. He may be different in war."

Cadmar stared ahead, showing no outward interest in their conversation.

She faced Caplin. "You sound wistful. Are you trying to prepare me or yourself?" His shoulders tightened. She had hit close to the mark. There was no need to push further. "I can assure you I have no expectations of Prince Yiloch. What he is like in this setting is of little importance. I made my choice. I am not here merely to escape an unpleasant situation. I'm here because I want to do this."

He held her gaze, his expression grave. "I'm glad to hear that. Whatever your reasons are for being here, don't get yourself hurt."

She pressed her lips together, taking a few seconds to rein in a burst of frustration. "I don't plan to, but let me worry about that. You have your own job to do."

He was opening his mouth to reply when someone called him. He acknowledged the summons with a wave. "You're right. Please excuse me."

He strode away, and she turned back to gaze at the water. The ship rocked with the waves as they picked up speed. A light spray misted the bow when it struck a larger wave. Indigo closed her eyes, letting the wind dry the dampness, leaving behind the sticky feel of salt on her skin.

"Do you go for him?" Cadmar asked in Lyran.

"You do speak Caithin, don't you?"

"I hear it. I do not speak it."

"Is that a personal choice?"

He didn't answer.

"You mean Prince Yiloch?" She wanted to see Yiloch and protect him, as foolish as that notion was. The prince had his own people for that. She also needed to escape Jayce, but she was looking for something else too. "I go to find myself, Cadmar. To see who I am."

Just as she started feeling foolish for saying it, he nodded, as though answering some unspoken question. She kept her eyes on the water, burning to know what he was thinking, but reluctant to ask.

"I wondered..." He hesitated, as if still working out what he wanted to say. "When Prince Yiloch risked the alliance for one night with a promised Caithin woman, I wondered at his actions." Her cheeks burned, and she stared hard at the swirling peak of the next swell. "He was quick to defend when Ian mentioned you. Now I think he may be more perceptive than the rest of us. For me, it has taken a few days of travel, but I see you are remarkable in many ways. I think it is that which drew him to you."

She felt stripped bare, as if he had peeled away all the layers of herself she couldn't seem to get through. It was the first time since the ship set sail that she felt at all nauseous. Gripping the railing, she used ascard to settle her stomach, her inward focus so intense that she jumped when he touched her hand, his skin like the night against the sunset of her lighter bronze. His hand stayed there, and her gaze traveled up his thickly muscled arm, rising to meet his bright eyes.

"My lady, I have much respect for Prince Yiloch. If you seek to find yourself, perhaps you should try looking through his eyes."

Her heart twisted in her chest. The sensitivity of this intimidating warrior amazed and moved her. She rested her free hand over his. "I can be nothing to him. You must know that."

He turned his hand—a hand strong enough to set the broken leg of a horse—and gave hers a gentle squeeze. "I know many things, Lady Indigo. That is not among them.

Perhaps what you say is true. If so, then maybe he can be something to you."

He released her hand and walked to the center of the ship. Her gaze followed him until she spotted Caplin, staring at her from where he now stood by the port railing, talking to one of his men. She looked away, using ascard to settle her nerves along with her stomach this time.

With a few simple words, Cadmar destroyed the careful wall she had constructed around her feelings for Yiloch. She didn't belong in his world, and he would never be part of hers, especially if he became emperor. She could play a part in helping him achieve that goal. Along the way, she hoped to find something within herself to negate her need for him and help her survive the life waiting for her in Caithin.

"How do you do that?"

She glanced at Caplin when he leaned against the rail beside her. "Do what?"

"You captured Prince Yiloch's interest at the feast as if you were the only woman in the room, and his captain took to you like an old friend. Today I leave you alone for a few minutes, and you turn an imposing warrior with the cozy disposition of a double-bladed axe into an adoring puppy. Have you considered going into politics?"

What would he say if he knew how it all started? "You exaggerate. Besides, Cadmar's far more sensitive than you give him credit for. A lot of men behave differently around a woman."

"Indeed, especially an attractive one." He ignored her look of warning. "But unless they know the woman well, all that usually involves is a lot of flattery and meaningless words. They actually talk to you. Why is that?"

"I don't know, Caplin. Why do *you* talk to me?"

The affection in his smile made her wish she hadn't asked. "I don't know. You're not like the courtiers and other high-born ladies I'm usually around. You accept people for who they are and are not so wrapped up in what a woman of breeding is supposed to be that you need to hide who you are behind gossip and fancy clothes. Nor are you so obsessed with being a healer that you can't enjoy an occasional lapse into the frivolity of being a noble lady. I find you to be an enchanting, well-balanced woman."

She turned away, unable to stomach his fond regard in combination with flattery. "I don't feel well-balanced."

"That's the waves." His teasing remark sparked off light laughter that broke the tension. "Besides," he said with a wink, "conversation is always better when there's a pleasant view."

"Caplin!"

"You wouldn't show yourself off if you didn't want to be noticed."

She tried to look angry and failed. "Honestly. I'm not about to wear canvas robes because you vultures can't manage your appetites."

He smiled, but his expression turned serious. "Do be cautious. You are a lovely woman, and we will soon be surrounded by foreign soldiers."

"I'm not overly concerned. There are women soldiers in the Lyran army, and I left my summer dresses at home. Besides, I don't think it's the soldiers I need to worry about."

He gave her a curious look that she pretended not to notice. Sometime while they were talking, the sun had gone down, its warm glow fading on the horizon.

Had the sunset been beautiful?

A yawn snuck up on her, and she covered her mouth. "I think it may be time to get some rest. Goodnight, Caplin."

"Sleep well, Indigo."

* * *

Morning brought heavy rain and rough waves. She stayed below deck through the early hours, providing aid to those who needed it in the turbulent water, herself included. As afternoon approached, she traded with another healer and went above to brave the rain for the sake of fresh air. Finding a lonely spot at the bow, she peered out, hoping to see some sign of the distant shore, but the heavy downpour obscured everything. Holding the railing, she let the spray from the water hit her. The rain had already soaked her through, and it helped rinse away some of the smells and grime of traveling.

She stayed there for a while, focusing on the simple act of balancing. Eventually, she reached out with her inner aspect and ran a tendril of energy away from the ship, using ascard in the water to extend her reach. When it came down to it, she wasn't sure which direction to search, so she pulled back without finding dry land.

By dark, the sea settled, and the rain stopped. In dire need of rest and drying off, she went below deck and changed into something dry behind the relative privacy of a screened-off corner, then retired to her sleeping roll in the stuffy, crowded sleeping quarters.

She woke up early from a restless slumber, packed her things into her sleeping roll, and took it with her so she wouldn't have to go back below deck. The washed-out light of early dawn revealed a crew busy unloading supplies into rowboats. They anchored outside a flat, sandy harbor in front of the walled village of Issaoula. The dock could barely accommodate one large vessel at a time for unloading horses. To speed things along, two of the ships had anchored in the harbor, and smaller rowboats were ferrying people and supplies to shore while waiting their turn to unload horses.

"Lady Indigo."

"Good morning, Caplin."

"Good morning." He gave her a tired smile. "Cadmar and I are going ashore on the next boat. If you're ready," he nodded to her bundle, "you can join us."

She glanced toward shore. The sky was clear. Morning light fell on a rough volcanic beach north of the port. The black, rocky landscape around that edge of the city reminded her of the prison and of Yiloch.

Yiloch.

Hopeless longing raked through her, sapping pleasure from her more pleasant memories of him. No matter how close she got to him, they would remain worlds apart. He was a Lyran prince, and she an engaged Caithin healer who, supposedly, only knew him from their encounter at the feast in Demin.

The city wall extended out on the volcanic rock, a deep red stone rising over black basalt. South of town, a rugged high desert stretched out as far as she could see. To the north, she could see the distant outline of hills and far-off mountains.

She nodded north. "That's where we're going?"

"Yes. Our route will take us north and east from Issaoula toward the mountains and then west toward the capital. Cadmar says the rendezvous is about a day and a half away. He was kind enough to add that it might take three or more days at our speeds."

She coaxed a reluctant smile to her lips. "I will go ashore. I've had enough of ships for now."

"Come along then."

Climbing down into the rowboat on a rope ladder draped over the side of the rocking ship required considerable fortitude, and her hands shook, making the process more difficult than it needed to be. The little boat itself felt tiny next to the merchant ship, but steady enough when she took a seat. Cadmar followed her down and sat alongside her, forcing Caplin to take another bench when he joined them.

She greeted the Kudaness warrior in Lyran, letting him keep his secret.

"Good morning, Lady Indigo. You look tired."

The concern in his voice compelled her to look up at him. The hissing snake head pommel of his sword hovered ominously over one shoulder, absurdly contrasted by the concern in his eyes. She swallowed a laugh and stared forward.

"I am well. I found the hold somewhat hard to sleep in."

"I do not know that you will find sleeping on the ground much better."

"You don't think I should be here, do you?" The big man shifted, rocking the boat with his weight. "I appreciate your concern, but I am a healer. I can manage."

"You are right, my lady. I worry more that those who care for you will not focus on their own safety with you there."

She resisted the urge to look back at Caplin, who would be listening to their conversation. Since he wasn't privy to the extent of her relationship with Yiloch, might he think he was the subject of Cadmar's concern? Would he be wrong if he did?

"I don't believe anyone among us would put themselves or anyone else at risk for my sake. My task is to aid, not hinder, and I intend to succeed at that."

Cadmar nodded as the little boat rolled over small waves toward shore, a different sensation when sitting that low in the water. Then a slow smile meandered across his face. "I believe you will succeed, my lady."

"You are welcome to call me Indigo."

He met her eyes and shook his head. "I do not think so, my lady, but I thank you for offering."

CHAPTER TWENTY-NINE

Yiloch's army left the manor at about seven-hundred and fifty strong with cavalry, foot soldiers, archers, and ascard users. Supplies sent out ahead of time via land and river to strategic points along their route enabled lighter and faster travel. More allied forces with additional supply wagons met them at the southern camp, where they would wait for the rest of the troops, including the force from Caithin.

En route, they had captured eleven imperial scouts, most surrendering quickly and all but one short-lived individual willing to swear allegiance to Yiloch. One of the allied troops absorbed a rogue unit of imperial soldiers on their way to the rendezvous. Three imperial adepts they encountered presented too much risk not to kill outright.

At this camp, they arranged two large tents for healers near Yiloch's private tent and set up similar private quarters for Lord Caplin. The gesture would strengthen their relationship, something that could only be beneficial in the days to come.

Standing on a rise with Adran, Hax, Ferin, and Ian, overlooking his army, what Yiloch saw pleased him. Once the Caithin force arrived, they would have a day or two to rest and go over plans. The Caithin ships had to attack Yiroth on the same day his army arrived. A force this large would never reach the capital undetected, but the seaward attack would provide substantial distraction. The faster they moved in on the heels of that attack, the more advantage it would give them.

A strange sensation startled him, like a caress against his inner aspect. He started erecting a defensive barrier, then recognized her ascard signature and stopped, dissolving the half-formed barrier to welcome her unexpected and intimate touch.

"They are almost here."

"How do you know?" Adran asked.

Yiloch glanced at Ian. "Can you not sense her?"

The young creator's brow furrowed, his focus turning inward for a second. He finally shook his head. "I can sense a large number of adepts and soldiers approaching, but no, I don't sense her."

Yiloch smiled. Her skill had grown, and the gentle touch had been for him alone. "She's there." He turned his attention to the roadway coming over the hill.

"You can't hide a connection that strong," Ian objected.

"We shall see."

Hax nudged Adran. "Is this *the* she?"

Adran sighed and nodded, impervious to Yiloch's warning glance.

The beat of hooves and feet on the ground, along with the soft creaking of leather tack and wagon wheels, reached them. Then a lone rider came into view and hailed them, waving a Caithin standard. Yiloch's sentries hailed the rider in return, and he vanished back over the hill. Moments later, the front line came into view—four mounted soldiers bearing Caithin standards. Behind them rode Caplin with several soldiers riding to his left. Off to his right rode a dark-skinned man with no visible weapons, probably the head of the healers, and beside him rode a familiar figure.

Yiloch's pulse quickened at the mere sight of her. Even many days of travel couldn't diminish her beauty in his eyes.

She glanced up once, and a small smile curved her lips. Then she leaned over to Cadmar, who walked alongside her. The dark warrior touched her hand, saying something while he made a wide, sweeping gesture with the other arm.

Hax stiffened. "Is your *she* the one flirting with my warrior?"

"She's the one he's talking to, yes," Adran answered. "I wouldn't read much into it."

Ian was squinting at the front of the army, his mouth hanging open. "That's impossible. You can't hide a connection that strong."

Yiloch answered with a smug grin. "Perhaps you can if you have a connection that strong."

Ian chewed at his lip, then asked, "That actually pleases you, doesn't it?"

Yiloch watched the rest of the wide column marching over the hill. "It does."

"It disturbs me." Ian continued to stare at Indigo, where she chatted amiably with Cadmar as they approached.

"It disturbs me to see Cadmar prattling on like that," Hax muttered.

The column stopped. Caplin, Cadmar, the dark-skinned healer, and another soldier continued forward. Yiloch forced his attention to the approaching men. Caplin, the soldier, and the healer reined in their mounts a few yards away and dismounted while Cadmar closed the distance. He bowed to Yiloch.

"You have done well, Cadmar. Thank you."

"It was my honor to serve."

Cadmar stepped around to flank Hax as the other three walked up.

"Prince Yiloch." Caplin bowed, the two men next to him mirroring the gesture.

"Lord Caplin." He reciprocated with a respectful nod.

"This is Master Siddael. He leads our healers." The dark man nodded politely. "And this is Captain Deryk, my second." The grizzled soldier gave a gruff nod.

"You are all welcome. Lord Caplin, you know Captain Adran and Ian. This is my second, Commander Hax." Hax's nod matched Deryk's in gruffness. "And this is Adept Captain Ferin, who heads my ascard users." Ferin nodded with deliberate grace, while all three eyed him warily. "Captain Paulin and Captain Eris will join us with additional troops over the next two days. We have tents set up for your healers and space around them for your soldiers to set camp. Captain Adran, Commander Hax, help Master Siddael and Captain Deryk settle their units. I wish to speak with Lord Caplin."

Caplin nodded to Siddael and Deryk, dismissing them, and Yiloch guided him out of earshot of the others.

"Did you encounter any trouble on your journey?"

"Nothing of note."

"I see you got Lady Indigo out of her situation."

Caplin glanced over his shoulder. "I only hope I didn't bring her into a worse one."

"I think you underestimate her."

Caplin gave him a terse look. "I know I do. How are things coming together?"

"Very well. I expect a major disaster any second."

Caplin glanced at him, and upon seeing his smirk, chuckled. "You don't strike me as the type to nurture doubts."

Yiloch grinned, easing back into the comfort of the young lord's disposition. "Perhaps arrogance becomes me, but the more complex a system, the more opportunities there are for it to fail. I would be glad to have your fresh, capable eyes look over our strategies."

Caplin flushed. "You honor me, Prince Yiloch."

Dismissing the other man's modesty, he gestured to the private tent he had arranged for Caplin. "That tent is yours.

You're welcome to settle in first if you prefer."

"You are most gracious, but I would rather familiarize myself with the situation before I worry about comfort."

Approving of the choice, Yiloch angled their course toward his own tent. When they entered, Terral was lounging in one chair. He rose with the elegance of one accustomed to luxury, regarding Caplin with open curiosity.

"Lord Terral, this is Lord Caplin, captain of our Caithin force."

Terral arched an eyebrow. "We have a Caithin force?"

"Yes. I'm certain you can understand why it was necessary to keep it quiet. Terral is my cousin," he added to Caplin, knowing Terral would point it out if he didn't.

"A pleasure, Lord Terral," Caplin greeted.

"Likewise, Lord Caplin."

Yiloch ignored his cousin's irritated look. "Come. Let us see what holes you can find in my plans."

Caplin grinned, accepting the challenge.

* * *

Indigo had touched Yiloch with her ability simply to see how he would react. His response made her giddy. He had started blocking her, then stopped, allowing and welcoming the contact. As Caplin warned, there might be sides of Yiloch he showed in war that she wouldn't like, but that didn't make him a different man.

The woman, Commander Hax, led Captain Deryk off to settle his soldiers, with Cadmar flanking her closely, his bearing conveying more devotion than obedience. That and the warning scowl the woman gave her suggested some depth to their relationship.

She turned her attention back to Adran, who was pointing things out to Siddael as they walked. Being Siddael's partner had unforeseen benefits. She traveled on horseback for much of the journey because he did, and now she got to follow along while Adran showed him around.

"We arranged these tents to provide privacy for your healers." Adran indicated two large tents with a sweep of his hand. "We are grateful to have them here. If there is anything they need, please don't hesitate to ask."

Siddael took it in with his usual calm. "Thank you, Lord Adran. How long do we expect to stay at this camp?"

"Another day, two at most. We are waiting for a few more troops."

"Very good. I will see to my healers now."

"When you are situated, there is food and drink available." Adran gestured to the cooking wagons, then turned to her. "Lady Indigo, it's a pleasure to see you again. How are you?"

Siddael gave her a puzzled glance.

"I am well, Lord Adran. And you?"

"Well enough. Prince Yiloch is in a fine mood now that things are progressing. That makes my life easier."

"He should be happy. He has us." She meant it in a broader sense, to encompass the healers and Caithin's soldiers, but also in a more personal sense for the two of them.

Adran's open smile let her know he caught both. "That he does. I will leave you to settle in." He nodded to them both.

She met Siddael's inquiring look as Adran walked away. "We talked for a while at the feast in Demin."

"I see." He said nothing more as he led the way back to the waiting healers.

When they finished getting set up in the tents, they went to get food and drink. The healers clustered together on a knoll near where they had entered the broad valley, with Caithin soldiers maintaining a casual buffer between them and the Lyran force. A precaution that was probably unnecessary, but not unexpected. Prejudice ran deep, and Caithin soldiers took their responsibility to protect the healers seriously.

Indigo sat apart to look over her new environment. There were soldiers, horses, and tents as far as she could see. So many people moving about the valley, along with their mounts and an array of cooks, blacksmiths, and other support units, made for an intimidating sight. Intimidating and fascinating.

She reached her ability out to touch Yiloch, where he now stood near his tent with several of his officers, figuring he wouldn't react violently if her masking was insufficient. When he didn't react to her guarded approach, she tried Ian. The stronger the subject, the stronger her masking had to be to avoid detection, a lesson she learned at the feast. This time the young creator, despite his considerable strength, didn't respond to her touch. Satisfied, she sent out seeking tendrils to discover the other ascard users in the army.

A methodical search found hundreds of adepts of varying strengths and a smattering of creators, all weaker than Ian. As she pulled back the seeking tendrils, an almost imperceptible ripple in ascard caught her attention. Closing in on it, she singled out a man at one of the tables, dressed in soldier's attire, with a complex barrier worked around his inner aspect designed to hide it completely.

Faintly aware of sweat forming on her palms, she sank into his barrier with a delicate tendril of ascard, layering masking as she went to blend it with the ascard of the barrier itself. When she broke through, he still showed no sign that he noticed her invasion. His strength, while not the equal of Ian's, was still substantial, turning her meal into a heavy lump of dread in her stomach. She eased out, then studied his appearance.

He looked like any other soldier. Why was he hiding his

ability?

Yiloch stood talking with Adran, Hax, and Ian. It wasn't appropriate to approach him directly given the difference in their stations, but he needed to know. Taking a deep breath, she got up and started toward him. About halfway there, she saw Caplin, currently talking with Siddael on the far side of one of the healers' tents, look up at where she had been sitting and tense. He scanned around until he spotted her. She ignored his puzzled expression and quickened her pace.

"Prince Yiloch, pardon my interruption." She bowed her head when they faced her. Her nerves danced.

What if she were wrong, and he knew about the adept? Perhaps he intended to keep the man a secret.

"What is it, Lady Indigo?" Yiloch asked, his regard impartial.

They had never interacted in such an environment. He didn't know what to expect of her any more than she did of him. She hoped she wasn't about to make a fool of herself.

"Who is that man?" She didn't turn or make any gestures toward the individual in question. "The one sitting at the far end of the third table on the right."

Noting her caution, Yiloch discreetly scanned the tables, then deferred to Adran with a glance.

"Ladon," Adran offered. "An imperial scout we picked up near Murvid."

"He's no scout," she asserted, clasping her hands to hide their shaking.

Yiloch's eyes narrowed. "What do you mean?"

"He's an adept. He has a barrier up."

Yiloch's nostrils flared, the hatred blazing to life in his eyes chilling her, but he believed her, and that was heartening.

"You're certain?"

She nodded.

He stepped closer, lowering his voice. "Can you take the barrier down?"

"I think so, but he might retaliate. I'm not sure I can take down the barrier and block him."

Holding her with his icy gaze, he said, "Ian, if she takes the barrier down, can you block him?"

Ian met her eyes, then shuddered and glanced away. He was afraid of her. The realization was a stab at her heart.

"I could... if I rode in on her power." His cheeks flushed bright as if he had suggested they have intimate relations. "Your masking is astounding, my lady." He glanced in her direction, not quite looking at her. "Do you think you could mask both of us?"

His compliment eased a little of the pain his fear had caused. It would be challenging to destroy the man's barrier while masking both of their abilities, but she had to try. "Yes."

She felt Yiloch and Ian both connect to the ascard.

Yiloch turned to his commander. "Let Hax get his attention first. I want him away from the tables. Then take the barrier down. Hax, lure him into an open spot and be ready to move clear."

The stern woman nodded and stalked toward the tables. Yiloch stepped away from them and drew his sword.

Indigo watched Hax out of the corner of her eye. At the same time, she reached out with the ascard and found Ian. Wrapping a tendril of ascard into his inner aspect, she drew his power with her, feeling a moment of resistance before he relinquished control. Hax approached the man and engaged him in conversation, leading him a few feet away from the table.

Indigo slipped inside his barrier again, finding it easier the second time, and drew Ian in with her, blending their presence with the barrier. She found the man's inner link to it and with a quick, decisive strike, severed it. The barrier shattered like so much thin glass, and his face contorted in sudden panic. She detected something beneath the barrier as it burst, a link with someone else's signature upon it. Then Ian rode up on the wave of her attack and slammed a block around his inner aspect.

In the same instant, Yiloch vanished, and Indigo gasped in surprise. He reappeared in front of the adept, swinging his sword in an arc through the man's chest. Before he could even fall, Yiloch swept the blade back again, slicing through the man's neck and severing his head. Blood sprayed across the grass, and the body hit the ground as nearby soldiers leapt back in alarm, several drawing weapons.

Yiloch turned to Hax and said something, making a quick gesture toward the body, then he strode back to them. Hax started barking orders. Soldiers jumped to do her bidding, cleaning up the mess.

Indigo's heart pounded in her chest, memories of the Watchman beheading Hadris bombarding her. Yiloch had executed the man with the same cold efficiency. Worse yet, she had played a part in facilitating his death.

"You were right." Ian stood by her left shoulder, his voice full of wonder. "Amazing. I didn't sense anything until you broke through."

A hand rested on her other shoulder. It was Adran. "Excellent work. You have good instincts."

She trembled under his touch, and he gave her shoulder a reassuring squeeze. "Is he always that…"

"Decisive? Frightening?"

She nodded.

"Usually, yes."

Yiloch was almost back to them. Caplin was also hurrying their way. Something in Yiloch's eyes gave her pause—a feverish glint, no doubt ignited by the thrill of conflict. Her gaze drifted to the blood on his sword. Biting the inside of her lip, she forced herself to step up and intercept him, knowing she only had a few seconds before Caplin reached them.

"Someone was watching him," she whispered.

"With ascard?"

"Yes. It was faint, but I noticed a link to someone else in him."

"Could you recognize the signature of that link if you encountered it again?"

"Yes," she said with more confidence than she felt. She might doubt herself, but she didn't want him to doubt her.

"Good. Stay alert for it."

Caplin stormed up next to them. "What was that?" His eyes locked on Indigo for a tense second before jumping to Yiloch.

Yiloch met his glare, irritation sparking in his eyes. "Lady Indigo noticed something strange about one of the imperial scouts we took in."

Don't tell him what I did. She touched his inner aspect, trying to convey her fear in the hope that he would understand.

He paused for a second, then said, "Ian investigated and discovered he was an adept. I didn't want to alarm anyone, but you can't take that kind of power lightly when it is being used against you."

"You alarmed plenty. My soldiers aren't used to adepts and creators running rampant."

Yiloch's hand tightened on his sword. "They had best get used to the idea before we go to war then, hadn't they?"

Caplin opened his mouth to speak, then hesitated, glancing at Indigo. The brief look told her his anger had more to do with concern for her than what Yiloch had done. "You're right, Prince Yiloch. Though that wasn't how I would have preferred to approach the problem."

"Understandable." Yiloch turned to her, and she bowed

her head, finding it hard to meet his eyes while that killing spark still burned in them. "Thank you."

"Yes, Prince Yiloch," she said, staring at his feet.

She felt a small warmth within, meant to comfort her. Yiloch turned away when she glanced up, but she recognized his signature. The maneuver of transporting himself with ascard the way he had must have exhausted him, and the gesture was sweeter for that reason. With the gentlest of touches, she used ascard to push his offered support away. He didn't need to waste his strength.

He strode to his tent without another word for any of them, nothing in his movement betraying their silent exchange. Following his example, she turned and walked toward the healer tents, the knot in her gut uncoiling when Caplin didn't follow.

As dusk crept in, she lay awake on her cot, tired and troubled. Yiloch was a killer, cold and efficient, but she wanted him no less for it. That she had helped take a man's life and felt more pride at having aided Yiloch than she did revulsion at the violent death, disturbed her.

When she tried to sleep, her thoughts lingered on the link she detected in the adept. Such a link would allow her to watch over Yiloch when fighting began.

She reached out with ascard, finding him easily. Using what she had found in the adept as a model, she probed into his inner aspect and linked the smallest tendril of her ability to him. That fraction of her ability would be unavailable for anything else, but it seemed a reasonable sacrifice. She withdrew then and closed her eyes. The link provided a comforting awareness of him, as if he held her in his arms again. She embraced the sensation and drifted to sleep.

CHAPTER THIRTY

Myac stumbled into the wall when a sharp pain tore through him, originating at his core and riding his nerves out to his extremities before vanishing. It only took seconds, but it left him breathless.

Ladon was dead. The agony of that abrupt separation caught him by surprise. He had never attempted such a link before. That he felt the ending of that connection so acutely suggested Ladon was close. Not close enough for Myac to have sensed him, but close enough that the sudden severing of the link had a potent backlash.

What might have happened if Ladon had been even closer at the moment of his death? He shuddered again at the thought. He would be more circumspect with such applications in the future.

Myac pushed away from the wall and continued to Rylan's private chambers.

The emperor sent out a call for troops the day after he returned from Yiloch's stronghold. Too little effort, too late in the game. Rylan had long known his son was building an army, but he refused to take the threat seriously. Yiloch, however, was taking the matter quite seriously. If Myac's sources were accurate, the prince had captured the loyalty of many of Rylan's lords and persuaded several others to adopt a neutral stance until things resolved.

It made no sense. Rylan embraced the false immortality Myac offered him. Yet, despite that apparent desire to live forever, he undermined his own position at every turn as if he didn't care to keep his throne. Did the emperor want his son to defeat him? Perhaps to satisfy some twisted need to have the strength of his bloodline confirmed. Did he think the prince would let him live? He couldn't be that foolish.

Myac stopped outside the tall, arched double doors leading into the emperor's chambers. Carved from pale wood and inlaid with silver in a delicate branching pattern that extended from the floor to the peak of the arch, they were as refined as the men and women who had lived behind them.

One guard stepped forward to open a door for him, inclining his head as he passed through. Myac stopped inside, and the door clicked shut behind him. The scents of roses, wine, and sex met his nose. The emperor was alone, but he hadn't been so for long.

Created crystal windows made up most of one wall, letting soft evening light shine in through sheer silver curtains. Lounging upon a chaise in that silvery light, Rylan looked like a marble statue.

Myac took a seat near where the emperor lounged and set his booted feet on a created crystal and silver table. When Rylan didn't speak, Myac closed his eyes and leaned back, losing himself in the flow of ascard as he swept it through the emperor. With meticulous detail, he invaded Rylan's body, using power to refresh flesh and bone. The process wasn't without a certain measure of pain, he knew, for he had used it on himself a few times, but Rylan maintained his composure. The only expression of discomfort was a small exhale when Myac stopped. Silence reigned for a while longer. The sun sank, and an attendant entered to light candles around the chamber.

Myac watched the candlelight reflect off the crystal windows and dance across the emperor's fine, chiseled features. "I believe Yiloch may be within a few days of the city."

"I would like to stop this battle before it starts, Myac," Rylan said as if commenting on the color of the sky.

Myac carefully considered his response. It didn't matter a great deal to him whether Yiloch or his father died in the coming conflict. He played this game with a mind to try any of several outcomes. He almost wanted Yiloch to win because it would be the more complicated ending and therefore more interesting. If Rylan won, however, there were fewer unknowns, so there was a sound argument there for striking Yiloch down fast.

"You know this land as well as he does, my lord. Where would you camp if you planned to lay siege to the city?"

A wistful smile touched the emperor's lips. Perhaps he recalled better days spent hunting with his family in the lands around the city. Days brought to an abrupt end upon the murder of his wife.

"By the river near Sendac or further west near Calif, depending on where he is moving supplies from," Rylan answered after a time.

"I can narrow it from there with a few carefully placed adepts."

"What are you thinking, Myac?" Rylan glanced at him for the first time since he entered the chambers.

"I think you know."

"Destroy my son, and it ends."

"Yes. Send a host against him. Seed it with strong creators and adepts and target him specifically. If he falls, his army will crumble."

"It must be a swift attack. Under cover of night or while they are setting up camp." Rylan tapped his fingers on one knee. "I need a mounted force that can move quickly and enough adepts to facilitate the isolation and destruction of my son."

Myac nodded. "I will send linked adepts out to sense

their approach. There should be enough range in a link to give us adequate warning." A chill swept through him with the memory of the pain from Ladon's death. Such links had their risks, but they were too useful to avoid.

"Do so and have Commander Nyak attend me in the War Room at dawn."

How nice it was to see Rylan taking an interest in finishing things. Serving a doomed man was hard to stomach, but maybe the emperor hadn't truly given up yet. Soon, Yiloch would have a little surprise coming to his camp.

* * *

Yiloch's sleep was restless that night. Indigo's display of power impressed and concerned him. Now more than ever, he saw that her ability could be a great asset, but the panic in her ascard touch earlier suggested that not even Lord Caplin knew what she could do. Trusting his instincts, he remained discreet when discussing the event with the Caithin captain and those of his own host who weren't already aware of her strength.

He needed her. Ladon went undetected for too long, and learning that someone was tracking the man remotely made her value obvious. He needed to speak with her alone.

Awake already, he went out to greet the force that rode in shortly after midnight before the sentry could notify him of their arrival. Eris accompanied Lord Vyram's host of one hundred and fifty heavy cavalry, five hundred and thirteen mounted archers, and another six hundred and ninety-eight foot soldiers. Vyram also brought two personal creators and an adept of notable strength. His reputation as a successful campaigner gave him substantial pull when he needed to recruit. The size of his force quieted some of Yiloch's frustration. Now they were only waiting for Paulin with Lord

Wallard's host.

Eris, in her typical restless fashion, rode back out after a few hours of sleep to meet up with Paulin and Lord Wallard. Once Vyram's host had settled, Yiloch slept for a time, but he rose again before dawn and walked out into the crisp morning air to ponder the dilemma of Indigo.

Walking around Vyram's newly erected tent, he started toward the gradual slope that rose behind the valley where his army gathered. He wasn't the first to seek that vantage point. Indigo stood there, staring out over his army. Delighted by his luck, he walked over to join her, stepping up next to her shoulder. She didn't react. Was her intention to remind him of the night of the feast? Recalling how she had welcomed his touch inflamed his desire, but he forced it to the background.

"What do you think of Lyra?"

She scanned the army in the pale gray light of predawn. "It's depressing."

"You're looking at it wrong." He took her hand. "Come with me."

She stood her ground as if she meant to refuse, but he kept a light hold and met her eyes. She searched his face as she had that first night in the prison, then nodded, allowing him to lead her to the top of the grassy hill.

"Wait," he murmured.

She did so, standing silent while the rising sun broke over the magnificent, rugged peaks of the Leras Mountains. It cast its brilliant light on the valley, illuminating the hilltop where they stood and moving down the other side, gradually lighting colorful wildflowers and golden grasses that blanketed the land. Her breath caught when the warm light washed over the landscape and a flock of songbirds took flight. The whisper of thousands of wings through the air mimicked the rushing sound of a light wind as they flew over.

It was beautiful, but not as beautiful as the woman next

to him, travel-worn, with her bronze skin tinted gold in the light and blue eyes shining with wonder. He placed a hand on her far shoulder so she wouldn't move away and leaned close to her ear.

"Look there." He pointed toward the far end of the meadow, near the tree line.

Several small spotted deer emerged from the trees, peering around as they stepped into the clearing on long, delicate legs. Facing those awesome granite peaks looming above the fragile nature of the meadow, the reality of the army behind them fell away. Standing on the hill, there was only the stunning landscape before him and her beside him. He became more aware of his hand on her shoulder and the delicious scent of her.

"You're right," she murmured. "I was looking at it wrong. Lyra is beautiful."

She looked up at him with those vivid eyes, a soft smile curving her lips. He longed to kiss her then, but he reminded himself where they were and how many people were there with them. Glancing back toward camp, he spotted Adran and Caplin standing near Vyram's tent now, watching them. Caplin appeared ready to kill something. Adran just looked resigned.

Indigo followed his gaze. "I believe we are drawing a crowd." Despite the caution in her tone, her attention drifted back out over the meadow to the deer.

He swept his arm out to encompass the scene. "This is all part of where I grew up. It is my home. I used to hunt these lands with Adran and his sister, Eris, when we were all much younger. I love it here."

"Thank you for helping me see it."

He removed his hand from her shoulder, but she made no move to leave, perhaps sensing that he had more to say.

Lowering his voice, he said, "I need your help, Indigo.

Your ability surpasses that of anyone else in this army."

"They don't know what I can do, and they aren't supposed to." She began picking at the nails of one hand with those of the other, and he grinned at the familiar nervous habit. He touched her hand, and she stopped, clasping them in front of her to keep them still as she had in the prison.

"Why can't they know?"

She bit her lower lip and gave him a pleading look. "It's complicated. Please understand. I'm not supposed to use my ability for anything other than healing while I'm here."

"I am trying to understand. All I need is for you to be attentive to threats from other ascard users. Any creators or adepts catching us unaware could devastate our ranks. Can you let me know if you sense anything? Even just a touch similar to how you let me know you arrived yesterday, but perhaps a little less... sensual."

She smiled, her cheeks flushing. "I could do that."

"You will help me then?"

A storm of torment filled her deep blue eyes when she looked at him. "How could I do otherwise?" She didn't let him respond to the curious question. "If you want me near when we're marching, ask Master Siddael to ride with you. I'm partnered with him, so I go where he goes."

"Thank you." He hoped the depth of his gratitude came through in his tone.

She nodded, and they turned in unison back to the camp.

"I think they're jealous," he commented as they started down the hill.

"Adran loves you, doesn't he?" A touch of startled revelation lifted her tone.

"Yes, and Caplin loves you." She gave him a sour look that he shrugged off. "You must have noticed."

"I hoped I was wrong. My relationships are confusing enough without adding that complication. But if you noticed it, I suppose it must be true. Cadmar told me you see things more clearly than most."

"Did he?" It surprised him to hear praise from the big warrior.

"He thinks highly of you."

"Did you two spend a lot of time chatting about me?"

"Yes." She gave him a coy glance. "Jealous?"

"And flattered," he said under his breath now that they had almost reached the others. "Good morning, Lord Caplin. Captain Adran. I hope the arrival of Lord Vyram's contingent didn't interrupt your sleep."

"Not at all." Tension put an edge in Caplin's voice. His eyes locked onto Indigo.

Adran gave Yiloch a warning look. He didn't need to ask what it meant. He had built up a decent camaraderie with the Caithin lord, and indulging his relationship with Indigo jeopardized that.

"Please excuse me, my lords. I must speak with Master Siddael." Indigo gave each of them a polite nod.

He admired her outward composure as she strode away. Already she had proven herself an exceptional woman, and he got the disturbing sense he was only scratching the surface.

A rider came charging out of the trees then. A fond smile curved Adran's lips as his sister catapulted towards them. Caplin watched her approach with widening eyes. True to form, she pulled up at the last possible moment. Her mount barely skidded to a stop before colliding with the tent. Yiloch struggled not to chuckle when Caplin hopped out of the way.

"Yiloch." He arched a brow, and she rolled her eyes. "Prince Yiloch," she amended, her weary tone almost making an insult of it, "Captain Paulin's a few miles out with Lord Wallard's host. Another nine hundred and twenty-three soldiers." As she spoke, her pale amber eyes wandered over to Caplin, appraising him with open interest. Her tone picked up a hint of sultry softness. "No ascard users, but he has a gorgeous heavy cavalry of one hundred thirty-four riders."

Caplin turned to Yiloch as though hanging upon his response, his rattled expression speaking volumes.

"Excellent. We will give them a chance to rest and move out first thing tomorrow. Captain Eris, this is Lord Caplin, commander of Caithin's force. Captain Eris is Adran's sister and one of my most vivacious officers," he added the last with a smirk.

"A pleasure, Lord Caplin." She raked the Caithin lord over with her fiery gaze.

Caplin's stern look faltered. "Uh, the pleasure is mine, Captain Eris."

Eris looked from him to Adran with a suggestive wink. "He's rather handsome, don't you think, Brother?"

The slight reddening of Adran's cheeks confirmed Eris's judgment before he looked away and tried to mask a chuckle by coughing into his hand. Caplin shifted uncomfortably and stared hard ahead.

Yiloch gave her a chastising look. "Could you not tease our allies?"

She gave him an indignant look, but before she could speak in her defense, Caplin spoke up. "It's fine. Military women are one of the things I need to get used to over here."

Eris grinned, looking amused, and tapped her horse on one shoulder, cuing it with the opposite toe. It stretched that foreleg, bending the other back and lowering its head in a bow. "My lords." She inclined her head.

Yiloch lifted a hand to get her attention as the animal rose. "As nice as that exit would have been, I need to speak to you in private. You can tend to your mount first if you wish."

She inclined her head. "I'll be right there."

As she rode away, Adran, a touch of flush still showing in his cheeks, smiled apologetically at Caplin. "She has a flair for making a spectacle."

Caplin shrugged. "It was refreshing. You surround your-self with fascinating people, Prince Yiloch. Perhaps I should not find it surprising that some of my own companions have taken an interest in you."

Yiloch ignored the indirect inquiry. "Fascinating is a good word for them."

Caplin pressed. "Might I ask what you and Lady Indigo were discussing?"

"She was there when I came out. I merely pointed out some of Lyra's beauty." Yiloch met his eyes, daring him to call it a lie. "I assure you she was in no danger unless the deer have recently become predators."

"There are many kinds of predators, Prince Yiloch."

Anger flared in him, and Caplin took a step back. Yiloch looked away, forcing calm. "We will break camp at dawn. I would like you and Master Siddael to ride with me so we can discuss how the healers will be utilized. It's important that we agree on that before they are needed."

"Agreed. We must leave no room for uncertainty. We will ride with you. Now, I need to prepare my soldiers. If you'll excuse me."

Yiloch inclined his head. "Thank you, Lord Caplin." He nodded a dismissal to Adran and returned to his tent.

Eris was already there, standing in the center of the main section, flipping a dagger up in front of her and catching it by the hilt. He watched for several seconds to pick up her timing, then stepped in and snatched it from the air.

"You haven't lost your touch." Her tone held approval. "Have I done something wrong to earn this exclusive audi-ence?"

He flipped the weapon, catching the blade, and handed it back to her. "When are you not doing something wrong? You push every limit you can."

She sheathed the dagger. "Have I ever gotten anyone

hurt?"

"There was that adept…" he teased as he dug through his packs.

"I was seven. She was fifteen. She should have known better."

He grinned and faced her. "I thought you might like to have this." He held up the pendant Myac had left with Dalce's sword.

She reached for it slowly, her eyes brightening with the shine of tears. "Delsan's?"

He nodded. She threw her arms around his neck in an unexpectedly fierce embrace. He wrapped his arms around her and held her while she clung to him for a few seconds. Then she kissed his cheek and disengaged, wiping at her eyes.

"Thank you. You're not half the bastard I tell people you are."

He responded with a wry smirk. "Be ready to leave tomorrow. And…"

"Yes?"

"Lord Caplin enjoys a good sparring match. Perhaps you could show him what it's like to fight a woman?" *Distract him. Give him something else to think about.* It was underhanded, but he could make use of the instant attraction between the two.

"With pleasure, my lord." She hung the pendant around her neck, gave him a wink, and hurried from the tent.

CHAPTER THIRTY-ONE

Caplin resisted the urge to follow Indigo and ask her what she and the prince had been talking about, and why they looked so comfortable together. Yiloch was a powerful man with strong ambition, and plenty of blood would be shed along the road to his goals. As much as he liked and admired the prince, he didn't trust him with her.

You don't trust anyone with her.

The prince had done nothing wrong, as far as he could tell. However, as the man charged with protecting the healers, he had the right to question their interactions, didn't he? Then again, maybe he was overreacting because Indigo was the healer in question. Many people were drawn to her, himself included. What bothered him most was the way she seemed drawn to Yiloch in return. Perhaps by clarifying the role of the healers, he could mitigate their contact without offending the prince.

By midafternoon, he had his soldiers organized and ready for a quick departure. Caplin searched out Siddael, not surprised to find the man working with the student healers. Indigo smiled at his approach, and he wondered again if his feelings toward her were leading him to be overprotective. Perhaps she was only being polite with the prince, as she was with everyone.

"Pardon the interruption, Master Siddael."

The master healer waved a dismissive hand. "We were finishing up. How can I help you, my lord?"

"We are departing early tomorrow. Your healers must be

ready to move at dawn. The prince requested that you and I ride with him to discuss how healers will be used during the fighting."

"Certainly," he turned to Indigo. "This will be a new type of learning opportunity for you, Lady Indigo."

Caplin shook his head. "There's no reason for her to ride with us."

Siddael gave him the firm, patient look of a teacher dealing with a stubborn student. "We are in unfriendly territory, Lord Caplin. As she is assigned to me, she goes where I go."

Caplin considered Indigo, but her guarded look offered him nothing. "Of course. I forgot about the partner assignments. Naturally, she will join the group."

Was he being paranoid? Could this be more than a coincidence? For an instant, he thought he caught the whisper of a smile on her lips, but he couldn't be sure.

"We shall prepare. Thank you, Lord Caplin."

He gave a nod and watched them go, yearning to call Indigo back, but the timing felt inappropriate. She needed to do her part in making them ready to head out. It would be wrong to pull her away now.

"Is that desire I see in your eyes, Captain?"

He glanced around to be sure none of the healers were close enough to overhear the comment, then turned toward Eris. She covered the last few steps with a swagger he would have found offensive in a man. She made it uncomfortably arousing. He stepped back from the heat of her presence, and she laughed, her pale amber eyes sparkling playfully.

Dusty blond hair, pulled back in a long braid, hinted at mixed blood, but her features were unmistakably Lyran in their refinement. The resemblance to her brother didn't detract from her allure. Neither sibling appeared particularly feminine or masculine, but each somehow struck a pleasing balance somewhere in between. Despite her lean musculature, Eris still exuded a very feminine allure.

"No." He clawed his way back to the question she had asked when she stopped and raised her thin brows in expectation. "Lady Indigo is a good friend. I'm merely concerned about her."

Her eyebrows inched higher, with skepticism this time. "Really?" She held up a hand, stopping his protest on his lips. "I was looking for someone to spar with. Would you care to be that someone?"

"I would love to," he lied, hiding his unease at the prospect of crossing swords with a woman. "However, I should go see if Prince Yiloch needs help with anything."

"He needs people to stay out of his way." She stroked the hilt of her sword in a way that broke him into a sweat. "Trust me, Captain, I have known him since he was a boy."

Evasion wouldn't work with her. Perhaps he should be blunt. "I'm not comfortable sparring with a woman."

"I find that hard to believe."

Caplin's cheeks warmed in response to her sultry smirk. He cleared his throat, struggling for composure. "With a sword, I mean."

She chuckled. "How do you do it then?" Her smile was teasing.

He laughed, self-conscious now. "I appear to be slaying myself with wordplay. Perhaps swordplay would be safer after all."

Eris grinned, victory flashing in her lovely eyes. "Come with me then, but I warn you, I won't be playing."

With a sense of nervous anticipation, Caplin followed. Watching the swing of her hips as she walked was a guilty pleasure, though he didn't get the feeling she would care even if she noticed where his attention was. She retrieved sparring swords from a supply wagon and tossed one to him. In his distraction, he almost missed it. To refocus, he ran through a plethora of fighting stances in his mind as he followed her to a small meadow in the trees beyond the supply wagons. The trampled grass suggested they weren't the first to put it to use. In unspoken accord, they walked to the center of the meadow and faced one another. Then she started prowling around him like a hunting cat.

"It's a shame you're not interested in men. My brother finds you attractive."

Determined not to let her distract him, he tracked her movements and responded with the first thing that came to mind. "Do you play matchmaker for your brother often?"

"Sometimes. I wouldn't in this case. I'd much rather keep you for myself."

The suggestive smile that curved her lips made his pulse quicken. He shifted to keep her in his field of vision as she continued her slow circle. "Are you always this blunt?"

"Only when I want something. Does it bother you? A woman speaking her mind so openly."

She was taunting him now, and he shouldn't let her, but she fascinated him. It was like exchanging taunts with any soldier before a sparring match, only charged with a sexual tension that enhanced the thrill. "Oddly enough, it doesn't."

"Does this?"

She darted in suddenly, swift and agile. It was all he could do to deflect her blade in time. He retaliated instinctively, but pulled his strike at the last second. Taking advantage of his reluctance, she ducked under his weapon and spun, striking a smart blow to his rear with the flat of her blade. Caplin twisted around and scowled at her little smirk, his rear stinging.

"Perhaps you'll follow through with your next attack."

She lunged in again. He didn't pull his strike this time. Some of the styles he had encountered fighting Yiloch were apparent in her technique, but adapted to accommodate her smaller, less powerful build. She fought with speed and precision, leaping nimbly out of range of stronger blows and darting in for quick jabs and swipes. When she had to block a stronger attack full on, he noticed it slowed her some, but her speed was a drain on his energy, and an abundance of failed attacks fatigued his arms.

For the next couple of hours, they traded victories, gathering an occasional audience. Caplin thought he glimpsed Indigo among the onlookers at one point, but by the time he could risk a glance, she was gone. Adran, Hax, and Deryk showed up together and left a short time later. Another two pairs took up sparring in the open area. A third pair took over their practice swords when they finally quit as dusk was creeping in.

Eris was flushed and panting, her broad grin contagious. Caplin chuckled and wiped sweat from his forehead.

"Come on, we can rinse off in the creek over there." She gestured away from the camp.

He considered pointing out that a branch of the creek ran closer to camp, but the idea of prolonging their intriguing encounter kept him silent.

"Are you married?" she asked as they walked. Pulling her braid over one shoulder, she began untying the band that held it.

"Engaged."

"To the right woman?" The band came free, and she unwound the braid, turning her long hair into a ponytail held by another band at the top, its length kinked in tight waves from its time in the braid.

Caplin said nothing. How was he supposed to answer that?

They came over a small rise, and he spotted the creek ahead. It was wider and deeper here, making it better suited to their purpose, but also quite secluded from the camp. Eris stopped beside the creek and turned her back on him.

"Can you undo the other tie? It's easier if someone else does it."

He inhaled, and the deeply feminine scent of her caught him off guard. The aroma was almost intoxicating, and he breathed in again, his blood heating as he undid the other band. Her hair fell out, still holding some of the shape forced by the tie. Without thinking, he ran his fingers through its silky length once, helping it to settle more.

She turned around, her body a warm, inviting presence mere inches from his. When had they gotten so close? Pale eyes gazed up at him, her features shadowed by the fast-fading light. He found it distantly amusing that he hadn't noticed he was several inches taller than her before this. Her bold demeanor added an illusion of greater height. She brought a hand up, letting her thumb caress along his cheek as her slender fingers slid into place around the back of his neck. It was then he realized one of his hands still rested on her shoulder, a lock of her hair wound in his fingers.

She applied gentle pressure to the back of his neck, and he relented, his mouth covering hers in a hungry kiss that she returned in kind. Caplin closed his eyes, tasting her, smelling her, moving his hand around her to draw her body closer. His other hand moved around her waist, seemingly with a mind of its own. The heat in his blood rose to a fever burn, raging through him like a river in flood.

When he released her mouth, she smiled, her face more flushed than it had been a moment ago.

"I'll take that as a no," she breathed.

It took him a moment to remember what she had asked. If he was engaged to the right woman. Shame scalded him then, flaring hotter when Indigo's face came to mind where Andrea's should have been. He moved away from Eris.

"I'm sorry. That was inappropriate. I..."

He trailed off at the sudden flare of irritation in her eyes. Her lips pressed together in a tight line, she stepped back, placed her hands against his chest, and shoved. Caught by surprise, he staggered back and fell, landing in the creek. The cold water shocked the breath from his lungs, and he inhaled, sucking in liquid. He came up sputtering and coughing to find her bent over on the shore, shaking with laughter.

Glowering, he climbed up onto the bank and reached for her, intending to return the favor. Rather than move out of his reach as he expected, she came forward, throwing her body against his and sending them both into the water. They came up entwined, and he met her eyes, the desire in them arousing his own yearning again. He untangled himself and climbed back out of the water.

Eris ducked under once to get her hair out of her face. Then she came up onto the shore with him.

"Your betrothed isn't here, is she?" She asked, squeezing water out of her hair.

"No, but that doesn't make it all right."

"She'll never know."

Her playful smile made him want to rebuke her almost as much as it made him want to kiss her again. "Eris, I find you very attractive, but I'm engaged and in love."

She met his eyes, her bright gaze probing into him. "I get the feeling you're talking about two different women when you say those things."

He gritted his teeth. Why had he said it that way? What was it about her that made him want to spill his soul to her, preferably while lying somewhere naked and sated?

"I'm going back to get dry clothes and food. You're welcome to walk with me if you like."

Eris shrugged and turned her back to him. "I'll be along shortly."

Caplin struggled for a moment with the deep-rooted need to escort her back to the others. She wasn't the type of woman who needed his protection. That was part of what made her irresistible. Deciding to put some distance between them, he turned away and walked back to camp.

He didn't see Eris again that evening. How amused she would be if she knew he could think of nothing else but the way she moved when she fought? When he entered his tent that night, he felt equal parts foolish and justified in pushing her away. Stripping down to a light layer of clothing, he climbed into his makeshift bed. Sometime later, he woke to someone climbing into the bed with him.

He would have cried out if not for the hand Eris placed over his mouth. He grabbed her slender waist with both hands, intending to push her away. Bare skin under his hands made him hesitate. He could make out her smirk in the faint moonlight that seeped through the thin walls before she removed her hand from his mouth and replaced it with her lips. In the dark, she could be any woman, even the one he wanted, the one with deep blue eyes.

Rather than push her away, he slid his arms around her naked body and pulled her closer.

CHAPTER THIRTY-TWO

For the next three days, Indigo rode at the heart of the army, close enough to listen to Yiloch's conversations. Caplin began the trip with his hackles up, responding curtly to the prince. When they discussed the healers, Yiloch deferred to Master Siddael's guidance, and Caplin gradually relaxed. By noon on the first day, the prince had engaged him with lively stories of many hunts he had been on in the woods they were passing through.

He was a prince in all ways—diplomatic, charming, and clever.

Along the way, she kept constant vigil with her ability, staying alert for scouts or ascard users. They captured an imperial patrol on the second day, incorporating the group into their army with little resistance. Early on the third morning, she sensed the searching tendril of an adept, but it withdrew too fast for her to track. She shared the information discreetly with Adran since Caplin didn't seem bothered by her interactions with him, perhaps having noticed the man's lack of interest in women.

As evening fell on the third day, they crossed a river and established camp. While support units erected tents and unloaded supplies from the boats that met them there, she scanned for danger in widening sweeps, sensing the ascard signature in millions of things within seconds—trees, animals, insects, villagers—and moving on. When she came upon a large group of riders approaching from the north, she narrowed her focus on them. The mounted force, heading their way at speed, had creators and adepts in their ranks. They would arrive within the hour, at nightfall judging by their pace and the remaining distance.

Alarm brought a cold sweat to the back of her neck. She spotted Yiloch overseeing camp arrangements. Ian stood near him, engaged in subdued conversation with a young female adept.

Reaching out with ascard, she touched Ian's inner aspect and wrapped a tendril into it. A barrier started going up, and she braced to fight it, but then he relaxed, letting her take hold. She drew him with her, masking his connection along the way, hoping he was strong enough to span the distance. When they encountered the approaching force, she divided the tendril of ascard, splitting his awareness along with her own to touch on the unique ascard signatures of the many riders in the approaching force, giving him a feel for their numbers. She lingered on the creators and adepts, hoping he could feel their strength as she could.

Satisfied that he understood her message, she released him. Despite her caution, he staggered when his control returned, then he met her eyes across the way, his face paler than normal. He waved the female adept away and grabbed Yiloch's arm. The prince's expression darkened as Ian spoke to him. When the creator finished, Yiloch ordered the Caithin troops and healers to the back of the camp, behind the rest of the army. They wanted to avoid tipping the emperor off to Caithin's involvement before the naval attack. While he prepared a host to face them, she continued tracking the riders.

Yiloch rode to the head of his host and led them out to meet the attack, hoping to surprise the enemy with their preparedness. Indigo joined Siddael and a selection of healers behind a defensive line of Lyran soldiers to await potential injuries. Dread formed a lump in her gut. With darkness falling, it would be impossible to see what was going on in the battle, so she reinforced her link to him and began picking at her fingernails.

"Don't worry." Siddael placed a hand on her shoulder. "Thanks to that young creator of his, Prince Yiloch will be ready for them."

"I hope so."

The approach of the enemy force sounded through the night like a barrage of drums, growing louder and louder. As the sound pressure was reaching its peak, the ground shaking with pounding hooves, it finally rolled to a stop. Darting her ability among the ascard users in the opposing force, she could sense four creators moving together in the center with adepts split out in pairs throughout. Several minutes passed in near silence, the occasional snorting and stomping of horses the loudest sound. Then a war cry sundered the night.

Seconds later, steel clashed. Voices cried out in anger and pain. When the first injuries came to them, the work kept her calm. Focusing on the needs of her patients made it possible to brace against the brutality of their injuries.

She continued to track Yiloch through the link and scan those around him while she worked. Little by little, a pattern emerged. The enemy adepts and soldiers were systematically isolating Yiloch from his soldiers, using a mix of illusion and precise attacks to clear a path for the four creators and one soldier now closing on him.

Indigo stopped and stared out toward the battlefield. Sweeping around Yiloch, she searched for his captains or anyone who might be available to come to his aid and found no one close. The enemy had isolated him.

"Healer Indigo, we have work to do," Siddael called, kneeling beside a moaning soldier whose bicep lay split open by a blade.

They had tethered injured horses and the horses of

injured riders nearby. Yiloch's mount, the dappled stallion he called Tantrum, was among them, which meant Yiloch was on foot. Her heart pounded in her ears, drowning out the sounds of battle. She could feel the creators closing in on him. He couldn't hope to face all four of them alone. Did they mean to kill or capture him?

She strode to the horse line, checking for an uninjured animal, and grabbed the reins on a slender bay. As she drew the horse away from the line, her sense of Yiloch disappeared. All uncertainty vanished, and she swung up, kicking the animal into a gallop.

"Indigo!"

She ignored Siddael's shout.

The link to Yiloch remained active to a point near where he had been, which meant a barrier of some sort interrupted it, but he was still alive. She pointed the horse in that direction, plunging through the rear defensive line with the element of surprise in her favor. While the animal charged out into the darkness, she erected barriers around them to protect them from physical attack and ascard detection. The horse stumbled over a body, and she lost one stirrup, but the animal righted itself and barreled onward, racing onward in response to her intensity. She got her foot in the stirrup seconds before the horse's shoulder struck someone as they charged past, sending the soldier reeling. She didn't notice if they were friend or foe, nor did she care.

Where Yiloch should have been, she saw nothing until she pushed through illusions the enemy adepts had crafted, then she saw five mounted men closing in around a lone figure. Yiloch still stood, but he had a crossbow bolt in his right shoulder, his sword hanging from his left hand. The four creators had a barrier secured around him, preventing him from moving or connecting to ascard. The fifth man was reloading his crossbow.

With a tendril of ascard, she bored through the barrier

and enclosed Yiloch with a barrier of her own, the same way she had enclosed the eggshell in her training with Serivar.

Under the nose guard of his helmet, she could see the fifth man smile when he leveled the crossbow at Yiloch's head. If they were aware of her approach, they didn't seem concerned. They were here to kill the prince, and their task was nearly complete.

Using the same method she used in training, she shoved out with all the ascard energy she could draw upon. The push slammed into the five men and their mounts, throwing them away from Yiloch. Her horse reared and twisted, panicking as the nearest creator and his mount came flying at them. When the terrified animal started to fall, she leapt from the saddle, somehow landing on her feet. Then she staggered, falling to her knees on someone's back as the exhaustion from her efforts crashed in on her. The person didn't move. The ascard signature of the five riders and their horses had vanished, but Yiloch, her link to him restored, was clear and strong.

An arm caught her, keeping her from collapsing among the bodies on the ground.

· "Indigo."

His voice, rough with pain and concern, filled her with validation. The shaft of the crossbow bolt still protruded from his arm, and blood darkened the leather of his armor. His sword hilt pressed into her back as he lifted her to her feet, and pain from that effort burned in his eyes. She longed to help, but her body wouldn't respond. He drew her close with his good arm, and she felt him gathering ascard energy. Panic burst through her when she realized what he meant to do, but overexertion spiraled her into darkness before she could protest.

* * *

Yiloch heard the enemy calling for retreat as he pulled on ascard. The abrupt loss of four creators and their commander devastated them. Pain from the crossbow bolt lanced through his shoulder. Indigo hung awkwardly in his good arm. He stared at her, trying to comprehend what she had done. The power behind it terrified him almost more than the realization that he would be dead if she hadn't intervened. He didn't have the strength to carry her back, but if he could gather enough ascard, he might transfer them both back that way.

"Yiloch!"

"Hax." He looked up at his commander. Concern and confusion furrowed her brow. "Give chase. Take down as many as you can, but don't follow too far. I don't want you charging into an ambush."

She spun her mount. Raising her sword, she let out a piercing battle cry and charged. The rest of his soldiers rallied to her.

Yiloch focused on the camp. He had transferred himself that far before, but he had never moved two people at once. Right now, he wanted Indigo safe and couldn't get her there any other way. Drawing on every reserve, he made the swap. They appeared in the camp next to the healers. Yiloch sank to his knees, Indigo still clutched against his side. Siddael fell upon them instantly. He put a hand on Yiloch's shoulder to steady him and knelt, laying his other hand against Indigo's throat. The master healer exhaled in relief.

"You." Siddael caught the attention of someone behind him. "Help me get the prince to his tent. And you." He pointed to someone else. "Carry her."

Strong arms helped Yiloch to his feet, and someone took Indigo from him. He stared after her unconscious form as they carried her away. She had saved his life, killing five men and their horses in one stunning attack. He wavered between horror and gratitude, but he understood Ian now. Her power scared him.

Back in his tent, they helped him out of his armor, and Siddael had him stretch on his bed. He placed a hand on Yiloch's forehead, and darkness descended.

* * *

Yiloch made a mental note to forbid healers from putting him to sleep. Hax's charge might have come upon an ambush, or the retreating opposition could have mustered for another attack while he was out. Neither of those things happened this time, but he was the leader of this army, and his disappearance at the wrong moment could be devastating.

Hax left a soldier waiting to report that they had killed or captured over a hundred imperial soldiers. There were minimal losses. The force sent against them hadn't been large. A special unit designed to isolate and kill him and then retreat. They had almost succeeded. If not for Indigo, the war would be over.

Caplin came storming into his tent shortly after sunrise. "What happened out there?"

Yiloch moved his shoulder, stretching it with care. Siddael promised another healing, maybe two, would have it as good as new. "How is Lady Indigo?"

Caplin glared at him. "She's resting. Answer my question. Why was Indigo on the battlefield?"

"I have no clue. It was chaotic, as battles often are."

"You're hiding something, and as long as it involves her, I will not let it go."

Yiloch met his furious glare unflinchingly. The Caithin lord could rage and accuse as much as he wished to. He had faced down far more intimidating opponents.

Hax stepped into the tent. "Prince Yiloch, pardon the interruption, but I must speak with you."

He nodded to her before addressing Caplin again. "I have

no command over Lady Indigo. If you take exception to something she has done, Lord Caplin, perhaps you should confront her. You may go."

Caplin stormed out. Yiloch felt a little guilty sending him to Indigo, but it was her place to decide how to deal with him. It was her secret.

"What is it, Commander?"

"Several people asked me what happened last night. I know what I saw, and I know you didn't do that. Fortunately, few others saw anything, and many who did aren't certain what they saw." She lowered her gaze. "I also know that I failed you—"

"Stop. My father made a bold move that almost worked. But I am still here this morning, and our losses were negligible. They lost four powerful creators and a commander, along with a substantial number of others. Those losses, followed by the Caithin naval attack, will shake their confidence. I don't need you to bemoan any perceived failings. I need you to focus on moving forward with me. Is that clear?"

She lifted her head, her stubborn devotion rising to the surface, as he knew it would. "Yes, my lord."

"Good. Do what you can to brush off the incident. Talk it down. We have more important things to focus on. Where is Indigo?"

"In Lord Caplin's tent."

"Have Ian keep watch and come get me when Caplin is not around."

Her eyebrows crept up. "An illicit rendezvous?"

Yiloch gave her a stern look. "She saved my life. I would like to thank her."

"You have always been generous with your thanks." Hax winked. "It shall be done, my lord."

He settled in to wait, taking advantage of the time to rest. By the time Ian arrived to let him know Caplin was away, he felt refreshed, if still quite sore.

"Ian, no one can overhear what I say to Lady Indigo. I need you to create a sound barrier once I am in the tent."

"Yes, my lord."

"Let's go then."

Yiloch wasted no time getting to Caplin's tent, keeping an eye out for the Caithin lord or anyone else who might try to interfere. They covered the short distance fast and ducked inside. Ian waited at the entrance as Yiloch continued to one of the divided sections. He drew back the flap to find Siddael sitting on a blanket next to the makeshift cot on which Indigo lay.

"Has she stirred?" Did her breathing change when he spoke?

"She hasn't woken, my lord." Siddael's eyes brimmed with questions that he somehow resisted asking. Through his sense of propriety, perhaps. "How is your shoulder?"

"Sore, but mobile. Might I speak with her?"

"Caplin asked that you not wake her."

He suspected Caplin was more adamant than that about his visiting her, but the master healer had a less confrontational way of presenting things. "I can sense that she's awake."

"Liar." She opened her eyes, earning a start from Siddael. "You can't *sense* a thing."

He smiled, relieved by the vitality in her eyes. "Your breathing changed."

She gave Siddael a hopeful look. "Might we have a moment, Master Siddael?"

"How do you feel?"

"I have a miserable headache, and nightmares plagued my sleep," she replied, her voice strained.

"I can help with one of those problems." Siddael put a hand to her head, and she grimaced, smiling her gratitude a few seconds later.

"Thank you."

He nodded and stood. "You have fifteen minutes."

When Siddael left them, Yiloch took the healer's spot next to her. A plague of distress stormed in her eyes that she had kept hidden in Siddael's presence.

"I've never killed anyone before."

"You made quite a spectacle of your first several." She gave him a sharp look, and he deflected it with a warm smile. "You saved my life."

"I had to. No one else would have gotten there in time." She reached out and touched his face. He caught her hand, kissing the fingers, his fear of her power fading before the pleasure of her company.

"How did you know?"

"I could feel everything. Every soldier lured away. Every life snuffed out around you, isolating you. The approach of the four creators and that other man." She shuddered.

Was it the trauma of killing someone, or did she dread losing him that much? Whatever the answer, more than a sense of duty motivated her.

"Then my link to you went silent."

Link? For a second, he didn't understand, then he recalled what she said about the enemy adept being linked to someone else. "You linked me?" Anger flared in response to her uninvited intrusion. "Like the link you found on Ladon?"

She gave him a patient, almost maternal smile, plainly unimpressed by his irritation. Her poise was disconcerting. "Don't look so annoyed. It allowed me to keep track of you so I could help when you needed it. Besides, you couldn't have stopped me."

It chilled him how true those words were. In ascard power, he was no match for her. The link made him subject to her supervision, an invasion of his privacy, but it also provided him valuable protection in their current situation, and the concern it represented moved him.

He leaned over, catching her by surprise with a kiss. She responded willingly, sliding her hand around the back of his neck and holding him close as she opened her mouth to him. When they parted, pleasure had replaced the distress in her eyes. He wanted her so much, but they couldn't get away with it here. He took her hand, settling for that limited contact while he considered her.

"I don't understand why King Jerrin would let someone with such a powerful ability come here. You should be too valuable an asset to risk on something like this."

She averted her gaze, her expression darkening. "The king doesn't know about me."

He narrowed his eyes. "Why wouldn't he? They carefully control their Ascard users in Caithin."

"I..." she paused, chewing her lip. "Headmaster Serivar is training me in secret. He wants to find out what I am capable of without someone else supervising the process. I used that to blackmail him into letting me come. The more I think about it, the more I fear he may have some nefarious purpose in mind."

"He may indeed."

She started sitting up, and he stopped her with a hand on her shoulder.

"I should tell Caplin."

He shook his head. Whatever the headmaster intended for her, right now, she was his secret weapon, and he wasn't willing to lose that. "Not yet."

"But he could be planning something awful."

"Or he really could be curious to find out what you're capable of. Besides, if he does intend to use you for something, he cannot do it while you're here." He brushed his fingers across her cheek to ease her troubled look. "Trust me."

"Trust you? Like when I trusted you and almost got eaten by a monstrous hound?" She let out a small sigh and continued before he could come to his own defense. "I do trust you, though I probably shouldn't."

"My lord." Ian poked his head in. "Master Siddael is returning."

As Ian retreated, they kissed again, lingering longer than was probably wise. They had already invited Caplin's scrutiny through their inability to keep away from one another. Yiloch drew away reluctantly and stood. The tent flap opened, and he stepped out of the master healer's way.

"Thank you, Lady Indigo." He met her eyes.

"Of course, Prince Yiloch." The slightest hint of frustration, a frustration he shared, came through in her voice.

"Master Siddael." He nodded to the healer.

"One moment, Prince Yiloch." Siddael laid his hands over the injured shoulder. Heat and pain flared, then faded to a dull ache. Siddael stepped back. "Once more this evening."

"Thank you."

The healer nodded.

Yiloch joined Ian outside the tent.

"Is all well, my lord?" Ian asked as they walked away.

"She will be ready to march on the city."

"Why don't we send just her in? She can kill everyone, and we can clean up when she's done." Yiloch gave him a severe look, and he shrugged. "Merely a suggestion."

"She may be powerful, but she is not invincible."

"My lord!" Paulin jogged up to them.

"What news?"

"A messenger arrived from the coast. Caithin's navy is almost in position. They plan to attack the port and outer wall at dusk."

"Excellent. Start assembling troops."

I hope you're ready, Indigo. Right or wrong, I need to use your power.

Guilt accompanied the thought of putting her in danger yet again, but he had a goal, and she was proving to be the greatest single tool at his disposal.

CHAPTER THIRTY-THREE

Myac!"

The sitting-room door flew open and Rylan stormed in, his face turned an unfortunate shade of crimson. Myac held back a sneer as he rose from the couch and bowed. Two haggard-looking men trailed behind the emperor, one a soldier with drying blood caked down his arm and the other one of the adepts who had gone after Yiloch.

"Things didn't go as planned, I take it." Myac barely kept the cynicism from his voice. How could they have failed? Yiloch should be dead. Again, the blasted prince thwarted him. Or was it the failing morale of troops who no longer trusted their emperor? Both, perhaps.

"Not at all! Yiloch was prepared for the assault, and someone killed all four of my creators and Commander Nyak with a single attack. How is this possible?"

"It's not." A chill swept through him, sudden anxiety forming a knot in his gut. "Someone highly sensitive might have detected the approaching host and warned Yiloch, but the prince's strongest asset is that boy creator. He could not have taken down your creators, not all four of them, and certainly not with a single attack."

Rylan gestured to the adept behind him. The man's eyes glazed over with exhaustion, and he put up no resistance when Myac dove into his mind with a probe of ascard.

"What happened?" He demanded.

"We proceeded as planned," the adept replied in a numb

monotone. "Yiloch was split off from his troops. The creators surrounded and blocked him. Commander Nyak was in position to finish him. It should have been over. Then someone killed all of them, even their horses. The attack threw them back several yards from the prince like children's toys."

Myac wanted to call him a liar, but the link to his mind revealed that he believed every word. "If the creators had him blocked, why didn't they kill him?"

"Commander Nyak wanted the prestige of killing the emperor's son."

Myac sucked in a breath, mastering his frustration even as the emperor's anger blasted his senses. "Yiloch has no one that strong. I would have sensed it even with the barriers they have shielding their camp." He stared at the adept. It couldn't have been a single person. They couldn't hide that kind of power. Through the barriers laid over the camp, he could still sense the young creator and several others with notable abilities. Perhaps if several of Yiloch's adepts synchronized an attack... But how could they time it so perfectly?

Rylan glared at him, pale eyes alight with anger, waiting for an explanation, but Myac was at a loss, and he hated it. It made no sense. With the creators they sent, Yiloch should have fallen. They were the emperor's strongest, as were the adepts who accompanied them. The only plausible answer was a combined attack, but that didn't feel right.

"Well?"

Myac tried to sound confident in his assessment. "It must have been a coordinated attack. Something multiple adepts had practiced together. We had four creators working in unison to secure Yiloch. They might have adepts trained to work together in his defense." As he said it, he found he could almost believe it. Almost.

"We suffered significant losses last night. I need more than speculation."

The emperor stepped in so their faces were only inches

apart, and Myac could feel the heat of the other man's rage. He flinched back. He could kill Rylan with ease, but the man still had a powerful presence. Disconcerted by the turn of events, he found it harder than usual to maintain his composure.

He stepped around the emperor and strode from the room. The storm of rage followed him. The other two men stayed behind, fear deciding their course for them. With the emperor on his heels, Myac made his way to the inner wall. Fresh morning air helped clear his head. He jogged up the steps, his desire to know, to understand what had happened, overpowering everything else. Rylan stayed close, rage still boiling, but tempered now by the need to find out what Myac was thinking.

Myac stood on the inner wall overlooking the city and closed his eyes. Rylan walked up next to him and stood silent, waiting. Reaching out with his ability, he stretched it south toward Yiloch's camp. Who was out there? He had done this once already—a cursory search before the emperor's special unit left the city—but he detected nothing of concern. At this distance, with the many protections they had in place, he could only feel the strongest connections, those that mattered. Several weak adepts could be a nuisance, but not enough to make a difference to the group they had sent after Yiloch.

He found the creator, Ian, young and stronger than most, but only marginally stronger than the four who had ridden with their host. There were plenty of adepts and creators of notable strength, at least thirteen strong enough to be troublesome. Perhaps some of them had joined to protect Yiloch.

There!

For an instant, he thought he sensed another. An adept, perhaps, but a second pass produced nothing. He searched again, hoping for anything to make sense of what had occurred, but he found nothing new. He opened his eyes.

"Anything?"

Myac shook his head. "There are several powerful abilities. None of them could have wielded that much power alone. It must have been a practiced synchronization. Not an easy tactic to pull off successfully."

"Why so difficult?"

"To combine power that seamlessly, the strongest adept must perform the working, and the others must give control of their ability to that individual. It requires considerable trust and perfect coordination, as well as significant strength on the part of the controller. Our creators layered four separate barriers over Yiloch. They did not combine their strength into a single working the way his must have been. An extraordinary accomplishment," Myac added with grudging admiration.

"Yiloch is no fool." Annoying pride came through in the emperor's voice.

"Unfortunately, it would seem that he is not." He swept the distant camp one last time, a pointless effort. "The young creator must have led them. He's the strongest."

Rylan spun on his heel and headed down the steps, leaving Myac to stare out over the city toward their enemy. That his recommended strategy had failed so completely grated on him, and the combined skills theory still didn't feel right. Even if Yiloch found that many adepts willing to relinquish control of their power, it would require substantial control and precision by the leading adept or creator. He had to be missing something, but what? He couldn't gather enough detail with the limitations of distance and several layers of masking. Soon, however, they would be closer, and he could try to learn more.

He stayed on the wall and looked out over the city. Hasty preparations were in progress for the now inevitable siege.

Troops were securing the outer walls and pulling in supplies from the surrounding area. The walls and city streets ran thick with soldiers, and people coming in to seek protection or fleeing for fear of the city falling crowded the roadways. Who was making the better choice?

* * *

When Indigo woke up again, she felt stronger. Siddael had handled her headache, but the nightmares had become less severe because of Yiloch. His visit diluted her horror at what she had done. It lingered in the back of her mind, but if she didn't think too much about the lives she had taken, she could be proud of having saved him.

She put her fingers to her lips, remembering his kiss. His desire for her still burned hot, and something in his eyes when he looked at her led her to believe the physical aspect was only part of the attraction. That helped her cope not only with the deaths she caused but also with knowing they might not be the last.

She pulled tangles out of her hair with her fingers and straightened her clothes before leaving the side partition. On her way out, she almost collided with a woman coming from the partition where Caplin's cot was. The woman sprang to one side with the same agility she had shown when Indigo saw her sparring with Caplin.

"Captain Eris?"

"Lady Indigo." Her amber eyes sparkled with delight. "I've been dying to speak with you. Perhaps we could spend some time together after we take the city."

"Perhaps..." Indigo glanced around the tent. "This is Lord Caplin's tent, isn't it?"

"Yes. I left my belt here last night. See you on the field."

As she skipped toward the exit, Caplin burst in, his hair

more disarrayed than normal and a wild look in his eyes. He stopped and stared as Eris darted past him, calling, "See you on the field, handsome."

He met Indigo's eyes, and she raised her brows in question. It appeared she wasn't the only one fornicating with one of their allies.

"We'll talk about that later. The main body of the army is moving soon. Prince Yiloch plans to be in position to attack by nightfall. The supply wagons will set up well back from the battlefield when we get there, and I think it would be best if you stayed with them. One cook has room in—"

"What?" She shook her head in bewilderment. "Why would I do that?"

His brow furrowed. "I don't know what transpired last night, but if something were to happen to you—"

"Caplin, I am a healer. I should be with the healers."

"That is not where you were last night," he snapped.

She shrank from the memory of shattered men and horses flung through the air. "I—"

He held up a hand. "There is something going on here I don't understand, but it's putting you in danger. It's as if you've become one of Prince Yiloch's soldiers. What is going on? What changed?"

I did.

The more she used it, the more she understood how strong her ability was. With that awareness came the courage to make the choices she wanted to make, to protect the prince rather than bow down to the demands everyone else made of her. She meant to help Yiloch, regardless of what that entailed.

And yet...

Her charge onto the battlefield had been foolhardy. She had taken time to erect protective barriers along the way, but sapping her strength in such a situation was suicidal. If she had not had enough power to kill the creators, Yiloch would have died, and she would have been at their mercy.

She shuddered.

"Indigo?"

"I can't explain, Caplin. I..." A faintly familiar ascard signature brushed over her. The link to the enemy adept, Ladon, had the same signature. She reinforced her masking. The touch moved on only to sweep back a heartbeat later. She almost reached out to trace its source, but here her own masking and the barriers Yiloch's creators had layered over the camp to hide the healers kept her ability hidden. Following the power to its source could expose her.

Caplin's hand rested on her shoulder. "What's going on?"

She met his eyes, yearning to explain, but Yiloch asked her not to tell him. How had her loyalties become so mixed up?

"It's nothing."

His gaze frosted over, and she braced for more argument, but then he exhaled, and the cold warmed. "Be careful. I won't have the prince putting you in danger. He will use you with no thought to your safety."

She wanted to argue, but no matter how Yiloch felt about her, his empire came first. Caplin's words rang true, though she suspected Yiloch wouldn't be quite so cavalier about her safety. Caplin would never understand because she didn't intend to explain it to him. Yiloch helped her find the courage to change her life in the short time they spent together in the prison. Even if she had no feelings for him beyond gratitude, she would help him now.

"I'll be careful, but you must focus on your task. I can't be a distraction to you."

Caplin's jaw tightened. He cupped her cheek with one hand. "I shouldn't have let you come."

"It's too late for that."

He took his hand away. "Grant me a favor. If you insist on being involved, stay with the healers."

"I will." She would go wherever Yiloch needed her, but Caplin didn't need to hear that.

The tent flap opened, and Siddael entered. He bowed to Caplin and gave her a nod, his gaze scrutinizing, assessing her condition. "Excuse the interruption, but the army is about to march."

Caplin nodded. "I am ready."

"Lady Indigo, you look rested. Will you be riding with us?"

She met Caplin's eyes, his distress as clear in them as if he voiced it. She turned to Siddael. "Yes, Master Siddael, I will be."

"Come along then."

She followed Siddael from the tent. The army waited in marching formation, catapults and ballistae carried up the river on ships lined up at the rear. They loaded the largest siege weapons in pieces onto wagons for assembly outside the city walls. Engineers still worked, building additional equipment that would follow later if needed.

Hax rode at Yiloch's side, Cadmar close on her flank. The other captains spread among other troops. Adept Captain Ferin rode at the front of the ascard users near the center, ahead of the healers. Various lords waited with their units. Horses stomped and snorted impatiently in the charged atmosphere.

Caplin cantered up to the head of his column to mobilize them while she and Siddael jogged out to join the healers. Several other stragglers hurried into position. The prince was through with waiting. She ran a gentle touch out to him along the link, and a glimmer of pleasure rose through the tense anticipation in him. She smiled and withdrew. He would use her for her power, but he would never intentionally harm her.

She believed that with all her heart.

From her position, she could only marvel at how the large force churned the ground, grinding grass into the dirt and making footing stickier the further back one marched. She yearned to have a bird's-eye view so she could see the change in the landscape before and behind. Wagons and leather tack creaked, joining the brassy chorus of metal armor and weapons and the deep bass thrum of hooves and feet marching. The powerful music of their advance both thrilled and frightened her.

Approaching dusk found their bold march changing to a weary trudge. The army came over a rise and, for a moment at the very top, she had a view of Yiroth, Lyra's capital. The immense outer wall encompassed a city nearly twice the size of Demin. Deeper in, closer to the ocean, a second towering wall protected a massive structure made up of gleaming spires and dramatic rooflines in icy whites and blues. One long, steep roofline shone like glass in the fading light. From this vantage, the palace looked made of ice and snow, stunningly beautiful.

Along the seaward side and in the port, the Caithin fleet already assaulted the city, and walls along those areas buzzed with activity. Fires blazed in the port, and she felt a sting of sorrow for the lives being lost, regardless of which side they fought on. As the army continued forward, she lost sight of the city amidst the mass of humanity and horses surrounding her.

The army stopped in the fields, out of range of the city's defenses, and the assembly of siege weapons and tents began. As night fell, attacks began against the walls, and healers soon had injuries to tend. Bolts from ballistae, set on fire with ascard as they reached their marks, wreaked havoc on the defenders, but the ballistae had limited range, so the soldiers running them were in the most danger. Yiloch held most of the army back, harrying soldiers on and behind the wall where he could while avoiding a full onslaught.

That familiar ascard touch searched the army constantly now, and its presence chilled her. The adept behind it didn't mask their ability, and she could now feel how great that power was. She wanted to warn the prince, but this wasn't the time. She took time to ensure that her masking held strong and tuned her senses to the enemy adept's power.

Cries of alarm rang out from the army's eastern flank. A swarm of heavy and light cavalry made a charge for that side. Yiloch, silver hair streaming out behind him, raced into the midst of the riders on his dappled stallion, Adran only a few strides behind him. She hurried to where Siddael stood talking with one of the foot soldiers.

"What's going on?"

Siddael gave her a solemn look. "Someone has come to the city's aid."

"But I..." *never sensed them*, she finished silently. Reaching out with her ability, she did a sweep and encountered masking over the attacking force. Not strong, but skillfully done. She had failed to notice it.

* * *

Yiloch wove Tantrum through the riders rushing to defend their eastern flank against the unexpected attack. There had been no warning, which meant the attackers were using masking. They had to be dealt with quickly. Whoever had come to Yiroth's aid could only have so many men at their disposal. They would try to do maximum damage as fast as possible and retreat.

He left Hax and Paulin to handle the restrained offensive against the wall, holding sufficient troops back to make sure the city's defenders didn't take this opportunity to sneak out and attack them from another angle. A few of Ferin's adepts joined the charge, though the majority remained focused on the city and would stay there unless called for. Ahead, enemy cavalry surged down the hillside. Behind them, the dreaded sight of a unit of mounted archers lining up, drawing their bowstrings.

Eris rode at the head of the charge, her troop's mounts stretched in a flat run at the oncoming riders. He maneuvered Tantrum to the front of the line of riders behind her troop, and they slipped in under the first volley of arrows from the hillside. Adran drew up alongside him as arrows flew over-head, taking down horses and riders behind them.

Yiloch pulled his sword free, engaging an enemy rider using ascard to add power and speed to his attacks. With his combined sword skill and ascard ability, few could stand against him as he charged in, searching for the ranking officer behind the attack. His blade bit into the side of a soldier, sending the man toppling from his mount to be crushed under the hooves of the many horses. As he felled another soldier, an unfamiliar war cry caught his attention.

Another troop charged out along the hillside, but this one was Caithin. Caplin had taken his cavalry around through the trees to come in on the left flank of the line of archers. Eris let out a whoop, and Yiloch grinned, turning to meet the next attacker.

The retreat sounded suddenly, and the opposing force scurried to make their escape, archers scrambling in an effort not to let Caplin's force cut them off. Eris led the chase, and Yiloch spurred Tantrum after her. Adran appeared alongside him again. For a moment, it felt like the hunts the three of them had enjoyed together in their youth, only this time the stakes were higher.

An arrow whizzed in front of him and plunged into Eris' thigh, driving through her leg and pinning her to the horse.

She cried out as the animal crashed to the ground, taking her with it.

Time stopped for Yiloch as he watched her fall, Tantrum leaping over her mount's legs to avoid going down with them. Turning, he saw Adran haul up on his mount and leap off before the animal stopped, running to his sister. Soldiers continued past, making good their rout. Yiloch pulled up, and Caplin took the lead, glancing back once with a look of genuine anguish before turning to the charge.

Yiloch dismounted and joined Adran.

Eris came free of the horse when it surged to its feet, part of the bloodied and broken arrow shaft still protruding from the saddle. Adran knelt over her. Her neck twisted at an awkward angle, her eyes gazing blankly at the sky. Blood streamed down her face from a laceration over her temple, but she wasn't in any pain now.

Yiloch laid a hand on Adran's shoulder. Nothing he could say would ease the misery, a fierce whirlwind of pain. Throughout his entire life, she had been there, almost as much a sister to him as she had been to her actual brother.

Adran brushed a strand of hair away from her lips.

They stayed there for several minutes. The riders came back down the hill, parting around them with respectful silence to rejoin the army. One horse halted alongside them.

"I'm so sorry." Caplin's voice cracked.

Adran kept silence wrapped around him like a shroud.

"Let's take her back," Yiloch prompted. When Adran didn't respond, he turned to Caplin. "Can you lead the horses down, Lord Caplin?"

Without a word, Caplin gathered their mounts, and even hot-tempered Tantrum went with him, subdued by the solemn mood. Yiloch knelt beside Eris and lifted her. Delsan's pendant lay on the ground beside her, broken. He left it. It had no value without her.

When he turned, Adran met his eyes, nodding approval.

This was right. Let them see that she meant something, not only to her brother but also to the man who would be their emperor. Adran followed him back to the camp. Her body hung limp in his arms, its lifeless weight devoid of passion. A lance of fresh pain pierced through the ache settling deep within him.

When they passed through the healers, a sharp intake of breath drew his attention. Indigo watched them, tears spilling unchecked down her cheeks.

Was that sorrow or guilt at failing to warn them?

He looked away. She didn't deserve the resentment he felt toward her at that moment, but he couldn't prevent it.

CHAPTER THIRTY-FOUR

As night fell on the seventh day of the siege. Yiloch watched the city, hands clenched tight on the reins. Tantrum shifted, pawing the ground. They were close to breaching the wall through two mining operations protected by ascard masking and illusion. They had the weaponry and ascard power to inflict considerable destruction inside the walls from here, but they restrained that power on his orders. He didn't want to crush the city and its people. They were his. Breaching the outer wall would get them inside, but Rylan's army would fall back behind the inner walls, and the costly destruction would continue.

Where are you, Leryc?

The plan was to sneak inside the city with Leryc's help and confront the emperor, but he either hadn't gotten an opportunity to contact them, or someone had discovered him. Rylan wouldn't willingly surrender any more than Yiloch would. Starving them out would take too long and take too great a toll on his troops, not to mention test the Caithin alliance to its limits and perhaps beyond. Leryc was the key to a less devastating victory. If he didn't turn up soon, they would have to resort to more destructive methods.

"Prince Yiloch!"

He spun Tantrum to watch Adran canter up. He had been in constant motion since Eris fell. Yiloch worried about him, but he knew better than to interfere. Adran would grieve in his way, and nothing he did was going to alter that or make it easier. There was a dark, hungry look in Adran's eyes, a look he recognized from his own experience with the loss of his mother. Hunger for revenge. The relentless need to make someone pay for his pain.

"My lord, you're needed at your tent."

Hope sprang up in Yiloch, and a slight nod from Adran confirmed it. He urged Tantrum into a swift trot back to the tents, swinging off before the stallion fully stopped and striding inside with Adran on his heels. Paulin stood talking to a young man with pale gold eyes and close-cropped light-blond hair. A small scar turned one corner of his mouth up in a permanent smirk, the result of a sparring match in which Leryc's overexuberance and inexperience brought him in too close for Yiloch to check his attack.

"Leryc!" Yiloch grabbed his arm and pulled him into a rough embrace that he returned enthusiastically.

When they parted, Leryc's broad smile twisted the smirk into a comical leer that Yiloch had often teased him about. "Prince Yiloch, it's wonderful to see you! I wasn't sure you'd recognize me."

"How could I forget that ridiculous smile?"

Leryc flushed, then glanced at Adran, and his expression sobered. He met Yiloch's eyes. "I can't be here long. I've been trying to get away from the palace for days. Myac pulled me off the outer wall and has been keeping me busy in the palace. I don't think he trusts me. Fortunately, the emperor's been demanding more of his time, so I finally got the chance to slip out."

Myac again. He itched to settle several scores with the adept. "Can you help us?"

"Yes." Leryc's eyes shone feverishly. "I can get you into the palace."

Yiloch eyed him. Another life to risk, but how much of the city might he save if he could get inside those walls and take down his father? "What's your plan?"

Leryc took a deep breath, and rubbed his trembling hands together. "I talked my senior officer into putting me back on normal duty. That means I'll relieve the outer wall patrol by the Northeast corner tower at three every morning. I broke off the mortar sealing up an old exterior access door in that tower. The space is being used for storage, so no one has noticed yet. You would have to get to the door undetected, but if you do that, I can let you in. If you avoid breaching the outer wall, the access doors in the inner wall will still be unlocked. Since your arrival, the emperor has spent every night until dawn in the throne room. You could confront him there."

"Can we do it tonight?"

Fear leached the color from his skin, but he nodded, clinging to his resolve. "Myac will be with the emperor."

"Good."

"He's dangerous. Don't underestimate him."

Yiloch smiled at his concern. "We will be at the door by three. Captain Paulin, see that Leryc gets safely back into the city and return here."

Leryc bowed. "Thank you, my lord." He donned the hood of his cloak and followed Paulin from the tent.

"I need Ferin, Hax, Cadmar, and Ian here now." He faced Adran. "And send word to hold off igniting the tunnels. We don't want the wall to come down yet."

Adran spun and strode from the tent.

Yiloch paced, wearing down the grassy floor of the tent until Paulin arrived to report Leryc's safe return. Adran arrived a few minutes later with the others.

"Leryc's getting me into the palace before dawn. I need all my officers to be visible while this is happening, and I need to be seen." He met Ian's eyes. "Can you create a convincing illusion of me?"

"If I have a subject to build the illusion over."

Yiloch turned to Cadmar. "How would you feel about leading the army in my stead?"

Cadmar flashed his teeth in a feral smile. "It would be an honor, my lord."

"Good..." He hesitated when Ian frowned. "Is something wrong?"

"I'll have to stay out here to maintain the illusion. I can't go into the palace with you."

Hax and Adran both opened their mouths to protest.

Yiloch held up a hand to stop them. "I already worked that problem out. I need you all to meet me back here exactly two hours after midnight. Ferin, I need someone you trust with a powerful skill in illusion to join us. You and Paulin will ensure the wall comes down at the right time."

"How will we know?" Ferin asked.

"I have a plan for that as well. Now go. We will meet here later."

He followed them out, stopping beside where Tantrum stood grazing. His gaze moved to the northeast tower. The wall there wasn't under heavy guard. They had focused the brunt of their attacks on the southeastern side, where the damage within the city wouldn't be as devastating, and on the western wall from the ocean. From the tower, he could sneak to the inner wall and from there to the throne room. The palace and city had been his playground for years. Sneaking through it was an old game. If they didn't breach the outer wall before he got inside, then the guard presence within the inner walls and inside the palace would be relatively light.

He mounted Tantrum, riding out to be seen before he made his move.

* * *

When the time came to meet again, Yiloch rode to where healers worked in shifts near their tents, tending injuries sustained from ranged weapon and ascard attacks. Indigo knelt a few feet from Siddael, healing a man with a torn abdomen. When she finished, she rose and turned to him, no doubt sensing him through her link. She looked weary, with bloodstains on her hands and clothes, but her eyes lit when they met his, and a faint smile touched her lips. How he loved having that effect on her. It lifted his mood even more than Leryc's visit had.

Such power you have over me, and you don't even have to touch ascard to do it.

He held a hand down to her.

"Healer Indigo." Siddael's voice carried a warning.

"I'm sorry, Master Siddael." She gave Yiloch her hand.

He helped lift her into the saddle behind him, where she wrapped her arms around his waist and pressed against his back in a manner unbefitting their supposed relationship. He didn't much care who saw or what they read into it at that moment. He savored the sensation of her clinging to him. It made it feel as if she might need him, despite the incredible power she could wield.

She is vulnerable, and you're about to ask much of her.

If she took comfort in being close to him, he refused to deny her that. He moved his reins into one hand and placed the other over her hands at his waist. She wrapped her fingers through his as he guided Tantrum to his tent.

"About Eris—"

"Indigo, don't. Ian said the masking was well done. No one blames you. Even so, you may not want to bring it up with Adran. Not yet."

She said nothing more.

Hax and Cadmar arrived at the tent just as they did, and Cadmar gave Indigo a hand down. One of Vyram's creators,

Dailin, also joined them, following Yiloch into the tent. Inside Indigo remained close to him, waiting like the rest to hear what he expected from them.

"Adept Dailin, I need you to come with us as far as the northeast tower and hide us from sight. Not only from those on the wall, but from my army as well. No one can see us. Can you do that?"

Dailin nodded, confident. "I can, my lord."

"Good. Ian, you need to maintain the illusion of Cadmar as me. He must lead one charge through the wall when the moment comes. Hax, I want you to accompany him with your troops. Adran, find Caplin. You will ride through the other breach with him and his host. They're efficient and follow his orders well. They will be an asset for keeping things under control inside the city."

"And it will keep him occupied, so he doesn't have time to look into other things." Hax glanced meaningfully at Indigo.

"Yes. Breaching the wall will keep my father's troops focused on our forces. When they learn he is dead, they will yield. The trick is coordinating the timing of the breaches. Indigo, can you communicate with Ian from within the palace when the time comes to take the wall down?" He met her eyes, seeing a touch of fear there as she digested his words. To her credit, her voice held steady when she spoke.

"Over that distance, a link would be the most reliable way, but..." She gave Ian an uneasy glance.

"Excellent. Ian, your moment has arrived."

Ian nodded, a faint trembling in his hands as his focus turned inward. Cadmar became a perfect mirror image of Yiloch, and Indigo gasped. She walked up to the disguised warrior, inspecting his appearance, then turned to Ian and smiled.

"Remarkable."

Ian flushed before her praise, and Yiloch shook his head. What an effect she had on people without even meaning to. Her effortless charm and sincerity won over everyone. He delighted in her in so many ways.

"It's nothing much, my lady," Ian said, downplaying his accomplishment. "A little visual trickery."

She glanced between Cadmar and Yiloch a few times. "It's marvelous."

Yiloch grinned as Ian's flush darkened. "Indigo, please create the link."

She gave Yiloch a curiously apologetic glance, then met Ian's eyes. "I haven't done this enough to know if I can undo it."

Ian took a deep breath. "I trust you."

Her eyes changed focus as she bent ascard to her will.

Ian shifted his feet a few times, then relaxed. "That wasn't so bad. I hardly felt anything."

"I'll be able to contact you through that link and let you know when it's time."

"We are ready then," Yiloch announced. "Cadmar, take Tantrum. Hax, stay with him and make sure he acts like me. Ian, you will send up the signal when it's time for the walls to come down. After that, do whatever is necessary to maintain the illusion."

"I will, my lord." Ian's sober expression reassured him. He wouldn't make a mistake like the one he had made on the way to Tunsdal.

As they left the tent, he turned to the remaining three.

"Indigo, Dailin, there are black cloaks in the rear partition. Find the ones that fit best."

When they went into the adjacent section, he set a hand on Adran's shoulder and waited for him to meet his eyes. "Can you do this?"

Adran's eyes brimmed with anger and with tears he refused to let fall.

"I can." He pulled away.

"I don't doubt your ability. I want to know if you can do this without taking unnecessary risks. I won't lose you both." Adran hung his head, and Yiloch used a finger under his chin to bring his gaze back up. "I *can't* lose you both. Can you do this?"

Adran exhaled. "Yes, I can."

Yiloch embraced him, encouraged by the strength with which his old friend returned the gesture. "I expect to see you in the throne room before dawn."

The smallest hint of a smile curved Adran's lips when they parted. "I'll be there."

"Go keep Caplin distracted and away from Cadmar. The clever young lord is far too likely to detect something out of place. I am off to see my father."

"Be careful."

He nodded and watched Adran leave before donning his own black cloak and drawing up the hood. Indigo and Dailin returned similarly attired.

He met Dailin's eyes. "It is time for us to disappear. "

As the ascard around them changed, Indigo's attention turned inward as well. Was she observing Dailin's process? In theory, such a working required the complex blending of ascard in the cloaks with ascard around them. Without the added uniformity and concealment of the cloaks, it would be more complicated. If Dailin slipped up, it could be disastrous, but the man had to meet high standards to be one of Lord Vyram's personal creators. Yiloch didn't expect him to fail.

"Indigo, can you mask his ability?"

She focused for a few seconds. "Done."

He offered her his hand, and she accepted it reflexively. They snuck into the night and made their way around to the northeast tower unnoticed. Yiloch led them to the door. It would only need to open for a few seconds for them to slip inside once Leryc arrived. They waited by the wall in silence.

Attacks from siege engines and the sounds of thousands of men and horses in motion made a din in the night. Indigo leaned against him, and he wrapped an arm around her. He kept his ears tuned for the sound of the inner latch on the door. When it finally clicked, they froze, waiting while it creaked open.

Leryc peeked through the crack, and Yiloch nodded to Dailin. The creator made them visible to Leryc as they slipped through the doorway, then he retreated, leaving them to their task.

Leryc shut the door and stared hard at Indigo.

"Is there a problem?" Yiloch prompted.

"Ah, no," Leryc replied haltingly. "I thought you'd bring someone less... fragile."

Indigo scowled.

Yiloch bit back a laugh. "She is not so fragile," he said before she could retaliate. But she was, he realized, looking into her fear-filled eyes. He needed her. He couldn't pull this off without her power, not with Myac in the equation, and yet. "If you don't want to do this..."

She placed a finger over his lips. "I understand the risks. I will help you."

Yiloch pulled her to him and kissed her. He could feel her heart pounding, betraying the terror she hid behind her brave words. He loved her for that courage.

Leryc coughed softly. "Excuse me, my lord."

Yiloch released her, keeping one of her hands to savor the silken softness of her skin. "Leryc, this is Lady Indigo. She is an extraordinary adept. Maybe you will have the good fortune of getting to know her better later, but for now, make yourself scarce. I expect you to survive this."

"I can help..."

Yiloch held up a hand. "If you want to help, go about your business as you normally would, and don't draw attention. This will be over soon, one way or another."

A new, willful resistance tightened his features. "There are many here who want to see you take the throne. We can get your force through the inner gates if they breach the outer wall."

Yiloch hesitated. He would be a fool to pass up such an offer. "All right. Do what you can. Try not to get hurt."

"Good luck." Leryc slipped through the door on the opposite wall, leaving it cracked. Tucking his thumbs into his belt, he strode away.

Yiloch led Indigo through, shutting the door behind them. They emerged in the far corner of the wealthy district, little disturbed by the assault on the city walls to the south and west. The residents probably holed up in their houses, hiding from an uncertain future. There would be few patrols while the focus was on holding the outer wall.

He led Indigo through the shadows, moving away from the outer wall where they were most likely to be spotted. When they neared the inner wall, they crouched in the shadows of some tall bushes, waiting while he got a feel for the timing of patrols on the ground and on top of the wall.

"I haven't much practice in stealth." She clicked her nails nervously behind him.

He glanced over his shoulder. "It is best done silently," he whispered.

She flushed and bit her lip.

He turned back to his task. When he had the timing, he moved them to the edge of the shadows. "Ready?"

"Yes." Her hand tightened on his.

"Now." They dashed across an open area between the last houses and the inner wall.

Panic shot through him when the door to the tower

didn't open, but with a little ascard behind his push, it gave. They ducked inside and hid behind a stack of crates stored in the tower's base, listening for anyone coming. With the outer wall still holding, a minimal guard would be in place along with adepts sensing for intruders. Given Indigo's skill at masking, he wasn't concerned about ascard detection.

Shadowed walkways and dark servants' passages served to get them from the wall into the main palace corridors. He knew every twist and turn, keeping to the hidden passages until he heard someone coming. Then he backtracked and opened a door into a marble-floored hallway with a high, arched ceiling. They started down that hall, stepping into a recessed doorway when two guards passed through a crossing hall in opposite directions. When the hallway was again clear, he moved, leading them from hiding spot to hiding spot, relying on dark nooks familiar from childhood forays. He finally stopped them around a corner from the throne room.

A cautious glance revealed two guards in the hall outside the massive arched doors. He gestured for Indigo to look. She peeked out, then tucked back against the wall beside him, the hand he still held trembling.

"Can you…" He trailed off when she paled, her eyes pleading for him not to ask. Yes, she could kill them, but she would suffer for it. He peeked around the corner again and changed his request. "Can you mask me while I take care of them?"

She nodded, relief and gratitude shining in her eyes.

He kissed her, then drew a dagger and his sword, careful not to make noise. Stepping around the corner, he swapped himself with ascard in the air between the two guards. Using his ability to enhance his speed, he buried the dagger in one man's throat, then spun, slicing into the other man's throat with his sword, nearly decapitating him. Still boosting his speed, he caught each of them before they fell and lowered them to the floor. Indigo walked out to him, her face paler now.

"There's someone powerful in that room," she whispered. "It's the adept who was linked to Ladon. He's been scanning the army since we arrived."

A ripple of unease moved through Yiloch. "Is he stronger than you?"

She shrugged. "I can't assess my ability the way I can someone else's. I know he's considerably stronger than Ian."

He grimaced. "It must be Myac. Can you block him?"

She met his eyes, her pulse racing beneath the soft skin of her throat. "As long as I catch him by surprise, I should be able to."

"Don't worry about anything else in that room, only him."

Her expression turned distant, already working on the problem, and Yiloch kissed her once more, just in case he didn't get another chance.

Her smile was shaky. "This will work." She searched his eyes, seeking reassurance.

"It will." They faced the doors together. "Let Ian know the wall can come down."

He watched her eyes trace the magnificent workmanship of the peaked double doors, a depiction of the view from the back garden terrace in spring carved into pale wood. Her focus turned inward. After perhaps a minute, she met his eyes and nodded. He shoved open the doors.

CHAPTER THIRTY-FIVE

They were waiting for a signal upon which the wall would come down in two places. Caplin's troop, along with those led by Captain Adran and Lord Vyram, would attack through the southernmost of the two breaches. Another force led by Commander Hax, Captain Paulin, and Prince Yiloch prepared to charge the other breach. Several adepts and archers rode with each invading force to protect them from overhead attacks. Adept Captain Ferin rode with Captain Adran, and despite how uneasy the man made him, Caplin was glad to have such an accomplished ascard user in their group.

Persistent attacks against the wall's defenders continued throughout the night, keeping them busy and distracting them from the careful redistribution of soldiers for the charge after the wall breach. It was masterfully handled. Throughout the process, Yiloch rode near the front lines of the assault with Commander Hax and Creator Ian, keeping his attention on those attacks to support the illusion.

Everyone was in position. Now it was a waiting game. Caplin's horse shifted under him, sensing his impatience. He wanted to check on Indigo before they entered the city, but Yiloch entrusted him with overseeing a portion of the wall assault during the day. Now he needed to be with his men. Captain Deryk maintained a protective buffer of soldiers between the fighting and the area where healers worked and rested. He had to trust that the man could protect them, especially if the invasion went awry. Besides, he could see Yiloch from where he waited, so at least the prince wasn't anywhere near Indigo.

Ian lifted a hand, his palm turned to the sky, and Caplin startled when a blue light flared above them. In response, someone sounded the call to attack, and the waiting troops sprang to life. Caplin signaled his men, and they charged, sweeping in from their apparently haphazard positions to blend seamlessly with the other two troops making up their force. Advancing in a column four riders wide, they surged toward the wall. Explosions boomed over the din of charging soldiers. Dust and debris filled the air as a wide section of the wall collapsed in front of them. Before it settled, the resulting rubble flew inward and to the sides, ascard power clearing the route of debris, pummeling imperial soldiers who rushed to defend the gap.

Then he understood the value of the diverse array of adepts in Yiloch's army. Healing was obvious in its benefits. The varied specializations of ascard users Lord Ferin had gathered for the prince showed their true worth now. As their column neared the breach, archers began firing from the intact wall on either side. A few riders went down before a massive wall of fire roared up in the opening, its flames lick-ing up the edges of the gap toward the defending archers, who fell back in panic. The riders ahead of Caplin didn't slow. They charged head-on into the flames filling the gap.

Illusion? The flame was illusion, though the heat coming from it was convincing enough. Caplin saw amazement and a trace of fear on his soldiers' faces. Things he could feel reflec-ted his own. His men would falter if he did, so he urged his mount onward. For a few seconds, stifling heat engulfed him, making it hard to breathe, then he was on the other side. A large troop came charging at them, weapons drawn and faces grim.

Adran and Ferin rode near the front of the force. Caplin

steered his mount in their direction. The adept captain looked absent, his eyes glazed over, and Caplin shuddered with the realization that substantial power was about to come into play. Then the front three lines of imperial soldiers skidded to a halt, falling into and tripping up the men behind them, some landing upon their startled comrades' ready weapons. A bitter smile curved Ferin's lips. As the confused men struggled to reform their charge, Adran signaled attack, and Caplin rode with them, driving into the disordered defenders.

They had only begun routing the first troop when horns blared from the inner wall. Bewildered looks met the sound, and the rear ranks of the imperial soldiers started falling back in retreat. Caplin cut out with a deadly sweep of his sword, catching a man at the gap between helmet and chest armor. Before his foe finished falling, he glanced at Adran, raising his brows in question. The defenders hadn't put much effort into repelling them. Why would they call retreat this soon?

Adran grinned.

As Caplin turned his attention back to the fight, searing pain lanced through his thigh. He grunted, sucking back a cry, and clapped a hand around the shaft of an arrow. It was a poor shot, going through at an angle, the tip emerging only a few inches from where it went in. Easy to heal, but knowing that didn't make it any less painful.

It recalled the injury that had taken Eris down.

Hatred flared in him, numbing the pain. He looked in the direction the shot had come from in time to see an archer tumble from the wall with an arrow in his back. The man struck the ground and stayed there in a broken heap.

Good riddance, you bastard.

Taking hold of the shaft on one side of the wound, he broke it with a pained grunt and pulled it free. Rage burned blood-red around the edges of his vision. He threw the arrow and kicked his mount into a gallop after the retreating defenders. Pain plagued the bleeding wound, a distant nagging, something he should attend to... later. It didn't surprise him to see Adran swing his blade and cut down the first soldier they overtook.

Caplin took down the next one. *For Eris.*

He could feel her arms wrapped around him, holding him in the aftermath of wild passion and smiling in a way that was somehow wicked and sweet at the same time. Pale amber eyes sparkled in his mind. Then they deepened, turning a vivid blue.

For those lost and for those who stood to be lost, they couldn't fail.

Some defenders turned and grouped together, knowing they couldn't outrun cavalry. Adran raised his sword, signaling the troop to alter direction and head down another street. As the column charged past the defenders, a group of adepts and soldiers broke off, preparing to take them prisoner. Caplin's rage was strong enough that he longed to cut them down where they stood, but Adran veered his mount into his path, steering him away.

Three riders who had pulled ahead of them went down, one with an arrow in his throat, the other two with gouts of flame pouring from their eyes. Caplin's stomach turned. Horror muted the anger sustaining him. Ferin moved, weaving to the edge of the column, and Caplin reined in a little, keeping his mount close to Adran as he watched. The adept pointed to a nearby building, and a woman next to him nodded. The building burst into a tower of flames. This time it wasn't an illusion.

Screams rang out, and a woman carrying a crossbow leapt from one window. She managed a few limping strides before a rider barreled down the crossing street and slammed into her. The impact threw her back against the side of the building, and she slumped to the ground like a rag doll.

Another column charged along the next street over, the leader riding an impressive dappled gray stallion with silver hair streaming out from under his helmet. A smaller troop was closing the gap and dealing with imperial soldiers caught between them. They appeared to be trying not to kill too many enemy soldiers.

On the next cross street, an entire troop of imperial soldiers knelt and tossed out their weapons in surrender. Several riders from each column pulled up and settled in to guard the prisoners.

Caplin looked questioningly at Adran.

"Put to the test, it seems many would rather follow Prince Yiloch than die for his father," Adran shouted.

Caplin nodded and pressed a hand to the wound in his thigh. His rage was fading, and pain started eking out a place in his awareness. The inner wall loomed ahead, its gates drawing together, another outer barrier ready to drop after the last stragglers rushed through. It would close before they reached it. They would have to take control of the city and start the siege anew at the inner wall.

A different pattern of horn blasts rang out from the inner wall then, and several answered back from somewhere within the prince's column. The gate stopped closing. Caplin knew enough about Lyran war customs to recognize that surrender had been declared and accepted, though he couldn't understand why it came so fast.

The columns slowed. Pain flared in his leg, and his foot felt wet in his boot. Blood? The wound wasn't that bad. As his mount slowed to a walk, he started reaching down and stopped abruptly, choking down a cry as pain tore through his side. The city tilted. He swayed in the saddle, and someone grabbed his arm.

Adran met his eyes, his brow furrowing. "Are you injured?"

"Only a flesh wound," he managed, gritting his teeth.

Adran leaned back in his saddle to look him over, then, to Caplin's surprise, he laughed. "You could say that."

"What?"

Ferin joined them, staring at him with raised brows.

"You've got an arrow above your hip," Adran explained.

"Oh." Caplin took a shallow breath, trying not to aggravate the wound. "That would explain the agony."

"It's well off to the side and shallow," Ferin offered. "Not likely to have hit anything vital."

"Lyran archers have wretched aim," Caplin grumbled.

"Maybe they noticed your striking good looks and pulled their shots." Adran chuckled again and turned to the soldier next to him. "Take my troop back and escort the healers in. Be quick about it. There are plenty of wounds that need urgent attention." He turned to Caplin. "You may want to stay on your horse and wait for a healer. Dismounting could worsen the damage."

Caplin nodded his agreement, the pain building rapidly now that there was no fighting to hold his attention. Keeping a tight rein, he allowed his mount to move forward with Adran and Ian. Prince Yiloch and Hax also approached the open gate. A substantial number of soldiers were coming out. Near the front strode a young man with a scar on one side of his mouth that gave a crooked twist to his pleased grin. He and others began kneeling before the prince, and Caplin suspected his grin had something to do with their abrupt surrender.

* * *

Indigo slammed a barrier around Myac's inner aspect. He immediately retaliated, and a cold sweat sprang up on her skin with the sheer magnitude of the power she was trying to contain. Stronger than her or not, he clearly wasn't as run down as she was after several long days of healing injuries. Yiloch seized ascard again and swept into the room, taking out two inner door guards in mere seconds. She couldn't help him now. The man standing to the left of the throne, his elegant Lyran features contrasted by eyes and hair blacker than ink, demanded all her ability.

Yiloch moved swiftly through the room, cutting down remaining guards while she kept to one side, following from a distance as he left a trail of bodies behind him until only the emperor, Myac, and a terrified attendant cowering in one corner remained.

Myac glared at her, the promise of pain in his cold sneer as he assaulted her barrier, sending a ripple through it. How long could she possibly hold him?

Yiloch stopped at the foot of the steps leading up to the throne. Emperor Rylan rose to stand over him. He reminded her of the prince in many ways, including the fierce determination that lit his pale eyes. Lifting his head high in defiance of his son, he walked down a few steps. Stubborn pride appeared to be a family trait.

"You came here to die," Rylan declared. "Myac can give me eternal life. I have no need of an heir."

"I hope he made you impervious to steel, because he won't be helping you." Yiloch's voice, thick with loathing, chilled even her.

The emperor glanced at Myac, whose eyes remained riveted on her. The little color in Rylan's face drained away. His gaze jumped to her, and he shook his head, his eyes widening.

"That is not possible. What is she?" He stumbled back to the top of the steps.

"She is my answer to your madness, Father. Your reign ends now."

Rylan shook his head again and, though he looked little

older than his son, she noticed the age in his eyes. Yiloch shifted his grip on his sword and advanced, a predator ready to make its kill. Rylan met his son's eyes, his expression hardening, and drew his sword.

"We finish this properly then." Determination surging to the fore again, he strode down the steps to engage Yiloch.

The two men fought with remarkable speed and grace. Fluid, dancelike movements brought their blades together and apart again as each sought advantage. Yiloch wasn't using ascard now, and she silently cursed him for it. He couldn't know what it cost her, but if an end didn't come soon, she would lose the silent battle she fought.

In a flurry of motion, someone's sword went skittering across the floor. Rylan dropped to his knees, and Yiloch leveled his sword at his father's throat. Unexpected sympathy swelled in her. For all he had done, the emperor was still a man, and a defeated one at that. They were all guilty of some sins. She shook her head when Yiloch raised his sword. She had seen so much death already. The edge of the blade glinted in the light of myriad candles around the room. Myac's power battered against her barrier with increased ferocity.

Yiloch's smile was devoid of compassion. "I don't need you to give me the throne, Father, because I am taking it."

He swung the blade. She met the emperor's eyes, seeing a familiar denial in them.

Hadris.

The blade cut through flesh and bone like soft cheese. Blood sprayed across the marble. His head hit the floor with a wet, crunching sound that turned her stomach, his body wavering for a second before toppling forward. Nausea threatened her focus.

Yiloch looked at the adept then. Spatters of blood stood out in vivid red against pale skin and silver hair. The Blood Prince stood before her, the terrifying killer her people gossiped about, his eyes burning with dark hunger. But he was more than that now. He was the emperor. His long strides took him up the steps to Myac. Blood dripped from the tip of his sword onto the adept's boot when he leaned close, his whisper amplified by the sudden quiet.

"All that power, yet here you stand, helpless before me."

The power within the other adept lashed out at her barrier in a panicked frenzy. Through their contact, she felt his terror and trembled with him.

"I can serve you." Myac spoke in a steady, almost seductive voice despite the intimate war he waged with her. "I can make you immortal."

Yiloch hesitated. His eyes narrowed.

Be greedy. Accept his offer. Let there be no more death.

Her strength faded, the barrier weakening as days of healing and masking caught up with her. Her mind played tricks on her, turning the head lying on the floor into that of Hadris and then her father.

Yiloch drew back his sword.

Her power faltered. Myac met her eyes and smiled. The barrier gave.

"Yiloch!"

Myac's sudden assault sent them both flying back from him. Her side struck the wall. Pain stunned her, and she hit the floor, struggling to breathe. Myac stalked toward her, the loathing in his eyes tearing into her. She tried to focus, to draw on ascard, but pain crippled her, searing agony filling her body and mind. Helpless, she could only stare, throat clenching with fear, lungs fighting for air.

Yiloch struggled to his feet near the throne, his movements sluggish. Blood streamed from a laceration above one eye. A glimmer of hope sparked, then pressure closed around her. With the pressure came more pain, blinding agony, and she tried to scream. With no air in her lungs, only a whimper emerged. Myac stood over her, his smile maniacal with rage at her near victory. Tears ran from her eyes. Pressure and pain steadily increased. Ribs cracked. Black swept in at the edges of her vision.

Yiloch struck Myac from behind and his blade bounced away, the failed attack leaving him staggering.

Yiloch.

Then Myac flew sideways as if struck by an invisible fist, and the pressure vanished. Ian appeared in her line of sight with Adran close behind him, the latter leveling a crossbow at Myac. He fired before the adept hit the ground. The bolt sank into his side, his physical shielding disrupted by Ian's attack. He struggled to his feet, clutching at the bolt shaft. Adran strode toward him, loading another bolt. The adept's black eyes rested on Indigo for a second, then he vanished.

She whimpered, still unable to breathe through the pain and too depleted to heal herself. Yiloch knelt beside her. His breath came in ragged gasps, and the wound above his eye still bled copiously, but she couldn't help him.

He clutched her hand. "Get a healer! Now!"

Adran and Ian sprinted from the room. A cough ripped through her, the pain making darkness threaten again, and she tasted the metallic tang of blood.

Yiloch stared into her eyes, oblivious to the blood running down his face.

"You will be all right." He spoke the words like an order.

Indigo squeezed her eyes shut against the agony, finding only darkness and fear behind her eyelids. Yiloch brushed her hair from her face, bringing her attention back to him. Was his face the last image she would see? Perhaps that wasn't so bad.

People rushed into the room. Adran, Ian, and a healer whose name she couldn't recall. The healer knelt across from Yiloch and laid her hands on Indigo's side. She glanced at the blood running down Yiloch's face and shook her head.

"I need more help. Another healer to assist with her and someone to take care of Prince Yiloch."

Emperor. Emperor Yiloch.

Ian dashed from the room again.

Yiloch glared at the healer, his gaze so fierce Indigo felt a pang of sympathy for the woman. "You will save her."

Indigo could feel the woman working ascard. "I can't fix this much damage alone."

Adran moved to the edge of her vision, leaning over Yiloch's shoulder.

"How did you get here so fast?" Yiloch held her eyes while he spoke.

"Someone sounded the surrender before we reached the inner gates. You have more supporters than we suspected. Leryc rallied them when we breached the outer wall, and they took control of the inner wall."

Indigo felt the healer working to ease her pain until someone else arrived, a commendable effort, though the agony was still enough that darkness continued to creep in at the edges of her vision. She almost let it take her, but Yiloch moved one hand to cradle her head, his face twisted with worry. For him, she fought to remain conscious.

More people entered the room. Siddael knelt next to her, unvoiced anger tightening the muscles in his jaw. He would never understand why she ended up here. Another healer knelt beside Yiloch to tend his wounds, but he sent the man away. Caplin also arrived, with a river of blood drying down his left leg. He was well enough to run off a substantial string of curses at Yiloch, who resolutely ignored him. The dismissed healer ushered Caplin back, silencing his tirade for the moment.

Siddael placed his hands against her side, meeting the woman's eyes. "I'll position and mend the bones. You follow and repair the lung tissue."

The woman nodded, placing her hands next to Siddael's. Then there was pain, lancing pain and white-hot heat searing through her as the master healer forced broken ribs into place with ascard. Yiloch wrapped his arms under her, keeping her head from striking the floor when she stiffened and cried out. At least she could now breathe well enough to voice her pain.

Siddael's voice cut through a haze of exhaustion and agony. "We can move her now. Is there a room nearby where she can rest before we do more healing?"

Yiloch nodded. The wound on his head was bleeding a little less now. He lifted her with care, leaving his sword where it lay. Above them, bright stars winked down through a ceiling of faceted crystal.

"Beautiful," she murmured.

He glanced up and then smiled down at her. "I'll show you that and many other beautiful things when you're healed."

They passed into a hall, and she closed her eyes, letting her awareness drift. She looked at Yiloch when they stopped. The blood on his face wasn't all his. Could she forgive him for that?

Someone moved past them to open the door. When he turned to carry her into the room, she spotted Caplin standing behind Siddael. His eyes churned with a storm of hurt, worry, and anger. She had lied to him. It couldn't have been different though, because she loved the man holding her. No matter who he was or what he had done, she loved him.

Yiloch laid her on a bed.

"Emperor Yiloch." Adran emphasized the title, an attempt to remind him of his responsibilities.

She shifted her hand enough to touch his arm. "Go. I'll be fine."

"I know." He stepped back and gave the healers a stern

look. "Heal her well."

"Yes, Your Highness," Siddael hissed, his expression no less severe.

When Yiloch and Adran were gone, Siddael sent everyone else away and shut the door. He sat on the edge of the bed.

"I don't know what you've done, but no good is likely to come of it." Fresh pain lanced through her ribs, drawing a gasp from her, and Siddael sighed, laying his hands against her side again. "A little more healing and you can rest. There are too many injured for me to spare energy sedating you. I'm sorry."

She bit her lip, tears streaming from her eyes as he manipulated bone and tissue again. When he finished, he placed a hand on her shoulder.

"Rest. I have a strange feeling you've earned it. Perhaps you can tell me about it later."

A small smile took most of her strength. "Perhaps."

* * *

Myac staggered into the night, slipping through the confusion of troops to where he sensed his father. How humiliating to have to seek help from the man, though not as humiliating as his own failure. For days, he had searched the army. Not once had he sensed her, not until she stood in the same room blocking him. Yiloch's presence in the palace should have been obvious to him as well, but she had hidden them both. He never put much effort into learning to mask because no one came close to matching his strength. She clearly didn't share his arrogance.

He could see her in his head and feel the invasion of her ability as if she still held him. So much power within her and without... such grace. Why did she deserve so much?

He spotted his father. "Lord Terral."

"Not now." Terral waved him away.

Myac grabbed his arm.

Terral turned and paled. "What are you doing here?" he hissed.

"I need your help."

He glanced down at the blood on Myac's hands. "Come with me."

Myac followed him, the bolt in his side causing a stabbing pain that worsened with every step. They walked to a tent at the back of the camp. Inside, he removed his cloak, and Terral watched him inspect the wound. The bolt entered below the ribs, its tip protruding in back. He considered burning it out, but he didn't want to cauterize the hole. Healing he could manage. Removing the bolt without causing more damage was another problem.

"Can you help?"

Terral took hold of the shaft with strong, steady hands. "I take it things didn't go as planned?"

Myac prepared to snap his response, but the words vanished behind a burst of pain when Terral yanked out the bolt. He doubled over, falling to his knees. After his confrontation with the Caithin adept, he had little strength left. He would have to use it wisely. With care, he began the excruciating process of mending the tissues, assessing and healing internal damage while he still had enough strength to do so.

"Yiloch didn't go for the immortality option?"

Myac bristled at his acrimonious tone. "He isn't his father."

"I could have told you as much if you would have listened."

Myac might have lashed out if he wasn't busy struggling to find the energy to finish healing. "Don't be disrespectful, Father. I am far from finished. I merely have to adjust my plans. In the interim, I need you to stay close to the new emperor and be as helpful and visible as you can."

Terral was fingering the dagger at his belt. "Where are you going?"

Myac met his eyes, and his hand moved from the weapon, still too afraid of his son's power. "Caithin. I must speak with an old friend, and I don't think I should show my face here for a while." His old friend needed to answer for not warning him about the Caithin involvement and that adept. If she survived her injuries, then she had to be controlled or eliminated. He would be happy to help with either option.

"How will you get there?"

"I'll manage. I need to rest. Is this your tent?"

Terral nodded.

"Wake me before daybreak. I'll need a horse."

"I will handle it." Terral left him.

CHAPTER THIRTY-SIX

Sleep came quickly, but so did Terral's return. The brief rest restored a little of Myac's strength. He took a few minutes to do a sweep with ascard. Was she alive? He found nothing. She was dead or masked. It didn't matter. If she lived, she would return to Caithin, and he would be waiting.

He turned to his father. "I am counting on you to stay close to Yiloch."

"I hope you know what you're doing."

Myac gave him a long, irritated scowl before leaving the tent. The somber gray light of dawn stretched over a surprisingly quiet landscape. Soldiers lay scattered about the fields, sleeping like the dead. Patrols marched the perimeter, but Myac used illusion to appear as one of them and mounted the dark bay tethered outside the tent. The horse wouldn't have the training that his favored mount did, but it would get him out of Yiroth.

He turned the animal north, riding into the cover of the trees before spurring him faster. Riding made the pain flare in his side where the bolt had penetrated. The healing was incomplete, but he needed more rest to finish the job. At least pain would keep him awake in the saddle.

* * *

Indigo woke a little after dawn, and Siddael healed her more.

Exhausted by pain and overexertion, she didn't wake again until afternoon. Siddael dozed in a deep chair near the foot of the bed in a well-furnished, but relatively simple chamber that probably normally housed someone high in the palace staff, a steward or similar notable individual.

Doing her best to ignore the deep ache in her ribs, she sat up.

The door eased open, and Ian stuck his head in. "Good afternoon, my lady. How do you feel?"

"Not too awful."

"I've been waiting for you to wake to ask a little favor. I am prepared to bribe you with the offer of a hot bath and clean clothes."

She smiled. "There is no favor too great, especially after your timely intervention with Myac."

He flushed and helped her up, then nodded to Siddael. "Should we tell him?"

"No. Let him sleep."

Deferring to her judgment, he led her out and down the hall to a large room with faceted crystal windows along the outer wall overlooking the coastline. A lavishly furnished sitting area faced the windows, and a large bed with sheer silver draperies matching those hanging around the windows sat on a raised floor near another run of windows. She stopped in the doorway and stared. The cool blues, grays, and whites used throughout the room drew in the majesty of the ocean beyond, creating a breathtaking spectacle.

Ian grinned. "Welcome to the emperor's rooms." He gestured to a set of carved double doors beyond the sitting area. "Your bath is in there along with a selection of garments that should fit well enough. When you're ready, I'm working in a room three doors down from the one you spent the night in."

She stepped close and rose on her toes to kiss him on the

cheek. "Thank you."

He turned a charming shade of pink. "Ah, it was Emperor Yiloch's idea." He offered an awkward bow and hurried out, leaving her alone in the luxurious chamber.

Perfumed steam rose from a round marble tub inset into the floor of the bathing room. Faceted crystal windows overlooked the ocean in that room as well. She shut the doors, shucked her grimy clothes, and sank into heated water to rest and wash. When she finished, she selected an ivory gown with a loose-fitting silver belt at the waist from the selection hanging from a tall mirror in one corner. It had tapered sleeves and a V-neck embroidered in pale blue. Fancy as it was, it was the least formal option, and the soft fabric felt marvelous against her skin.

Dressed and refreshed, she wandered along the beautiful pale marble halls to the room Ian had indicated. When she knocked, the door opened a crack and Ian peeked out.

"Lady Indigo, I hate to bring you into this, but I think you may be more qualified than I to puzzle this out."

"I'm happy to help."

His doubtful look concerned her. Then he opened the door and stepped aside. A body lay stretched on a table in the center of the room. She entered, and he shut the door behind her. Using a sparing touch of ascard, she freshened the air and approached the table.

"Nice trick," Ian commented, following her.

She shrugged. The more she worked with it, the easier it became to adapt her ability to different applications.

The late emperor's head lay positioned in its proper place, the effect almost grislier than if they had left it off. When she looked at his face, she saw much of his son's surreal handsomeness there, even in death. Tears stung her eyes.

"Emperor Yiloch wants to know what Myac was doing to control his aging," Ian explained. "He looks younger than he did when I was last here, over five years ago. I found traces of remarkable creation throughout his body. It's extraordinarily detailed, but there's more there, and I don't have the skill to make sense of it. I thought you might have the flexibility in your ability to figure it out."

She walked to the other side of the table, pondering the fallen man. With the sweep of his own son's blade, he had gone from a magnificent and powerful ruler to an empty gray shell. Did Yiloch regret taking his father's life? Did it matter? More importantly, why did he want to know what Myac was doing? Was it curiosity or a desire to recreate the process for himself?

She touched the pearlescent white hair that kept its luster even as the rest faded in death. Then she met Ian's eyes. The lanky youth watched her with reverent curiosity.

"I'm flattered you think so highly of my ability, but what point is there in prying into this?"

An unexpected fondness warmed his smile. "I thought you'd ask. Prince... Emperor Yiloch hoped it might help us understand Myac's power. They've found no trace of him since last night, but he doesn't think this is the last we'll hear of him."

She shuddered at the memory of that power. Steeling herself, she swept out with ascard, searching as far as she could reach. Nothing. No trace of his ascard signature. Memories of pain and helplessness before those pitiless black eyes made her shudder again, and Ian reached across the table, hesitating shy of touching her arm.

"Are you well, my lady?"

"He won't come around for a while. His injuries were severe." She turned her attention to the body. "I'll see what I can find."

Drawing on her power again, she sank it into Rylan to examine the signature and nature of the workings. What she found was an exquisite tapestry of skills laced into every fiber of his being. Bone, muscle, everything woven through with Myac's ascard signature. She searched for flaws in the work, admiring the precision and patience it must have taken. Layer upon layer of regeneration tied flawlessly together. Creation and healing combined to refresh life in a manner she would never have dreamed possible.

The door swung open, and she startled, jarred from her exploration.

"Ian, have you..." Yiloch trailed off, stopping inside the door to stare at her.

She felt like a giddy courtier before his favorable regard. A flush warmed her cheeks. He looked striking in the fine clothes he wore, freshly groomed with silver hair cascading over his shoulders. When he smiled, she automatically reciprocated.

"Indigo, you look well. Breathtaking even."

Ian, who still faced her over Rylan's body, glanced down. She caught a hint of approval in his smile.

"Thank you, my lord. You look rather remarkable yourself."

He openly admired her for a moment more, then, recalling his purpose, shut the door and approached. "I see Ian asked for your assistance."

He came to stand beside her, and she breathed in the scent of him. His hand came to rest on her shoulder—a simple gesture infused with intimacy by the tenderness of his touch.

"Have you found anything?"

She glanced at Ian, not wanting to offend him by taking charge. He met her eyes and nodded.

"It's a remarkable blend of creation and healing. Myac truly was regenerating the emperor's body. I've never heard of anything like it." Admiration and envy crept into her voice.

"Just Myac? You don't think anyone helped him?"

"No. His signature is on all the work."

His hand tightened a fraction on her shoulder. "Where would he have learned that kind of healing?"

"I don't know, but he did it well. The work is seamlessly blended and woven permanently into his body."

"And you can determine all of this from examining a dead body?"

She met his eyes. "Yes. Does that bother you?"

He kissed her forehead, and Ian glanced away selfconsciously. "Honestly? Yes. Your power intimidates me."

"I believe this adept, Myac, is at least as strong," she warned.

Someone knocked, and Yiloch nodded to Ian. While the creator went to answer it, he said, "I have people searching for him, but I suspect he is well away from here."

"He is." She shivered.

He squeezed her shoulder, his touch gentle and comforting.

"Lord Caplin," Ian greeted loudly.

Yiloch removed his hand and took a step away from her. Ian opened the door for Caplin. Someone had also loaned him nicer, clean garments. When he looked from her to Yiloch, his weary expression darkened.

"Emperor Yiloch." His greeting was curt. "I had hoped you would refrain from taking inappropriate advantage of Lady Indigo's skills once you had your throne. I suppose that was too much to ask."

"You are mistaken, Lord Caplin," she said before Yiloch could give voice to the sudden anger in his eyes. "Creator Ian requested my assistance."

Caplin met her eyes. When she held his gaze, he relented. "My apologies, Your Majesty."

Yiloch inclined his head in acceptance of the apology. "What do you need?"

"I wanted to discuss the withdrawal of Caithin's troops. Although I would like to speak with Indigo for a moment first, if I may."

She nodded. "Excuse me, Your Majesty. Creator Ian."

"Thank you for your help," Ian said.

Yiloch inclined his head to her.

Her hand brushed the dead emperor's shoulder as she walked around the table. The image of Yiloch delivering the final blow, his eyes cold and unforgiving, drove to the forefront of her mind. That image refused to reconcile with the warmth in his eyes when he looked at her or the gentleness of his touch.

Forcing the image from her mind, she followed Caplin from the room.

"Walk with me." He started down the hall, heading away from the throne room.

She fell into step with him. "Did we suffer many losses?"

"Very few, thanks to healers and Emperor Yiloch's allies inside the city. I'm relieved it's over. He has much to sort out, but his support here is more than sufficient. We can return home."

A dagger of sorrow twisted in her chest. Perhaps Yiloch didn't need them here now, but no one in Caithin needed her either. "Then we'll depart soon."

"I'm afraid so."

She stopped, puzzled by the apology in his tone. He faced her, pain and frustration casting a shadow over his features. "I don't know what's going on. I don't understand the connection you have with that man and his companions. Whatever it is, it has ignited a fire within you. I would hate to see that fire go out, but you don't belong here, Indigo. We both know it. I—"

"Caplin, please. I know where I belong, even if nothing but problems await me there. I have felt needed here in ways

I never felt needed before. Yes, I probably took too many risks along the way, but I wouldn't do anything differently if I could." She softened her words with a gentle smile. "You have been patient with me, Caplin, and you're right. I know my place. Please trust me."

He stepped close, putting his arms around her, and she let him hold her, sensing that he needed to.

"I thought you were going to die last night." His voice cracked.

So did I. She pushed away memories of fear and pain. "I'm too stubborn to die that easily."

"I'm glad to hear that." He released her.

She stepped back, her smile weighed down by the sorrow of the coming separation. "We'll be home soon, and I will have other problems to deal with. Right now, I would like to continue assisting Ian, and I believe you wanted to speak with the new emperor. Please remember that I put myself at his disposal. He is the same man you got along with so well back in Caithin."

Caplin nodded, though she could see resistance in his eyes. "I'll try."

"That's all I can ask."

CHAPTER THIRTY-SEVEN

Yiloch watched the door. The room felt empty without her.

"Are you going to make her stay?" Ian stared at his hands resting on the edge of the table.

Yiloch laughed, a sound edged with bitterness. "I do not believe any of us could *make* her do anything."

Ian looked at him. "I didn't mean that. She would stay if you asked her, wouldn't she?"

How he wanted to believe that. "I don't think so."

Ian's hopeful expression wilted. "It's too bad. She's useful to have around and…"

And you adore her.

He had achieved his greatest goal, and all he felt was disappointment. How could an entire empire pale next to her deep blue eyes and sincere smile? If he had known the effect she would have on his life before he pulled her into the prison, would he have done anything differently? Most likely not. She had no obligation to do any of the things she had done for him. Nor did she owe him her loyalty. She certainly didn't owe him her life, which she had almost sacrificed for him more than once.

He looked at his father, relishing a flicker of satisfaction.

Rylan used him after his mother died, taking advantage of his hunger for revenge, his anger, and his sorrow to convince him to destroy an entire village. Those villagers had never sheltered his mother's killer. Rylan fed Yiloch lies, using him to clear the land as a political favor to a lord who never ended up putting it to use. As far as Yiloch was concerned, his father had killed her. Now he was dead. There must be some justice in that.

"How's Adran?" Ian's question interrupted his thoughts.

"Without Eris, he seems lost, though Leryc has been distracting him with an endless barrage of questions about our years in exile." He couldn't imagine how losing her felt to Adran, who had been her shadow most of his life. Ian had also walked in the shadow of her energy for years. He considered the young creator, noting the dark circles under his eyes. "How are you holding up?"

"I'm furious," Ian admitted, "but it doesn't help."

"It never does."

"At least we won. That would have pleased her."

Caplin and Indigo returned then, and Caplin bowed with more respect this time. Yiloch met Indigo's eyes at the depth of that bow, wondering what she had said to change the man's attitude. She flashed him a quick smile and went to stand near the table.

"Emperor Yiloch, I would speak with you if you can spare a moment."

"Certainly, Lord Caplin." He turned to Ian and Indigo. "If there is more you can discover here, please do so. Send for attendants to prepare the body for burial when you are done."

"Yes, Your Majesty," Ian replied.

Yiloch turned to leave and felt her gentle caress within him. Was Indigo asking him to be easy with Caplin or just seeking contact? Perhaps both.

He led Caplin past the throne room. He hadn't gone back in there, though palace attendants had long since cleaned up the mess. The early morning he had spent sorting soldiers with Hax and one of Ferin's adepts who specialized in sensing emotions. They carried out an exhaustive sweep of surrendered troops, searching out those who weren't willing to bend knee to Yiloch as emperor. Perhaps because he was the legitimate heir, or because so many of them had followed him in the past, most accepted the change. The result of the process, losing a scant few soldiers and ascard users, raised his spirits.

Adran had gone to oversee repairs on the walls and damaged structures within the city, a task Leryc enthusiastically offered to help with. Ferin, with his myriad creators and adepts, also joined them. Paulin directed the cataloging and removal of the dead, a task Yiloch didn't envy. After working through the surrendered troops, he turned Hax to the task of finding the palace steward to sort out wages for the army and address the needs of individual lords who had provided soldiers. He would review the final numbers, but it would take a day or more for the steward to get the rolls and individual needs lined out.

He led Caplin through a doorway beyond the throne room onto a terrace overlooking the Gilded Strait. Caithin ships cycled through the port, resupplying and repairing for the journey home. He leaned on the railing and gazed out to sea. The departure of the ships meant Indigo's departure, not something he cared to contemplate. Caplin stood beside him, mimicking his pose without obvious intent.

"Your soldiers and healers were a phenomenal asset, Lord Caplin. And your routing of the archers on that first day was brilliantly done. I don't believe I ever thanked you for that."

"It was lucky timing. We were in an excellent position when they arrived. I merely wish we could have been faster. It might have saved Eris."

Yiloch caught the sorrow in his voice that struck off a fresh pang of loss. "Many things might have saved her. There is no point in looking back. My companions and I will mourn the loss of her life for the rest of ours."

Caplin was silent.

Yiloch waited, breathing in the salty ocean air.

"I don't mean to rush things, but I believe we have ful-filled our part of the agreement. The ships will be ready to leave by tomorrow. I see no reason to linger."

Yiloch struggled to extinguish a spark of hatred for this man who would take Indigo away from him. The weight of unspoken words hung heavy between them. The young lord loved Indigo. It showed in every look he gave her, but he didn't know what he loved. In the time since Yiloch first met her in the prison, she had changed. He loved watching her grow in strength and confidence. Caplin was unwilling to let her be more than she had been before. In that way, he was no better than her useless fiancé.

Wresting control of his resentment, Yiloch broke the tense silence. "You are eager to take her away from here, aren't you?"

A muscle twitched in Caplin's jaw. "She says you are not at fault. All I know is that when I saw her lying there in the throne room, I was ready to kill you or die trying. I don't know why you insisted on putting her in danger, but arguing about it now won't change anything. She belongs in Caithin."

Yiloch's anger grew with every word. He was close to saying or doing something he would regret. "I demanded nothing of Indigo. The choice to help me was always hers. I never wanted to see her hurt. I still feel that way. If you believe it is your duty to rush her away for her own protection, then I expect you to protect her. The danger she faces in Caithin may be more subtle, but it is no less deadly."

Caplin's hands tightened on the railing, his knuckles whitening. "What am I supposed to do? I can't leave her here."

He considered arguing that point, but the decision didn't

belong to them. Even his authority as the emperor held no sway in this. She wasn't one of his subjects. "If you care for her, do what you can to help her or stay out of her way. She deserves that much consideration."

Caplin turned on him, eyes blazing. "Don't presume to tell me—"

Yiloch took a threatening step forward, his hand dropping to the hilt of his sword. "You think you love her, Lord Caplin? I know I do." The ring still hanging around his neck grew heavier with the declaration. "I would keep her here if the decision were mine to make, but it is not. Nor is it yours. Perhaps you can take time on the way back to Caithin to get to know the woman you think you love."

Caplin stared at him, surprise overpowering the rage in his eyes. He took a step back and faced out to sea. For a long time, he said nothing. Yiloch watched waves rolling onto the shore. Dusk brought its gray veil down over the landscape, and an adept somewhere lit lanterns in the port, glimmering beacons in the fading light.

"How could you come to love her so quickly?"

"Do you really have to ask?"

Caplin scowled.

Yiloch yielded a little. "I leave that to her. If she wants to, perhaps she will tell you. It is enough to say that without her, I would not be where I am now."

"Excuse me, my lords." Terral stepped out to join them on the terrace. "Emperor Yiloch, if it would please you, my troops and I can stay until things are situated here."

Yiloch appreciated the interruption more than the offer. "That would please me greatly, cousin. If you will both excuse me, I have other business to attend to."

He left them. He did have business to attend to, but he avoided it, lurking in the quieter hallways of the palace and eventually ending in the throne room. It sat empty, every trace of the battle waged under the crystal ceiling less than a day ago now gone. He walked to his throne and sank into it, gazing down the length of the room. An extraordinary work of art, every detail carefully considered and precisely worked to blend with or enhance some other detail. Beautiful. Desolate.

Night had fallen, and stars sparkled in the black sky, their light shining radiant through the faceted crystal ceiling. He took a deep breath, considering all that was now his. All the power and responsibility that came with this station wasn't enough to get him the one thing he wanted.

A side door opened, and Indigo entered, her gaze telling him she had come looking for him. He drank in her graceful movements with his eyes as she approached. Her hair hung loose in thick, dark waves around her face. The gown she wore molded over her curves. The link must have told her where to find him, and his misgivings about it faded as she glided up the steps. Without a word, she moved to sit on the step below the throne, and he stood.

"No. Sit here." He gestured to the throne.

She shook her head. "I can't sit there."

"I insist."

She met his eyes, then settled on the throne, putting her arms on the sides, her posture rigid. She traced some of the elegant workmanship with her fingers, then smiled up at him, eyes shining with mischief.

"Can I issue orders now?"

He leaned down and kissed her, savoring her taste and the feel of her skin under his fingers when he caressed her neck.

"You can order me," he whispered.

"If only."

He sat at the foot of the throne, leaning against one corner, and gazed up at the sky. "You are leaving tomorrow?"

"Yes." Regret and sorrow tightened her voice, a reflection of his feelings on the matter.

"Will you come back?"

"What for?"

He turned. Did she take him for a fool?

She blushed and looked at her hands, beginning to pick at her fingernails. "What can I be to you?"

"I cannot marry you." The nobles here would never tolerate a woman of anything but the purest Lyran lineage on the throne. "But with your abilities, you could help Ferin train adepts." He took one of her hands and kissed it. "Who will protect me from Myac if you leave?"

"So I could be useful to you."

He saw a glimmer of hurt in her eyes. Would it harm anything for her to know she was so much more than a tool to him?

"Up." He rose, and she stood with him, moving aside to let him rest his back against the front of the throne. At his direction, she sat in front of him. He wrapped his arms around her and leaned close to her ear.

"Look up." He felt a small shiver run through her when his breath tickled across her skin.

She leaned into him and looked up through the created crystal ceiling. Her head rested on his shoulder. "It's gorgeous."

"I would share so much with you, given the chance. But this? This is who I am."

"The emperor of Lyra?" She twisted around to face him.

"Yes."

She kissed him, and he reciprocated, her passion always a welcome surprise.

When they parted, she murmured, "It's our last night."

Standing, he drew her up with him. "Come with me."

From there, he led her to his chambers, trusting that she

would warn him if anyone were around to catch them. They didn't bother to light candles. Moonlight coming in through created crystal windows cast a silver glow over the room. They took their time undressing one another. With only her ring resting against his skin, he put his arms around her and drew her down into his bed. She wrapped herself around him, and he delighted in her touch, her scent, and the softness of her skin that had been so close and so long denied him.

CHAPTER THIRTY-EIGHT

The bright silver glow of early morning filled the room with cool light. Yiloch smiled, and she gazed into his eyes, rising to kiss him. They made love again, and she understood with no need to hear him say so that it was love they made. It was clear in his eyes and the way he touched her.

Afterward, they lay entwined on the bed, and she picked up her ring, admiring the stones. He folded his hand over hers on it.

"You can't have it back." A hint of teasing lightened his tone.

She released the ring, drawing his hand to her lips to kiss it once. "I wouldn't want it anywhere else."

They lay in silence a while longer. She listened to his heartbeat, comforted by the steady rhythm. When he stirred again, sorrow pierced her chest. They couldn't stay there any longer. The palace occupants would be waking. Did it matter? No one would judge him for their illicit romance. Only she would be judged, and not by the Lyrans, but by her own people.

"I hate to leave you, but there is still much I must do."

"We could run away and live like peasants, hidden in a remote village somewhere," she teased.

"I doubt they would look kindly on me if I abandoned the empire a day after seizing it."

She pressed a hand to his chest and traced her link to him

with her power. She had created it with her inner aspect, but it had since changed, becoming a perfect blending of the ascard within each of them with no obvious way to separate the two.

"About the link. I'm not sure how to undo it. It…" she trailed off when he kissed her forehead.

"I don't care. I like the thought of being connected to you, and I am sure Ian won't mind either."

He got up and offered her his hand, drawing her up with him when she took it. She followed him to a set of doors that opened into an enormous wardrobe, half of which bloomed with a garden of gowns. The other side held a vast assortment of fine men's clothing.

"The gowns belonged to my mother. Judging by how the other one fit, you can wear anything in here."

"I'm leaving today."

"Consider it a small token of my gratitude. I wouldn't be here if not for you. You realize that, don't you?"

She flushed. "I did what was necessary."

"You did far more than that."

She met his eyes, a twisting ache in her chest. "I love you."

He drew her into his arms and held her close. She melted into the embrace, longing to stay, but it could never work, not for them. There were things she needed to do, and he had an empire to rule. She poured all her longing into a single kiss.

When it ended, he stepped away. "Let me dress you."

She watched him hunt through the gowns and pull out a delicate, pale turquoise gown with a low-cut back. A train of material gathered at the back of the waist and trailed down the back of the loose-hanging skirt. The bodice was elaborately embroidered in silver thread, and loose sleeves hung off the shoulders with a small gather at the wrist. It was an elegant blend of styles, and the color was unlike anything she had ever seen. She drew upon her inner aspect and inspected the material.

"The color is created. Remarkable." She touched the silken material. "I can't wear that on a ship."

He set it in her arms and dug deeper into the wardrobe, drawing out a soft gray cloak. "It will be a quick crossing from here. Wear this over it on the ship."

She donned the gown and stepped in front of the mirror to admire it. Then she ran a brush through her hair and worked a few decorative braids into the sides, using them to bind it partially up. He came up behind her in a flattering jacket and pale gray pants with silver and dark blue accents. Brushing her hair aside with one hand, he kissed her neck.

She shivered and smiled at his reflection.

"I will see you before you leave."

She turned to kiss him, then watched him leave the room, picking up his sword on the way out. She took the cloak and scanned for people in the hall before stepping out. After getting something to eat, she wandered to one of the ocean-side terraces and watched the port until the thought of leaving brought the sting of tears to her eyes. Then she turned her attention to the waves rolling out over the Gilded Strait until Siddael found her.

"Lady Indigo."

"Yes."

"Lord Caplin asked for you. He is in the throne room. Carriages wait to take us to the ships."

Reluctance weighed down her limbs. She forced herself to face him. "Thank you, Master Siddael. I will attend him momentarily."

Siddael inclined his head and left.

She grudgingly left the terrace and went to the throne room. Adran lingered near the main entrance alone. Ian stood close to where Yiloch and Caplin were speaking at the foot of the dais, with Adept Captain Ferin waiting quietly next to them.

She approached Adran with an ache of sorrow swelling in her chest. Despite the circles under his eyes and the sorrow etched in his features, he found a smile for her. It didn't touch his eyes.

"I'm sorry about..." She trailed off when he shook his head and drew her into an unexpected embrace.

"I know you weren't at fault, though I tried to blame you at first. I needed someone to blame, but..." His voice cracked and he fell silent.

She hugged him in return, then gave him a light kiss on the cheek. "Take care of the prince."

"I will, my lady."

She squeezed his hand, hoping the gesture offered some comfort. Then she walked to Ian, nodding once to Ferin, who returned the gesture with a polite smile. The adept's eyes shone with approval, making her wish she'd had the opportunity to talk to him during her time in Lyra.

"Creator Ian, about the link..."

He shrugged, an endearing, boyish grin striking down her unease. "Emperor Yiloch already told me. Besides, I was prepared for it to be permanent when you did it."

"You aren't angry?"

He stepped forward and gave her a quick hug, then hastily retreated, a blush coloring his pale features. "It's been a pleasure working with you, my lady."

"Likewise, Creator Ian."

"You're welcome here, always."

"Thank you."

When she turned from Ian, already fighting the sting of tears, she found Yiloch and Caplin watching her. Caplin shook his head, looking bewildered. Yiloch's smile was strained by sorrow. Under his gaze, she felt her heartbeat quicken, the ache inside building.

"Excuse me, my lords." She offered a curtsy directed at neither of them specifically.

"Are you ready, Lady Indigo?" Caplin looked at her gown and the cloak draped over one arm, his eyes brimming with unasked questions.

"Yes, Lord Caplin." Did he hear the tremor in her voice?

"Very well. Good luck, Emperor Yiloch. May your rule herald a prosperous time for both our countries."

"Thank you, Lord Caplin. Have a safe journey home."

When Caplin walked away, Indigo moved to follow, but a hand caught her arm, turning her back. Her heart pounded, feeling as if it might explode when she stepped into Yiloch's embrace, all need for secrecy crushed by the more potent need to touch him again. Wrapping her arms around his neck, she kissed him with all the passion in her being. She could feel Caplin's eyes on them and felt a pang of sorrow for him, but it paled next to the suffocating anguish of leaving. She tasted her tears when their lips parted, and he brushed them away with one hand, his other holding round her waist to keep her close.

"Stay," he whispered, staring into her eyes.

She hesitated, savoring the warmth of his touch. How she wanted to do as he asked. "I cannot."

His jaw tightened. "You will not."

"You've done what you had to do," she said. "Now it's my turn."

He closed his eyes for a moment, clenching his teeth. Was his pain as great as hers? Part of her hoped it was.

His pale eyes opened again, drawing her in. "Be careful, Indigo."

He kissed her again, the contact sweet and lingering, as if no one watched. She returned it with a hint of desperation. They parted a little, and his smile warmed her through, bringing a matching smile to her lips despite the tears.

"You can always return."

She kissed him again, just once more, before stepping back, and he caught one of her hands.

"Remember those words," she said. "They may come back to haunt you."

She started turning away, and he let her hand slide free of his, little by little, reluctantly.

"I hope so."

She took a deep breath to steady herself and walked away, their hands parting. Each step drove the blade of sorrow deeper into her heart. Caplin watched, waiting, and she avoided his eyes, not ready for the anger or hurt that might lurk in them. She made a point of not looking back. Yiloch wouldn't linger. He had an empire to bring to heel, and he would move on to that without dwelling on regret or sorrow. It was his way. She would do the same and never regret the time they shared or any of the things she had done for him.

Caplin remained silent on the short ride to the docks. The last ship awaited them, and she donned the gray cloak before walking to the bow to gaze out to sea. Tears ran down her cheeks. She held onto the rail as the ship left the dock, and Caplin joined her. He glanced at her once, then stared out over the waves. She knew then that she still had an ally, regardless of what hurt she might have caused him.

"You love him." A hint of bitterness sharpened his voice.

She nodded.

He placed a hand over hers on the railing and squeezed it, offering support despite the jealousy in his eyes. "You seem to have trouble picking relationships."

She breathed a small laugh, though the grief in his eyes stung. "I do. I'm sorry, Caplin."

"Don't be. Some things can never be. I'll help you move

into a new residence. I already know a place. You shouldn't give Jayce a chance to retaliate. I want to protect you, Indigo. All else aside, you have always been a dear friend to me."

"Your help with moving out of the residence would be welcome." She let him keep her hand, taking comfort from the contact.

"Do you intend to come back here?"

"I can't be a part of his world the way I want to be," she answered, carefully choosing her words. "Still, I might come back when I have finished my schooling. There is much I could learn from the Lyran adepts."

Caplin looked torn. He shook his head, not voicing the misgivings in his eyes. "You are right. There's much you could learn."

Afternoon sun lit the water, creating brilliant reflections of light on the waves that reminded her of the faceted crystal ceiling in the Lyran palace. She almost looked back, almost sought Yiloch through the link that would fade with distance, if only to know where he was in the palace, but she didn't. Someday, if everything worked out, she might return here. Only then would she indulge the link, if only to feel him again for just a moment.

THE END

CHAPTER ONE

Yiloch sat upon his newly won throne, patient and wary, watching the black-skinned man approach up the length of the magnificent room. Guards, adepts, and creators stood alert along both sides. Even the eyes of the men and women in the subtle etchings along the blue marble walls seemed more attentive than usual. Two lines of three warriors flanked the man, each carrying an ornate spear topped with a slender, curved blade. Elaborate markings down the length of the shafts made them appear more ceremonial than functional, but he knew better than to doubt the effectiveness of those weapons or that of the men bearing them. Kudaness warriors were skilled fighters. In their hands, those delicate-looking blades could practically decapitate a horse with a single strike. Allowing armed visitors into the room at all was a declaration of his confidence in the many ascard users present.

The thin, sand-colored straps of a few satchels he carried were all that covered the leader's chest, exposing a broad, muscular build. A warrior at first glance, but prior experience with the Kudaness, coupled with years of political education, gave Yiloch the knowledge to translate a few of the messages written on the man's skin. An elaborate tattoo on his right cheek marked him as part of the Ithik Ani, the Kudaness priesthood. The black swirling tattoos over his arms, shoulders, and legs announced his role as a suac, a high priest. Another tattoo with three black lines running parallel to the line of his jaw on his left cheek and two black dots beside his left eye informed others he belonged to the Murak tribe. Long black hair, braided back into countless strands, several woven through with patterns of beads, swung heavily down to his lower back. He wore intimidation in place of armor, and his copper eyes, discolored by the potion the Ithik Ani used to initiate a connection with their gods, gleamed with feral intensity.

Only a month into his reign and Yiloch was hosting a most unusual visitor. The presence of a suac in his halls could be a gesture of respect or a warning. Perhaps both.

"Emperor Yiloch." The Lyran usher, his light skin stark white beside the dark Kudaness, offered a deep bow to Yiloch, then inclined his head toward the visitors. "I am honored to present Suac Chozai Galal un Murak un Ani."

The usher's introduction confirmed everything Yiloch read from the tattoos. This man was very important among his people. Kudaness high priests held more power than their tribal chieftains did. Even among other tribes, this man's rank made him second only to their suac.

Before the throne, the high priest lowered his chin in the slightest intimation of a bow, his odd metallic-eyed gaze never leaving Yiloch's.

This is a man whose power is never challenged.

That would make him frustrating to deal with. Yiloch needed to proceed with caution, though, especially given the unexpected nature of the visit. Whatever the reason for his unannounced arrival, the suac had the political advantage for the moment.

Yiloch nodded to the man, offering reserved respect. "Suac Chozai, your visit honors us."

The suac's answering expression curled his lips into a predatory snarl, and his eyes sparkled as if he found something amusing.

The irrepressible twitch of a muscle in Yiloch's jaw was the only thing that might expose his annoyance, but only a careful observer was likely to notice. A heightened sense of vigilance rose in him in reaction to the thinly veiled animosity lurking behind those eerie eyes, but he kept his expression neutral. Kudaness priests had a notorious lack of respect for rank outside of their own culture and, at least in his limited dealings, they treated most everyone with some amount of disdain. It made them challenging to work with, but the Kudaness were a powerful people and the border they shared with Lyra boasted a long trade history beneficial to both countries. His father's madness nearly destroyed that trade, and Yiloch wouldn't risk its revitalization over such a small measure of insult.

"The Murak have seen that Lyra's new Emperor respects the trade relationship with Kudan," the priest began, his accent thick enough that Yiloch had to listen closely to understand him. It might have been easier if the man spoke in his native tongue, but using the Lyran trade dialect was appropriate here, showing some deference to Yiloch's rank in this setting. "The Murak, the greatest tribe in Kudan, wishes to express our gratitude for your efforts."

He resisted a smirk. How many of the tribes would lay claim to that status? "It has long been a beneficial arrangement. Emperor Rylan insulted both of our peoples by disrespecting that relationship. That will not happen under my rule. However, while I appreciate your gratitude, I do not believe you traveled all this way to express a simple thank you. Why have you come here?"

Tension rippled out from the high priest. His copper eyes glinted in the sunlight shining down through the faceted crystal ceiling as he returned Yiloch's measuring regard, perhaps trying to determine whether he intended some insult with his abrupt manner.

Yiloch could have been more tactful, wasting time on niceties, but the mere rarity of a visit from a Kudaness suac was enough to inspire interest and unease. He itched to know the reason.

"I am suac to the Murak tribe, chosen by the gods to bear the burden of their gifts for the benefit of my people." Suac Chozai's somber expression and weighted tone communicated the significance of his status. "One of those gifts is the ability to foresee possible futures. The gods have shown me that our lands and people will soon face a terrible threat. Not only the people of Kudan, but all our people"—he swept a hand out to suggest a wider area—"are under threat from a tribe not of Kudan. This tribe is mighty. They come in great numbers and use ascard in ways none here have seen before. They ride on the backs of sturdy horses and will decimate all in their path if not dealt with through quick and decisive action. We require the aid of the Blood Prince to defeat this threat."

Yiloch narrowed his eyes, making little effort to hide his disapproval of the old, hated title. His hand itched to move closer to his sword. Whether Chozai's use of the title was a mere slip from long habit or an intentional insult, the suac tried his patience. A careless approach, considering he was requesting military aid.

He waited a moment to see if the suac would apologize. When he didn't, Yiloch spoke, biting off his words with the effort of keeping them civil. "I would be a fool to extend my resources so soon after taking the throne. My empire is recovering from significant upheaval. I have many soldiers and adepts out hunting for the adept Myac, who remains a threat. What benefit is there to Lyra in sending aid to the

Murak against an enemy who is, as yet, mostly unknown even to you?"

The suac's smile broadened, giving a glimpse of incisors filed to a subtle point. It enhanced the predatory appearance, but he wouldn't intimidate Yiloch with tribal gimmicks. The confidence in his smile, however, was a trifle unsettling.

"You need us, Blood Prince," Chozai stated, making it apparent that the use of the title hadn't been a slip.

Yiloch scowled, losing the struggle to contain his irritation. Kudan and Lyra held an uneasy peace balanced on the benefits they could offer one another and a shaky mutual respect for the extreme differences in their cultures. That balance felt even more precarious at the moment.

This one man is not worth the destruction of that peace.

"You insult me in my palace, then expect me to accept on your word that I should extend you aid at a time when I have need of my soldiers here. You had best be able to offer more concrete proof of how this will benefit Lyra." He infused his tone with an edge of warning. He would not continue to suffer disrespect in his own palace.

Like a man struck dead, the suac's face lost all expression. His eyes clouded over, a translucent white masking the brilliant copper, and his voice assumed a deep, rhythmic cadence. "The emperor of Lyra will be thrice betrayed; by ally, by family, and by love. To escape the dark consequences of those betrayals, he must send forth his army to the aid of those favored by the gods. In return, salvation will come from beyond his borders to mend the rifts created by those betrayals. If such aid is not given, salvation will not come and his empire will fall in a storm of fire and blood to a savage power from beyond the Rhuakine."

Yiloch glanced at Ian, the youngest and strongest creator in his army. The young man shook his head. If the suac was using ascard to change his eyes and voice, Ian couldn't detect it.

A chill passed through Yiloch, and he noticed his cousin, Lord Terral, shifting his feet near the foot of the dais. Was that from the same unease they all felt at the suac's dark fore-telling, or something more insidious?

Betrayed by ally, by family, and by love.

The Rhuakine was a canyon-scarred desert to the east of Kudan, implying that the savage force the suac spoke of was the same one that threatened the Murak. If so, his people would fall before this new power first if Lyra didn't send sol-diers to their aid. Under those circumstances, he would have expected a more respectful approach from the man. Was the disdain for foreigners so ingrained that he couldn't overcome it even for the sake of diplomacy?

Yiloch stood. With his sword riding comfortably at his hip, he descended the steps and walked up to stop a few feet from the high priest. Suac Chozai was a big man, several inches taller, but his eyes, which had regained their usual abnormal color, took on a hint of wariness. The Murak war-riors tightened their grips on their weapons, and some of Yiloch's guards took hold of their swords. His bold approach had extracted some reluctant respect from the arrogant high priest and his guards.

He met those deep copper eyes with a steady gaze. "You have intrigued me, Suac Chozai. I give little credit to fortune-telling as a rule, but if I discounted all such things completely out of hand, I would not be where I am now. Perhaps we could discuss this in a more casual setting."

Chozai nodded, and two of his warriors moved up closer behind him. Adran, one of Yiloch's captains and a lifelong friend, and Ian came forward from either side of the dais to flank him. It was a given that they would attend him, just as the two lead warriors of Chozai's retinue accompanied him. The suac stepped aside to let Yiloch walk ahead of him, more out of a lack of trust, he suspected, than any show of deference to his rank within the realm. Among the Kudaness, the suacs were exempt from the laws of men. Knowing that, Chozai's manner wasn't surprising, but it still chafed him.

Yiloch led them to a set of doors on one side of the main room. The usher hurried ahead, opening the doors into the map chamber. Maps hung on the walls and covered the surfaces of every table. Old maps, new maps, maps of places he knew as well as he knew his own bedroom, and maps of places he wasn't certain even existed. A few chairs sat along the walls to provide the option of comfort if desired, but the room served primarily as a place to peruse maps and plan strategies.

Adran and Ian flanked him as he walked around the back of a table with a map of Kudan stretched across it, then they moved off to the sides where they could keep watch over him and his visitors and still be close enough to react to an attack.

The map they stood over was a rare, beautifully detailed piece. Yiloch's father, the late Emperor Rylan, purchased it from a Kudaness sea captain before Yiloch was born. The tribal borders within Kudan had changed since its creation, as they often did, but it still gave a reasonable approximation of reality, and he appreciated the artistry of it.

Suac Chozai approached the opposite side of the table while the usher shut them into the room. His dispassionate gaze fell upon the map.

Yiloch considered the situation for a moment. He had noticed Lord Terral's unease when the suac mentioned betrayal. It might have merely been discomfort caused by the suac's strange display, but Terral was one of very few left in his empire who could claim to be family. If there were any truth to the suac's prophecy, Terral would be a prime suspect, a possibility that prompted the relocation to a more private setting. If guilt brought about Terral's unease, then perhaps the desire to find out what occurred behind these doors would drive him to carelessness.

"From your words, Suac Chozai, I gather you believe the Murak will fall to this savage foe if I refuse to send aid." Yiloch kept his eyes upon the map to avoid showing too much interest in the answer. The suac expected no more courtesy than he gave when dealing with unbelievers from outside his lands. It was tempting to meet his expectations.

"You understand correctly. If our fates were not intertwined, I would not be here."

Yiloch pinned the Murak priest with his gaze. "Then tell me, who will betray me?"

Chozai reached a tattooed arm across the table. One finger, tipped with a thick, cracked nail, came to rest upon the ring that lay hidden under Yiloch's shirt, pressing it against his skin. "Your greatest undoing shall come from here," he stated with conviction.

Defensive rage, wild and unreasoning, blazed to life in Yiloch. He wanted to tear the man's hand off. To leap across the table and strike him down. Chozai drew back from him in response to the change in his bearing. The ring, Indigo's ring, burned against his skin for a few seconds, blazing with the intensity of the emotions tied to that delicate band. Every second he had spent with her, all the sacrifices she had made and risks she had taken for him, rushed to the forefront of his mind. His ascard ability flared, rising with his emotions so he had to wrestle back control.

Ian, highly sensitive to ascard use in others, tensed, his eyes growing wide.

"All this talk of foresight," Yiloch snarled, fury driving the words past his lips. "I saw that display out there. I thought the Kudaness considered it sacrilege to use ascard."

He attacked their religion, seeking to repay some of the turmoil the suac's accusation caused him, and it worked.

Chozai's copper eyes flashed, and his two warriors shifted into a wider stance, moving their weapons out of ceremonial position to something far more threatening. Adran's hand dropped to his sword hilt, and he too moved into a combat-ready posture.

Calm washed over and through Yiloch then. He glanced at Ian, whose pale eyes had taken on a familiar inward-facing intensity. The manipulation was unsolicited and unwanted, but not unwise.

Chozai followed his gaze, reading something different into the glance. He motioned to his warriors, who assumed their previous stance. The suac wasn't fool enough to pit his men against the power of a creator, and Ian had become renowned for his exceptional ascard strength since helping Yiloch take the city from his father. Ironically, several of the acts that earned the youth the respect he now held were Indigo's accomplishments, but allowing Ian to take credit for them increased his influence and allowed her to keep her power hidden. It also made the creator an effective political asset.

"I do not manipulate the power of the gods for my visions. The gods grant them to me." He turned a sneer on Ian, not so wary of his power that he wasn't willing to express his disdain. "Not stolen."

The tension in his tone told Yiloch he had gotten under the man's skin, but if the suac, as representative of the Murak un Ani, had no more respect to offer him, the tenuous relationship between their people was not apt to change anytime soon, certainly not for the better.

"Suac Chozai, I require more to build a military alliance on than prophecy and brash accusations. I have an empire to fortify, one the former emperor made a fair attempt at destroying the foundations of, and a dangerous criminal to bring to justice. I need my army at hand until I have brought all my lords to heel, preferably with as little bloodshed as possible. There is much to be done to secure my rule. If you can offer me no greater proof of your need, or of my own, if you cannot even respect my rank, then we have nothing more to discuss. You are welcome to return and present your case again if these things change. For now, all I can offer is refreshment and rest before you depart."

Suac Chozai's expression darkened, growing more hostile with every word. Disregarding the man's foretellings and his confidence in their accuracy made Yiloch uneasy, but as Emperor, he couldn't allow the man to disrespect him. Gambling resources on mere prophecy might also make his subjects wonder if he shared the madness his father suffered from in the end.

Chozai's lip lifted in an animalistic snarl, exposing one sharpened canine. "You will destroy yourself and your empire with your arrogance."

"Just as your arrogance will destroy your people if your visions come true," Yiloch countered. "You have not offered me enough sound information to work with. As I said, come to me with more, and I will reconsider my position."

The suac narrowed his eyes and gave a curt nod. "So it shall be."

Chozai turned from Yiloch, and his warriors fell in behind him. Yiloch watched them stride from the room, making no move to follow. The suac hadn't stood on ceremony, nor had he behaved in a manner respectful of Lyran customs. As such, it seemed appropriate to let him show himself out of the map chamber. The usher would see to him from there.

Yiloch turned to Ian when the door shut behind them. "The foretelling he did, where did he draw his power from?"

Ian stared at the door, lips pressed in a troubled line. After a few seconds, he looked at Yiloch and shrugged. "I don't know. I didn't sense him connecting to his inner aspect or drawing on ascard around him, and he wasn't masking anything that I could tell."

Yiloch stared at the closed door. Silence filled the room. Several minutes passed before Adran coughed and Yiloch met his worried amber eyes. His slightly darker skin and dusty blond hair betrayed impure blood, but he was a lifelong friend and advisor. Lineage carried little weight before the trust that existed between them.

"The suac didn't look pleased." Adran's tone carried a trace of displeasure with the way the situation had gone.

Yiloch nodded once, dismissing the underlying message. "I have been thinking, Adran." He walked to another map. This one depicted the allied kingdom of Caithin across the Gilded Strait. "We need healers in our army. Not borrowed healers, but our own formally trained healers."

Adran walked to the other side of the table and rested his hands on it. His fingers tapped the surface a few times, the only expression of his annoyance at the change of subject. "We could ask King Jerrin for an instructor, though it might be more beneficial to send some of our adepts to train at their academy."

Yiloch touched the city of Demin with one finger, trying to ignore the ache in his chest at the thought of Indigo there. "Discuss it with Ferin and see what he thinks of sending adepts to Caithin for training. Ask him how many he would send and who, then prepare a missive to King Jerrin and bring it to me."

"My lord." Adran inclined his head, the concern in his eyes taking on a more personal nature.

Yiloch looked away. They had been friends far too long for him to expect Adran to miss the distress that hid behind his carefully controlled regard, but he had no wish to discuss it until his head was clearer. Besides, there were more urgent matters to worry about. "Any news of Myac?'

"Still nothing."

He nodded, suppressing the chill of dread that always came with thoughts of the dangerous adept who had nearly killed Indigo. "You may both go."

The two men left him, Adran lingering in the doorway a few seconds before moving on. When the door clicked shut, Yiloch reached down the collar of his shirt and brought out the ring that hung there. Two clear stones nestled in a delicate band to either side of a larger gem the color of her eyes—the color of her name.

"Indigo." He let her name roll off his lips like a caress.

Holding the ring, he closed his eyes and played back every touch they had shared, every kiss and intimate moment, in his mind. Extraordinary power filled her, hidden beneath a gentle beauty and charming vulnerability. She had helped him take the throne from his father, using her uncommonly strong ascard connection to assist him to the point she had almost lost her life more than once. She gave everything for him because she loved him, and though his motives for using her power had been selfish at the start, he couldn't help reciprocating that love by the end. Still, she was Caithin, and the exalted pure blood of Lyran royalty was part of its power. He could not ask her to be his bride, not without losing the approval of his people, and she had her own battles to fight in Caithin. Now he had only her ring and a deep ache in his chest.

No, betrayal couldn't come from Indigo. She would never turn against him after all they had gone through together. His trust in her made him suspicious of everything the suac said after implicating her. And yet, as he twisted the ring about in his fingers, a deep disquiet took root in his heart that hadn't been there before.

TO BE CONTINUED...

ACKNOWLEDGEMENTS

I'm fortunate to be surrounded by amazing people who have believed in and supported me along this journey. I may not mention everyone, but you all hold a special place in my heart.

I want to offer thanks to the following people.

To Michael for years of supporting my dreams and letting me read you every book I wrote.

To my mom, Linda, for loving these characters as much as I do and helping me struggle through endless edits to get to this point.

To Rick and Ann for always being willing to read and give feedback on my books and for always believing in me.

To my fellow author Eldritch Black for sharing long rides to the coffee shop full of cathartic rants and commiseration every Thursday, and for being an amazing writing companion.

To Aradia for *knowing* I would succeed from the first time we met and for being an inspiration in your dedication to your own art.

To my cover artist, Robert, and my interior designer, Brian, thank you for your fantastic work and your patience with me through this process.

I must also thank my sixth-grade teacher, Mr. Johnson, for being so encouraging when I told you I was going to be an author, and to my eighth-grade algebra teacher, Mr. Siebenlist, for allowing me to ignore lessons because you were so pleased I was writing books in class rather than notes.

AUTHOR BIO

Outside of her career as an author, Nikki is a professional technical and creative writer, spider wrangler, animal lover, and devoted cat mom. Writing fantasy and science fiction stories has been a lifelong passion for her. She loves to draw on her myriad life experiences, doing everything from wild cave exploration and competitive horseback endurance riding to practicing iaido and archery. She invites you to join her on some fantastic adventures.

* * *

Thank you for taking the time to read this novel. Please consider leaving a review if you enjoyed it.

* * *

For more information about Nikki and her work, visit her website at http://www.elysiumpalace.com.

OTHER WORKS BY NIKKI MCCORMACK

THE WARDEN'S SON (A Vanris Series)
Child of Vanris
Blood of Vanris
Heart of Vanris
Throne of Vanris

DAUGHTER OF VANRIS (A Vanris Series)
Wave Dancer
Wave-Touched
Wavelord

SILVERBLOOD RAVEN
A Path of Blood and Amber
A Path of Secrets and Dreams
A Path of Storms and Reckonings

CLOCKWORK ENTERPRISES
The Girl and the Clockwork Cat
The Girl and the Clockwork Conspiracy
The Girl and the Clockwork Crossfire

FORBIDDEN THINGS
Dissident
Exile
Apostate

ELYSIUM'S FALL
Dark Hope of the Dragons
Dark Savior of the Dragons

STANDALONE NOVELS and SHORT STORIES
Golden Eyes
The Keeper
Warden's Rise (A Vanris Short Story)
In Silence Waiting (Short Story)
And They All Look Just the Same (Short Story)
Making Monsters (Short Story)

www.ingramcontent.com/pod-product-compliance
Lightning Source LLC
Chambersburg PA
CBHW030649120726

47905CB00001B/122